"Egomaniacal cad! How dare you?

"Laying your filthy hands upon me as if I were but a common streetwalker! Have you no decency? Ah, but of course, this is the manner in which all you London rogues treat your *wenches,* thrusting your loathsome attentions upon them. If my father . . ."

Her last words brought his wandering eyes quickly to heel, and he threw back his head with a hearty laugh. "Oh, heavens, a Daddy's girl."

"I most certainly am not!" Trista huffed.

"To my mind, you rather enjoyed the actual kiss, did you not?"

Trista fairly flew at him. "How dare you?"

Quick as a flash, Nicholas caught her wrists in a steely grip and pulled her close against him. With eyes glittering dangerously into hers, he spoke slowly and deliberately. "Rest assured, my hot little lioness, you will come to realize that *I dare much.*"

Dear Reader,

This month, Harlequin Historicals celebrates the arrival of spring with stories by four fabulous newcomers.

In *Steal the Stars* by Miranda Jarrett, the author uses her firsthand knowledge of the Rhode Island coast to weave a passionate tale set against the backdrop of America's struggle for independence.

Ana Seymour's delightful heroine finds herself the unwilling guest of an American *bandido* in the camp of the infamous Pancho Villa in *The Bandit's Bride*.

Arabesque by Kit Gardner, for those of you who like a touch of mystery, is the story of star-crossed lovers who discover the seamier side of London's upper class.

Set in medieval Wales, *A Warrior's Heart* by Margaret Moore is an unforgettable story of a soldier, wounded during the Crusades, and the spirited gentlewoman who turns his bitterness to love.

We hope you enjoy our March titles. And please be sure to look for more books by these four talented authors in the coming year.

Sincerely,
The Editors

Arabesque

Kit Gardner

Harlequin Books

TORONTO • NEW YORK • LONDON
AMSTERDAM • PARIS • SYDNEY • HAMBURG
STOCKHOLM • ATHENS • TOKYO • MILAN
MADRID • WARSAW • BUDAPEST • AUCKLAND

Harlequin Historicals first edition March 1992

ISBN 0-373-28717-8

ARABESQUE

KIT GARDNER,

a former C.P.A., lives in Southwestern Pennsylvania with her husband and two young sons. When her busy schedule allows, she enjoys skiing, golf, travel and reading anything from romance to the latest in sensationalistic thrillers.

To Joanne, Donna and Colleen
for their unwavering support and enthusiasm,
and especially for Lee,
who, with one innocent tap on the shoulder, threw
wide the doors to the publishing world for me and
proved that dreams can come true.
To my sons, Max and Ben,
for taking three-hour naps.
And to my husband, Dave,
who's taught me more about romance and chivalry
than any hero, real or fictional.

Prologue

London, April 1823

Making his way through the steady drizzle, the lone figure huddled within his greatcoat and clutched at his top hat as a sudden gust of rain nearly drove his legs from beneath him and threatened to snatch from him what little protection the hat provided. The wind eased and the man scurried along with head bent low, hugging the building at his side for fear of another lashing. Had it not been for his preoccupation, he may have paused to wonder at the black coach parked at the curb and a similar conveyance not ten paces farther up the street along the opposite curb. Any vehicle lingering on this particular street so early in the day was rare indeed, more so a pair so handsomely turned out. As it was, the man glanced up only when he reached one particular business establishment. After fumbling in his pocket for his keys, he struggled with the lock as another sheet of rain whipped his coat about him. With a muffled oath, he shoved the door open, then slammed it shut against the raging elements. Doffing both hat and coat, he shuddered and hurried to stoke the fire to take the dampness from the air. The tinkling of the bell drew his attention momentarily from the coals and, with a frown, he glanced at his pocket watch. Shaking his head, he snapped the stove door shut and rose to greet the early customer.

He was surprised to find not one but two gentlemen gracing the front room, the water dripping from their coats onto the rough plank floor. The shopkeeper's attention was immediately drawn to the younger man, whose powerful presence filled the small room. Even without the top hat he held at his side, the man stood extremely tall, though the intensity of his manner proved far more unsettling than either his height or his breadth of shoulder. Indeed, the dark-haired man held himself like a tightly coiled spring, a barely contained rage evident in the depths of the fierce blue eyes. For a moment, those eyes narrowed beneath stormy dark brows and the chiseled features grew harsh, causing the shopkeeper's gaze to dart to the small white-haired gentleman at his side. The older man leaned a gnarled hand heavily upon his cane, lifted his aristocratic chin a notch and peered keenly from beneath bushy white brows at the shopkeeper.

Neither of the patrons spoke, confining themselves for several moments to intense observation, which caused the shopkeeper no small measure of confusion. With eyes darting between the two, he managed a wan smile and spoke in a shaky voice, "Gentlemen, may I be of service?"

Leaning forward slightly on his cane, the older man peered intently at the shopkeeper, then in a smooth voice that rang of breeding he stated flatly, "You're not Sleeth."

"N-nay..." the shopkeeper stammered. "You refer to Oswald Sleeth?"

The old gentleman nodded. "The same. I was quite certain he conducted business from this establishment, though many years have passed since I had occasion to speak with him."

"Indeed, you find yourself in the proper place, though I fear Oswald met an untimely demise only a fortnight past." The shopkeeper paused as the tall gentleman muttered under his breath and turned abruptly to fix that stormy glare upon the gently falling rain. With a shudder that had little to do with the dampness in the air, the shopkeeper drew a deep steadying breath and swung his gaze to the elderly man. "Perhaps I can be of help, for I, too, make my living as a solicitor."

Waving an unsteady hand, the old man shook his head. "'Twas a personal matter with Oswald Sleeth that brought me here, though I cannot speak for this gentleman." His gesture toward the tall gentleman drew a surprised look from the shopkeeper, who harbored the mistaken notion that the patrons were together.

The younger man turned sharply and spoke in a deep timbre. "With whom shall I speak regarding Sleeth's business matters? You?"

Beneath the intensity of the man's regard, the shopkeeper found himself more than a tad elated that he was not the man this tall fellow sought. "Nay! Not I! 'Tis Oswald's brother, Archibald.... Aye, that's the chap's name. Not two days after Oswald died he cleaned the place out. Took everything. Perhaps he is the man with whom you should speak, though he's a Society fellow and knows nothing of the business. I know not where you might find him."

"And what of you?" The tall gentleman fixed an unwavering glare upon the shopkeeper. "You appear somewhat knowledgeable of Sleeth's affairs."

"Oh, nay, sir!" the shopkeeper hastened to reply. "Just recently I came to share this small space with Oswald. Paid half the rent, for Oswald had fallen upon some rather hard times. I barely knew the man, and much less of his business affairs."

For a moment the stormy gaze narrowed upon the shopkeeper until the gleaming eyes were but slits. Then, apparently satisfied with the man's response, the tall gentleman donned his hat and with a curt nod turned to leave the small shop. His hand stilled upon the doorknob as the shopkeeper's voice rang out.

"And if Archibald Sleeth should come round, sir, whom shall I say was calling?"

"Brennan is the name. Nicholas Brennan. Good day to you." Drawing the door wide, he stepped into the misty drizzle and, pulling his collar close about him, hastened to his waiting coach. The tinkling of the door's bell behind him and an insistent tug at his sleeve stilled his booted feet and snapped his head about. At his elbow stood the elderly gentleman, peering up at him through the rain with a peculiar look in his eye.

"Brennan. Forgive me, for this may appear a rather odd request, but I believe our business with Sleeth was of a similar nature. Would you care to join me for a bit of tea? I know of a place just round the corner."

For a moment, Brennan studied the old man. "Very well." He turned to mumble something to his waiting coachman, then followed the old man to the small corner pub.

The dimly lit establishment was deserted, save for a scattering of single patrons and a serving wench. With a gleam in her dark eyes, she descended upon their table as soon as Brennan eased his long legs beneath the heavy wooden table and ran a hand briskly through his dark hair. Through bushy brows, the older man carefully observed the saucy wench's posture and pose as she thrust her ample charms all but beneath the young man's nose. Brennan paid her little heed; indeed, he appeared entirely unaffected by the attractive girl, who, apparently unaccustomed to such treatment, sauntered away in a huff to fetch their tea.

They sat in silence for several moments, carefully assessing each other until the serving girl placed their tea none too gently upon the table.

The old man lifted a shaky hand to his teacup and fixed his eyes upon Brennan. "I can spare you the trouble of searching for this Archibald chap, Mr. Brennan. He is not the man you seek."

"Indeed?"

"You're skeptical, of course. I assure you it was entirely coincidence that we should meet thus, though, I must admit, a remarkable stroke of luck for us both." At Brennan's wary look, the elderly man waved a gnarled hand. "You shall see, my young friend. I believe we may be of some help to one another."

Brennan leaned his forearms upon the table. "Go on."

"I am an old man, Mr. Brennan, and though my limbs fail me at times, my mind is as sharp as it was twenty-six years ago when I first met Oswald Sleeth. At the time, Oswald harbored a certain fondness for brandy, both fine and not so fine, which, one can only conjecture, eventually led to his untimely demise. This penchant for drink also rendered him rather loose-tongued, and he found in me a ready ear. It was during one of his exceptionally long tales that I learned of the fate of your family business, Trent Shipping, and of the man responsible for the tragedy. He told me this some time after the actual event, but Sleeth was still quite proud of himself for cooking up the scheme, then managing it so divinely. He received a hefty purse for his trouble." The heavily wrinkled face rose slowly to Brennan and the corner of the old man's mouth lifted in a sneer. "Sleeth was not the man ultimately responsible, Brennan. That man is here, as we speak, in London."

Nearly leaning out of his chair, Brennan spoke fiercely through clenched teeth. "Speak the name, old man!"

The old man raised a hand beseechingly and slowly shook his head. "Revenge burns deep within you. Perhaps 'tis not so good."

"That's not for you to say. I've suffered great loss. Suffice it to say, I deem my cause just and worthy."

"I'm quite certain you do. You are still in shipping, I presume?"

"Aye." The broad shoulders settled against the tall wooden back of the chair and he eyed the old man with no small measure of caution. "I arrived from Richmond late last evening. I have this business to attend to with Sleeth, and other business matters. I've also the Trent family home in the country, which requires my attention."

"Ah, yes, family honor and all that, a lesson I was too late in learning."

"What do you propose, Mr.... ?"

The old man waved a dismissing hand. "The nature of my business requires that I remain anonymous, even with you, my friend."

A dark brow lifted and the blue eyes flashed a warning to the old man. "It's not my wont to conspire with those unwilling to divulge their given name. Such was the very nature of my family's undoing with Sleeth. Forgive me, but I would find you a trifle difficult to trust, which quality I deem essential in all my transactions, be they business or personal. Good day to you, sir."

Quick as a flash, a hand clawed at Brennan's sleeve as the young man pushed his chair from the table. "Brennan! Don't be a fool!"

"I think perhaps I would be more foolish to remain."

The dim green eyes widened with sudden desperation. "I implore you, my hotheaded young friend! I respect your hesitancy. Indeed, your reticence attests to the vital importance you place on this most personal matter. However, do not let your caution blind you even for a moment. You needn't trust me, for that will take time. But you must believe that I know of the man upon whom you will have your revenge. And if we are to help one another, my identity must remain anonymous."

For several long moments, the wary blue eyes carefully assessed the older man, then Brennan relaxed slightly in his chair. "As you wish, though 'tis against my better judgment."

A hint of a smile tugged at the old man's wrinkled mouth. "Believe me, you will never rue our meeting this day, my friend."

"I shall be the judge of that." His gaze grew thoughtful. "In exchange for the man's name, what is it that you wish from me?"

"You are able to move about freely in the man's circles with little fear of detection, for I am quite certain he will not recognize your name. It's imperative, however, that you keep yourself disassociated with the Trent name lest he become suspicious."

Brennan peered closely at the old man. "You say the man will not recognize my name, yet you realized who I was the moment I spoke the name Brennan?"

"Of course I did. My good man, once Sleeth told me of that tragedy and I learned who was responsible, I felt compelled to pass the information along to your family. By then, however, Trent Shipping no longer existed, your Grandfather Trent was dead and buried, and his only living relative, your mother, had sailed for the States with her husband, Jason Brennan. Ah, my knowledge of your family lends me an air of plausibility, eh? The burden of Sleeth's information weighed heavily upon me, Mr. Brennan. So much so, in fact, that I employed every possible means to locate your family. I was fairly well connected in this city, thus I experienced little difficulty obtaining the information from the Trent family solicitor, a business associate who happened to owe me a favor."

"And if Sleeth could avail himself of the same methods?"

The old man shook his head firmly. "Sleeth was a ruthless man, I admit, but his interest in your family extended only so far as the completion of the transaction. No doubt his collaborator knew less than he. Brennan, if I believed he would recognize you, I would not risk your detection."

"The documents in my possession bear only Sleeth's signature and that of my mother's father. I'm almost certain that Sleeth retained similar documents and perhaps others naming the man responsible."

The old man shook his head. "If you are seeking proof you'd best forget it. I'm quite certain any incriminating documents still existing have either been destroyed or are in very safe hands. Indeed, the gentleman you seek is of a stature that keeps him rather protected from the typical courses of action in situations such as this."

"You're after the same man, I gather."

"Aye, I have a vested interest in exposing him for what he is. 'Tis of a personal nature, though I would gladly do so simply for your sake, Brennan."

"I'm rather curious about your visit to Sleeth. Your reaction to the news of his death leads me to believe you were not aware of it."

"Indeed, it was a shock. Only recently I became aware of certain circumstances that require me to act against the man you seek. I deemed it necessary to renew my acquaintance with Sleeth if only to determine whether he and Sleeth were still doing business together."

"Oswald took that to the grave. Perhaps his brother may be of some help."

"Perhaps."

A twinkle in the depths of the green eyes piqued Brennan's interest. "You have a plan."

The old man shrugged, but the gleam in his eyes and the hint of a smile tugging at his mouth belied the casual response. "Perhaps."

For the first time in a long while, Brennan allowed himself a softening of manner. In fact, the old man was quite certain he glimpsed a shadow of a smile forming on the handsome face as Brennan finally loosened his greatcoat and settled comfortably in his chair as if in anticipation of a lengthy stay.

"Wench!" Brennan bellowed, raising an arm at the passing serving maid, who hastened to his bidding. "Bring me a tankard of your finest ale, and the same for my friend here. I fear the tea was not to his liking."

With a chuckle, the old man settled comfortably in his chair, as well, and they remained thus for quite some time, even after the shopkeeper ventured past in search of a tasty midday meal.

Chapter One

Oxfordshire, England
April, 1823

"Marry me, Trista."

"Oh, for heaven's sake, Peter, surely you jest?" Trista Fitzgerald cast him a sideways glance and shoved an elbow into his beefy side. "You're like a brother to me—nay, my very best friend. Why on earth would I want to marry you and ruin all that?" Plucking at a growth of newly sprung heather, she surrendered to a laugh, then leaned back upon her elbows and stretched her trouser-clad legs before her. Absently, she fingered the heather as her eyes scanned the sloping countryside. The sun warmed her face, the fragrance of spring teased her senses, the solitude broken only by the occasional snort of one of the horses as they grazed. She closed her eyes. "Marriage is for fools."

Peter shifted at her side. When he spoke, he sounded as if he swallowed half his words. "'Tis what awaits you in London and well you know it."

Her eyes flew open to fix heatedly upon the sturdy young man beside her. The sun caught in his golden curls, in the blond down of his first whiskers. How painfully young he seemed, though he was already twenty-one. Still, he was far too young to bear the horrific burden of running an entire farm and providing for his six siblings, his mother and rum-sodden father. His skin was weathered, worn like his makeshift boots; his dark eyes dim, lifeless at times, the visible testament to the hardships he bore. In all the years she'd known him, Trista had but glimpsed the inner ravages. Their friendship, however, was based upon forthrightness. Thus, despite her concern, she hesitated not a whit before replying in a less than congenial tone.

"Peter Fleming, I am no addlepated fool. I know very well that Aunt Esme's thinly disguised invitation for the Season is merely an excuse to peddle me off to some insufferable limp-wristed, lily-livered London dandy who postures and shows a leg and has more lace handkerchiefs to his name than I. God only knows, the woman must be bored to distraction, in *desperate* need of some project, all cooped up in some enormous London manse." Trista erupted with a hollow laugh. "Have I news for her." She shook her head and plucked at Peter's leg as his attention appeared to be focused upon something very distant. "Her letter mentioned that new husband of hers . . . that Count Something or other. Some godawful Italian name. He's a businessman, *inordinately* busy. Poor woman . . . must be dreadfully lonely. No doubt she misses Paris, and Gaston, of course."

"He died, what . . . not six months ago?"

"If that. I must say, Father displayed little of his business tact when he heard the news that she'd remarried so soon. Of course, Father tends to be rather cynical about love and all that."

"Little wonder he's never remarried."

Trista settled back upon the soft grass, her eyes on the cloudless sky overhead. She sighed and gave a casual shrug. "Attorneys are very busy men, Peter, even those tucked away in the country. Besides, Maggie has tended to us very well since the day Mother died. Why on earth would he need a wife?"

Peter's gaze remained fixed before him, his voice hollow and dull. "So why are you going?"

"To London? Why, Father left me little choice. This business matter of his just so happened to coincide with Maggie's annual visit to her family." Trista scowled and heaved an agitated sigh. "According to Father, I am far too young and headstrong—though I believe if I were old and headstrong 'twould be far worse. In any event, I cannot remain at home, in our cozy little cottage, all by my lonesome for three months. You know, Esme's letter was so blasted *timely* in its arrival, one has cause to wonder if she perhaps planned it all thus."

Peter fidgeted with a blade of grass, studying it as if he chose his words carefully. "Don't go, Trista. Don't leave, not even for a day. As I know the sun will rise on the morrow, I know you shan't return."

With a laugh, Trista grasped Peter's rough hand and shook it with conviction. "Oh, Peter, for heaven's sake, stop it. I *abhor* all that London Society rubbish, all that posturing and posing, all those fashionable frocks and the entirely proper thing to do. Surely you cannot envision me dressed as I am in a stable hand's old trousers amongst a gaggle of breathless paramours eagerly awaiting summons from London's most notorious roué of the day? Why, I..."

"Marry me." The words were spoken so softly they were nearly snatched by the wind.

"Oh, Peter, stop teasing."

Quite suddenly, he leaned over her, his bulky shoulders blocking all view of clear skies. His hands were on either side of her, his head bent so low she felt the heat of him. "Marry me, Trista. This is no joke. I want you as my wife...tonight...and you need never go to London."

Trista blinked with confusion and forced a half smile. "Peter, I cannot marry you."

The familiar curve of his lips twisted painfully and he pinned her hands beneath his. "Damn you! How can you say that when I—I love you! I've loved you since the day I met you. Wanted you for my wife from the very start... dreamed of you forever at my side!"

Trista swallowed over the knot in her throat. "Peter, please, you know I never wish to marry. What the devil has come over you? Perhaps 'tis something you ate."

"Oh God, Trista!" he croaked, his voice breaking, hoarse with emotion. "Blast you, how could you not know that

I've come to feel about you thus? How could you not know that I adore the very sight of you...that keeping myself from you has become a daily torture? How I long for you...in my bed..."

"Peter! What the devil do you mean? Dear God, you are my one dearest friend, the one I confide in, the one I trust! How can you betray me so?"

"Betray you?" he cried. "I love you! I want you as my wife. I cannot bear the thought of you with...some... some..." His voice cracked. "He'll be some damned blue blood, some dandy with more money in his purse than I'll ever see in my entire lifetime!"

"No, Peter! I desire no husband, truly I don't! You more than anyone should know that."

"By God, have you no sense? Look at yourself, Trista. Do you think men blind to such beauty? Do you think *me* blind? They will want you, no matter the clothes you wear, just as *I* want you. 'Tis your hair, like liquid fire and gold, and your skin. Your eyes, as green as the first spring grass, and—"

"Stop it!" Trista squirmed in his grasp, experiencing the first twinges of fear when his grip upon her only tightened and his chest pressed firmly against her breasts. "Release me, Peter, I wish you no harm."

"No harm!" he cried. "'Tis done, Trista. This notion you have that you shall remain unwed—hidden away with all your perverse loyalty for a lonely old recluse of a father, destined to become as lonely and jaded as he—'tis utter foolishness when you could be mine!"

Trista clenched her jaw with mounting indignation. "How dare you besmirch my father's name! I shall belong to no one but myself. Least of all to a man I do not love or find forced upon me. Now release me!"

Had she slapped him, Peter would have looked less dumbstruck. As it was, he stared at her, a cold, hollow stare. "You don't love me." It was a statement of sudden, chilling realization.

"Oh God, Peter, I..." But her words died in her throat as his eyes glazed and fell to her lips, then lower to her breasts, which suddenly seemed crushed against him. She heard the rasping of his breath through the mounting din in her ears, and then a mind-numbing terror, a terror borne of some instinct—surely not of experience, for she was as innocent as a maid could be.

Before she could summon coherent thought, he fell upon her, his bulk trapping her, his mouth seeking hers with all the fervor of a young man long denied that which he desires most. Trista gasped, twisting her head violently then shuddering with revulsion when his slackened mouth slid past hers, glancing off her cheek then sliding along the length of her throat. She knew a sudden helplessness, then anger, which manifested itself in a strength borne of desperation. With all her might, she shoved against him.

"Peter... release me!"

He paused, shuddering, then rolled from her, pressing his head against his knees, his limbs trembling. "If I were less of a man, by God, Trista, I would..."

Trista scrambled to her feet, clutching the worn shirt about her as if seeking some protection, and attempted to draw a clean breath. "If you were man at all, you would never betray me... force yourself upon me! You're no better than those dreadful rogues I'm forever reading about, deceitful louts who dabble in debauchery and play upon feminine weaknesses."

"'Tis as the villagers say," he rasped hoarsely as if he hadn't heard her, his eyes fixed heatedly upon her. "You think yourself above us all. You and all those damned highbred notions. Go, go find your lord! That's what you long for, what you truly desire, though you're far too spoiled and proud to admit it. I know you well, indeed. 'Tis *me* you do not want!"

Despite his callous words, words that sliced through her heart, she found herself reaching a hand to him. "Peter, stop this foolishness...."

He bared his teeth and growled, "How dare you pity me! *You*, who shall find yourself bound to some man you do not want, living a life you abhor. 'Tis *you* who should be pitied, Trista, not I."

Something in the pit of Trista's belly constricted, a pain both fierce and poignant. "I'm sorry, Peter," she whispered, turning to seek her mare through the blur of her tears. With trembling hands, she caught hold of Gypsy's bridle and led the mare to a nearby tree stump. Mounting, and without a backward glance, she guided the animal from the clearing.

"Trista, some attempt at a smile and a cheery disposition would serve you well."

Trista pursed her lips and cast her father a reproachful glance before fixing her gaze once again upon the coach window and the passing streets of London. "'Tis the rabbit stew settling, Father, nothing more. It was far too greasy."

"Humph!" was her father's blustery reply. "Indeed. Would I be remiss in assuming you've reconciled yourself to your dreadful fate?"

"Hardly that. I shall bide my time, Father, humor dear Aunt Esme if it will please you and make the time go any faster. But I shan't enjoy myself."

"Oh, for heaven's sake, don't enjoy yourself."

Trista glared at her father, all dashing and debonair in his topcoat of deep blue, peering at her through bushy white brows with just a hint of a smile tugging at his mouth. "Don't mock me, Father. You know very well that one need only read the *Times* to glimpse the squalor plaguing the city, the blatant disregard for human life, save for that of the privileged classes."

Winston Fitzgerald's gaze turned thoughtful for a moment. "A sad state of affairs indeed. However, an entirely different London is depicted by the society pages you blatantly disregard in your haste to consume every bit of newsprint that finds its way into the house...and you needn't wrinkle your nose with such feigned distaste."

"'Tis not feigned, Father, I assure you."

"Be that as it may, I feel compelled to remind you that limiting one's variety of reading material never once contributed to a suitably well-rounded character. Indeed, my dear, some may even find you rather *mulish* in your opinions."

"So be it." She sighed and toyed with a reticule she found more cumbersome than convenient. "'Tis only that the thought of finding myself flung into the very heart of a society for which I harbor naught but contempt..." At her father's raised brow, she mumbled grudgingly, "Albeit a contempt borne of ignorance."

"You're making me wonder if perhaps I've done you a disservice educating you myself, keeping you all tucked away in the country. God only knows, Esme has requested you visit her since the day you turned sixteen."

Trista shook her head and gave a hoarse laugh. "Dear God, the poor woman shan't rest until I am properly wed. Oh, to be all of a dreadfully nubile nineteen years! What *shall* I do?"

"You might try enjoying yourself, my dear. 'Tis only for three months."

Trista gazed wistfully from the coach window. "Will you be staying at least the night before this trip of yours commences? One would think you'd be rather anxious to visit with Esme."

"Indeed, I shall remain overnight, at least to meet this new husband of hers. This Count Catalani. However, my business commitments necessitate my *abandoning* you after one short evening."

"*You* labeled it abandonment, not I," Trista replied with a smile. "It's always business with you, Father. Why, Aunt Esme shan't recognize you. To hear Maggie tell it, you were quite a rogue when you first met Mother and Esme."

"Rogue? Ha!" Winston scowled from the window and shook his head with feigned disgust. "That blasted woman and her infernal loose tongue. You'd think she'd known me since I was a wee babe the way she gibber-jabbers. No, Trista, I was but a fledgling attorney with one badly worn pair of shoes to my name. I struggled for every farthing."

"Perhaps, though Mother took an instant liking to you. Esme, as well. She must have, or she wouldn't have helped arrange your marriage as she did."

Winston's eyes grew clouded. "Aye, 'twas Esme who snuck Helene from the house, from beneath her meddlesome father's very nose. Perhaps 'twas my rather zealous pursuit that proved my undoing. Aye, but Helene was barely seventeen at the time and, I suppose, too young to marry, especially a penniless Englishman." Winston chuckled. "I disrupted the household, I can tell you that, though Renaurd put forth little effort in my regard. He composed himself with equal bluster and obstinace when Esme wished to marry Gaston Beauregard. A dreadful shame, I tell you, for we haven't seen Renaurd since the day I married your mother, though even to this day I harbor little but contempt for the man, wherever he may be."

"Surely Aunt Esme had maintained correspondence with him."

"Perhaps, though she was so deeply hurt by their rejection of Gaston that I believe she returned to Paris with him shortly after they married. And there she remained until his death. Who knows whatever happened to Renaurd." He paused rather abruptly as if struck by a sudden thought. Consulting his pocket watch, he muttered to himself then drew several documents from his attaché, scanned them briefly before replacing them in the case and snapping it shut. He mumbled something about the blasted city traffic, then started abruptly as the coach pulled to a stop along a quiet, tree-lined street before a small business establishment.

"Ah, we're here. I'll be but a moment, Trista. 'Tis a small matter I simply must tend to. Then I shall deliver you to Esme. Just wait here, my dear."

With mounting curiosity, Trista observed him fumble with his attaché and walking stick, then duck his head and mutter a mild oath when his top hat caught the top of the doorway. She gazed after him as he hurried up the walkway to the front door, which burst open at his knock.

After a time spent fidgeting with her hair and a ridiculous hat Maggie had procured for this trip, Trista pushed the coach door wide and called for the coachman.

"Ian, if you please, I fear the coach has grown a bit stuffy and I wish to take some air. If you could help me from this thing..."

Offering his hand, the coachman assisted her, then spoke rather firmly, though this caused her not a moment's pause as she turned to stroll off down the street. "Lass, don't ye go strayin' too far. Yer father, he'll be comin' soon, and not too pleased he'd be with yer wanderin' off."

"Oh, Ian, for heaven's sake," Trista scoffed, waving a gloved hand to indicate the quiet street where but few buggies passed and only a handful of pedestrians lingered. "'Twould be most difficult to get myself lost. Not to fear, I will stroll but a short distance."

His mumbled reply was lost upon her. Without a moment's thought, she loosened the ribbon beneath her chin and drew the hat from her head. The sun warmed her skin and she reached to free the lace from her throat, unhooking the buttons of her dove gray traveling jacket as she did so to reveal a cream lace underbodice. She continued on, her head tilted toward the setting sun and her eyes nearly closed. Her hands hung loosely at her sides, carelessly dangling her reticule and hat. As such, she was oblivious to the bulky figure waddling toward her with lowered head as pudgy hands fumbled with a topcoat that refused to remain closed over an ample girth.

The sudden impact of soft bosom colliding with unresisting paunch sent hat and purse sailing unceremoniously into the street. Trista's head snapped and her eyes flew wide as she realized she'd bumped headlong into a London gentleman. Thoroughly flustered, she apologized profusely and raised trembling hands to her flaming cheeks.

Her victim was a short, stocky gentleman of her father's age, she guessed, who graciously swept off his top hat to reveal a shining bald pate. His considerable bulk was stuffed like a sausage into a lemon yellow topcoat and flaming red breeches that strained at the seams. Gleaming, beady eyes popped at her from a sweat-streaked countenance, and he licked his puffy lips feverishly and shook his head, which, to Trista, suddenly appeared too small for his body.

"Nay, nay, my sweet lady. 'Twas my fault, without a doubt! My most humble apologies!" He bowed low before her, extending a white-stockinged leg. Straightening himself with obvious difficulty, he paused, eyes bulging when his corset popped ominously, then gave a heavy puff and eyed her closely. "My dear, may I be so bold as to introduce myself. Archibald Sleeth, at your service."

"Mr. Sleeth . . ."

He seized her slender hand in his fleshy one, squeezed it and drew it beneath his arm. "Archibald, please, Miss . . . ?"

"Fitzgerald, Trista Fitzgerald," she offered, suddenly wishing to draw her hand from the clammy grip permeating her glove. "Archibald, forgive me. You see, 'tis my first trip to the city and—"

"Ah, I see, no doubt a lovely young lady such as yourself seeks to become a member of the ton, the social elite." He pulled her just a step nearer.

She stiffened. "I truly harbor no such aspirations, Mr. Sleeth. To be perfectly honest, someone is expecting me shortly and I must return—"

"Ah, but they will snatch you up, my lovely, clasp you to the very bosom of Society, embrace you within their fold, beautiful as you are." His puffy lips quaked as if this all proved nearly too much to bear. "The landed gentry, my dear, a class to which I myself belong. And as such, I shall be your escort."

He took several steps and she stumbled after him, aware of some inner alarm screaming a warning. Twisting her head, she knew a sudden panic at her distance from the coach. Ian was nowhere to be seen, and of a sudden the street seemed eerily deserted. Spinning toward Sleeth with heightening desperation, she planted her feet and sought to free her arm from his unrelenting grip.

"Mr. Sleeth, my arm, if you please!"

"Archie . . . please call me Archie," he breathed, leering at her, then pulling her along. "Come with me, little Society minx, let me show you London. We shall set this bloody town on its ears."

With eyes widening in panic, Trista clawed at his hand, a terrified scream lurching from the depths of her throat, when suddenly Archibald Sleeth was lifted off his feet and set soundly upon his rump with a whoosh and a mighty tear as his stays ripped asunder.

From out of nowhere, and before Trista could flee, a very tall, dark form descended upon her. A strong arm slipped about her waist, a warm mouth settled against her tumbling hair, and a deep voice murmured softly in her ear. "Didn't I ask you to remain at home for me, little love, while I completed my business? Missed me too much, as I did you."

The hand at her waist pressed possessively against her, a thumb rubbing brazenly against the fullness of her breast. Trista stiffened with mounting rage. She turned her head, opening her mouth to vent her anger, only to receive a mouthful of crisp, wavy dark hair as the unseen face nuzzled her somewhere above the lace at her throat and below her ear, then shifted to nibble at her earlobe. Shivers ran along her spine and she squirmed against the solid frame of her captor.

"Play along, darling," the stranger's resonant voice warned smoothly, speaking only for her ears, and the hand at her waist tightened again.

"I say, dear fellow!" Sleeth's voice rose an octave as he furiously shook his walking stick at the stranger. "What is the meaning of this?"

"Many pardons, my good man," the stranger apologized smoothly. "But 'twas my bride with whom you were romping, though I scarcely blame you. I'm certain you'd agree that I'm the luckiest man on earth to be forever bound to the marriage bed with as fetching a wench as she."

Trista's eyes widened in humiliation, though words stuck in her throat. She could do naught but gape at the man.

As he leaned toward her, Trista's gaze rose and she glimpsed chiseled features and eyes the color of the ocean. "I fear we've just embarked upon newly wedded bliss," he murmured.

As those softly spoken words swirled about her, Trista was acutely aware that his thumb rubbed at the base of her throat, then moved under her chin to tip her head up to his. With eyes widening in disbelief and her arms dangling uselessly at her sides, she felt her mouth drop open at the outright gall of the man even as the bronzed face descended and firm lips brushed hers in a feather of a kiss.

At Archibald Sleeth's muffled cough, the stranger lifted his head and smiled apologetically at the other man. "You'll forgive me, of course, for I fear I can't keep my hands from her."

Imprisoned in her abject horror and uncharacteristically at a complete loss for words, Trista was seized by an uncontrollable urge to kill this rake...this...this... Why, those eyes of his were all over her, from head to toe and back again!

"Darling," he drawled wickedly, the look in his eyes causing Trista to clutch her parted jacket close with hands that trembled with rage. "In the future, *do* try to keep your clothes on." He winked slyly at Archibald Sleeth. "She has developed this charming aversion to clothing ever since we wed."

Sleeth muttered something beneath his breath, obviously considering himself rather lucky to have chosen as his prey the wife of an extremely understanding chap. He stammered an apology beneath the handkerchief pressed to his beaded upper lip, then turned on his heel and, without a backward glance, beat a hasty retreat, waddling up the street whence he came.

"'Twould appear the ruse proved a success," the stranger murmured, his hooded eyes still fixed upon the retreating form. He turned, releasing his hold upon Trista, and bestowed a dastardly grin upon her.

Trista, however, was not the least bit aware of this scoundrel's disarming good looks. Nay, she was far more concerned with laying a stinging blow upon the stranger's jaw.

"How dare you?" She gulped for breath, her ire knowing no bounds when the cad seemed rather amused by all this, looking about as pleased as a fox in a henhouse despite the imprint of her fingers that he wore. "Posing as some love-smitten groom! How shockingly intimate your portrayal of the devoted spouse! Egomaniacal cad! How dare you?" She shook her tumbling locks with a stubborn toss of her head and took a step toward him. "Laying your filthy hands upon me as if I were but a common streetwalker! Have you no decency? Ah, but of course, this is the manner in which all you contemptible London rogues treat your wenches, thrusting your loathsome attentions upon them. If my father..."

Lending her half an ear, the stranger drank in this tousled, trembling young beauty, the green eyes flashing unabashed contempt, the burnished chestnut locks tumbling about her shoulders. She was irresistibly charming, and he found his gaze traveling leisurely over the upturned nose, the flushed cheekbones to a full, pouty, totally kissable mouth and slightly cleft chin lifted haughtily with her anger. She stood tall, slim and proud before him, despite her dishabille, so self-righteous and defiant, claws bared and ready for a fight over her hardly blemished honor, that it was all he could do to suppress another grin, take her in his arms and kiss all that anger out of her.

Her last words brought his wandering eyes quickly to heel and he threw back his head with a hearty laugh. "Oh, God, a daddy's girl."

"I most certainly am not!" Trista huffed, pursing her lips and clenching her fists against her skirts lest she use them on this rascal. Unwittingly, she found her eyes drawn to the length of his strong brown throat, which appeared almost rawly masculine against the stark white of his collar. He was rather fierce-looking for a rogue, with icy dark features and longish hair, and was attired almost completely in black, with a simple black cravat at his throat. The cut and cloth of both topcoat and trousers suggested he was a gentleman of good taste, if not some wealth. He was extremely tall and powerfully built, with a tapering waist and very long legs....

What the devil? Her cheeks flamed, and before she could summon a coherent thought, he spoke in that godawful deep voice.

"Rest assured, I meant only to dissuade your friend Sleeth in his pursuit. If I in any way offended you, I apologize."

"Indeed, you did!"

"Ah, I see. Perhaps you wish I'd ignored your plight and left you to defend yourself against his all but honorable intentions. I'm more than aware of the man's less than remarkable way with the fairer sex, though I have to admit, the fellow has an eye for a beautiful woman. Nevertheless, I believe my only fault lies in expecting some token of appreciation for rescuing you. Perhaps if I were to fetch your hat and purse..." Before she could reply, he retrieved the articles from the cobblestones, though not before another passing coach had all but flattened them beyond repair.

She snatched the articles from his ever-so-helpful hand. "Ha! The day shall *never* dawn when I will even consider entertaining the thought of thanking you for either my ruined hat *or* my still-intact virtue, which I doubt was seriously threatened until *you* came along!" She peered as haughtily as she could down her prim nose. "Despite what you believe to be *your* dreadfully honorable reasons for doing so, please be advised that this maid abhors mauling and kissing forced upon her without consent in some brazen display—"

"And here I'd thought 'twas simply the display you abhorred. To my eye, you rather enjoyed the actual kiss, did you not?"

Trista fairly flew at him. "How dare you?"

Quick as a flash, his hands caught her wrists in a steely grip and pulled her close against him, so close that her breasts were nearly flattened against his hard chest. His eyes glittering dangerously into hers, he spoke slowly and deliberately, the warmth of his breath upon her cheeks. "Rest assured, my hot little lioness, you will come to realize that *I dare much.*"

Trista felt the bottom fall from her stomach, for she realized that she had met not only the embodiment of all she despised in a man but her match of wills. She could almost believe she hated the cad.

At the sound of a door opening at a nearby shop, he released her wrists abruptly and bowed mockingly before her. He gave her a lopsided grin, displaying even white teeth. "It was most pleasurable."

The azure eyes slid from hers to peer over her shoulder, and Trista turned about to spy Ian quickly approaching. She spun about as the stranger retrieved his hat from a nearby bench, tipped it in farewell, then presented her his back as he purposefully strode to take the arm of the very young, very beautiful blond girl alighting from a nearby shop. Clad in a lovely ice-blue-and-white striped satin gown, her golden locks swept saucily beneath a matching plumed hat, she presented the stranger with a dazzling smile, laid her gloved hand upon that black-clad arm and allowed him to escort her from the shop and a fuming Trista, who, for the first time in her life, felt annoyingly tousled and severely underdressed.

Clenching her fists, Trista turned and bristled past Ian.

The coachman skidded to a halt, spun about and hurried after her. "Lass, whatever happened to ye? Are ye all right, child?"

" 'Twas nothing but a rather unpleasant encounter that I shall soon forget," she grumbled over her shoulder as she strode determinedly toward the coach. "Not a word of this to Father."

With a disgusted sigh, she tossed the useless hat into the coach and hastily rebuttoned her jacket to the throat. Try as she might, fumbling and fussing for what seemed an eternity, she could not achieve the careless crisp fall of lace at her throat. Abandoning that task, she poked and tucked at her hair and was contemplating what to do with a wayward tendril hanging down her back, when of a sudden a door burst open and her father and a female companion stepped into the sunlight.

Trista gaped openmouthed, a state to which she had of late grown somewhat accustomed, as her father fairly bounced down the walkway, speaking animatedly and guffawing at the slightest remark made by his companion. She was a small woman of perhaps thirty with rich-hued auburn hair, milky skin and large emerald eyes, the exact color of the beautiful gown she wore. She spoke easily with Winston in a voice both smooth and refined, and when she laughed, laying a slender hand upon his forearm, Winston beamed down at her with eyes twinkling. They stood facing each other, their voices low, oblivious to both Ian and Trista.

Could *this* be Isabel Kingsley, the so-called client her father would be accompanying on a month-long business trip throughout the Continent?

Their conversation apparently at an end, Winston bowed lingeringly before the woman, then tipped his hat and sauntered toward the coach, breezing past Ian and Trista with barely a nod.

He bade them to the vehicle with a smart "Shall we? No use in standing about idly. Esme awaits."

For several long moments, Trista could only stare, mouth agape. Then, with one thoughtful glance after her father's "client," she gathered skirt in hand, lifted her chin and, with Ian's assistance, boarded the coach.

Trista paused to tug angrily at her neckline for what seemed the hundredth time since she'd donned the blasted gown not three minutes past. Why hadn't she succumbed to Maggie's incessant mumblings that all her gowns were in desperate need of altering? She'd grown, she realized that, but in places she'd paid little heed to over the years and to proportions she'd never dreamed. She gave the impossibly low, scooped neckline a wary grimace. Dear God, she felt as if her breasts were completely displayed, and worse yet, she could barely draw a breath. Perhaps if she didn't eat too much at dinner...

With skirts lifted, she hurried down the sweeping stairs and through the enormous entryway, her heels tapping against the marble as she hastened toward the parlor, toward the unmistakable sound of her father's voice. Skidding to a halt just outside the open doors, she took a deep breath, adjusting her neckline with a scowl and swept as gracefully as she could into the room.

Her father stood before the fire with drink in hand, facing the doorway, immersed in a lively conversation with the tall gentleman before him. A third gentleman lingered near the windows, bent low over a table, refilling his drink from a crystal decanter.

"Trista, come join us!" Winston greeted her with a bit too much enthusiasm, slapping his friend amicably on the back before hurrying toward Trista.

"Ah! So this is Trista!" The gentleman at the windows spun about as Trista took a pace into the room. His voice was smooth and elegant as he moved as gracefully as a man could to take her hand in his and bend low over it. "Allow me to formally welcome you to my home. Esme has talked of little else these past weeks but your visit with us."

Dominic Catalani was a tall, regal-looking man with sleek dark hair, a swarthy complexion and pencil-thin mustache above a dazzling, thin-lipped smile. He was elegantly attired in a dove gray topcoat and trousers, his peacock blue waistcoat and matching cravat superbly contrasting with the crisp white ruffle at both collar and cuffs. The hand he laid upon Trista's was perfectly manicured, and diamonds glittered from the ring on his little finger.

Beneath his unwavering regard, Trista felt the color climb in her cheeks and experienced a moment's trouble retrieving her voice. "I . . . thank you, sir. I fear an apology is in order for my tardiness. I fear I napped a trifle too long."

The Count waved a bejeweled hand. "My dear Miss Fitzgerald, I am known simply as Dominic. Indeed, one so beautiful and charming needn't concern oneself with trivialities like tardiness. Besides, we've lingered over a drink or two, though I fear Esme and Bianca will be a trifle puffed up as they preceded us to the dining room some time ago. Your father, Mr. Brennan, here, and I had a bit of business to discuss." The Count released her hand and gestured toward the broad back of the man still standing before the fire. "Nicholas, shall I introduce you?"

When this Nicholas fellow turned from the fire, Trista felt the bottom drop from her stomach. It was him! The scoundrel! The rogue! He was here! And not two moments past her father had slapped him amiably upon the back, behaving as if they were old friends! Her pulse hammered in her ears as he sauntered toward her, the intensity of his gaze as it swept the entire length of her snatching away what little breath she possessed.

Chapter Two

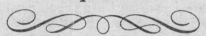

"Nicholas, may I present Miss Trista Fitzgerald, newly arrived from the country for an extended visit with my wife, her Aunt Esme. Trista. Nicholas Brennan, businessman *extraordinaire.*"

He has a name! Trista thought wildly as he took her unyielding hand firmly in his and bent that dark head low over her trembling fingers. At the soft brush of his lips upon her skin, Trista, seeking to escape his touch, found her hand soundly encased in his larger one. She cast furious eyes at him, only to bristle anew as he lifted a smoldering gaze to the shocking display of her bosom. Unconsciously, her free hand moved to her décolletage in a valiant and entirely vain attempt to shield herself.

"The pleasure is all mine, Miss Fitzgerald," he drawled, and at long last lifted his eyes to hers.

I'll bet! Trista fumed, forcing a curt nod, which she prayed revealed every last ounce of her contempt. Her eyes darted to his, so full of some wicked promise, and she realized with a start that her hand was still firmly entrapped in his. Gritting her teeth, she snatched her fingers from his so suddenly that the movement drew a raised brow from her father.

"As I was saying, Trista," Winston remarked, eyeing his daughter with some speculation, "you can well imagine my surprise when I realized that Nicholas's grandfather was a highly regarded business associate of my father's." He frowned, as if struck by a sudden thought. "And now you're in shipping. Brennan...Brennan. Seems to me, though I may be wrong, that your family was involved in that shipping empire that went under some years ago. Whatever was the name?''

"I'm sorry, but I do believe you are mistaken," Nicholas replied. "Most of my ancestors were farmers, Mr. Fitzgerald, hardworking people, though quite unremarkable, and certainly bearing no relation to a shipping empire."

"So sorry. I was quite sure." Winston shook his head and smiled. "Old age, eh? So glad to hear you've experienced such success with your business in the States. I wish you all the best in London, as well. How long did you say you were planning to stay?''

The brilliant blue eyes flickered to Trista. "One never knows what opportunity may present itself, and I have never been wont to let *any* slip away. In all truth, I haven't given the matter much thought, though I must confess—'' that damnable grin curved his mouth ''—if your daughter is any indication of the beauty to be found in London, perhaps I will lengthen my stay...interminably."

Oh, spare me! Trista clenched her fists in frustration. She spun about and headed with definite purpose for the dining room, feeling the anger rise like acrid bile in her throat. Was there no limit to the man's audacity? Despicable, he was. *Worse* than despicable. Behaving as if this were their first encounter, plying her father and Dominic with that conjured-up business gibberish as if he were some noble, astute businessman instead of the swaggering rake he most certainly was. For heaven's sake, didn't noble gentlemen employ tailors to refit pants that were far too revealing for anyone's taste?

How was she to right the matter? She could boldly accuse this well-respected businessman, a man whose ancestors were once highly regarded associates of her own grandfather, the same man with whom her father was so dreadfully and erroneously impressed—accuse him of what? Rescuing her from some vile lecher named Archibald Sleeth? Nay! Was there to be no justice?

Dinner began as a consummate disaster when Trista, wishing to locate her place at the table, stumbled headlong into Nicholas's unyielding, very solid frame.

"Why, Miss Fitzgerald," he murmured softly. "Bumping into gentlemen today has brought you nothing but trouble. Is that what you're after now?"

"Heavens no!" she flared at him through gritted teeth. "Out of my way, you cad, for you are no gentleman!"

She pushed past him, bristling at the low chuckle following her, and found her place beside her father. Not long thereafter, she grew all too aware that Nicholas had taken his place directly opposite her, a vantage from which he could easily keep her in his sights. Which he did. Flagrantly. She attempted to fix her gaze upon the elegant white-and-gold bone china, nearly unable to bear his staring at her, so relaxed and cocksure he was, as if daring her to play the ruse further. Businessman *extraordinaire*, pah! He was much too busy rescuing damsels in distress and juggling handfuls of beautiful blond women to be any kind of businessman, much less an exceptional one. To Trista's eye, the man's only quality remotely approaching extraordinary was his dauntless capacity for staring.

Esme played no small part in the disaster, entirely ravishing in an elegant blue silk gown, her glossy dark hair piled high atop her head, the diamonds glittering at her ears and wrists. She gaily assumed the role of doting aunt, bubbling forth with half a dozen "oo-la-la's!" amidst all her plans for Trista to set the entire city agog. No expense would be spared! After all, a girl must have something to wear if she's to become the rage of London! *Mon Dieu*, but the gentlemen would be in pursuit and the ladies raging with envy!

Trista merely hung her head or averted her eyes or toyed with her food, roast duckling and salmon soufflé, which did not stir her in the least. She found the wine, however, very much to her liking and sipped long and often from her glass.

And that rascal across the table continued to stare.

Then, of course, Dominic's niece Bianca, who had ventured from Milan with the intent of remaining for the Season, made her intent this eve painfully apparent. From the moment Nicholas occupied the seat beside hers, she'd laid her jewel-encrusted hand upon his long brown fingers lying on the cream damask tablecloth, and there they lay for the remainder of the evening.

After a lengthy perusal, accomplished with the aid of no small amount of wine, Trista finally decided Bianca had a rather earthy, feral look about her with her slanting black eyes beneath a fall of jet black curls. Her full lips were bow shaped and revealed a mouthful of gleaming white teeth whenever Nicholas spoke, whereupon she leaned toward him with nostrils flaring as if she intended to inhale the man. She wore a sophisticated crimson silk gown with cap sleeves slipping just off her rounded shoulders and a low scooped neckline revealing her bountiful bosom. Of this, she was quite obviously proud, for every now and again she raised a hand to her collarbone, then traced a crimson fingernail past her breastbone to her deep cleavage, then up again, repeating the motion very slowly, her liquid eyes fixed intently upon the hulking figure at her side. The dim glow of the candlelight bathed her skin a smooth burnished copper and the ruby-and-diamond jewels sparkling brilliantly at her ears and throat only enhanced the rich hue.

Trista felt sick. Lowering her eyes, she sipped again from her wine, then attempted a bite of roast duckling, though the lump in her throat barely allowed passage of the liquid. Her stomach immediately rebelled. Just as she was on the verge of gagging, her eyes lifted momentarily and locked with those across the table.

Devil take him but he was handsome, so handsome she momentarily forgot her near hatred of the man and the lump of food sitting innocently in her mouth. As if with a will of their own, her eyes followed the tousled fall of his hair to the chiseled cheekbones and firm lines of his jaw, then fell unabashedly to the broad chest, where muscles strained against the satin fabric of his waistcoat with every breath. After a moment, her eyes rose to his once more, and for the first time in her life she experienced a feeling of such sensual awareness she nearly died of fright.

Reality swept upon her as her throat violently constricted, and she quickly averted her gaze, instinctively reaching for her linen napkin. Without a second thought, and before her rebellious stomach could embarrass her beyond measure, she lifted her napkin, unceremoniously depositing in it what remained of a bite of duckling. At that moment, a servant materialized at her elbow and she nearly jumped from her skin, though she managed to lift her wineglass yet again for him to refill, nodding her thanks and attempting to concentrate on the conversation swirling about her like a thick haze. She focused her attention on Bianca, who was chattering on excitedly about a murder. *Murder?*

"And, according to Darcy Langston, the girl had been savagely molested and beaten before she was killed!" Bianca's hand fluttered wildly at her décolletage.

Esme hastened to scold. "Charming girl that she is, Darcy Langston is no expert on murders and such goings-on. You cannot believe all that you hear, Bianca."

Lifting a shoulder haughtily, Bianca sniffed. "Read the *Times* for yourself tomorrow. Why, Darcy was all but best friends with the poor girl and understandably distraught at the news."

"As we all are, I'm afraid," Dominic interjected. "The police are involved, are they not? Though no clues to the Boudoir Murderer's identity have come to light. The victims were both young, beautiful society maidens. Quite tragic."

Winston spoke gravely, the concern etched upon his brow. "Boudoir Murderer, eh? No doubt 'tis a tale worth hearing."

Dominic leaned over his dessert of flaming rum cake. "The bodies were all found in the women's own private rooms, with no visible sign of forced entry. All were quite savagely beaten and ravaged before they were killed, either by a blow to the head or strangulation."

"Please, Dominic, not here." Esme raised a jeweled hand to her throat and made little effort to suppress a shudder. "If the gentlemen would like to discuss the matter further, they may retire to the drawing room with my heartfelt blessings. I'm quite certain that the ladies would much rather discuss our plans for the remainder of the week, yes? Besides, such ghastly talk is hardly appropriate for Trista's delicate constitution."

Trista pushed aside her untouched dessert. Delicate constitution be damned. What was it about women that banished them forever to inane gossip and frivolous, albeit frightfully tedious, orations on maintaining a household? She supposed she should take to her bed with a fit of the vapors over talk of murder! No doubt it was the *proper* thing to do, though her mutinous spirit of late fixed a look of vexed frustration across her brow and set her toe to tapping beneath the table.

Seizing upon Esme's suggestion, the gentlemen strolled leisurely from the room, proclaiming themselves in search of brandy and a good cigar. Bianca sashayed promptly after them. Intent upon seeing herself to bed, Trista started to her feet, then suddenly caught herself, her hand bracing the table as she struggled to get her wobbly legs beneath her. The room spun about her and she raised a hand to her temples to ease the dizziness.

"Trista, are you quite all right?" Esme's voice filled with concern as she hastened to the girl's side. With one knowing glance at Trista's sudden pallor and sluggish response, Esme laid an arm gently about her niece's shoulders. "Your first time with wine, yes? Best that you found your limit tonight and not at your ball, where this could cause you certain embarrassment."

Trista raised a grateful smile and leaned heavily on Esme's arm. They proceeded slowly from the room toward the staircase, a path that led them directly past the open drawing room doors. Trista's stomach heaved with every step, threatening complete embarrassment before her aunt and any poor soul within earshot. As they passed before the drawing room, she dared a bleary glance inside the room, spying only Nicholas's broad back. Assured that she would escape virtually unnoticed, she breathed a measured sigh of relief, only to inhale the pungent cigar smoke wafting into the hallway. Blanching, she felt her legs buckle beneath her as her stomach heaved violently and the bile rose in her throat. Leaning all her weight upon her aunt, she knew a certain dread as Esme's firm hold upon her arm was jarred loose. Then, just as she expected to dissolve in a wine-sodden heap, powerful arms swept around her back and beneath her legs, and a solid chest imposed itself close against the side of her bosom. Lifting widening eyes, she found herself surprised not by the rugged visage looming close above her but by Nicholas's amused smirk as he strode easily with her to the staircase.

The disaster was complete.

Her dull senses grew instantly aware of the heady scent of brandy mixed enticingly with the clean smell of *him,* even as she wondered what to do with her flailing arms. "Dear God, put me down, you brute..." she managed to slur.

He slanted flashing eyes at her, then took to the stairs. "Not enough supper and a bit too much wine for our little visitor, hmm? Or is this some little game you're playing so that I may rescue you yet again? If it is, I think I like it." He paused and adjusted her in his arms so that her bosom pressed full against his chest. When he spoke, his wayward thoughts lent his voice a low, smooth drawl. "Are you quite certain that London is prepared for a country maiden incapable of handling men, food and drink? I think not."

Trista allowed herself a huge yawn, which dissolved into a pout. "Who the devil cares what you think? You're nothing but a despicable..."

The laughter rumbled deep in his chest. "Ah, our second meeting has not improved that lovely little disposition of yours, eh?"

"Heavens, no," Trista mumbled with an annoyed frown, then yawned again as she felt herself drifting dreamily into sleep. What would it hurt to allow her head to fall against a muscular shoulder...her arms to loop about his neck? Let the cad smirk.

"Blasted pants...businessman *extraordinaire,* my horse's arse..." she mumbled, conscious only of the dull buzzing in her ears . . . and that solid chest against her cheek . . . and then, only darkness.

"I believe the man is newly arrived from America, that wild, heathen land." Dominic shuddered and sipped his tea. "Little wonder he proved a most entertaining guest."

Trista glanced up sharply from her breakfast fare of ham, eggs, cold boiled beef and currant buns. She could lay blame for the sudden fluttering in her belly to her overindulgence of spirits, though Esme's liquid concoction she'd rather glumly imbibed seemed to have tempered the ill effects. Then again, when one despised a man as she did this Brennan fellow, a certain fluttering in one's belly could certainly be expected. The sunlight spilling through the floor-to-ceiling windows made her head ache and she squinted through a crystal vase of freshly cut white tulips for a better view of Dominic.

"I do so enjoy lending an ear to his business philosophies, as New World and, dare I say, coarse and untried as they are," he remarked, directing his comments to Winston. "Though the man *is* a Yankee, which speaks for itself. He is sure to raise a few eyebrows with his unrefined methods, be they business or social, eh?"

Winston raised a curious brow. "Then again, to successfully build a shipping empire, perhaps he sees fit to apply new methods. My father knew of his family. Good business people. No doubt Brennan acquired several of these traits from his ancestors."

Trista almost snorted into her teacup. The previous evening's activities had obviously done little to temper her father's infatuation with Nicholas Brennan.

Dominic shifted uncomfortably in his chair. "Indeed, though I may not altogether agree with him, his business venture warrants closer scrutiny, especially with the sum he suggests—a tremendous sum indeed, though the man balks at specifics. Did you notice that, Winston?"

"I did, though to my eye his hesitancy to expose all to a potential investor indicates a man of sound judgment. Or perhaps he simply sought pleasure last evening."

"That may be." Dominic spoke with forced levity, then raised a haughty brow, as if a trifle miffed at Winston's response. "Though I dare say, I am not simply another potential investor. Brennan would be more than a fool not to realize that. After all, I've had the man to my house on more than one occasion for the express purpose of discussing business."

His voice rang shrilly through the breakfast room and Esme glanced up quickly. "Oh, shush, Dominic, not here."

Dominic raised brooding eyes. "Yes, of course, 'tis only a minor business venture at that. Business aside—though in his case, one finds it difficult to separate the business from the man—he is a rather odd sort, lacking in *breeding,* for want of a better word, or perhaps 'tis his blasted arrogance. And quite a gambler, I might add. I've lost a farthing or two to the man myself. One wonders why I bother with him."

Trista nearly choked on a mouthful of ham and eggs. Indeed, she rather liked this Count fellow!

"Nothing to become upset about, I dare say," Dominic murmured half to himself, then turned to Winston as if dismissing all talk of Nicholas Brennan. "Must you be off so early today? Perhaps we could detain you. I'd wager you'd find London nightlife a wee bit more, shall we say, 'gay' than you may recall from years past."

"'Tis quite dreadfully true," Esme remarked. "Now that all the awful wars are over and that heathen Bonaparte is tucked away where he belongs, England is enjoying herself once again, and has been for several years now, though I fear the streets are not safe for a respectable family after dark. All the gaming houses, not to mention the brothels and prostitutes! Surely, Dominic, you're not suggesting..."

"No, of course not, darling," Dominic assuaged, patting her hand. "The gentleman's club I frequent is all very proper, though I've encountered our friend Brennan there on a few occasions. Why a Yankee would be allowed in such a place, I'll never know."

This was more like it. Gaming houses, brothels and prostitutes sounded more like the Nicholas Brennan Trista knew.

Winston waved a hand, begging off, and soon departed amidst several misty-eyed farewells. Soon thereafter, Dominic appeared bearing walking stick and top hat, claiming urgent business to which he had to attend, then sauntered casually from the room, whistling a cheery tune.

"Always business," Esme murmured. "He enjoys dabbling in various business ventures, for he has the means and finds it exciting, much more so than tending to matters back in Milan, which he and I find *dreadfully* boring. Besides, his mother, the Marchioness, lives there and..." She waved a slender hand as if to dismiss the mere thought. "Suffice it to say, I feel less for her than I do for my own father. It pleases me to come back to London, though I do miss Paris terribly at times. 'Tis best, I suppose, to be far from the memories of Gaston." The dark eyes grew clouded for a moment.

"You miss him very much," Trista murmured.

"Oh, *cherie,* at times too much," came the whispered response. For an instant, Trista was certain she detected tears shining in Esme's luminous eyes. Then her aunt gave a shrug and drew herself up with a wide smile. "Darling, I have found London pleasantly exciting, and you shall, as well. You needn't concern yourself with all that idle talk of murder." She paused, glancing toward the doorway. "Tsk, that Bianca. Sleeping well into the day as usual. Enjoyed herself immensely last evening with M'sieur Brennan, I must say, though who wouldn't, hmm? My, my...so tall and dark he is, with that allure of mystery. Keeps himself decidedly removed from all the social goings-on, much to the dismay of femmes fatales like our Bianca." Daintily, she sipped from her teacup, then waved a hand. "Bianca has set her sights on him and will certainly wheedle out of him as much as she is able. Oh, here she is now. Bianca, darling, sleeping so long, tsk, tsk, 'tis nearly dinnertime!"

Bianca swept into the room on a wave of sweet musky perfume that all but obliterated the scrumptious aroma of the food. "I fear the evening ended far later than expected," she informed them in a low, husky voice, and her dark eyes twinkled mischievously. She moved languidly, like a sleek cat swathed in a crimson-and-white striped satin gown. She purred her good-mornings, which Trista returned with forced gaiety.

"And what hour was it that finally saw you to bed?" Esme inquired. "I retired rather late myself. I trust you found Monsieur Brennan entertaining."

"Very much so," Bianca murmured, toying with her dangling ruby earrings. She smiled secretively and sighed. "He's so devilishly handsome, it's almost wicked. Those eyes when he looks at you..."

Trista gulped her tea. The cad.

"And he lingered well into the evening, I fear the birds were already about!" Bianca shivered with unabashed delight.

"Surely you were chaperoned?" Esme scolded, lifting a brow disapprovingly.

Bianca lowered her gaze to admire her manicure. "Uncle Dom was enjoying a bit of a struggle to keep apace with the conversation, so I assured him that we would be fine unchaperoned. Besides, that bloody servant Emerson was skulking about all night, popping in and out so unexpectedly to serve this or fetch that. I do believe the man floats about, for he makes no sound at all."

"It pleases me that Emerson is attending to his duties properly," Esme remarked.

"Really, you needn't get puffed up, Esme. Then again, perhaps you should. In all truth, the man can be most insistent, a quality I find irresistible. Actually, I had quite a time keeping his hands from me, but who could blame the man! All that *hot* Yankee blood!"

Esme raised her hands to her temples and moaned softly, "Oh, Bianca, no..."

"Esme, please! I intend to have him as my beau for our ball and every other ball this season. Any girl with eyes in her head will be green with envy! Now, I must be off. Luncheon at Darcy Langston's."

Esme cast Bianca a sidelong glance. "One would think Darcy incapable of entertaining so soon after the murder of her *dearest* friend."

Narrowing her feral gaze upon Esme, Bianca sniffed, "Why, we're *all* upset, Esme. Really! There's little sense in keeping to one's very bed over this."

Esme cast Trista an amused glance. "And what with the gossip *abounding.*"

"Of course!" Bianca exclaimed. "One must keep informed, you know. So sorry you shan't be there, Trista. Don't feel too left out of the fun. Ooh! Perhaps Nicholas will be about!"

"Monsieur Brennan does not strike me as a man harboring much interest in little luncheons and idle gossip. However, lest you so happen to bump into the man, do try to maintain some decency of manner, Bianca." Esme shook her head hopelessly.

"I'm well aware of proper behavior in public with a gentleman!" Bianca huffed, smoothing her skirts and apparently ignoring Esme's dubious expression. "Besides, I wish to keep Nicholas a delicious secret until the ball, so not a word, either of you, yes?"

"Of course, darling," Esme assured her, then added, "if you can also manage such a feat, hmm?"

"And what are you two about today?" Bianca asked, purposefully ignoring Esme's prod and raising a lofty brow at Trista.

"Shopping!" Esme breathed, rising and nearly clapping her hands with glee. "We're off to Adelle's for some new gowns for Trista!"

"How charming!" Bianca retorted through a stiff smile. "Though I don't believe Adelle carries high-necked muslin gowns and white cotton bonnets. Really, Esme, isn't Trista a trifle young for silks and brocades?"

"Young! Oh, for heaven's sake! Trista is about to acquire a magnificent wardrobe, perfect for her London debut! Let us be off, Trista, before the sun sets on us!"

* * *

"Do not move, Trista,' Adelle, the lively French couturiere, warned over her shoulder as she and Esme hastened to the back of the tiny shop in search of the proper shoe. "The pins are quite sharp!"

"Mmm, and well I know," Trista murmured, almost afraid to take a breath for fear of being pricked by a pin and bursting from her bodice. Willing herself to stand very still before the mirror, she gazed at her reflection and found herself taken aback. The girl in the glass could not be her. She was... quite beautiful. Her hair tumbled in glossy disarray about her shoulders, her eyes a deeper jade against the pale pink of the gown. The dress was spectacular, made of the finest peau de soie, with capped sleeves caught at the shoulder with pale pink rosettes, a scandalously low neckline, fitted waist with cream sash and a full billowing skirt, flounced at the hem with pink rosettes, and with a cream silk underskirt. The fabric shimmered in the sunlight when she turned gingerly from side to side. Blast Adelle for fitting the gown so snugly about her waist and bosom with those pins of hers.

Trista glanced about the empty shop, her gaze following the bobbing bonnets and top hats just visible through the high windows. Turning back to her reflection, she twisted ever so slightly from side to side to view the wide sash and swinging skirt, so intent on the play of sunlight upon the shimmering silk that she was completely unaware of the tinkling of the bell over the entrance announcing the arrival of another customer. Indeed, only that deep, resonant voice could have brought her crashing to her senses so rapidly, her stomach plummeting to her bare toes and her heart slamming against the walls of her chest.

Chapter Three

"Why, Miss Fitzgerald, one can't help but be surprised to find you out and about so early in the day." Nicholas Brennan removed his top hat and tossed it carelessly onto a nearby chair. He sauntered toward Trista, slim hips swaggering, his hooded gaze capturing hers in the mirror before sweeping unabashedly over her from head to toe. "And no worse for wear, indeed," he remarked as if half to himself.

"Surely you have some sordid business in yonder back alley which requires your immediate attention," Trista mused with forced levity, even as she wondered why her blood suddenly pounded within her veins. It was anger, of course, nothing more. After all, hadn't the man displayed naught but blatant disrespect for her, her family, while perpetuating his guise of swank and noble Yankee businessman? Indeed, that alone was cause enough to set her teeth on edge. With a haughty lift of one shoulder, she attempted to focus her decided lack of concentration on her gown once more, though one eye strayed to the hulking figure looming at her side.

Nicholas loosened his topcoat as if in anticipation of more than a brief stay, and the laughter rumbled deep within his chest. Leaning against a nearby stool, he folded muscular arms over his chest and inclined his head, gracing Trista with yet another leisurely sweep of his eyes. "We're certainly frisky this morning, hmm? A trifle high-strung, perhaps? Need I remind you that you now owe me a token of thanks for two separate acts of unmitigated valor. At this rate, you may have to marry me by week's end and bestow upon me your virtue—worth a king's ransom, I'd wager my life—plus a substantial dowry just to repay my gallantry."

Trista choked on her response. She couldn't be sure, but hadn't he just likened her to a blasted horse? Of all the... Marry him! She retrieved her voice and ground out through clenched teeth, "'Twould seem your idle and depraved existence has left you not only blissfully ignorant of the meaning of the word *valor*, Mr. Brennan, but also grievously self-impressed. To my eye, your behavior has been anything but gallant, warranting naught but a scathing reprimand as repayment from me."

"Ah, I see a night's rest has done little for your surly disposition." His gaze swung about the shop. "Of course, if you're anything like a typical woman, a new frock or two should bring a smile to your lips and a lightness to your step for, oh, several hours at least."

"Spoken like a true connoisseur," Trista muttered, scowling in his general direction, then presenting her back in a futile attempt to ignore him.

"Has anyone ever told you that you frown and stomp your feet entirely too much for one so young and beautiful? Would I be remiss in assuming that you're not finding London to your liking?"

"Actually, since you've asked, 'tis certain of its creatures forever *lurking* about that I find especially distasteful."

"Ah, then I presume you've found your Uncle Dominic's welcome lacking in some way?"

Trista glanced sharply at the beguilingly innocent expression he suddenly wore and immediately leapt to her aunt's defense. "Hardly! Both he and Aunt Esme have been nothing but gracious."

"Then surely you worry needlessly over our friend Sleeth."

"'Twasn't *he* that came to mind, either."

"He truly believes that you are reveling in all the passion of newly wedded bliss, sweetheart."

"Ha! No thanks to you!"

"Precisely my point. You have yet to thank me. Of course, we could settle the score now, very simply." The sensuously smooth drawl of his voice wreaked far greater havoc upon her senses than the sudden realization that he had moved very close behind her. "I am very willing," he murmured softly.

In the mirror, Trista watched his smoldering eyes fall from hers to sweep over her hair, then drop to linger on her bosom before rising to fix upon her mouth. The unmistakably hungry look in his eyes left her feeling not unlike an overripe lamb being led to slaughter.

"Must you forever stare at me, Mr. Brennan?" she sniffed, though her voice had taken on a decided breathlessness due perhaps to the bodice from which she felt on the verge of bursting. Indeed, she seemed suddenly incapable of drawing a deep breath. Gingerly, she raised her arm to adjust the gown, only to be pricked nastily by a pin. "Or perhaps 'tis my likeness to horseflesh that you find so intriguing, hmm?"

His chest pressed against her back, and his cleft chin just brushed the top of her head. His gaze lowered and fixed somewhere... "I didn't realize that I was staring. Though I must admit to having a decided penchant for long-legged, full-chested mares."

"Mr. Brennan," she began firmly, taking a step from him.

"Nicholas to you, sweet Trista," he drawled, stepping close behind her once again. "There's little need for formalities. God, but you're unbelievably beautiful in pink."

His gaze dipped again to her bosom, and Trista had to fight the nearly overwhelming urge to squirm from the blasted gown. "I prefer Mr. Brennan, thank you just the same," she informed him, then peered down her nose at him. "However, methinks Boudoir Murderer could possibly suit you, as well."

Nicholas erupted with an easy laugh. "Ah, but you wound me, lovely Trista. However, since the only maid's bedroom I have frequented of late is yours, you may call me Nicholas, or even darling, if the mood suits you."

"Had I known—"

"Would you like me to refresh your memory? 'Tis a most pleasant one for me."

"Heavens no!" Trista exclaimed heatedly. "Actually, I do seem to recall a somewhat vague, though quite unpleasant memory of late last evening. Perhaps that would explain my nausea and throbbing, aching head, hmm?"

"Highly unlikely," he replied, moving to her side. "Although I've never been accused of bringing on nausea, I have been known to cause throbbing and aching . . . but not of the kind you've yet experienced, I'm more than certain."

His voice was so deep, so husky, so close to her ear and so seductively laced with innuendo she most certainly did not understand that of a sudden Trista felt like a fox caught helplessly in a trap. To escape from that silky voice, his bold words so eloquently spoken, she would gladly have chewed off a treasured limb. Her prison, however, was a row of prickly pins that unceasingly reminded her of her straits.

"Mr. Brennan, must you stand so close? My aunt is just behind yonder counter."

"The fear of detection only heightens my purpose, Trista." The lopsided grin faded. "I could hardly believe my luck last night, running into you again."

"Luck?" Trista cried. "Surely you jest! Playing me for a fool before my family! All but daring me to expose you for the insufferable rake you are!"

He lifted a curious brow. "I seem to recall you had every opportunity to blaspheme my character, if that was your purpose, Trista. Perhaps you do indeed harbor some small measure of appreciation."

"Oh, please!" Trista nearly snorted with disgust. "You had my father so entirely captivated with your talk of business, he would have paid me little heed."

"Is that so?" His lips twisted into a smirk. "And here I'd thought your inability to speak was merely the result of wondering what to do with the food in your mouth."

Trista stared at him, feeling the color sweeping to her cheeks. "You're detestable."

"I've been called worse."

"That doesn't surprise me. Now be gone. I wish nothing from you but that you leave me alone."

"That may very well be what you believe you *should* wish, Trista, though your enchanting green eyes tell an altogether different story."

"Simply another trick of your insufferable ego," Trista replied testily, though for the life of her she could not meet his gaze and found herself, much to her horror, staring at his blasted, formfitting trousers. With cheeks flaming, she whirled abruptly from him, only to be pricked viciously by the stabbing pins. In heaven's name, where were Adelle and Esme? *Making* her shoes or simply locating a pair?

"Be off with you!" She waved a hand toward the door, aware of an inner trembling that had little to do with despising the man. "Your drawing room fancy, Bianca, awaits, though I'm sure you have a fine blond miss stashed on some nearby corner."

"I do believe beneath that prim and pristine veil within which you wish to cloak yourself, a green-eyed monster bears her mighty claws." His white teeth flashed in what could only be deemed a self-satisfied grin, one Trista itched to slap from his face.

"Believe me, 'tis God's truth," Trista half whispered, aware of her fiercely pounding heart, of the danger of this man. "I want nothing more to do with you."

"Are you quite certain, sweet Trista?" he murmured, raising a hand to lift a wayward tendril of gold-streaked hair that lay against her bosom. Instantly, Trista stiffened, lifting furious eyes to his and opening her mouth to speak.

"Shush, darling." He pressed a finger against her lips. "There is no further need to lash me with your quick tongue." His gaze dipped again to caress her trembling breasts. "You're bewitchingly beautiful."

His voice had lowered to a whisper and Trista stood rooted to the spot, her legs suddenly weak as a swelling tide of feeling lapped at her gently, cajoling, willing her to lower her eyes to the mouth moving closer and closer to hers. She was suddenly powerless as his arm slipped easily about her waist, and her eyes widened and rose to his. She stiffened, anticipating his intent, knowing that she should sweep his hands aside, slap that look from his eye, flee if she had to…but she was unable. He raised a finger beneath her chin and tipped her face to his.

Unhurriedly, his lips moved over hers, willing a response from her in a kiss so languorous, so feather light, Trista's every thought was banished to the four winds. A trembling seized her, from rage, shock, she couldn't guess, nor did she care as she realized her hands had risen to grasp his arms. With a soft, agonizing moan of despair, she felt her lips part beneath his and her will crumple in a heap.

At her sweet surrender, his kiss grew bold, intensifying, as he slanted his mouth over hers with increasing fervor and his arm flexed and drew her hips full against his powerful length. His fingers traced molten heat along her collarbone and the side of her breast, and Trista's eyes flew wide with startling realization. His hand moved boldly to cup her breast, nearly pushing it from her gown, as his lips blazed a path from her mouth to her ear and along her throat, causing Trista to struggle in earnest. Liquid heat threatened to dissolve her legs beneath her as he lowered his head and she felt his mouth upon the high curves of her breasts. His breath was ragged and hot against her skin and she sagged against him, pushing vainly at the powerful shoulders. She gasped, stunned by the liberties he took yet unable to catch her breath for his mouth was upon hers yet again, drawing her very life's breath from her.

Through the crushed silk of her gown, she felt the lean, hard length of him pressing unabashedly against her and she knew a sudden panic, a desperation to escape this man and his wicked intentions. She had to make him stop. She must….

And then, quite suddenly, Nicholas released her. To her horror, she realized that her aunt and Adelle were coming from the back of the shop, their animated voices apparently rousing him from the depths of depravity much quicker than she. She opened her mouth to speak, her trembling hands fumbling over her breasts.

Nicholas brought a finger to her lips to shush any words poised on the tip of her tongue. "Our friends arrive, Trista, and not a moment too soon." His warm fingers brushed intimately against her skin as he assisted in the reparations, and he spoke in a husky whisper. "Stop your trembling, darling." Gazing upon her with eyes still blazing with desire, he lifted her chin and brushed his mouth lightly over hers, murmuring against her parted lips, "We'll continue this at a later date, rest assured," then moved with catlike speed to retrieve his hat.

"Wha...?" Trista could manage only a muffled croak in his general direction, so outraged was she by his assumption. The arrogant buffoon! Spinning to the mirror, she raised trembling hands to cool her flaming cheeks. Dear God! One look at her swollen lips, flushed skin, tumbled hair...

"Monsieur Brennan! What a surprise!" Adelle exclaimed as she spied him perched casually and, to her eye, quite magnificently against a stool. "I was not expecting you! Your patronage has been missed, *mon cher,* for very few men share your impeccable taste in women's clothing." She winked at him and patted one brawny arm.

Rising to his full height, Nicholas greeted the two women.

Esme offered him a pleasant smile. "'Tis quite a surprise, though a pleasant one, indeed, to happen upon you...*here.*"

The rays of sunlight streaming through the windows played upon his broad shoulders. "Being that it was such a beautiful morning, I thought to enjoy a leisurely stroll and happened to spy, through yonder window, Miss Fitzgerald intently admiring herself."

"Well, you're welcome anytime!" Adelle winked wickedly, then her mouth dropped open in surprise as if at a sudden thought. "Since you're here, perhaps you could save Mademoiselle Cooper a trip and deliver to her the new silk stockings she recently purchased. They've but just arrived from Paris early this morning. Ooh, Esme, you should see them! Our lovely Trista *must* have a pair!"

The rather vivid image her words inspired caused Nicholas to raise a devilish brow at Trista, who was contemplating the ceiling and blushing to her toes.

As Adelle scurried once again to the back of the shop, Esme moved to Trista's side and set about smoothing the pink silk skirts. "My, my, but the gown *is* awfully wrinkled. Even more so in this light. No matter, darling, Adelle will have it pressed crisp and beautiful for your upcoming ball." Entirely oblivious to her niece's plight, Esme raised a brow in Nicholas's direction. "M'sieur Brennan, 'tis highly improper that you linger so."

With half an ear to her aunt's gentle chiding, Trista fixed her deeply troubled gaze upon the polished wooden floor. Her anger rose in her throat, begging for release, as she struggled to remain beneath her aunt's soothing touch. With every fiber of her being she ached to scratch the man's eyes from his arrogant head. How dare he seduce her, then casually, flippantly, agree to deliver silk stockings to this Miss Cooper? She'd heard tale of the London rakes, infamous for their sweet seductions, intense pursuits and cold, calculating rejections, but never before had a man so perfectly embodied that which she had grown to despise most.

"After all, 'tis rather unseemly to be spied in a women's couturiere shop," Esme remarked.

Nicholas shrugged casually. "I've never concerned myself with seemly and unseemly behavior, Countess, though I fear my presence may have offended Miss Fitzgerald. She looks rather peaked of a sudden."

"Trista, darling, you do look rather pale. And your hair... such a state! Are you finding shopping a trifle trying?"

Trista shook her head as her eyes skidded about the room in search of a safe haven and her mind scrambled for words. "The pins..."

"Oh, goodness, of course!" Esme breathed. "You have been so good to remain so still. Thank heavens we finally found these lovely shoes so that Adelle may properly examine your hemline." Glancing sideways at Nicholas's tall form perched casually against the front counter some distance from the pair, Esme couldn't resist. "Monsieur Brennan, can you deny that my lovely niece looks exceptionally beautiful in this gown, though the fit is not what it should be, of course. With the necessary alterations..."

Nicholas's appreciative gaze swept Trista's rigid form, lingering overlong and, quite obviously, on her swelling bosom. "Yes, she is exceptional. Leave the gown as is, unaltered, and I would be more than happy to pay for it myself, Countess."

Esme's mouth sagged open, then snapped shut when Adelle emerged and handed Nicholas a small bag overflowing with crisp white tissue.

"Many thanks," Adelle gushed, brushing her hand against his. "Do not make yourself so scarce."

"*Madame.*" Nicholas bestowed a dazzling smile upon Adelle. Donning his hat, he turned to the pair before the mirror. "Countess, *mademoiselle,* a pleasure." Tipping his hat, he turned and strode from the shop with only the tinkling of the bell echoing his departure.

"My, my!" Esme breathed, fanning her face dramatically. "That man does not mince words!"

"You were able to concentrate enough to listen to him, *cherie?*" Adelle exclaimed, dropping to her knees beside Trista to examine the hem. She gave a throaty and deliciously wicked laugh. "I fear I have trouble keeping my eyes in my head and my hands to myself whenever Nicholas Brennan is about!"

Trista rolled her eyes heavenward in a silent plea.

"Of course, one cannot deny he is handsome," Esme remarked, though her tone was reproachful. "But his manner is so *awfully* bold."

"*Cherie,* I fear you may have been in London far too long, for you have forgotten the thrill of such a man! Unfortunately, his kind are scarce in these midsts."

"Thank heavens," Trista muttered under her breath, drawing startled expressions from the two women. "I—I mean...'twould be...difficult, at best, to properly handle oneself with such a man."

Adelle laughed throatily at Trista's remark. "Why, in heaven's name, would you *want* to handle yourself properly with him? He calls to mind all sorts of delicious, improper thoughts! *Mon Dieu,* the things he could do with those big powerful hands, and such long fingers! You know what they say about men with big hands?" She glanced at Trista's befuddled expression. " 'Tis said that the size of a man's hands reveals the size of his more private parts, like—"

"Adelle, shush!" Esme scolded her friend. "You're positively wicked! Our innocent Trista is blushing to the tips of her ears at such talk!" She raised a hand to smooth Trista's tumbling curls, ignoring Adelle's chuckling, and spoke soothingly to her niece. "Trista, do not listen to our Adelle. 'Tis obvious what *she* needs in her life!" she teased, ignoring Adelle's dramatic "Ha!"

Much to Trista's relief, Adelle soon rose from her task and their business was completed. As they emerged from the tiny shop, their hasty retreat to the waiting buggy was interrupted by a pleasant male voice.

"Why, Countess Catalani! So good to see you again!"

"Kendall Barry. Such a surprise!" Esme greeted the young gentleman and extended a hand. "May I present my niece, Mademoiselle Trista Fitzgerald. Trista, Kendall Barry."

He was young, perhaps twenty-five or so, of medium height and build, with amiable features and an easy smile that climbed clear to his dark eyes. He was impeccably attired in a pale blue topcoat, trousers and matching waistcoat, with crisp white ruffles flowing at collar and cuffs and a striking blue-and-white striped cravat knotted at his throat. Beneath his handsome regard, Trista found herself blushing, and she peered at him through lowered lashes. He bent his fair head over her fingers, then raised twinkling brown eyes to hers and grinned broadly. "My pleasure, Miss Fitzgerald."

"Trista has just arrived for a visit," Esme explained, linking her arm through that of her niece. "We are, however, in a bit of a hurry today, though I'm certain we shall have further occasion to meet at several parties this Season. And of course, you will attend the ball in Trista's honor.''

''I wouldn't miss it, Countess!'' His eyes fastened upon Trista. ''To have such a lovely young lady gracing the streets of London...why, it lightens my heart and my step immensely knowing that we *shall* meet again, Miss Fitzgerald! I shall make certain of it!'' With a sweeping bow, he beamed at Trista. ''Do enjoy your stay, Miss Fitzgerald.''

''Mr. Barry.'' With a smile, Trista nodded again as Kendall tipped his hat, then Esme virtually dragged her to the buggy as she bade the gentleman a cheery farewell.

''Oh, Trista,'' Esme breathed. ''M'sieur Barry is a fine young gentleman, of excellent stock. Quite a catch! And, I must say, you made the proper impression! The fellow couldn't keep his eyes from you! Which is all well and good, for if he *does* spread any news about London's newest arrival, 'twill surely be good news, eh?''

''I suppose,'' Trista replied as she climbed aboard the waiting buggy and settled against the plush velvet seat. ''Thank heavens London harbors one gentleman amongst the cads.''

''Oh, *cherie,* pay M'sieur Brennan little heed for *his* kind are a rarity, thank heavens. My dear, London Society abounds with wonderful young gentlemen who understand proper decorum.'' Esme gave her hand a reassuring pat. ''Rest assured, you shan't have to deal with the likes of M'sieur Brennan. He is simply not of our circle.''

Her aunt's words offered Trista little encouragement. By virtue of some baser instinct, she knew she would indeed be dealing with Nicholas Brennan far more than any swank Society gentleman. Her flagrant inability to function normally with the man caused her far greater distress than any doubts she harbored regarding her adherence to proper decorum. With brows drawn together in deep concentration, she unconsciously nibbled on a fingernail and received a quick scolding from Esme. Lowering her hands docilely to her lap, she stared at her trembling fingers, the memory of the strong arms flexing beneath her fingertips looming so vividly her heart flip-flopped, and she quickly turned flaming cheeks to the bustling city streets.

The blasted rake was off cheerily delivering silk stockings to his Miss Cooper and he still had the power to set her stomach aflutter. At least Esme appeared less than enamored of the Yankee, which should have eased her plight somewhat, though some baser instinct dictated that Nicholas Brennan could indeed prove her doom, were she to allow it. He could ruin her, her family name . . .

"I fear you will have not one free moment at the ball! M'sieur Barry is certain to attend. Perhaps with a wee bit of encouragement, he will ask to court you!" Esme dissolved into a sigh. "How splendid!"

"I trust the sole ambition of every Society maiden is to acquire an adequate suitor at these functions? After all, that is the very reason for having these balls, is it not?"

" 'Tis not the *sole* reason, Trista darling, though I, for one, am at a loss for anything more fun than flirting outrageously with dozens of eligible young men at a party." Esme fanned herself with a gloved hand. "Of course, I am well beyond that now and merely enjoy observing the chase. Trista, these functions afford us idle rich something with which to occupy ourselves. *Mon Dieu!* To think of laboring over a dreadful sampler all day or simply tending to the business of the household with no lovely diversions such as shopping or planning a heavenly ball! 'Twould be unbearable! Though this is what is expected of a good wife, nevertheless."

"Expected by whom?"

"Why, our husbands, of course, darling creatures that they are! 'Tis the reason we must find you a rich one, darling, someone who will keep you in a grand style."

"I don't wish to be kept, Aunt Esme, in a grand style or otherwise, and you needn't gape at me."

"Surely you don't mean that, Trista! Whatever would you do with yourself married to some poor lout?"

"I don't wish to be married, either. All this posturing and posing like some pampered poodle, simply to attract the proper rich gentleman . . ."

"For heaven's sake, darling, don't be thickheaded! Do anything to *get* the proper man, then behave as you wish once you've got him! Believe me, eligible men are a rarity, and *rich* eligible men even rarer, so you must use your cunning to get them." Esme gazed at her niece in earnest. "Darling, men would have you believe marriage is a trap, and within its confines you will be expected to stay. Appease them, cater to them, smooth their furrowed brow, ease the tension. Make the home a warm haven with your simple, gentle ways and they will leave you to your business, whatever it is you choose. The higher the station of the man to whom you cleave, the more deliciously wicked your 'business' may be. Understand? 'Tis the nature of marriage these days, like it or not."

" 'Tis the very reason I find it distasteful," Trista grumbled. "Why do I need a man at all?"

"Darling," Esme soothed, squeezing her niece's slender hand, which was clenched angrily in her lap. "I fear you will have little choice. They will be perched upon your doorstep, one atop the other, awaiting a mere glimpse of you! And if you should choose to bestow a hint of a smile upon one eager swain... *Mon Dieu!* But for heaven's sake, be choosy, Trista, though not overly so. The chase is most fun, after all!" Esme heaved a melancholy sigh. "Enjoy the thrill, for once you're married..."

Trista shook her head. "And therein lies the reason for the much-needed distractions, hmm?" She threw up her hands in disgust. "I simply do not understand!"

"You needn't understand, darling," Esme cajoled, "simply play the game."

Play the game? Ha! Nicholas Brennan had perfected the pastime, no doubt to *avoid* marriage as fervently as she was expected to seek it. For the life of her, Trista could not envision herself in a marriage, much less one in which she catered and cajoled, tiptoeing about when in her husband's presence, dangling insignificantly upon his arm like some decorated ornament with no tongue in her head, then, when not beneath his watchful eye, behaving as she truly wished. Was this to be her destiny? To be something she was not simply to satisfy her role in current Society? Never!

Chapter Four

On the evening of Trista's ball, nary but the slightest fragrant breeze filtered through a cloudless sky, a full yellow moon slowly rising above the distant horizon. Gas lamps flickered to life along the cobblestone streets and the curving drive before the Catalani manse.

A pair of impeccably attired footmen stood before the brilliantly lighted house, patiently awaiting the arrival of the guests, who soon drew forth in their highly polished black coaches. The guests were graciously ushered into the marble foyer, where the lyrical melodies of the orchestra's waltz played about them and the elegantly attired Count Catalani and his beautiful Countess Esme waited to greet them.

The house brimmed with crystal and sterling vases overflowing with pale pink roses. Soft candlelight flickered in the wall sconces and at every table, creating a dusky, romantic ambience about the magnificent ballroom where the elite of London Society clustered.

Dusky, romantic ambiance, however, was furthest from Trista's mind. She stood, poised at the top of the stairs, in a grip of pure unmitigated terror. Never mind that she detested these blasted Society functions, that she had attended more tiresome luncheons and intimate soirees than she could bear in the past week, that since the moment she'd awakened this day, she'd been bathed, polished, powdered and pressed at least thrice over by that twittering little maid Aileen, and that she had endured it all with smiles and nods and appropriately timed oohs and aahs, if only to please

Esme. It mattered little what she thought of all these goings-on. The fact of the matter was that she suddenly realized how entirely out of her element she truly was. How
blastedly naive. How confoundedly *common*. An unwel-
come thought to a maid who considered herself above all
this.

Her fingers trembled over the lustrous three-strand pearl
choker Esme had clasped about her neck. She'd bestowed
that and the matching pearl-and-diamond earrings and
three-strand pearl bracelet upon her niece with a teary sniff
and a perfumed embrace before bustling about smoothing
invisible wrinkles from the shimmering pink silk gown. A
gown not unfamiliar to one particularly troublesome rake.

Dear God, if Nicholas Brennan would find himself any
place but here this eve, Trista would be eternally thankful,
though some entirely hateful part of her prayed he would
come. What *did* she want? Blast, she knew not what, except that it wasn't to be here. She wanted to go home, that
was it! Back home to Peter and . . . marriage and babies and
mounds of soiled clothing and an embittered husband, old
before his time because of endless labor—

She was quite certain she didn't want that.

Her eyes flickered anxiously over the crowd milling about
the foyer and settled with relief upon her aunt and Dominic, standing just inside the front portal. With a last deep
breath, she began her descent, her smile wavering, her grip
upon the banister like a stranglehold. Her eyes locked with
those of her aunt when Esme turned at the ensuing hush, a
safe haven amongst the stares, appreciative and otherwise.
When she had nearly reached the bottom, Dominic moved
to take her hand. Then, suddenly, a dark shadow filled the
entry, a shadow that moved in a familiar manner, a large,
tall shadow with broad shoulders and impossibly slim
hips. . . .

Her heart nearly stopped. The intensity of Nicholas
Brennan's gaze rooted her feet to the spot, and for a brief
moment the world about her careened out of control. She
was aware of her hand fiercely gripping the banister, of the
music sounding as if from a distance, of those damnable

eyes penetrating the very depths of a resolve she had so valiantly tended this past week.

When he moved forward, the flickering candlelight danced upon his rich dark hair and shadowed those chiseled features. Trista's legs turned to liquid. Her eyes flickered over his immaculate black attire, rising to meet his once more, only to sweep away beneath his bold appraisal of a gown he knew all too well. She could almost *smell* the man. How in God's name had she ever thought to ignore him?

Through a haze she felt Dominic's firm hand upon hers as he climbed the few steps and guided her to stand beside her aunt. Esme spoke in a very distant and muffled voice, and Nicholas spoke, as well, though Trista remained unmindful of the words, aware only of that deep resonance reverberating in her muddled mind. And when his lips brushed her fingertips as he bowed before her, she felt suspended in midair, until his gaze slipped away and she tumbled helplessly to her senses at his casually spoken words.

"May I introduce Miss Ivy Cooper."

Miss Cooper of the infamous silk stockings!

Trista had enough wits about her to snap her mouth shut as quickly as it fell open. With a stiff smile, she greeted the other girl, instantly recognizing her as the beautiful young blond woman in ice blue satin, the woman with the dazzling smile she seemed to reserve solely for Nicholas. With an uncharacteristically critical eye, Trista assessed the honey gold locks, the exquisite features and lovely brown eyes, the peach silk-and-brocade gown, which displayed curves of which Nicholas was most assuredly aware. The girl spoke in a sweet lilting voice, smiled a dimpled little smile.

And Trista hated her completely. Resisting the nearly overpowering urge to yank this Ivy Cooper's dainty hand from Nicholas's arm, she watched with mute frustration as they turned to make their way to the ballroom. Hateful man!

Rather suddenly it occurred to her that Esme had been speaking to her in that low conspiratorial whisper she employed for all these blasted functions. Something about Kendall Barry arriving ever so promptly....

"Remember our little talk, *cherie?* Make yourself inconspicuously available, yes? Oh, and, darling, the dress that wicked Bianca has chosen for this evening is positively scandalous. Dominic refuses to speak with her, let alone *look* at her! Oh, the disgrace to the family name shall endure for years!" Esme raised a gloved hand to fan herself dramatically, then nodded and smiled graciously at a passing guest before bending to Trista again. "Bianca insists upon making a spectacle of herself simply to win the favors of Monsieur Brennan. There is no denying the man is sinfully handsome. It's a shame one feels continually compelled to remind him of his manners."

Trista could only mumble her agreement and remained beside her aunt for some time as she was introduced to a multitude of guests. Try as she might to concentrate on the names and faces of those she met, she found, much to her chagrin, that her traitorous eyes were forever wandering to the ballroom in search of...

Esme pinched her arm and spoke close to her ear. "Darling, hullo... I have someone whom you should meet."

Grateful for the interruption, Trista turned, blinked several times and felt her heart lurch. Standing before her, clad in kelly green topcoat and breeches, a flaming orange silk waistcoat and cravat, and looking not unlike a very warm, well-greased, overly fed pig, was Archibald Sleeth.

"Enchanted," Sleeth murmured after Esme performed the unnecessary introductions. He smeared puffy lips over Trista's stiff fingers, his marble eyes gleaming wickedly at her.

Cold dread and revulsion prickled along Trista's spine. Nearly yanking her hand from his, she visibly winced at her aunt's casually spoken words.

"Monsieur Sleeth, so good to see you again. My niece has just recently arrived, but only for the Season, though I hope to find her a beau to delay her."

"Indeed." Sleeth raised a colorless brow, peering curiously at Trista. "*Miss* Fitzgerald, I trust you are enjoying your visit to our fair city thus far?"

Trista eyed the repulsive man coolly and lifted her nose a notch. "I am enjoying a truly marvelous time, though I fear I have found some elements of London more distasteful than others." Seeking to assuage the panicked expression that suddenly racked Esme's face, Trista laid a hand upon her aunt's arm, her level gaze meeting Sleeth's hooded eyes. "On the very day of my arrival, I fear we happened upon some unsavory characters who harbored rather lewd, debauched notions of proper behavior with a lady."

"Oh my..." Esme breathed, fanning herself with a gloved hand and directing her comments to an unusually red-faced Sleeth. "'Tis shameful the vermin allowed to plague our city streets! Oh, thank heavens you arrived safely, *cherie.*"

Trista lifted a brow and leveled a haughty gaze upon Sleeth. "Mr. Sleeth, it was *truly* a delight to meet you."

With a curt nod, Sleeth turned on his heel and waddled off toward the ballroom.

"A most amusing man," Esme remarked. "Somewhat of an eccentric, dreadfully common. I can assure you he has not met with favor in Society." She wrinkled her nose delicately. "In any event, Dominic does some business with him, though whatever for, I could not even guess. One can't help but wonder why the devil he's here. Why, just look at the man. Oh, to be so *desperately* in need of a new tailor!"

It was then, amidst the surge of satisfaction at putting Sleeth in his place, that Trista glanced toward the ballroom and spied Bianca and Nicholas. He was leaning against a doorjamb, drink in hand and dark head lowered, to listen no doubt, though he was doing a bloody fine job of ogling, as well. So intent was he upon Bianca's low, dusky voice, he loomed but a scant few inches from her swelling bosom, thrust forward provocatively by her gown, a gown so daringly cut that Trista's mouth fell open in shock.

The entire dress was of a very clingy fabric completely covered with black lace. Sleeveless, the bodice molded Bianca's sleek waist and rose to barely cover her breasts. The skirt hugged well-rounded hips and thighs, then flared to a sweeping skirt behind her. Her jet black hair was pulled severely from her face to fall in an untamed cascade down her back, and the only jewelry she wore was a spectacular ruby pendant that sparkled between her breasts. To Trista's eye, she looked as if with every fiber of her being she wished to devour the man before her. And *he* seemed intent upon becoming the first course.

Trista spun about with a disgusted snort. Where the devil was his Miss Cooper? Better yet, why the devil did she care?

With little thought, she snatched a tall glass of champagne from a passing servant and gulped at it, relishing the warmth spreading through her limbs. Raising the glass once more, she opened her mouth, then nearly choked, attempting to swallow, when a hand touched her in the small of her back and a resonant voice assailed her befuddled senses.

"Don't drink too hastily, Trista sweet, lest you forget yourself in front of all these ever-so-honorable gentlefolk." His murmur was close to her ear, then he moved before her like some big, black fortress. Those damnable eyes flickered over her, the look unmistakable in its appreciation. "'Twould be a breach of conduct from which, I fear, you would never recover."

She managed to swallow the entire gulp of champagne, though half fizzed uncomfortably in her nose and set her eyes to watering. "You're despicable."

"You're delectable," Nicholas returned, and his smile broadened, crinkling the corners of his eyes. "Though I didn't think it possible, you're even more beautiful tonight than you were...what...has it been a week? I've missed you, sweet. Perhaps 'tis the soft candlelight playing upon your tawny skin."

"Cease your addlepated prattle!" Trista hissed, seeking to avoid that mocking glimmer in his eyes, and found her gaze wandering over his simple starched white collar to the mother-of-pearl buttons of his shirt. The image of masculine fingers tending to those fragile buttons loomed vividly. She presented him her back. "Go away."

"I fear I cannot." He was before her again, that enigmatic smile, that silky murmur. "Trista, God's truth, do you know that when I look at you all thoughts flee but one. Have you any idea what that might be?"

"Heavens no!" She fanned herself heatedly. "Stop looking at me in that awful manner!"

"Am I staring again? Perhaps 'tis all I'm capable of doing when you're about. God only knows, conversation manages to elude me. Have you missed me, sweetheart?"

"Missed you? How dare you—"

"Oh, no, not the how-dare-you's again. I was hoping we were well beyond that point."

"Of course, 'twas but a momentary oversight. How could I have forgotten that you are the fervent embodiment of lowly swine. You're quite right, your most debauched, depraved behavior shouldn't surprise me in the least. Indeed, I've come to expect it."

"Then perhaps you would offer little resistance if we were to steal away to yonder terrace to pick up where we left off a few days ago. I do recall thinking that the bodice of your dress would be far more flattering worn about your waist."

"Nicholas!"

"Ah, you remember my name."

"Have you no manners?"

"None. Come dance with me."

"You're beyond contemptible...a vile, despicable cad—"

"A brute."

"Swine..."

"Don't forget bloody arrogant heathen. Come dance with me."

"No! Cease, this instant!"

"Cease what? We're merely enjoying a conversation, a very innocent one at that, much to my frustration." Nicholas took her empty champagne glass and handed her a full one. "Come, since we've run out of appropriate names for me..."

"Ha! Never!"

"...and since the idea of the terrace doesn't tickle your fancy at the moment, dance with me. It's a lovely waltz. You *do* dance, do you not?"

"I most certainly do!" she huffed. For a moment she allowed his hand upon her elbow to guide her toward the ballroom. After all, the scoundrel didn't think she could dance. She would show him.... And then she realized what she was doing. She jerked her arm free, stopping dead in her tracks. "Get your hands from me, you brute! Be off with you! Go find your Miss Cooper—"

"I'm afraid she's powdering her nose."

"Bianca should suffice."

"Tending to some problem with her dress, I believe."

"Indeed! Why, 'tis a wonder the woman can dance in the thing!"

"As a matter of fact, she can't. I believe she has resorted to champagne."

"Then find some other maiden to pester and fondle. I have no use for you." Lifting her chin, she turned to breeze past him, only to find her wrist soundly encased in a steely grip.

"I've no desire to be with any other maiden but you." His voice was low, very close to her ear.

"Ha!" Trista attempted the impossible, trying to free her wrist while battling his effect upon her senses. Damn that voice. "Bianca and her lame excuse for a dress would find that a trifle difficult to believe."

Nicholas raised a curious brow. "Lest you harbor some misconceptions, my lady, I am a red-blooded man with a penchant for beautiful women. In all honesty, would you prefer me any other way?"

"You're despicable," she sneered.

"You're still delectable. And you're repeating yourself. Come dance with me."

"Never! I hate you!"

A dark brow shot up at her words. "Then tread lightly, my sweet innocent, for but a hairbreadth separates hate and love."

Trista's heart slammed against her chest and she felt as if the wind were knocked out of her. *Love?* What had love to do with anything? She raised shining eyes to his, so clear, so blue...

With cheeks flaming, she spun about, attempting yet again to pull her wrist free. His husky voice stilled her feet. "Trista, don't go...."

"Ah! So *there* you are! Trista! Brennan! I've been looking all over for you!"

Trista snapped her head about in the same instant that Nicholas released her wrist. Dominic approached, Bianca sashaying behind him as quickly as her confining dress would allow. Trista endured Bianca's hateful glare as the girl shoved herself next to Nicholas, linking an arm through his and managing to melt all over him.

"Nicholas, darling," Bianca purred huskily. "Did you miss me overmuch? I'm so dreadfully sorry I was gone so long, but I fear my dress is just a wee bit small in the bodice and requires adjustment now and again. Perhaps next time *you* may make the adjustments, hmm?"

"Bianca, really!" Dominic gasped. "Compose yourself like the well-bred young woman you are!"

With a husky laugh, Bianca waved her full champagne glass at her uncle and swayed against Nicholas. "I'm only enjoying a bit of fun, Uncle Dom. Even we well-bred young women do *that* from time to time. Isn't that so, Trista darling? Oh, but you wouldn't have the slightest idea about such things, would you, being from the country and all. Whatever does one do for fun on a farm? Chase cows and clean up after the horses?"

Trista opened her mouth but for the life of her was unable to call to mind some witty retort, though she knew she would have ... eventually ... had Nicholas not interjected.

"There are those who harbor a certain fondness for horses, Bianca. Myself for one." He cast a glance at Trista as Bianca wrinkled her nose with distaste. "Do you ride, Miss Fitzgerald?"

"Occasionally," Trista murmured.

"Perhaps we could enjoy a ride together one day." He gave her a grin that nearly rendered her breathless. For a brief, entirely shameless moment, all but that rugged bronzed visage ceased to exist. And then she was swept away by a firm hand upon her back toward the ballroom...but it wasn't Nicholas.

Dominic guided Trista onto the dance floor with a hopeless shake of his head in Bianca's general direction. "You seem to be enjoying yourself, Trista."

"Indeed," she managed. "It's a splendid ball. Aunt Esme has truly outdone herself."

"She's a remarkable woman. Quite capable, though the champagne and roses alone cost me a bloody fortune." The last he muttered as if to himself, then his eyes fell from hers to her throat, and his dark brows swept together in a sudden frown. "Where did you get those?"

Trista's fingers played idly upon the pearl choker. "They were a gift from Aunt Esme earlier this evening."

A tic in his cheek drew her gaze, as did the sudden chill in his eyes. "I see..." He then gave her what looked to be a forced smile. "You're very good at this waltz, you know, very light in my arms."

Something in Dominic's voice and the manner in which his hand moved upon her back momentarily aroused some sixth sense in Trista. Hastily, she banished such thoughts as foolishness and averted her eyes, only to spy Ivy Cooper sweeping past on the arm of Kendall Barry.

Trista stared after the pair. This nonchalant dallying with other guests seemed readily accepted behavior at balls of this sort, though she never would have expected it of anyone except Nicholas Brennan.

At the end of the dance, Kendall Barry's huge expectant smile caught Trista's eye from across the room as he attempted to shoulder his way through a sea of full skirts toward her. As fate would have it, however, the orchestra struck up another waltz before Kendall reached her, forcing him to abandon his quest. Trista turned to squeeze her way from the dance floor when quite suddenly she found herself caught up in a pair of muscular arms that all but flattened her against a powerful chest. She stared at the fine cloth of his topcoat as they swung about the ballroom several times in silence, all too aware of the eyes she could not meet smoldering above her, of that chest pressed unabashedly against her soft bosom. The shoulder beneath her trembling fingertips was solid brawn, enough to split asunder the last shreds of any resolve.

With a sudden overwhelming sense of panic and delirium, she pushed against his shoulder to create at least a whisper of distance between them, only to feel his hand at her back draw her closer. "You're not going anywhere."

As she dared herself to glance up at him, Trista realized with a shock how close their faces truly were. Quickly lowering her head, she focused once again upon his shoulder, conjuring her best haughty tone. "Do you always find it necessary to force women to your bidding? I find it rather distasteful."

"Nay, Trista, 'tis only with you that I feel compelled to behave in this manner. No other maiden has yet proven as troublesome."

"Perhaps more maidens should consider doing just that, for some small shred of humility would bring about a marked improvement in your character."

"If you would find me more to your liking, then perhaps I..."

"You needn't bother. You would still be the most despicable of cads."

"I see. The lady has passed a harsh judgment upon me, eh? It would serve me well to know why you detest me so completely. I am at a loss."

"At a loss?" Trista raised blazing eyes to his. "Certainly you're not *that* thickheaded? Perhaps all this chasing about of maidens has left you daft."

"Chasing about?" Nicholas's dark brows drew together in a puzzled frown. "Trust me, sweetheart, I've had little time to chase any maidens about, only you."

"'Tis comforting to know that I am distinctive in some small way," she snorted derisively.

His gaze flamed and dropped to the soft breasts pressed against him. "Trista, you've many distinctive qualities, several of which are in no way small."

"I insist you cease your blatant ogling of me."

"I fear I cannot, try as I might."

"You've never tried! Stop distracting me!"

"You're distracting *me*, lovely Trista. My thoughts are still on the terrace."

"Then perhaps you ought to indulge such thoughts and steal your Miss Cooper and her silk stockings away to yonder balcony to have your bold, seductive way with her."

"It is highly improbable that I will ever be found bold and seductive with Miss Cooper or her silk stockings, for that matter, though I find the thought of *your* silk stockings arouses many bold, seductive impulses."

"Your lack of regard for Miss Cooper is utterly shameful. Has she any idea of your less than passionate feelings for her?"

"I certainly hope so, my inquisitive little mouse. I doubt she would have it any other way."

"Thank heavens there exists one other maiden in this city who feels as I do."

"For altogether different reasons. Ivy is my cousin."

"Oh, *please*, you think me some simpleminded wench to believe that?"

"Trista, trust me, nothing about you is simple. Believe what you will. Now relax for a bit. Enjoy the dance. You're all surly and tense once again."

Trista felt his hand rub softly across her rigid back, those long fingers brushing against her skin above the back of her dress and sending traitorous shivers along her spine. She bristled anew as the orchestra began yet another waltz and Nicholas appeared nowhere near releasing his firm hold upon her.

" 'Tis indeed shameless what you are doing," she admonished.

"If you could but read my mind."

"You're creating a spectacle of yourself... of me, and I shan't allow it."

"Is that so? We shameless rogues are wont to make far more than spectacles of ourselves, Trista. And we care dreadfully little about what others think."

"How eagerly you embrace your role! Ha! But I suspected little else of you. 'Tis highly improper that I dance only with you."

"Improper? To whom, Trista? I have a sneaking suspicion you pay not the slightest heed to what all these highbrow Society gentlefolk think or say. But you are a woman after all, and will resort to anything if it suits your purpose, will you not?" He silenced her blustery reply by drawing her tightly against his entire length. "And speaking of improper, I know of several truly improper things I would be more than happy to teach you...."

"Nicholas!"

"Trista, sweet fiery little kitten, did you believe for the briefest of moments that I would idly stand by this evening and allow you to dance the night away on the arms of a dozen or more eager swains?" His voice was a husky murmur. "I have every intention of monopolizing you for the remainder of the evening, whether you like it or not."

"You're a beast," she managed, attempting to fathom why her heart suddenly felt as if it soared, her legs as if they would dissolve beneath her. How on earth had all her anger simply vanished, abandoning her at the most inopportune moment?

His mouth pressed against her hair, his breath warm upon her cheek. "Indeed I am. Now, sheathe those claws and for heaven's sake don't look at me like that. A man has only so much control."

She bit her tongue. It was all she could do, for words, all sense, eluded her. Without thought, she swung her eyes to focus on his throat, which was a grievous mistake, for her movement brought her fragrant tresses to brush against his jaw.

She felt him tense, his body rigid against hers. An entirely foreign, delicious anticipation spread through her limbs, bubbling low in her belly. How easy it would be to lay her cheek upon his chest, to feel his capable arms encircle her. She sighed, a truly wanton, guileless sigh, and relaxed completely against him, her entire body trembling against his sinewy length. They barely danced at all.

Nicholas murmured something unintelligible, and she lifted her eyes to his. Molten fire ignited deep within her, a sudden, irrefutable sense of destiny enveloping her.

"I—I must get some air..." she breathed, lurching from his embrace, somehow making her way through the blurred sea of colorful gowns and topcoats and curious stares, through the opened doors onto the terrace. A fragrant breeze caressed her burning cheeks and she paused, inhaling deeply of the fresh air... but only for a moment. Warm hands caressed her upper arms, a hard chest pressed unabashedly against her back, a voice murmuring softly, so seductively, and she fled mindlessly... across the terrace, down several stone steps and into the shadowed gardens.

Through the thundering of her pulse, she heard him behind her, his strides both long and sure, unhampered by cumbersome skirts. She stumbled, uttering a helpless cry of frustration, and felt hot tears stinging her eyes. She clutched her skirts, stumbled again, then fell...against a wall of solid brawn, right into his arms.

And then his mouth was upon hers, his arms molding her body to his, his tongue plundering her mouth, still open with disbelief. She gasped for a breath, for sanity, when his lips released hers to sear a trail of fire along her throat, his husky voice murmuring incoherently against her skin. And then his hands were beneath her hips, boldly cupping her derriere, brazenly lifting her against him... and her world spun crazily. She felt his hot breath upon the high curves of her bosom...his hands cupping her breasts...his mouth aflame upon her skin... and then fire exploded in her brain and reason washed over her as if a bucket of icy water had been dumped unceremoniously upon her head.

With all her might she pushed against him, breaking free with a desperate cry. "Nay!" Her fingers trembled uncontrollably as they clutched at her bodice. "Nay! 'Tis a dreadful mistake...a shameless, heathen act. I—I don't even know you!"

He took a step toward her, his eyes in the moonlight glowing like those of the fiercest of wolves. "Oh, but you do, in ways you can't even comprehend. It's called passion, lovely innocent."

"No!" she railed, choking on a sob. "I swear if you lay a hand upon me again... You've tricked me...woven your evil web. So wicked."

"I am naught but a man, Trista, and with every fiber of my being I desire you, in ways you could never dream of. 'Tis not evil or wicked, I can assure you. Attempt to deny it, fight it, but one day you will come to believe these words I speak."

"No!" She raised her hands to cover her ears. "You must cease..." Her voice dropped to a fervent whisper. "Heed me well, Nicholas. From this moment on, do not attempt to seduce me."

"It was not I who initiated tonight's seduction," he drawled, folding his arms across his chest. "From the moment I entered yonder manse, you were slanting those cat's eyes my way, swinging those luscious hips, rubbing those soft breasts against me."

Blinding rage and humiliation surged through Trista so quickly she didn't pause to consider that he only chose to bait her. Her eyes widened, her fists tightened, the blood pounded at her temples and she lunged at him with arms flailing. "God, how I hate you!" she choked, pounding useless fists against that solid chest as tears of frustration slipped from her eyes. "Be off with you! Out of my life! I hate you so."

His arms swept about her, pulling her fiercely against him until her nose pressed into his chest. His low murmur reverberated through her senses. "No, you don't. You could never hate me."

She rubbed tearstained cheeks against him, feeling his hands massaging gently at her back, and hers stilled to lie innocuously against his chest. How tragic that struggle could be so entirely futile, that he alone aroused this wanton weakness.

"I do hate you so," she choked.

His hand caught in her hair, pulling her head back until her eyes met his. The harshness of his expression sent a new shiver along her spine. "You don't despise me."

"I do," she murmured shakily, wishing that she could simply lie down and die, rather than tremble anew as his hands slid her sleeves from her shoulders.

"You want me." His voice was a silken purr as his mouth brushed softly against her collarbone then across her shoulder, sending delicious ripples of delight dancing along her spine. "Say it, Trista."

"Oh, God . . . please don't do this. . . ." For the life of her she couldn't stop him . . . or herself. She swayed against him as the flame of his mouth again ignited the smoldering embers deep within her.

"Say it, sweet, wicked, witchy Trista. You want me. . . ."

From deep in her throat Trista moaned as his lips brushed hers, so softly, achingly sweet, full of promise, and she drowned in that heady feeling. "Oh, Nicholas, yes . . . I do want you so." Wantonly, she swayed against him, parting her lips beneath his, when suddenly a gnawing began low in her belly, a warning that something was dreadfully amiss.

She opened her eyes to find Nicholas staring at her, his mouth set in a rigid line, his eyes glowing devilishly. "It would serve you well to heed your own words, spoken from the depths of passion with surprisingly little encouragement from me. It's a lesson I do not wish to teach you again. Cloak yourself tightly in your virginity and surround yourself with obedient swains whilst you still can. Henceforth, it will serve you naught." He leaned perilously close to her. "Heed *me* well, Trista. I will have you."

And with that he released her abruptly, then turned and disappeared into the night.

Chapter Five

"Such a likable young woman, that Miss Cooper. 'Tis a shame she had to depart so suddenly. Some unforeseen business entanglement involving Brennan... the businessman... yes, Nicholas Brennan, her cousin."

Trista stared at Kendall Barry and gagged on a mouthful of canapés. "Her wha...?"

"Miss Fitzgerald! At the risk of being too forward, may I suggest that perhaps 'tis time to forego the champagne? I fear you may have overindulged."

With a dismissive wave of her hand, Trista gulped from her champagne, her thoughts racing. *His cousin?* "Indeed, I too found Miss Cooper rather delightful," she lied gracefully.

"Oh, delightful, yes, and frightfully young. Just barely seventeen. She's from America. Richmond, I believe." Kendall paused and flushed scarlet behind his white kid glove, pressed to his mouth. "Do forgive me. 'Tis not my wont to gossip so. I fear I may have begun to bore you."

"Oh, heavens, no. Do go on."

Kendall hesitated not one moment and leaned toward Trista as if he positively ached to divulge the latest news. "Her family owns the famous Yankee Cooper shipping conglomerate. Dear God, you must have heard the name. In any event, she's in London attending boarding school and visiting with her cousin at that enormous country home of his. It seems she and Brennan grew up as close as brother and sister."

"I find the man rather forward," Trista sniffed.

"Oh, indeed! At the risk of being bold myself, I must say that the manner in which he conducted himself on this very dance floor with you—why, it was an utter disgrace!"

"Perhaps he doesn't know better."

"His lack of breeding is so dreadfully obvious, no matter his family's success in the States. All Yankee upstarts, if you ask me." Kendall lifted his chin and peered down his thin nose, though the stock wound tight and high beneath his chin prevented him from doing little else. "One shouldn't be overly surprised at his lack of decorum. According to the rumors—to which, mind you, I pay frightfully little heed—he's a brilliantly shrewd businessman and matchless at the gaming table, to boot. How well I know."

"You gamble?"

"Why, Miss Fitzgerald, have you no ken of White's Club? My heavens, whist and faro are the games of the day! Of course, 'twould be highly unseemly for a young lady such as yourself to be found in so crude an establishment. Lest you mistake my meaning, the club lacks little in the way of elegance. To the contrary. 'Tis only that women of your station are not usually the type found gathering round those gaming tables. I, for one, find the gaming most intriguing and quite rewarding, though not with Brennan at the table. Perhaps I shouldn't be so bold, but I've heard talk that your uncle, the Count, has found tremendous misfortune at the Yankee's table."

"Indeed?"

"Perhaps it's idle talk. In any event, Brennan surely has a way with the women, especially those at the club. Developing quite a reputation, I must say. Obviously, not so much so with the ladies of the ton, who wouldn't find him to their tastes, of course." He paused, obviously mistaking Trista's shudder for one of revulsion. "I'm so sorry to have insulted your tender sensibilities. 'Twas most remiss to have gone on so about a man you quite obviously find distasteful."

"Yes, most distasteful."

It was at that moment that Esme materialized at Trista's elbow with a pinch and a terse smile directed at the ever-so-gallant Kendall, who busied himself over the table of canapés. Esme whisked Trista into a shadowed corner of the room and leveled a stormy gaze upon her.

"*Cherie,* you seem intent upon worrying me into apoplexy this evening! Where on earth have you been?"

"Why, uh ... the terrace. The champagne ... "

"Ha!" Esme scoffed. "Are you suggesting your disappearance had nothing to do with that ... that brazen display of ... of ... *coupling* your Monsieur Brennan mistakes for waltzing?"

"He's not *my* Mr. Brennan!" Trista whispered hotly.

"Ha! Tell that to poor old Lady Wigginsham. The woman all but swooned dead away when she caught glimpse of you and that...that... Oh, *cherie,* you have managed to set the entire place agog, and for all the wrong reasons! Not only did you agree to dance with that...that *Yankee,* but you allowed him to carry on in that shameless manner for what seemed hours on end, in front of an entire roomful of people who shan't forget this! It will be on their tongues for months!" Glancing about, Esme fanned herself heatedly. "How awfully pleased Monsieur Brennan must be with these new waltzes that allow him every opportunity to fondle his partner. In days past, when court dances were the rage, scoundrels like him had to steal away to yonder terrace to fondle their women."

Trista nearly choked on her fresh champagne.

Esme paid her little heed, so distraught was she. "Stick with Monsieur Barry, Trista, dear God, do me that favor. He's such a fine young gentleman, accepted among the beau monde and Dominic's set. I'm quite certain *he* knows how to waltz properly!"

Trista endured Esme's chastising with agreeable little nods and found herself musing, as the night wore on, that Kendall Barry was indeed her safest harbor. No matter that the handsome young man failed to stir her blood, that all his talk of Almack's Assembly Rooms and the prior evening's soirees bored her nearly to tears, that his eagerness to court her manifested itself in a gross lack of masculine bravado that left her yearning for just a glimpse of Nicholas Brennan's heathen spirit. He promised to escort her on a trip through Hyde Park, to the Duke and Duchess of Leighton's ball not a week hence. He would call upon her, fill her ear with delicious gossip and perhaps venture quite boldly to take her hand in his. He promised to keep her as occupied as a maid could hope to be. Beneath that handsome blond regard, what maiden in her right mind could resist him?

If only Trista didn't know the unfortunate answer to that.

She pondered this as she bade her good-nights and hurried through the deserted entry toward the stairs. As she rounded the banister, she was gripped roughly about her wrist and unceremoniously yanked into the shadowed entrance to the parlor. Her head snapped against the damask-covered wall and she stared terror-stricken into the shadows for some clue as to her assailant. She abruptly abandoned all thoughts of fleeing when a walking stick shot out to press painfully against her shoulder.

"Looking for your devoted bridegroom Brennan, Miss Fitzgerald?" Archibald Sleeth sneered, emerging from the shadows.

Trista's stomach heaved at the mere sight of the man and she made little effort to hide her obvious distaste. Swallowing the acrid bile welling in her throat, she averted her face from his fetid breath and the awful stench permeating the air about his bloated figure. The many hours spent sweating profusely in too-tight clothing had taken their toll upon his toilette, as had his obvious penchant for drink. "Unhand me, you cad!" she demanded.

"What is this? You do not enjoy my attentions, Miss Fitzgerald? Ah, of course, you think me some—how did you so delicately phrase it—lewd, debauched character with little notion of proper behavior, isn't that right? Thought to have a little joke on Archie, eh? That damned Yankee upstart Brennan! Thinking to make a laughingstock out of me!"

Trista gritted her teeth. "I've little notion of Nicholas Brennan's intent, nor do I care. I simply wished then, as now, to be left alone. Now unhand me!"

"Left alone? Ha!" He snorted sardonically. "The man had his hands all over you on that dance floor, and got from you naught but a teasing smile in return. 'Twould make for some very juicy gossip, indeed, if I were to divulge that you and that cur were seen cavorting like a pair of lovesick birds in broad daylight. And such a *shameless* display it was! Why, I was nearly taken with a fit of the vapors! Imagine what that would do to your reputation . . . and your lovely aunt's."

"No one in their right mind would ever believe the filthy likes of you."

"Indeed, then why am I here, Miss Fitzgerald, attending the event of the season, mingling with the upper echelons of Society folk, hobnobbing with the ton, if I am naught but a highly regarded member of Society, hmm? Why, simply ask your dear Uncle Dominic. *He* more than anyone knows how profoundly secure my position is, and growing more secure with each passing day. Your Brennan, why, he's Yankee scum. And you? Why, you've the most to lose, innocent lamb, struggling to protect your honor, for if you lose that, what do you have, eh?"

A mind-numbing hatred filled Trista. "What is it that you want from me?"

Rheumy eyes dropped to linger on the swelling curves of her breasts and Trista thought she would retch. "My dear, you are painfully naive but simply too perfect just the same. How long I have waited for a ticket into the very bosom of Society. You, my dear, shall be that ticket." His eyes met hers and his tone grew suddenly menacing. "And while you're at it, tell that bastard Brennan that I won't forget what an ass he made of me. I will have my revenge, upon him and you, as well, sassy minx."

Licking his lips again, he ogled her bosom feverishly and just a moment too long, for his pause provided Trista ample opportunity to bend one leg and, with all her might, drive her knee between his pudgy legs.

With a strangled, high-pitched scream, not unlike the squeal of a stuck pig, Sleeth fell from her, doubled over in pain. His hands clutched at his groin, his face grew a mottled purple and he rocked back and forth with a desperate moan.

Backing away from the prostrate figure, Trista sneered contemptuously. "Don't *ever* threaten me again, Mr. Sleeth, or we shall see who has the most to lose." She turned and stumbled up the stairs, seeking the haven of her room.

Clad only in shift and pantaloons, Trista sat at her dressing table three days hence, peering with much concentration and a furrowed brow at her reflection as she pulled, twisted and coiled her hair this way and that. With a despairing sigh she threw up her hands, and the glossy curls fell hopelessly about her shoulders, the gold-streaked strands ablaze in the midday sun streaming into the room. In the mirror she caught sight of the pile of gowns tossed hither and yon about the room, and groaned. The entire morning had been devoted to the selection of the *perfect* gown for the day's outing with Kendall Barry, and at the moment she was no closer to making a decision than she had been three hours before.

Of a sudden, her chamber door burst open and a breathless and flushed Aileen skidded into the room. "He's here, miss!"

"He's what?" Trista choked, lurching to her feet. "So soon? 'Tis but midday! Doesn't all this riding about in Hyde Park commence at 5 p.m? No matter, he obviously knows better."

"Oh, miss, he's divine, an absolute dream! And in our very drawing room! Ooh, to be you! A dress, miss?"

"My hair, Aileen?"

Not more than a quarter of an hour later, Trista emerged from her chamber wearing a stunning high-necked, pale green satin gown with full three-quarter-length sleeves and a spray of cream lace at collar and cuffs. The waist was fitted, the skirt full and sweeping, rustling crisply with every step she took. Her hair was coiled demurely at the nape of her neck and secured with a pale green pearl-encrusted satin bow.

The first thing she saw upon entering the drawing room was an enormous sterling vase overflowing with gorgeous white calla lilies, sitting in the center of a mahogany table directly inside the room.

"Why, Kendall!" She rushed forward with a smile. "The flowers are exquisite. You shouldn't have."

The second thing Trista saw upon entering the drawing room was Nicholas Brennan, swaggering toward her in that manner that was his alone. The sun spilled about his impeccably attired shoulders, setting his hair aflame, and Trista's smile faded fast. With whitening knuckles, she gripped the gilt edge of the table before her as the floor seemed to tilt beneath her feet.

"So sorry to disappoint you," he drawled with more than a hint of sarcasm. "I must say, I've never seen such a bewitching smile on any maiden. Methinks I should bring you flowers more often. Then again, perhaps the culprit is our friend Barry. Not an unenviable chap, after all."

He stopped not an arm's length from her side, and Trista hastily averted her gaze to the beautiful flowers. *He* had brought them? She raised a remarkably steady hand to the delicate petals of the lily closest to her, feeling his eyes upon her... watching, waiting, probing.

"Thank you." She spoke in even, measured tones despite her sudden distress.

"I came to apologize," he muttered hastily and not altogether convincingly as he gestured to the flowers.

Trista lifted her chin a notch. "Is that all you came for?" For an instant she was certain a flame leapt in those smoldering eyes and her heart skipped a beat, stopped, then tripped along.

"No...." He folded his arms over his chest, drawing Trista's gaze momentarily. "So, you're expecting a call from the reigning bon vivant *extraordinaire.*"

Trista's jaw tensed. "And if I am, it's none of your business."

"Indeed? For the life of me, I can't fathom what you could possibly find of interest in the man."

"You wouldn't. The man is a gentleman, a characteristic which I am quite certain you are inordinately incapable of fathoming."

Nicholas gave a short, caustic laugh. "I gather you place a high degree of importance on that particular asset, judging by the breadth of your beautiful smile not moments ago. It would interest me greatly the qualities a man must possess to be so nobly labeled by you."

"I care naught for what interests you, Nicholas." Trista moved around the table away from him, trailing a slender finger along the gilt edge of the table. Lifting her eyes to peer at him through the lilies, she watched his gaze travel a slow path up her arm, past the lace at her throat to lock with hers.

"In all truth, I would prefer not to join ranks with your 'gentlemen' if Kendall Barry is your idea of an acceptable beau," Nicholas remarked, studying the lily closest to him. "One has to admire the lad's initiative. By week's end, I wouldn't be surprised to find him upon bended knee."

"Do you think so?" Trista asked airily, smiling to herself as Nicholas scowled and thrust the lily aside.

"You can't be serious! The man—*man?* Ha! He's but a lad."

"Why he's *years* older than I."

"That's a truly frightening thought. You needn't remind me. He's a daddy's boy, Trista, Society's plaything. Doesn't understand the first thing about money."

"He's very kind and thoughtful..."

"And gentle with children and animals, too, I suppose, eh?"

"Charming, polite and well respected in the best circles."

"As if you really care, Trista."

"My Aunt Esme is quite taken with him, and I, too, if you must know."

"You could have spared me that," he growled, moving close to her side once again.

Trista sensed a quivering begin deep in her belly and made a career out of studying the calla lilies. "And why should I? He is my beau. I shall attend the Leighton affair with him. I enjoy spending time with the man. And for your information, he listens to me when I speak."

"A remarkable quality."

"And he is gracious, ever so eager to please. A true friend."

"Are you sure you wouldn't be as satisfied with a puppy, Trista? Indeed, they're far more pleasing to look upon and certainly easier to house-train."

"You're contemptible!"

"And Barry is a fool."

"Pardon me?"

"Trista, if I were he, there wouldn't be a chance in hell for another man to get this close to you. You'd be far too busy with...other things...." She felt his gaze upon her bosom, the heat emanating from him, and her pulse hammered in her ears. "To my good fortune, Barry is doing little to protect his interests."

"His interests require little in the way of protection, even from cads like you," Trista sniffed.

"Is that so? Tell me, what do you think his reaction would be if I were to divulge my rather intimate knowledge of the scent of your skin, the silky texture of your hair, the softness of your—"

"Cease! You wouldn't dare!"

"Is that so? Would you care to wager on that? One could easily surmise that I have far more to protect here than Barry."

"You?" Trista blinked with disbelief. "The gall! *You're* the fool!"

"Perhaps. You *are* the only innocent with whom I have ever dallied, and God knows, I should have my head examined for it."

"A splendid idea. Now, take your leave."

He didn't move one brawny muscle. "Trista, you have perfected the art of denial and have succeeded in fooling no one but yourself. You're hopelessly naive with respect to affairs of the heart."

Trista bristled. "Tell me, Nicholas, how do you survive an entire day and still manage to walk erect with the oppressive weight of your ego about your shoulders? I will have you know that my heart is in no way involved and I am guilty of denying nothing! I simply stated a fact—you've no interest to protect because I have no interest in you! Be gone." She waved a hand at the door. "You've no further purpose."

"Oh, but I do...." With catlike speed, his hand slipped about her waist, drawing her against him, his lips pressed against her ear. "I can't stay away. I want more...."

His mouth was a searing flame against her throat for the briefest of moments and, oh, how she wanted more, just as he. Yet she lurched from his arms, sweeping his hands aside with a cry. Retrieving her scattered wits, she raised a remarkably steady gaze and held a hand before her as if to fend him off. "Heed me well, Nicholas. In spite of these prehistoric notions of male-female interaction you have honed in your heathen homeland, I regret to inform you that in London, more than a cad's pagan desires is required for any measure of interaction." She stared into fathomless eyes. "You may want more, but I most certainly do not."

He gave but a derisive snort in reply and looked bored.

"The truth, Nicholas, is that I have foolishly allowed my baser instincts to govern my behavior with you. Unfortunately, this has led me to immeasurable shame and you to all the wrong conclusions. Oddly enough, and to your credit, I suppose, your experience thus far has been with, shall I say, more *mature* ladies who have known the thrill of a first kiss or the spark of newfound passion. Their ardor is born from true desire for you and I fear you've erroneously assumed the same with me."

His stormy silence filled the sun-dappled air.

"Nicholas, in short, you've mistaken a wide-eyed maiden's infatuation with romance for an honest desire for only you. You see, I find I've become a rather fickle maiden, and though I do find you vaguely attractive in a purely physical, rather primitive sense, my tastes have suddenly taken a turn for a more suitable, shall I say proper, young man, who shall appeal to all of my senses and with whom I can explore the physical—''

"You're lying," Nicholas growled suddenly, gripping her upper arms, his eyes blazing beneath angry dark brows. They swept over her face, then fell to her mouth, and her knees buckled as his intentions hit her full force. He meant to kiss her! Now? Despite all her treacherous words?

He pulled her so close her breasts pressed heatedly against his unyielding chest, the contact igniting smoldering embers deep within her. Her lips parted, breathlessly, in a soft gasp, wantonly awaiting a kiss . . . that never came.

"Damn," he muttered, thrusting her from him. "You can close your mouth, Trista. I'm not going to kiss you . . . though it's the only time you make any sense to me." He shoved a hand through his hair and narrowed his gaze upon her. "Don't make me think you're not worth all the damned trouble you've caused me." He shook his head and gave her a final sweep of his eyes. "Women." And with that last, low, menacing growl, he turned on his booted heel and strode from the room.

Trista drew a deep breath, painfully closing her eyes upon shoulders that had never looked so broad, long-muscled legs that strode much too purposefully away from her, bearing that hypnotic voice, those damnable eyes. The front portal banged with finality and she jumped, her eyes flying open to fix upon the lovely flowers. With a cry of sudden savage fury, she swept her arm before her, sending the vase crashing to the floor. Calla lilies lay strewn about the polished mahogany, the vase rolling over once, then settling against the leg of a settee, but Trista was already halfway up the stairs.

When Kendall Barry arrived promptly at 5 p.m., Trista cheerily greeted him with a saucy smile, which she hoped revealed not one trace of her troubled thoughts. They departed soon thereafter, Trista upon a grossly docile gray mare and Kendall astride his bay gelding. He conversed mostly about his horse, his most prized possession, he declared, adding that he had recently acquired the mount for a small fortune at Tattersall's, the auctioneers near Hyde Park corner.

"The gentlemen of Society use this Hyde Park rendezvous to vie with one another in being the best mounted," Kendall explained. "They will spend incredible sums to acquire such horses as England alone can produce, Miss Fitzgerald. Myself, as well. Indeed, I've heard tale that the horseflesh in this country is better off than a majority of the common folk. Though that state would not be difficult to attain. Of course, 'tis certainly not something with which *we* should concern ourselves!"

Trista nodded and smiled despite the sudden chill that swept through her. She brushed this aside and slanted a glance at Kendall, wondering why he insisted upon addressing her with such blasted formality despite her countless requests to the contrary. Little wonder courtships endured interminably, with couples spending countless hours discussing the seemly and unseemly manner in which to simply address each other. Surely it would take years for Kendall to address her as "Trista, sweet," not that *that* particular nickname warmed her heart any small measure.

They passed through Hyde Park's wrought-iron gates and into a huge expanse of tree-shaded lawn. Beyond the immediate area, Trista spied a throng of men and several women, such as she, on horseback. The gentlemen were elegantly clothed in fashionable riding attire with quirts and top hats, which they tipped to the ladies as they passed. The majority of the splendidly attired ladies were in superbly appointed carriages, attended by powdered footmen in gorgeous liveries and elegant coachmen with top hats and white gloves.

Kendall drew up on his reins. "If I may be so frank, Miss Fitzgerald, you will not see any of the lower or middle classes of the city intruding themselves upon areas such as this, which are given up exclusively to persons of rank and fashion. This is Society's playground."

Glancing sharply at Kendall, Trista mused on his rather pompous statement, then brushed off her idle thoughts, for he obviously spoke the truth. Indeed, as they made their way through the park, Kendall hastened to point out the Society folk in attendance, from the most celebrated beauties to the most conspicuous of horsemen.

"We may even have occasion to see the King himself," Kendall remarked impressively, and received a greatly anticipated gasp of awe from Trista.

Soon they approached a crowd of perhaps a dozen or so young gentlemen on horseback. With some surprise, Trista noticed that the men were gathered about a smartly appointed black carriage, lined in pale blue satin, and upon whose plush satin seat was poised a striking, petite, auburn-haired young woman. She was exquisitely attired in a pale blue satin frock, which hugged her voluptuous bosom and tiny waist to perfection. Unabashedly, Trista looked on as the young woman raised the daintiest of hands to her billowing hat, casting a saucy look at a gentleman nearby, who had apparently been overhungry for some smile of recognition. This small gesture seemed to inflame the remaining would-be swains all the more, and they crowded about her closer still. She postured and pouted, then, with a wicked grin, made some fabulously witty remark, which drew a round of guffaws from the group.

"I see court is in session," Kendall remarked with derision, drawing a frown from Trista. He nodded at the auburn-haired young woman. "Clothilde St. John, the most celebrated of all the Fashionable Impures." At Trista's questioning glance, he grew a trifle flustered. "Forgive me for being so brazen. At the risk of offending you, Miss Fitzgerald, the fair Clothilde is a professional courtesan, a category of wench known as the Fashionable Impures by our set. And she is the most sought after of her kind, by half the Dukes of England and all the fashionable young Lords rich enough to enjoy her...er, charms. The unmitigated idol of the masculine half of the beau monde. I hear she was recently set up in a new town house by her latest lover, whose identity, of course, is still a mystery, as it always is until the unavoidable falling out. I suppose it lends her more of an allure." Kendall paused and Trista noticed that his eyes were fixed intently upon Clothilde St. John. "That is, of course, if one had a penchant for that sort of thing."

As they passed slowly by the entourage, Trista stared openly at Clothilde St. John. Here was a woman who refused to oblige Society by living strictly by its morals and standards, a woman who shunned the myriad rules governing marriage and the proper behavior of a wife. Trista mused on this for the remainder of their ride. Perhaps the life of a courtesan was far better than that of a wife. A courtesan. Lover of fabulously wealthy Dukes and Lords.... It was certainly worth a thought.

It was but two days hence when Trista first noticed the uncharacteristically bland, almost overtired expression Esme acquired, an expression undoubtedly brought on by the unexpected arrival of the Marchioness, Dominic's mother.

Trista caught but a fleeting glimpse of pale gray silk skirts and a bobbing white head as the Marchioness was led on her son's arm to the drawing room, the sweet scent of rose water clinging in her wake. The drawing room doors closed with soft finality behind the pair. Trista drew herself up quickly beneath Emerson the butler's stern gaze, lest she be found trespassing, and attempted, quite successfully, to loiter inconspicuously outside the door.

A flustered Esme appeared, fanning herself furiously and commenting that indeed 'twas most fortunate for everyone that Dominic hadn't any business appointments until later that day. Or, *mon Dieu,* she would have had to entertain the crotchety woman herself! She then disappeared within the drawing room for what turned out to be a brief "hullo," then emerged and, with a miffed expression, swept by Trista, who could have sworn she detected "Blast that woman!" among her aunt's mutterings.

The Marchioness's visit was decidedly short, and Dominic offered little in the way of an explanation. Indeed, after the woman's departure Trista noticed his drawn, tense demeanor and curt tone whenever he spoke, especially to

Esme, who appeared to be fighting some inner battle, as well. The Marchioness had upset the household and Trista knew not why. Nor could she speculate, for she was swept along on a flurry of luncheons and afternoon teas with Esme, who presented a cheery face to her close circle of friends and never once hinted at the trouble caused by her mother-in-law.

Chapter Six

On a soggy gray morning seven days hence, a handsome coach and six left London's city limits and lurched along a narrow dirt road that at one time had resembled a navigable thoroughfare. The week's incessant rain had since rendered it a quagmire that hindered travelers far more than it aided and left the once polished black vehicle and its four attendants sodden and dirt-splattered. A fine mist fell and the murky sky clung to the treetops, casting a shroud of gray gloom over the rolling countryside and the trio within the plush confines of the coach.

Trista peered from the coach window into the fog, hoping that Kendall was achieving some protection beneath the broadcloth greatcoat and wide-brimmed hat he had chosen for his ride to the Leighton country estate. He was out there, somewhere, behind their coach and that bearing the three ladies' maids and twice that number of trunks, braving the elements alongside Dominic, astride his dirt-splattered mount.

"A fine day for a picnic," Bianca huffed in an uncharacteristically nasal tone. Raising a dainty handkerchief to her swollen red nose, she sniffed none too softly. "In God's name, how did I catch this miserable cold? I am truly vexed, and just in time for the event of the Season. What miserable luck!"

"Perhaps you should have remained at the house," Esme scolded from her seat opposite Bianca.

Frantically shaking her head, Bianca attempted a response, only to be engulfed by a tremendous sneeze.

"*Mon Dieu!* I shall have Hastings turn about."

"Don't you dare!" Bianca rose half out of her seat with her vehemence. "Never fear, dear Esme, for you shan't be seeing much of me and my blasted cold." She dabbed her handkerchief to her nose. "I *refuse* to sulk about all day sipping weak, tepid tea with a bunch of mealymouthed women, wasting oodles of time discussing nothing of importance, while Nicholas could quite possibly be about!"

Trista rolled her eyes and studied the fog.

"For far too long I've made do with his games of cat and mouse. At this rate, I shall be an old maid before the man comes calling! No more. Besides, this ball is the perfect opportunity. I fear I shan't be able to sleep tonight knowing full well that bronzed Adonis is beneath the same roof."

Esme leveled a stern look upon Bianca. "Need I remind you to conduct yourself with dignity and respect? Do not fool yourself, *cherie,* this is no innocent soiree. No wee faux pas will go unnoticed. Rest assured the tongues will be wagging viciously and relentlessly if you commit the slightest transgression. Heed my words, and please, do everything possible to remain in your own bed."

"Alone?" Bianca sassed with a hint of a smile, then dissolved beneath the onslaught of another sneeze.

Esme could but wave a dismissive hand and sigh helplessly.

Not more than an hour later, Trista found herself amongst a group of women upon the Leighton terrace, fervently embroiled in a conversation concerning the weather. Her only contribution had been several huge yawns, which she hurriedly stifled behind a gloved hand. She then found herself next to Bianca, whose dark eyes darted feverishly about the sweeping lawn and the gentlemen on horseback as they prepared for the hunt. Trista could have told her that the one she sought was not among the group of gentlemen. Not yet, at least.

"Blast him!" Bianca hissed as if half to herself. "I simply will not subject myself to this nonsensical gibber-jabber while I wilt miserably in this air. I can hardly breathe.... Ah, thank heavens! Why, look who's here! Ivy Cooper, *darling*, so good to see you! And Chorlis Beckwith. It's been simply *ages*, darling. How are you?''

Chorlis Beckwith was a striking young woman with a sweep of honey blond curls and friendly brown eyes twinkling from beneath her hat. To her misfortune, she had acquired a rather shaky reputation of late, after being discovered flagrante delicto with a married man in a broom closet. Prior to this indiscretion, however, she had been known to have a propensity to lift her skirts for just about any Society gentleman.

"Chorly has a new beau," Ivy informed them in a low voice, drawing her parasol against prying eyes.

"He's not my beau . . . yet!" Chorlis giggled. "I've but known him two weeks, but I do believe I may be in love for the first time!"

"For the first time? *You*, Chorly?" Bianca snorted. "My dear girl, time is of no consequence. I've found that a decided fondness and depth of feeling can result from one or two meetings—with the right man, of course. Oh, Ivy darling, by the way, you *did* say that Nicholas was coming."

"*Cherie?*" Esme materialized at Trista's elbow. "Is it some custom from your part of the country to venture forth in a half-dressed state at all times? Your parasol? *Mon Dieu*, you would forget your head if it were not attached! Now go fetch that thing before someone notices! Oh, and *cherie*, the Duchess remarked just a short time ago that the house has proven quite difficult for guests, and even for some of the newer servants. Don't get yourself lost."

With a murmur of apology, Trista excused herself from the group and made her way from the terrace back to her room with relative ease and only a bit of direction from a passing servant. She retrieved the parasol from a flustered Aileen, who insisted it was her fault for burying the thing beneath her cloak. So intent was Trista upon returning to the party, though God only knew why, she paid little heed to the direction she took and inadvertently descended a set of stairs that led to a deserted, unfamiliar part of the house. Glancing about, she bit her lip and frowned. She peered down the long deserted hallway to her right, which was lighted at the end by a large window and what appeared to be a door. Hesitating not a moment, she lifted her skirts and hurried along the hallway, clutching her parasol.

Much to her relief, the door opened upon a beautiful flower garden enclosed by high brick walls and a wrought-iron gate, which led to the empty lawn beyond. Over the brick wall to one side, she heard the muffled thunder of horses' hooves and the faint chatter of the women. The gate swung open easily at her gentle push and she turned to make her way along the path skirting the high walls, then stopped dead in her tracks.

Standing before her was a magnificent riderless black stallion, eyeing her coolly with ears pricked and delicate nostrils flaring. Sleek black muscles glistened in the sun and a slight breeze ruffled the flowing ebony mane and tail, which nearly reached the ground. Hesitantly, lest she scare him off, Trista took a step toward him, noting the highly polished leather of both saddle and bridle. He was obviously under excellent care and exceedingly well trained, for he stood his ground at her approach, his wary dark eyes upon her, his ears pricked. Slowly she moved before him, speaking low as her gaze flickered over the powerful chest and legs, then swept to the arched neck, the small, finely shaped head, clear, wide-spaced eyes and tapering muzzle.

Drawing off one of her gloves, she raised her bare hand to rub gently upon his nose, the heady smell of horseflesh and polished leather invading her perfumed senses. He lowered his head such that she scratched between his ears, then at the side of his head.

"Oh, my ebony prince," Trista said with a laugh. "You're not such a beast after all, hmm?" She giggled when he took a step toward her and boldly nuzzled her arm, then the length of her bodice. She had to retreat a step, laying a firm hand upon that seeking nose. "Such liberties you allow yourself and we've but just met! What a love you are! Where in heaven's name is your master?"

"Nero!"

The stallion's head lifted suddenly toward the deep voice and Trista started, dropping her glove and parasol clumsily at the sudden interruption of that all-too-familiar voice. She should have known.

Nicholas stood before her, just as his horse, tall, regal looking, eyeing her warily as he idly twirled his quirt between his fingers. He was clad in formfitting fawn-colored breeches and polished knee-high black boots, which matched his tailored black riding coat. His shirt was crisp and immaculately white and the stock wound tightly at his neck was tied in a knot high beneath his cleft chin. Unlike the other gentlemen, however, he wore this attire as casually, as comfortably, as he did a shirt opened to the waist, as if he were born to it. The breeze ruffled his tousled hair. Those startlingly blue eyes simply stared.

Trista felt her throat constrict.

"You'd best retrieve your silly umbrella or Nero will make a meal out of it."

"Oh! Of course..." Trista murmured, averting her gaze as she bent to coax the parasol from a playful Nero.

"Nero!"

Once again, the stallion turned at his master's call but made no move. Trista detected an almost imperceptible flicker of annoyance and something indiscernible in Nicholas's fleeting expression as he finally swung his eyes from her. Nero gazed at his master with what Trista could only label an air of open defiance. The stallion nickered and tossed his dark head, pawed the soft ground, then eyed his master. With another nicker and a sassy toss of his head, Nero bent playfully and nuzzled at Trista, searching for the parasol she had concealed behind her back as she struggled to keep a smile from her face.

With no more than three long strides, Nicholas was beside her, sweeping any hint of a smile from her face as his arm shot out to grasp Nero's bridle and still the horse's play. Nero showed his master the whites of his eyes with a sidelong glance and Nicholas scowled back, then fondly patted the stallion's neck and spoke to the horse in a voice tinged with sarcasm.

"So, I see the lady has cast her spell upon you, as well, my friend. Heed my words, Nero, she is a self-proclaimed fickle wench, the worst kind, and by day's end will swing her sultry gaze and her saucy hips toward another—perhaps the dapple gray or bay gelding in yonder field. Able mounts, but certainly lacking the fortitude, the strength and the vitality—aye, all the qualities that make for the finest, the most virile of thoroughbred stallions."

As if in response to his master's voice, Nero nickered and bobbed his head at Trista, who stared with clenched jaw and clenched fists at the pair of cohorts.

"Oh, indeed, I most agree," Nicholas drawled. With his eyes upon her, he agilely mounted. " 'Tis indeed a mystery why a mare of such fine breeding and possessing such decidedly pleasing attributes should find interest in anything less. A gelding, you ask? Perhaps her blood runs a trifle cold. She is, lest you forget, as pure and chaste as the freshly driven snow. You'd best confine yourself to other pastures, my friend, and mares that will stoke the fire in your loins. Not some virgin ice goddess capable only of frosty glances and one or two quite unremarkable and decidedly frigid kisses."

Trista fumed and glared up at Nicholas, who sat his horse easily, leisurely, giving her his cool, unreadable look, daring her to offer forth some barrage of emotion to feed that insatiable ego. And Nero simply eyed her suspiciously. Traitor! Well, she would not give the scoundrel and his well-trained mount the satisfaction of a response, much less anything but the cool back of her head. Thus, despite the nearly overpowering urge to slap his handsome face and fill his ear with a good chastising, Trista sniffed, gave them both a last deprecating glance, then turned on her heel. Snapping her parasol open with far more angry force than she would have liked to display, she strode purposefully away from the pair.

She rejoined the younger women, lending half an ear to their idle chitchat, while her eyes strayed to the decidedly more interesting activity farther out on the lawn. Kendall looked dashing astride his sleek mount, though, much to her discomfiture, she soon found her gaze drawn to the powerful, sweeping strides of the magnificent black horse and his masterful rider.

"Well, finally!" Bianca raised her hand as Nero cantered past. "*Niii*-cholas! Oh, *Niii*-cholas!"

Nicholas tipped his hat in greeting, then swung Nero about to rejoin the others.

"Well! He does know how to sit a horse!" Bianca gushed.

"I should certainly hope so," Ivy replied. "There's no finer horseman in all of Richmond, in fact. Even England, I would wager."

"Oh, I would never doubt that," Bianca breathed. "Tell me, Ivy, being the accomplished man that he is, 'tis a wonder that Nicholas has never married. Perhaps the right woman hasn't come along."

"That very well may be, though I must say it's not for lack of eager young ladies." Ivy smiled at Bianca, displaying little outward sign that she was at all aware that the other girl hung on her every word. "My cousin is a rather particular man, though rumor has it he's indulged his share. I suppose he prefers it that way, no burden of a wife and all that. And with his work and all, especially lately with this project here, he hasn't the time. Nor the patience. Why, just the other day he was muttering something about fickle maids and...flowers. Yes, that was it."

"Flowers? Really?" Bianca purred.

"I believe he said they were a terrible waste of time and effort, or something like that."

Bianca lifted a knowing brow. "All that man needs is the perfect woman to turn his head, to show him the error of his ways, and he'll be married in no time."

"I'm not so sure about that," Ivy countered with a sweet smile. "Rumor around Richmond has it that a herd of wild buffalo couldn't drag Nicholas Brennan to the altar."

Bianca gave Ivy a sharp look and drawled, "Well, God only knows what a wild buffalo is, but I can tell you this, mark my words, when it comes time, 'twill take no more than a gentle nudge to get a ring upon one of those long fingers." Lifting her chin confidently, Bianca dabbed at her nose and cocked her head at Ivy. "Are you quite certain that Nicholas is unattached?"

"As sure as I can be, Bianca, unless you'd like me to sidle over and ask him for you?" Ivy gave Bianca her sweetest smile. "I wish you the best of luck with my cousin. You'll need it. Come along, Chorlis, Trista. Let's get some lemonade, shall we?"

The men were soon off for a rousing game of cricket, leaving the women to their own pursuits. Harboring no great desire to watch the men run about a soggy playing field, Trista retired to her room and found solace in a brief nap and a steaming bath. Her young maid, Aileen, had been busy all afternoon preparing Trista's cream silk gown, as well as the multitude of underclothing and accessories, which she spread carefully upon the bed as Trista sank low into a steaming tub. Aileen excused herself with Trista's blessing to seek out an afternoon snack, leaving Trista to revel in the lilac-scented soap, which she ran idly up and down a slender arm, her mind wandering.

"Ah, Nicholas, thief of hearts..." she murmured softly, then started, her eyes flying open at the soft plop of something hitting the water lapping between her breasts.

"Aileen..." For the briefest of moments, Trista smiled at the young girl's foolery until her eyes focused on the green glove floating innocently before her. Her glove. The glove she'd dropped when she'd discovered Nero. Her smile evaporated, her mouth fell open, and her heart gave a violent lurch. Instinctively, she raised her arms to cover herself just as her head snapped up to meet Nicholas Brennan's cool gaze.

He leaned casually against a dresser nearby, his arms folded over his broad chest. "Your glove, Miss Fitzgerald," he drawled in his casual tone, though his expression was entirely serious. The smoldering eyes flickered over her hair tumbling from the knot atop her head, then slid over her neck and shoulders and lower into the soapy water that barely hid from view that which he sought.

"H-how dare you!" Trista sputtered. "I presume saun-
tering into a woman's chamber while she bathes is some sort
of Yankee custom."

"Actually, it's part of a centuries-old mating ritual."

"Mating?" Trista's mouth fell open and she drew her
arms tighter about her. Glancing about for a towel, which
Aileen had obviously forgotten to set aside, she snapped,
"Be gone from here, Nicholas, this instant."

He moved to the foot of the tub and Trista found her eyes
drawn to his fingers, dangling into the water where her toes
had been splashing not moments before. She didn't need to
lift her gaze again to know in her heart that he looked so
completely handsome, so magnificent in his rugged way,
with his dirt-splattered shirt loosened and his hair wind-
blown and smelling of spring-fresh meadows. She felt that
familiar ache growing in her belly, mocking her anger and
frustration at his blatant disregard for her privacy. Despite
the screaming in her mind to do otherwise, she raised her
eyes to his and felt her anger dissolve in a heap.

His gaze flickered over her once again, a fleeting expression of impatience and something akin to pain scudding
across his features. Abruptly, he turned from her toward the
bed, presenting her with a feast of the broad planes of his
shoulders and tapering back, the sloping lines of a narrow
waist, the flexing buttocks. Hastily, she averted her gaze.
Color flooded her cheeks. He lingered far too obviously
over her flimsy undergarments displayed upon the bed, and
she swallowed past a parched throat when he extended a
hand to the dainty pink ribbons of her chemise. His touch
was achingly gentle yet so intimate that she reacted as if the
warm fingers brushed against her own skin. For several
moments he stood thus, silently, his face in profile drawn,
tense, his hooded gaze on the fine linen before him. Then,
without turning, without another word, he strode from the
room.

A dashing and gallant Kendall presented himself promptly
when Trista first appeared later that evening in the ballroom. He swung her onto the dance floor, his hands lightly

about her, his conversation flowing, dance after dance and throughout a light supper. Trista listened halfheartedly, smiled when she felt she should, ate like a bird and blushed profusely throughout the entire evening, for once Nicholas appeared, he did nothing but stare. At her.

He stared casually, through hooded eyes, leaning a shoulder against a doorjamb, drink in hand. He stared intently, poised upon the edge of the dance floor, not a hand's breath from her as she swept past on the arm of another. He stared as he ate, as he drank and as he carried on conversations. He stared blatantly, obviously, and to the exclusion of all else, including Bianca, who earlier had taken a liberal dose of foul cough medicine, then drowned her sorrows in too much champagne and was now finding it a trifle difficult to remain awake.

Nicholas continued to stare, and others around him began to stare, as well, and murmur amongst themselves. Even Kendall summoned a frosty glare or two, which only served to momentarily lift the corners of Nicholas's mouth. It was only a matter of time before Esme swooped upon Trista to warn her about "that man!" "That man" had replaced "Monsieur Brennan" after the Duchess of Leighton herself took Esme aside to whisper her concerns.

Esme cast Nicholas a furious look across the room. "Whatever is the matter with him? He's all but undressing you with his eyes! He has no decency! Perhaps if I speak with him..."

Which she did, and rather unsuccessfully at that, for Nicholas resumed his behavior and Esme reappeared at Trista's side, flustered and seething with anger. "Damned Yankee!" she muttered, then closed her eyes and pressed a hand to her heaving bosom. "He completely ignored my pleas—spoke only of the weather and inquired of Emerson, of all people, then thanked me again for such a lovely time at our ball! The gall! He pays Kendall so little heed one doesn't know what to do! Thank heavens he has not asked you to dance— Ha! Whatever am I thinking? 'Twould be far better to *dance* with him than allow him to *watch* you in that manner." Esme shook her head, then gave Trista a startled look. "Why, Trista, you needn't look as if you're enjoying this in some perverse way! I realize the attentions of a man can be intoxicating, but please confine yourself to Kendall."

Not surprisingly, Kendall finally grew so tired of Nicholas's behavior that he insisted upon a stroll onto the terrace for some privacy. For a time they walked in silence, then he paused and clasped Trista's hand about his arm.

"Trista..." He pulled her to him and she felt herself stiffen. "May I call you darling?" His look brimmed with such unabashed hope that she could not tell him otherwise. And then she was in his arms, pressed tightly against him, his lips finding hers clumsily and with an urgency that left her shaken but otherwise unmoved. She pushed against his heated chest and he released her abruptly, only to catch both her hands in his and bring them to his lips. Then, to her horror, he fell to his knees before her.

"Darling Trista..." he moaned. "How long I have waited to address you thus! Darling, my heart is on my sleeve—you have captured me—I am yours!" As he spread passionate kisses over her hands, Trista searched frantically for the proper words.

"Kendall...I..." A sudden movement in the garden beyond drew her attention. She peered closely into the shadows, leaving Kendall blissfully unaware of her distraction as he pleaded into her hands. She heard not a word he spoke, for into the dim light cast by the open terrace doors stepped Dominic and Archibald Sleeth.

They, too, appeared unaware of prying eyes, though their heated words did not lend either of them to glancing about idly. Indeed, Trista expected them to resort to their fists at any moment. If only she could venture closer, perhaps she could discover the reason for their obvious disagreement.

"Oh, say you feel it, as well, my darling. I have waited so long for you...for the perfect woman. Darling...marry me. Say you will and make me the happiest man on earth!"

Trista glanced at Kendall with a distracted frown. What had he said? Ah, they were moving closer now. If only Kendall would shut up!

"Just say yes, my darling, and we will be rid of that Yankee. He shall never bother you once you're mine. I've spoken with my father...."

Trista gave Kendall an encouraging smile, though she knew not the reason for the desperate look in his eyes, the slackness of his mouth as if he anticipated something from her. In another moment, Sleeth and Dominic would be very close.

"Darling, I've thought about this moment since the day we met on the street! You needn't say anything. You are so sweet, so pure, so innocent. You must forgive me if my depth of feeling embarrasses you, my darling. I shall keep you in such a grand style! Worship you! I've so much to offer. What is your answer, my sweetest darling?"

Growing unbearably frustrated with Kendall and his incessant gibberish, Trista swung her gaze to him and replied, "Yes, Kendall?"

His boyishly handsome face lit up like a beacon. "Yes? Yes! You'll agree to be my wife!"

Trista's jaw sagged. "Wha...!"

"What's this! Trista, did I hear you correctly? Why, it can't be! Did you say you were going to *marry* Kendall?"

It was Bianca, sashaying upon them in a remarkably unobtrusive manner despite her dizzy state. Shaking her head, Trista opened her mouth to correct this gross misinterpretation but found the words caught helplessly in her throat. Bianca surged onward, waving her empty champagne glass, her voice raised an octave or two.

"Why, *no one* is happier than I to hear the news of you two wedding. Esme! Uncle Dom! Such wonderful news! Trista and Kendall are betrothed!"

Trista was later to remember the following sequence of events as a blur through which she was forever saying "No!" At the news, Esme whooped with joy, clapped her hands and danced about, kissing her niece countless times and babbling on about the wedding of the decade. Dominic congratulated a befuddled-looking Kendall, then embraced Trista, muttering that she was doing the smart thing.

For what remained of the evening, Trista was embraced and kissed more than she would ever hope to be again by people she barely knew, hopelessly caught in a swirling sea of champagne-soused Society folk. They allowed her barely one word, misinterpreting her confused looks as those not inappropriate for a blushing bride. They also managed to keep her separated from Kendall for the remainder of the evening.

Even the soggy-nosed Sleeth loomed before her to smear his lips against her stiff hand and to murmur his most "heartfelt" congratulations. It was after the Duke of Leighton allowed himself the liberty of fondling her rounded hip—bawdily suggesting, as he did so, that once she was conveniently married, perhaps she would consider becoming his mistress—that Trista decided to leave the guests to their play.

She dismissed Aileen immediately after being helped into her cotton nightgown and wrapper, then sat before the dressing table idly running a brush through her cascading curls and staring dumbfounded at her reflection. The muffled sounds of revelry below drifted to her through her open window. What in God's name had happened?

With a troubled sigh, she moved to the plush chaise before a softly crackling fire. Settling against the velvet cushions, she gazed thoughtfully into the gently leaping flames and found herself wondering where Nicholas had been for the latter part of the evening. A damned bloody nuisance he was becoming, invading her thoughts at the most inopportune moments. She should be contemplating her next move, the entirely graceful manner in which she was going to extract herself from this sham of a betrothal. *He* should be furthest from her mind. Yet, he wasn't...he never was. What the devil was she to do?

And then it dawned on her, at first a thoroughly ghastly notion, which, after several moments of thoughtful contemplation, became a remarkably viable option. After a good hour, it was the only thing to do.

She would marry Kendall, or at least allow them all to think so.

* * *

With a start, Trista awoke, perhaps at the crackle of a last dying ember or the settling of the house and its occupants for the night. Or, which was far more likely, from the incessant and frightfully inappropriate growling in her belly.

Rising on shaky legs, she drew her wrapper close against the cool night air. What she wouldn't give for one morsel of that scrumptious-looking bread pudding, pigeon pie or the thinly sliced beef, all of which she had idly toyed with at supper while her wayward thoughts strayed to a tall dark gentleman. Perhaps a juicy apple to satisfy her until morning....

Licking her lips, she lit a nearby candle and moved to the bedroom door, opening it gingerly to peer up and down the deserted hallway. She strained for the slightest sound, the merest evidence that anyone was about; the servants even, who most assuredly were readying for the huge breakfast feast. Perhaps they would be willing to give her a bite or two. Her stomach rumbled again, urging her to step into the shadowed corridor and close the door softly behind her. Her heart thumped a bit faster as she moved cautiously down the hallway toward the rear staircase. Her candle, held high before her, cast oddly shaped shadows against the silk-covered walls and flickered wildly as her feet moved noiselessly over the plush carpets.

Her stomach twisted with anxiety. Although her mission was far from clandestine, she viewed the idea of prowling about a huge manor in the wee hours of the morning with certain trepidation and for a moment wondered at her bravery in attempting to navigate a house that left her confused in the light of day.

She slipped past countless closed doors on either side of the hallway, then moved stealthily down another long corridor to the staircase. Once on the first floor, she glanced about to get her bearings and frowned, unsure as to which direction would be the most likely to lead her to food. Turning to her right, she proceeded into another hallway, pausing at a half-opened set of double doors. Hesitantly, she peeked inside the dimly lit room. She breathed a sigh of relief that this small library was indeed empty, though the cozy fire and empty glass on the table before the hearth indicated that the room had not been deserted for long.

When she reached yet another corridor, she frowned and glanced up and down the hallway again, thoroughly confused. An ominous anxiety twisted in her belly, prompting her to return to the safety of her room.

Just as she turned to retrace her steps, a muffled sound from behind a nearby door snatched her attention and sent gnawing fear prickling along her spine. With wide eyes and little thought, she deliberately moved toward the closed door and the sound that appeared to be more and more like a muffled scream. Her heart raced as she stepped before the door and pressed her ear close to the wood.

Someone, a female, sounded as if she were attempting to scream, but it was muffled, a gurgling almost, as if it were being forcefully suppressed. Raising a trembling hand to the doorknob, she turned it ever so slowly, then pushed the door open.

Chapter Seven

Illuminated in the ghostly flickering light of her candle was a huge black shadow bent over a much smaller form—a woman...gurgling...not screaming any longer. She was being strangled.

Choking on a scream, Trista struggled for reason, attempting to keep her legs beneath her as the room spun crazily. And then the shadow turned, faceless in the dark, then became human and uttered a growl, throwing aside the limp form. With a terrified scream, Trista whirled, crashing heavily into the door and dropping her candle. Her hands fumbled for the door in the darkness and she flung it wide, stumbling down the dark hallway as her robe caught about her legs. She didn't pause to think, couldn't act quickly enough, had little notion where she was running. He was behind her, and with every thud of heavy footsteps closed the distance. Staggering around a corner, she crashed headlong into a table, uttered a cry and stumbled past. Her robe caught on a chair, and she tore it from her without thought. Desperately, she lurched through the deserted ballroom, daring to glance wildly behind her. Dear God... He was so close...not ten steps behind her...swooping upon her....

Into another dark hallway she surged and without hesitation stumbled down a steep flight of wooden steps. It was dark...very dark and cool...a damp, musky coolness. She could hear him...heavy, ominous footsteps thundering on the steps, getting closer...and she lunged down a dark narrow passageway toward a very dim light. Then, sud-

denly, there was nowhere to run . . . a dead end. Her head
twisted frantically, searching . . . and then a door, a way out!
Feverishly, she squeezed through the narrow opening and
with all her might slammed the heavy door shut, falling
against it with a sob. When the heavy footsteps stilled just
outside the door, she nearly died of fright. Through the
frantic pounding in her ears, she heard the scraping of a key
turning in the lock.

Whoever it was had locked her in.

"Noooooo!" she sobbed, and in reply received only a
low, terrifying growl and the muffled sound of footsteps
retreating.

"Well, if it isn't Society's golden girl. To what do I owe
the pleasure, Trista sweet?"

With a shriek of pure terror, Trista spun to face none
other than Nicholas Brennan. He stood casually before her,
grinning from ear to ear, his bold gaze raking her scantily
clad form from head to toe.

"Oh, Nicholas!" she sobbed, and unceremoniously threw
herself into arms that instantly wrapped about her. "It was
so awful . . . he was after me . . . I . . . think he k-killed someone. . . ."

"What?" He grasped her shoulders and held her from
him, gazing urgently into her eyes before crushing her
against him with even more fervor. She sobbed uncontrollably into his shirt, attempting to speak through trembling
lips, clutching at him as if he were her last vestige of reality.

Soothingly, he spoke against her tumbled hair, telling her
not to speak of it just yet. Beneath his gentle coaxing, her
sobs diminished and she hiccuped, burying her face against
his shirt. With a sniff, she lifted her eyes to him, encountering a gaze so intense she grew suddenly all too aware of the
feel of him against the length of her, of his hands caressing
her back.

"Where are we?" she asked, dragging her eyes from his
to glance about the small, dimly lit room.

"The wine cellar." He drew a handkerchief from his
trouser pocket. "Here. The shirt is useless now, sweetheart." He smiled as she made good use of the linen. "I

couldn't sleep. Too much in need of a good draft of brandy, I suppose. Seems the festivities did away with the brew upstairs. I'll give them that much—these Society folk truly have a knack for throwing a good party.'' His finger beneath her chin brought her gaze to his. ''For God's sake, what happened?''

She retold her tale in a trembling voice. ''I've this wine cellar to thank. Had this door been locked, he would have k-killed me....''

Nicholas drew her close and stroked the wayward curls from her face. ''You needn't think on what could have happened, Trista. It sounds as if he only meant to frighten you. Otherwise, he would have followed you into this room. After all, he had no way of knowing I was about. Have you an idea who he may have been?''

Trista shook her head and choked on a hiccup. ''No...he was very dark...big...wearing a cape or a full coat that swirled about him like an evil thing.''

''No help there,'' Nicholas murmured against her hair. ''Not one of the gentlemen guests was without his greatcoat today due to the weather. Then again, our killer need not have been a guest. Did you get a look at the woman?''

Trista shook her head, feeling her teeth chattering uncontrollably and Nicholas's arms tightening about her.

''And you're quite certain 'twas an act of violence that you happened upon?'' Trista raised a befuddled expression and he lifted a hand to gently sweep the curls from her face. ''Perhaps 'twas a manner of lovemaking with which you are unfamiliar.''

''Dear God, I may be an innocent when it comes to that, but I can assure you 'twas no act of love that I witnessed!'' She gave him a wary look.

''Oh, rest assured, my lady, I've only heard tale of such things. Believe me, my methods are of a far more gentle nature.''

Trista gulped and averted her gaze from his devilishly raised brow, willing her trembling to cease. ''N-no, I am certain 'twas a violent act. Why else would he have come after me?''

Nicholas drew her close, then reached behind him and brought forth a full bottle of amber liquid. "Here. A swallow or two of this and you'll feel much better."

Trista cast a hesitant glance at him, then at the bottle he held, unsure of his motives for a moment. In reply, she received naught but a look of genuine concern as he urged her to take a sip. She leaned forward and managed one gulp of the liquid, which instantly blazed a trail of fire down her throat to spread warming fingers through her belly and trembling limbs. With a cough and a wan smile, she raised a watery gaze to his arched brow and placed her hand next to his on the bottle, tipping it toward her once more.

"You surprise me, Trista. You do this remarkably well. What would dear Esme say of such things?" His twinkling eyes found hers, then fell to a tiny drop at the corner of her mouth.

Self-consciously, Trista licked her lips, retrieving the droplet that held Nicholas's rapt attention, and lowered her eyes as he helped himself to a liberal dose. The brandy was having far more than a calming influence upon her, and she realized this with a sinking heart when her gaze was unwittingly drawn to the parted neck of his shirt, the rugged column of throat exposed as he tilted his head back. Her eyes slid to his hand clasped about the bottle, and she found herself admiring his hands for the thousandth time, those long, tapering fingers that possessed the strength to bend steel, she was sure, but were equally capable of an achingly gentle caress.

Suddenly, she was unbearably conscious of her sheer cotton nightgown despite its high-necked semblance of innocence, and her trembling intensified when his eyes traveled the length of pearl buttons to the lace under her chin, then settled on her mouth, just inches from his.

"Thank you... yes, I do feel much better." She eased herself from him slightly. "I do believe I can stand on my own." Turning, she wrapped her arms around her shoulders to ease the burning of his touch. Yet she still felt him, even at a good arm's-length distance. His breathing was short, caught in his chest for a moment, and her breath caught, as well. Silence hung like a tangible barrier between them, though the air crackled with unspoken words, desires . . .

Nicholas's eyes narrowed upon the slender form, the alluring curves illuminated by the warm glow of the lantern that played upon the sheer cotton of her gown and set aflame the golden streaks in the tresses tumbling down her back. So frail she was, and so painfully young, terrified half out of her mind, needing comfort—aye, strong arms to protect her. Yet all he could think about was parting the cotton gown, feeling her soft and yielding beneath his seeking hand. Even in her vulnerability, she possessed that come-hither look with those full pouty lips and liquid eyes that boldly caressed, invited, as if she were begging to be ravished.

Feeling his eyes upon her, Trista knew another uncontrollable trembling, brought on by something other than sheer terror, and she risked peering at him through lowered lashes. This nearly proved her undoing.

"Perhaps we'd best be gone from here." She gestured to the door. "We should get help . . . do something."

"I'm afraid that's quite impossible."

Trista's eyes widened. "Impossible?"

"Quite. You see, I have no key—anymore. 'Twas the one that your pursuer used to lock us both in."

"You mean *you* haven't got a key?" Trista squeaked disbelievingly. "Locked in? We can't be."

"We are." How devilishly pleased he looked!

"No!"

"Yes." Slowly, he set the brandy aside.

"What shall we do?"

"I have an idea." He was beside her, warming her with the fierce heat of his body, all those desires held in check. His fingers brushed like liquid fire over her shoulder to lift a stray lock of hair, caressing the silky strands, then pressed it to his lips. When her eyes met his above that lock, her defenses crumbled. That one movement, so slight but done with such tenderness, revealed a side of him she could not fathom and sent her senses reeling. With a groan, she lurched from him, pressing her flaming cheeks against the locked door, her palms pounding uselessly upon the solid wood of her prison. She groaned again as his chest pressed against her back, warm hands encased hers and a deep voice murmured low in her ear.

"At this moment, and I may be damned to hell for it, it matters little to me who the killer could be. In fact, I feel I owe him a token of thanks for bringing you here. Now turn around. Look at me."

With a trembling sigh and an overwhelming sense of destiny, Trista turned to face him. With solid oak at her back and solid muscle against her breasts and along the entire length of her, she knew, in no uncertain terms, that she was on the brink of losing herself. She had no will, no power to resist him. She could not....

His eyes were everywhere—on her tumbling hair, her trembling mouth, then burning into hers. "You won't marry him—you know you won't."

Trista focused on the cleft chin so very close above her. "B-but I must...I...oh, I cannot marry Kendall or anyone else, for that matter."

His lips curved into a lopsided smile. "Is that so? Will you tell me why, darling innocent?"

Trista's eyes widened as he bent his mouth to nuzzle the side of her neck. She closed her eyes, willing the words to her tongue as tiny shivers of delight rippled through her. "I...I have little desire to be naught but a decorative ornament upon some man's arm while he keeps his mistresses and goes about his life."

"Indeed?" His hands brushed along her upper arms, warming her skin through the thin cotton.

Molten fire coursed through her and she sagged against the door. "Marriage holds little appeal for me. Surely you understand, for your feelings on the subject run along the same vein."

"Do they now?" His lips brushed over her forehead, his palms lay at her collarbone and his thumbs slowly caressed the flushed skin of her neck. "And how would you know my ‎lings on the matter, sweetness?"

Trista barely heard him for the sound of the blood rushing in her ears. His touch left a trail of fire along her quivering skin, a flame that only he could quench. Of their own accord, her hands left her sides to press against his chest, her eyes lifting to his. "Ivy was full of tales of your purposeful avoidance of that trap."

His hands cupped her face and he lowered his mouth to brush with infinite tenderness over hers. "Tell me, darling love," he breathed against her trembling lips. His arms slipped about her and crushed her soft breasts against him. "Why do you talk so much? Forget about everything, sweet angel...yield to me, everything soft, beautiful..."

Trista pushed gently, ineffectively, against him and turned her lips from his with a groan, only to feel his mouth again at her throat, hungrily...urgently...

"Nicholas...please...you mustn't."

"I must."

"We must cease this foolishness."

"This isn't foolishness, love." His voice was husky, hoarse with emotion. "No one but your pursuer knows that you are here, and he would never risk detection by even suggesting as much. 'Twill be hours before we are discovered. Until then, I shall not be dissuaded."

With a groan, he lowered his mouth to hers. With all the fervor she had suppressed within her, all the passion long denied, she returned his kiss. And then, she knew not how, his shirt was gone. She barely glimpsed his powerful length of naked torso before heated flesh seared her skin through the sheer gown. His muscled back rippled beneath her fingers, his mouth claiming hers in a fiery kiss as deft fingers teased the tiny pearl buttons at the top of her gown. As if in a last plea, Trista lifted her own trembling fingers to lie gently upon his, stilling his quest momentarily.

"Oh, no..." he murmured huskily as he grasped both her hands and brought them to his lips. "You can't stop me now, sweet angel, no more than you can stop yourself." His hands returned to the buttons and hers slid helplessly about his neck to caress the dark hair curling beneath her finge

With a trembling sigh and a fiercely growing need, she drew his mouth to hers again and melted full against him.

With a moan, Nicholas abandoned all hope of unbuttoning the gown and, with one swift movement, tore the thin fabric from neckline to waist. Trista's eyes flew wide and she gasped as her naked flesh met burning steel.

"Trista . . . sweet love . . ." His breath rasped against her mouth as he gently eased what remained of the gown from her shoulders to fall in a heap at her feet. She shuddered as the cool air caressed her bare skin, then again as Nicholas eased from her slightly and his passionate gaze fell to her unbridled charms. She closed her eyes, suddenly embarrassed, supremely self-conscious, and attempted to cover herself, but his hands stilled any such movement and drew her full against him.

"You've no need to shield yourself from me, sweet. You're so beautiful . . . you've no idea . . ." His eyes flickered over her upturned face, over those wide fathomless pools of emerald where a man could lose himself. "Trista, I've wanted you like no other woman I've ever known . . . ached for your golden skin beneath my hand . . ." As he spoke, his hands caressed her bare shoulders, then lowered to cup her full breasts, and Trista groaned, clinging to him as wave after wave of delicious sensation flooded through her.

"Nicholas . . . please . . ." she moaned softly as he began to caress her breasts, gently teasing the rosy peaks that swelled beneath his hands.

"Please what . . . ?" His voice was a whisper and his mouth a trail of fire along her neck, over her collarbone, teasing, enticing, inflaming her beyond reason. "Please stop? Is that what you want, my sweet virgin? I *will* stop, if that is truly what you wish. I won't continue unless you're willing."

His hands fell from her aching flesh and he gazed upon her with passion-filled eyes, though Trista knew in her heart he spoke the truth. Yet she ached for him . . . for a release only he could provide, and without hesitation she reached for his hands, placing them again on her breasts. "No, my darling Nicholas,'' she murmured huskily. "My wish is that you never stop...."

In one quick movement she was shoved against the door, her feet all but lifted from the floor beneath the force of his unleashed passions. He spread kisses along her throat, his hands at her shoulders pressing her against the door. His tongue was aflame against her breasts, over the quivering flesh of her softly rounded belly and lower still. With a moan, she drew him closer, kneading the muscles of his back and shoulders and his mouth claimed hers again.

And then her legs collapsed beneath her and they sank as one to the floor. She was dimly aware of the tangled remnants of her gown and his shirt beneath her, but she cared naught for that bed upon which she lay. At that moment, no better place on earth existed. Nicholas kissed her passionately, ferociously, until she had to turn away to catch her breath, and found her mouth at the hollow of his throat. She tasted of his skin with tongue and lips...savored his scent, and her arms wound about his neck. She pressed herself closer, rubbing against him until his mouth found her breasts, teasing, nibbling at the peaks, then engulfing each. With one hand, he pressed the soft mounds to his face as the other found the smooth skin of her lower back.

And then his mouth caressed the skin between her ribs, swept lower to the taut quivering flesh of her belly as his hands boldly claimed slender hips, trembling thighs. Her legs parted easily beneath his touch and he groaned as he lowered his mouth to the soft curls where her limbs met, nuzzling, seeking....

At this most intimate touch, Trista stiffened, arching her back, pressing her palms against his shoulders. Yet reason flew from her like a frightened bird and wave after wave washed over her, lifting her higher and higher until she unconsciously lifted her hips to him.

And then he was kneeling over her, kissing her mouth hungrily. For a moment, he raised his head and gazed upon her, his words a breathy rasping. "How I want you, virgin witch...." In one swift movement his trousers were gone, and Trista gasped again as naked, hot flesh came against her. His hands were in her hair and his mouth upon hers, bruising her lips, drawing her breath from her. As one powerful leg parted hers, he raised himself above her and Trista glimpsed the magnificent sinewed length of his bronzed body for the first time, and something more—suddenly frightening—and she lifted wide eyes to his.

"Nicholas...I know not what to do...I...have never...you must be gentle..."

"Of course," he breathed against her ear. "Just relax, sweet love. Put your arms around my neck, that's it."

Trista felt him *there,* so fiercely hot, incredibly swollen with a consuming desire, a passion that would not be denied. He caressed her breasts, her waist, her hips, soothed her fears until her legs parted with but a sweep of his hand. His mouth claimed hers as he surged into her, and she jerked against him, arching her back, uttering a muffled scream at the pain of her virtue being torn asunder.

Clinging to him fiercely, she became aware of the slow languid movements of his hips against hers and his voice murmuring unintelligibly against her throat. From deep within her the yearning began anew, only stronger, even more consuming, like an ember ignited, then flaring, intensifying to a sweeping flame, devouring her. And she was his, arching against him, sweeping passionate kisses over his face, his throat, his shoulder as the waves crescendoed for them both, lifting them higher and higher as one, until they were poised on the edge of glorious discovery...and they tumbled with limbs quivering and muffled sighs against each other's warm parted mouths as the sea of desire washed over them, then slowly retreated, bathing them in the sweet afterglow of sated desire.

Trista's breath stirred the dark hair at the base of Nicholas's throat. She turned her head and her lips found the strong forearm at her side. He nuzzled her breasts, then, with a groan, rolled from her onto his back, half leaning against the wall, and pulled her full against him. She tucked her head beneath his chin, her hand brushing over his chest, her hips nestled against him. With a sigh, she closed her eyes, snuggled closer and surrendered to the sweet lure of slumber.

Trista knew she slept, but at some point awakened to the caress of hands upon her skin, fiery kisses drawing the sleep from her. With breathless gasps of pleasure, she clung to him, her body a finely tuned instrument plucked and played to perfection beneath his masterful touch. Throughout the night he made leisurely, passionate love to her again . . . and again. And as the palest fingers of dawn streaked the early morning sky, he brushed his lips over hers one last time before peaceful sleep found them both.

In retrospect, Trista would never be quite certain exactly what it was that drew her from her dreamless slumber. Perhaps it was the scrape of a key in the lock, or even Nicholas's softly muttered oath as he drew the meager garments about them for what little modesty they would provide. One thing was certain. The sound of the door slamming open unceremoniously jolted Trista fully awake and she rose up against Nicholas's furred chest, blinking the sleep from her eyes.

"Hush, sweetheart," Nicholas murmured, tenderly pressing a finger against her passion-swollen lips. "We have company."

A strangled groan from the doorway snapped Trista's head about and her eyes instantly locked with Dominic's gleaming black orbs.

Despite his need to grasp hold of the doorjamb for support, the Count's gaze was remarkably steady. It flickered over the slender sweep of Trista's naked back as she sensuously reclined against her strapping Yankee lover. He paused in his perusal at the spot of blood on the tattered cloth lying smoothly over Trista's legs and rounded derriere, held in place by the hand lying possessively at the curve of her hip. Blazing black eyes locked with a hooded gaze of ice blue, and Dominic started, entirely flustered, angered beyond measure by the casual, almost leisurely manner in which the Yankee simply sat there, openly caressing Trista's bare back as if this were an everyday occurrence.

The fellow at Dominic's side, the Duke himself, managed to speak first, though he seemed quite unable to tear his eyes from the display before him. "Oh, dear...what have we here?" He ran a beefy hand through the flyaway red thatch upon his head, which appeared in desperate need of a comb. The man looked as if he had been unceremoniously yanked from his warm bed, his bare feet peeking from beneath silk pajamas. "Ahem...er, Dominic...perhaps we should allow them a moment to dress themselves, eh?"

With her gaze purposefully averted and her cheeks flaming, Trista glanced helplessly about for her gown, which she spied in tatters at her feet. Myriad emotions tumbled through her causing her to shudder uncontrollably as Nicholas drew her to her feet, then eased his shirt about her.

Her hands fumbled with the buttons until able fingers swept hers aside and flew to the task as she fiddled with rolling up the sleeves that hung past her fingertips. Her focus settled unconsciously on the taut, rippled stomach before her, where smooth dark hair grew into a thin line that tapered and disappeared into his trousers. She hastily glanced away, closing her eyes.

His arm slipped about her waist, turning her, and he pulled her back against his sturdy frame. Her pulse hammered in her ears, her belly churning beneath the heat of his palm pressing against her. Then Dominic swung about and fixed a murderous look upon them.

"I'm ever so glad to see that you two are safe and unharmed," Gaylord ventured cheerfully, clasping his hands together and rocking back and forth on his toes. "I'm afraid that we've had quite a shock. You see, sometime during the night a woman was murdered."

Trista blanched visibly at the confirmation of her worst fears and sagged against Nicholas. Raising a trembling hand to press against her throat, she murmured hoarsely, "Dear God, who was she?"

"Chorlis Beckwith," Gaylord replied solemnly, peering through his bushy brows as Trista groaned, then all but collapsed in Nicholas's arms.

"Take your filthy hands from her this instant!" Dominic's voice crackled through the air. "Haven't you done her enough harm already, Brennan?"

"'Tis neither the time nor the place for disagreement," Nicholas replied smoothly, though his gaze was deadly and rooted Dominic to the spot. "However, at the moment, I believe the lady could use a bit of comfort, for she was indeed witness to the murder."

"Oh my, how bloody awful!" Gaylord exclaimed, shaking his head in disbelief. "Poor lass. What in God's name was she doing about at that hour?"

"I believe the lady was hungry."

"Ha!" Dominic sneered with a disparaging sweep of black eyes.

"Has she any idea who the killer could be?" Gaylord asked. "We have none—no clues, though I must say this has thrown the house into a complete uproar, all that talk of boudoir murders."

Nicholas shook his head.

"I myself would certainly question *your* motives in all this," Dominic jeered. "Perhaps you were behind the entire incident simply to get your filthy hands on her."

"Ah, yes, fate dealt me a cruel blow last evening," Nicholas drawled. "I believe you are barking up the wrong tree, Count. I trust that my motives or any connection with the killing will not be questioned again. One does, however, have to wonder what led *you* here?"

Dominic's face grew mottled with anger and he shook a fist furiously at Nicholas. "Damn you to hell, Brennan! How dare you even suggest your actions be casually brushed aside! Listen to me, Yankee cur, if I had it my way, you would be castrated for what you've done to this girl. Rape carries a heavy sentence in this city."

Trista gasped and Gaylord hastily moved his bulk between the two men, who appeared close to knocking each other's heads off. Nicholas fixed a narrow gaze upon Dominic and simply loomed, stoic, silent, head held high, feet spread apart, as his hand at Trista's shoulder began to move slowly over her arm.

"Swine! Take your hands from her!" With a muffled curse, Dominic lunged at the Yankee but received a burly hand in the chest from Gaylord.

"Now, now, gentlemen." Gaylord scowled. "Brennan, no one doubts your word. You see, we found Miss Fitzgerald's robe and this key to the cellar beside Miss Beckwith's, er, body. I realize the gravity of this situation, murder and all, and I assure you that the matter will be given the appropriate attention. However, I have to feel some compassion for the Count. 'Tis undeniable that something went on here."

"I was in no way insinuating that it had not," Nicholas replied.

"Oh, of course you weren't...and I, er, 'tis certainly none of my business how the matter is handled—with delicacy, I can only hope—but as host, one has to concern oneself with proprieties, you know. I fear the Duchess's reaction, as well."

"I say we hang the bastard!" Dominic sneered, turning away from the rumpled pair as if the mere sight of them sickened him.

"Barring that, of course, if at all possible, I...oh dear, no..." With widening eyes, Gaylord paused at the shrill, decidedly frantic, undeniably female voice echoing down the narrow passageway.

Suddenly, Esme burst into the room with silk robes flowing about her. "Dominic! Did you find her...?" She stopped midsentence as her eyes met Nicholas, then widened as they slid slowly, with hesitancy, but as if unable to resist, over the bare chest, down a bronzed arm to the hand resting upon Trista's shoulder. Esme's jaw sagged as her gaze swept over Trista and down the length of a shirt that was obviously not hers to the shapely calves and bare feet, beside which lay the telltale remnants of a nightgown. A shaking hand rose to her throat as her eyes sought Trista's, but her niece's gaze was shamefully averted.

"Oh, *cherie*...no..." Esme groaned and sagged against her husband, who murmured something soothing to her, one could only surmise.

"Upstairs, both of you," Dominic snapped. "Trista, to your room. Brennan, find some clothing to cover yourself and meet me in the library in half an hour."

"As you wish," Nicholas murmured with a mocking bow. Pausing, he allowed Trista to find her legs beneath her and, with a hand at her back, followed her from the room.

With trembling fingers, Trista swept the tears from her cheeks as Aileen smoothed her mistress's skirts, pressed a handkerchief into her hand and gave a hopeful smile. Squeezing the young maid's hand, Trista turned to follow the butler, Sloane, to what most certainly was her doom, that which she had been fearing like the pox since her arrival. Her heart fluttered like a frightened bird within the confines of her chest and her limbs moved slowly, dreamily, as the hallways passed in a blur and sounds fused and became one. Dimly, she was aware that Sloane paused and drew wide a set of double doors. And suddenly she was in a richly decorated room, where a cozy fire crackled before an imposing, tall dark form. He turned and azure locked with jade, driving her breath from her as a distant memory flooded her mind.

He had been standing before another fire, that first night in her aunt's house, and had turned that lopsided grin upon her, stealing her breath away then, as now. How long ago that seemed . . . if only they could go back. . . .

"Ah, Trista, I see you've managed to compose yourself quite well." Dominic's strained voice filled the room and Trista found him standing stiffly beside Esme, seated in a nearby chair.

Esme's soft brown eyes filled with pain at the sight of her niece, and she dabbed gently at them with a lace handkerchief. "Oh, *cherie,* what you have done. . ." Esme's words dissolved into a moan and Dominic's free hand dropped to her shoulder.

With the other, he raised a glass of amber liquid to his lips and gulped feverishly, then leveled a narrow gaze upon Trista. "I believe one matter has yet to be determined before we can decide upon the manner in which to proceed. 'Tis the matter of your consent, Trista."

Trista's lips parted with confusion and she clutched her handkerchief as if to draw strength from that fine linen. "Whatever do you mean?"

"Was it rape, Trista?" Dominic sneered. "Or did you consent?" Piercing black eyes flickered disgustedly over a stoic Nicholas. "Brennan, here, is of little help on the matter, though I would question every vile word that falls from the Yankee vermin's tongue." At Esme's soft reproach, he continued in an even tone. "'Twas *he* who insisted that we ask you. So noble of him, wouldn't you agree? Stupid, if you ask me, to lay his fate in the hands of a willful child." He paused and peered closely at Trista. "If it were up to me, the cad would be hanged and you shipped off to a convent or strict school for wayward girls until your father returns."

Trista swallowed hard and raised shining eyes to the Count, quite certain that only her aunt's influence saved her from such a fate.

"Well, Trista, which was it . . . and you'd best think long and hard on this one, much longer than you did before you found yourself in this situation."

"Dominic, you're all but accusing her," Esme murmured, though her husband seemed oblivious to her words.

"Listen to me, Trista," he continued. "No one would question that it was in fact rape. Everyone with eyes in their heads was aware that Brennan was sniffing after you as if you were some bitch in heat. And you, the innocent, newly betrothed maiden." He paused, gulping again from his drink, then his lips curled with a vile sneer. "He's a Yankee, Trista. From a land of outlaws and misfits, heathens capable of far worse than rape, let me tell you. Undoubtedly, he has been in this position before. 'Tis understandable, of course, for he's an opportunist with a burning greed for wealth, for position, for *you*—the epitome of a freshly bloomed English maiden of Society from excellent stock, money . . ." A dark brow lifted suggestively at Trista and he paused, allowing his words to sink in, then smiled thinly as Trista cast wide eyes at Nicholas.

To no avail, for the tall, silent Yankee appeared as if he hadn't heard one word that Dominic put forth. His gaze was so steadfastly locked upon her that Trista felt as if his eyes were the vise about her trembling soul.

"Trista, we only wish what is best for you," Esme murmured weakly. "We simply wish to guide you as your father would. You have been irreparably tarnished by this act—God only knows what poor Kendall will think of it all—but perhaps we could salvage some measure of decency. If in fact it *was* rape, Monsieur Brennan will be properly dealt with by the authorities, perhaps thrown from the country. Sullied though you will be, perhaps one day you will find a man who could bring himself to forgive this—perhaps Kendall even. Do you understand what I'm telling you?"

" 'Twas not rape."

Those words, spoken shakily, barely above a whisper, brought Esme's hands to clutch frantically at her breast and Dominic to utter a muffled curse. "You stupid girl! Have you any idea what you're doing?"

Shamefully, Trista lowered her head and her eyes fixed upon the handkerchief she clutched with both hands. "I speak the truth. Nicholas should not be unjustly punished for my indiscretion, my lack of common sense."

"*Your* indiscretion!" Esme breathed. "Darling, you were not alone in that godforsaken cellar! I beg of you, perhaps your thinking is somewhat clouded on the actual events. If he in any way forced you..."

Regretfully, Trista shook her head. "I was not forced in any way, I fear. I am ashamed more than you will ever know, Aunt Esme, and my dearest wish is to spare you further grief. So that I shan't tarnish your name or the family any longer, on the morrow I shall be gone from London back home...."

"Oh, no, *cherie*. We cannot possibly allow you to do that." Esme shook her head woefully. "I'm afraid that propriety dictates only one possible course of action, and this breaks my heart, for 'tis the harshest of all possible punishments.'' She paused, dabbing at her shining eyes, then grasped Dominic's hand and lifted a mournful gaze. "I'm afraid that you will have to marry Monsieur Brennan. And the sooner the better.''

Chapter Eight

"Noooooo!" The sole word, borne on a trembling sob, escaped Trista's lips unheeded as the import of Esme's words struck her in the belly like a fist. "No! Aunt Esme, please! Dear God, no!" On quivering legs, she flew to her aunt, dropping to her knees beside her and grasping the soft hands. "I implore you! Please do not force this action! Anything but this!"

Esme stroked the wayward curls from her niece's feverish brow, though her tone remained firm. "I'm so dreadfully sorry, Trista. 'Tis the only way. Perhaps you should have considered the results your wanton behavior would bring."

"Perhaps if we wait until Father returns..."

"'Tis of no consequence. I'm afraid that your father would agree with this decision. You simply have no choice."

"But I could leave! As if nothing happened."

"Oh, but it did, and the whole dreadful lot of Society knows it. We simply cannot allow this act to go unacknowledged. If you were to leave here, Monsieur Brennan would go off on his merry way and the only conclusion to be drawn would be that it was not rape. Forever, you would be cast as the fallen woman, while he enjoyed the remainder of his life, unscathed, proud to have added a sweet innocent to his conquests." Sadly, Esme shook her head. "At least this way you may be able to save face, perhaps enjoy some measure of happiness with the man. Dear God, how could you have allowed this to happen?"

Trista's disbelieving eyes fell from her aunt as frustration and humiliation rose within her, a dull ache lodging in her throat. Lifting her handkerchief to her nose, she raised a teary gaze to Nicholas, but he was gone . . . his space before the fire empty. She swung widening eyes upon her aunt.

"Let him go," Esme murmured from beneath her own handkerchief. "He is well aware that he narrowly escaped prison, perhaps an even harsher punishment. I believe Monsieur Brennan will henceforth be more than amenable."

"Indeed," Dominic snarled from behind his glass. "You're too kind, Trista. I had no idea martyrdom ran in your bloodlines. You've sacrificed yourself for that man, you do realize that? Are you quite certain you'd rather not change your mind?"

Trista stared openmouthed at the Count. Surely he wasn't suggesting that she *lie* to save her skin and condemn Nicholas, living that lie for the rest of her life? Though, condemning them both to a sham of a marriage could be far worse.

"Nay. I don't wish to speak anything but the truth."

"As you wish," Dominic snorted, then swept a deprecating gaze over her. "You know, 'twas quite amazing the Yankee's manner before you joined us. He agreed to marry you. Offered little resistance. I do believe he even said he had anticipated as much. Bold words for a man ruled by what lies between his legs." Esme gasped and Trista felt her cheeks flame at the callous words. "I would imagine that he will keep you on your back and breeding for a good part of the remainder of your life. Do I paint too grim a picture, Trista? So sorry. 'Tis the truth, and I feel only contempt for both of you."

"Dominic!" Esme scolded, rising to her feet to lay a steadying hand upon her husband's arm. "Stop it this instant! You've no need to berate the poor child further. Look at her! Frightened half out of her mind, poor lamb. Now go, Dominic. Someone must speak to poor Kendall of this. We certainly owe him that much, no?"

* * *

Esme, apparently certain that *she* would be the subject of many drawing room and tea party conversations for months to come, launched herself into the planning of the wedding with all the fervor of one who waits an entire lifetime with breathless anticipation for such an opportunity. Trista, however, deemed the flurry of preparations entirely baffling and grossly hypocritical. This sham of a wedding should consist of nothing more than a few hastily spoken vows, certainly not some farce of a production. Surely all those pinched countenances that had for the last two weeks peered scornfully down their well-bred noses at her would not attend her wedding, smiling warmly, whispering words of congratulations. Bloody hypocrites, the entire lot!

"Ah, *cherie,* 'tis your wedding day! So lucky you are, no?" Adelle fluttered about, her clucking and idle musings drawing Trista from her thoughts. "And Nicholas—when he sees you! He will not be able to keep his hands from you!" She winked wickedly. "Such a hot-blooded man, no? Why, of course, you must know, eh? Tsk! Tsk! Young love! So hot, so exciting!"

Trista raised ice-cold hands to press against cheeks flaming beneath Adelle's wicked words and raised twin pools of jade to her reflection in the full-length mirror. With a breathless gasp, her mouth fell open. "Oh, Adelle . . ."

"You like, eh? 'Tis *magnifique!* The most beautiful gown I have ever seen! Was it not worth every candle that burned late into the night?"

In the soft glow of late afternoon candlelight, the fabric shimmered richly, a creamy white taffeta that cast Trista's skin in a tawny glow. The sweeping skirt was incredibly full, complete with three crisp underskirts and double flounced at the hem with cream bows and clusters of seed pearls. The pearl-encrusted bodice, daringly cut in a low neckline, hugged Trista's waist and bosom to perfection. The enormous poufed sleeves narrowed at the elbow and were fitted to her wrists.

Her eyes swept over her left hand, the trembling ice-cold fingers bereft of all jewelry. Soon she would be wearing that simple gold band that would seal her fate. With a shudder, she turned to peer over her shoulder at the low-cut back and the long row of silk-covered buttons. Suddenly, unbidden, a vision loomed of long masculine fingers tending to those buttons.

"Ooh, *cherie,* such a catch he is! Oh, but you must realize this!" Adelle secured upon Trista's head a band of the palest pink roses woven with baby's breath, then smoothed the floor-length veil, which fell from the band beneath Trista's coiled locks. "Keep him happy, eh? A man such as he—oo-la-la! Two, maybe three, even four times a day! Oh, to be you, *cherie!*"

Trista flushed scarlet, mumbled some incoherent reply and failed miserably at securing her diamond-and-pearl earrings.

"Ah! Before I forget..." Adelle fluttered to Trista's open trunk nearby and plucked a flimsy, very tiny piece of white silk from the contents, dangling it sassily from one hand and arching a wicked brow. "My wedding gift to you, *cherie,* though God only knows when that Nicholas shall allow you a stitch of clothing!"

Trista stared with mute horror at the silk swatch as Adelle resumed her fluttering. "Always remember this, to keep your man happy, my sweet innocent. To the outside world, you must always be a refined, elegant lady. A sparkling jewel upon your husband's arm. But behind closed doors you must be his whore, his mistress, everything he desires. This will keep him forever at your side and from the arms of another. Believe me, I speak truth."

Trista's heart plummeted to her quaking knees at those brazen words. Nay! She could not! How could she even think of becoming everything he desired when she most assuredly embodied everything he detested! A tarnished bride forced upon him...

At that moment, the bedroom door burst open and Esme, resplendent in peach silk, bustled into the room. Words poised, unspoken, hands trembled, unheeded, and tears brimmed, unshed, as an enormous bouquet of pink roses was thrust into Trista's hands and the firm pressure at her back and along her arm guided her from the room. Candle-light flickered and her gaze grew clouded as powdered cheeks brushed hers and Esme's lilting voice swirled about her, the words a low buzz, the tone, which was meant to soothe, only heightening the claw of anxiety scraping at her insides. The crisp rustle of her skirts served to assure her that her feet, indeed, moved, as if lead-filled, yet she floated to the top of the stairs. The marble entry, the glorious garland of pink and white roses wound about the banister swam before her clouded gaze as the hushed murmur of voices rose from the ballroom below. Below, where another waited, as well.

On Dominic's arm, Trista drifted up the long aisle past a sea of blurred faces, her feet barely whispers beneath her as the lyrical strains of a harp captured her in its soft melody. Her eyes were unseeing through the fine netting of her veil, yet later she would remember the faces of certain guests quite clearly and the distinct fragrance of so many blooming roses.

Then *he* was before her, looming larger than life, firmly clasping her hand beneath his arm. The heat emanated from him and seeped through her fingers into her quaking soul, yet she could not look at him.

The pleasant-faced man before them spoke, his words of love, of sacred vows, settling like a shroud upon Trista. Tears welled unbidden and her legs threatened for the thousandth time to buckle beneath her. She bit her lip, drawing deep, unsteady breaths.

Suddenly, Nicholas's resonant voice reverberated through her, those vows so gravely spoken...the prison within which she would endure her days...his voice settling upon the hushed crowd like a rumble of distant thunder. Then a whisper, borne on the fragrant breeze wafting through the open terrace doors, spoke her vows. Warm hands encased hers, stilling their trembling momentarily, and she was suddenly facing him. Her eyes fluttered to the fingers grasping hers. With a sureness Trista knew *she* would never feel, those fingers slipped the ring upon her left hand.

This was no simple gold band.

Her heart lurched and she swayed until his firm hand at her elbow steadied her. The stone, a brilliant emerald surrounded by a dozen or more diamonds, was so large it nearly reached to her knuckle. She felt the weight of it, like that upon her heart, as she murmured the vows and managed to ease the gold band onto Nicholas's steady hand. Her right hand was once again firmly clasped in his and they turned again as the parson spoke of God and unions that no man should divide. Then, suddenly, she felt his hands at her waist, turning her, drawing her to him, and cool air swept over her cheeks as he lifted the veil. Her gaze flew up to his, and her lips parted, her breath snatched from her as his head lowered to hers.

His lips brushed over hers, lingering like dew upon a freshly bloomed flower, then suddenly flaming, devouring, as he crushed her to him. Her hands fluttered against his chest, the blood rushed in her ears and she was lost, caught in a tumble of skirts. He released her, perhaps at the muffled sound of an uncomfortable cough from one of the guests, and then she was drifting down the aisle once more.

Trista had but a moment to whisper a teary farewell to her aunt before her silk traveling cape was swept about her shoulders and the firm pressure of Nicholas's hand at her back guided her to the waiting coach. Momentarily, she glimpsed the magnificently appointed black vehicle, the matched team of black horses, before a stern-faced coachman bowed curtly and swung the door wide to reveal a plush gold velvet interior. Nicholas assisted her aboard, then, nodding to his man, ducked inside and settled himself upon the seat opposite her.

The coach lurched forward and Trista's unsteady gaze fixed upon the passing city streets. A murky fog was rapidly descending, a steady drizzle obliterating all with its consuming shroud of gray. Unconsciously, she shivered and snuggled closer within her cape, though the silky fabric offered little in the way of protection from damp chills. Or penetrating gazes, for that matter.

She shifted in her seat, wishing with all her might that Adelle had not deemed it necessary for her blasted gown to require *three* underskirts, which all but filled the entire coach. Indeed, with every slight bump or sway of the coach, Trista grew increasingly aware that Nicholas's thigh brushed intimately against hers, *beneath* the mound of skirts. She drew her knees together, yet not a moment later the muscled thigh brushed against her once more. She shifted yet again, drawing her legs to the side, only to find her path blocked by his other leg resting against the side of the coach. Trapped—between the longest legs in the kingdom.

She lowered her gaze from the window and found her eyes drawn to her hands clasped tightly in her lap. The brilliant emerald weighting her hand sparkled and winked mockingly at her, causing her to shudder again and close her eyes upon that symbol of their union.

After a time, she raised her eyes hesitantly, then visibly started as she encountered a visage so harshly intense, so fierce in its stern perusal that her breath was momentarily snatched from her. How easily his rugged good looks could become so stark, the high cheekbones sheets of ice, the sculpted jaw chiseled granite. His eyes were shards of glass that sliced through her scattered resolve, her shattered dreams, to her quaking soul. She knew a sudden prickling fear, a fear that split asunder the unease she had experienced at the thought of marrying a man she barely knew. The philandering, the swaggering, the flippancy and the audacity, the quick wit and, yes, the undeniable charm, even the irresistible sensual hold upon her—with *these* qualities she felt somewhat prepared to deal. Not with *this* man, who looked as if he would do anything he bloody well pleased, and charm would be the least of his methods. Unconsciously, she shivered, unaware that her movement caused the folds of her cape to part. Unfortunately, she became very much aware of this when the hooded eyes lowered from hers to stare openly at her bosom, though whether it was passion or contempt she viewed within the depths of those ice blue orbs, she could not be certain. Growing even more flustered, she attempted to gather the cloak tighter about her, when, quick as a flash, he grasped her hand, stilling her quest.

"Don't."

The harsh command brought a frown to Trista's brow and a flush to her cheeks. She returned his stare, drawing shallow, unsteady breaths, entirely uncaring that her heaving bosom was all but laid bare before him as the cloak fell to her sides. For a moment, the grip on her wrist tightened as he pulled her toward him, and she resisted, bracing her legs.

" 'Twould serve you well, madam, to remember that you are now *mine*. And *I* prefer you without the damned cloak." With a sweep of his hand, he snatched the cloak from beneath her, tucking it beside him and settling against his seat once more.

Trista gaped at him. "*Yours!* I will be no man's chattel!"

"Chattel, wife, call it what you will."

"What?"

"Surely, my fickle bride, the nature of modern-day marriages doesn't surprise you. 'Twas you who coined the phrase 'decorative ornament,' was it not?"

A gnawing ache began low in Trista's belly. Indeed, she'd known not what to expect of him as her husband, but she'd never anticipated a Nicholas so snide, so cynical. Surely this was not the true nature of the man to whom she would be joined for all eternity?

"I know little of modern-day marriages except what has been told to me," she replied haughtily, flinching at his derisive snort.

"Ah, indeed, your dear aunt found a moment's time from her planning of our blessed event to tutor you on the trials and tribulations of married life. Of these, dear wife, she is more than aware."

Trista's cheeks flushed with embarrassment. "Aunt Esme only means well, and events of that sort serve as her diversion. Indeed, I'll have you know I had little to do with that lavish affair."

"Fare for the idle rich," Nicholas muttered. Her head was turned from him, affording him a view of sweeping dark lashes, the fine-boned delicacy of her jaw, the fullness of her lips. The smooth column of her throat beckoned, as did the tantalizing swell of her bosom, the creaminess of the gown in the soft light of the lantern only heightening the lustrous tawny hues of the jewel nestled within its folds. Yet his gaze strayed for the briefest of moments before coming to rest on her furrowed brow.

His *wife*—so beautiful in her shame and degradation, even more so, if it were possible, as the unwilling bride; snatched from his arms only to be forced into a marriage she had wished to avoid at all costs. Even at the expense of her reputation, that most highly valued of all Society's virtues. It was certainly rare, and decidedly disconcerting, to come upon a maiden who would have suffered the pain and retribution served up by Society's finest rather than wed him, even if, by so doing, she would save face and be found in good graces once more. Was he so loathsome a candidate for husband that she would have gladly sacrificed her honor to avoid speaking those vows with him? And what of their passionate night spent together, a night he would not soon forget and one that he wished to repeat tonight and every night hereafter? Was she the type of maiden to indulge her fancy, then move on to another paramour without a moment's hesitation? Had she perhaps been speaking the truth when she'd proclaimed to have a fickle heart . . . this fickle maiden capable, even in her innocence, of probing the depths of his passion, of stirring feelings he'd never thought possible, then wishing for any punishment but that life sentence she had been dealt?

His eyes narrowed upon her, as if simply staring at her long enough would bring him solace, and his jaw tensed with his troubled thoughts. Surely this was not the true nature of the woman to whom he would be joined for all eternity?

"Perhaps it would be best to speak of this arrangement, dear wife." His bruised psyche added more than a bit of sarcastic bite to his words, words borne from the depths of a battered ego that allowed little in the way of forethought. "It's only fair that the marriage be just that—a vehicle for us both to maintain our reputations while we go on about our lives as before, with some deference toward the arrangement and a good bit of discretion, of course. I'm more than certain that you will find this to your liking, for you will have full access to the house and the grounds, and you need only ask for anything else you may wish.''

Trista raised an uncomprehending, slightly wary expression to the brooding man before her.

"I must say," he muttered with a cold sweep of his eyes, "I admire your conviction to speak the truth, faced with a fate worse than death, no doubt, though one could surmise that you have thought long and often since then about changing your mind."

"Perhaps, though if the scene were replayed, I'm certain that I would not speak otherwise."

"How very noble and self-righteous."

"I have never been, nor do I ever hope to become, a liar, Nicholas, *especially* because of you. I believe if I have committed some transgression, then I should take my lumps, so to speak."

"Your lumps...ah, I see. Well, then you needn't fret, for I will not demand much in the way of wifely duties from you. You needn't look so wide-eyed, Trista. I'm simply saying that this will be, for all intents and purposes, a marriage of convenience." He lowered his gaze momentarily to her abundant charms, which all but beckoned for a man's caress—*his* caress. Gritting his teeth, he growled, "You will not be expected to share my bed, and I have little intention of forcing you. I do expect, however, that you will conduct yourself properly as my wife, bearing the Brennan name with honor—and, of course, if you *do* choose to take a lover, find it within yourself to employ the utmost in discretion. Do I make myself perfectly clear?"

"Quite," Trista managed, gulping past the lump in her throat. For a moment, she dared not breathe, as if that slight movement might somehow shatter this understanding between them. *This* from him she had not expected, and though his mood certainly disturbed her, his pronouncement that she would be left to her own pursuits, without the threat of him seducing her will from her, left her with a lightened heart, a measure of her dignity. To find oneself forced upon a man was humiliating enough. To be bent to his will by his seductive powers, then stand idly by while he resumed his gambling and wenching life...why, that would be unbearable.

That he detested her was grossly apparent, and his desire for her had surely been appeased by their one night of passion. He had even suggested that she take a lover. How like the true philanderer.

"So, you are pleased, woman?" he growled.

Trista gave a small shrug. "And why shouldn't I be?"

Nicholas scowled and sought what he could from the fog-enshrouded windows. This smiling acceptance of her fate descended upon him like a crushing blow, and he nearly drove his fist through the coach window with frustration. Had he actually expected anything but that from a fickle wench? Now what the hell was he going to do?

Sometime later, the vehicle slowed to a stop, and though Trista was eager for some glimpse of her new home, the impenetrable curtain of fog afforded her little view of the structure. Nicholas swept her cloak about her shoulders, then alighted from the coach. Drawing the cloak about her as best she could, Trista struggled through her mountain of skirts and ducked her head as Nicholas clasped her hand. So intent was she on maintaining her balance as she stepped from the coach that she was completely unaware of the low neckline of her gown gapping provocatively from her breasts, allowing Nicholas full view of their swelling fullness. His attention was captured so entirely that for a moment his hand wavered. At that precise moment Trista caught her heel on the edge of the floorboard and, seeking the strength of his hand, found herself teetering precariously, a mere hairbreadth away from tumbling head over heels to the ground.

Without a moment's hesitation, Nicholas swept her up in his arms and strode purposefully toward the looming entrance.

"My shoe!" Trista exclaimed breathlessly, gesturing over his brawny shoulder to the coach, where her shoe dangled.

"I'll buy you twenty more just like it," Nicholas muttered, his gaze purposefully averted from the woman squirming in his arms. Although he was all too aware of his wife's sleek, long-limbed attributes, at the moment he was experiencing difficulty keeping his thoughts from those that were soft, very round and pressed enticingly against him.

"Fleming, the bags!" he barked as he passed the young lad, who painfully lowered his eyes from the newly wedded couple and hastened to his employer's bidding.

Trista's head snapped up. "Peter!"

Nicholas's feet stilled midstride, and his stormy gaze settled upon her. "You spoke, wife?"

"I..." Her eyes darted incredulously to her friend tending to the bags. "I...he's my...Peter."

A dark brow lifted in reply, causing her to flush beneath his regard. She felt the heat of his gaze upon her and unconsciously tensed for what was certain to be a caustic remark. None came, and Nicholas continued on, nodding curtly at the tall, placid-faced gentleman servant standing at the opened doorway. He lowered Trista to her feet before the older man.

"Fritz, my good man, may I present my bride, Trista." Extending an arm toward her, Nicholas swept his eyes over her from head to toe, then leaned toward the older man and, under his breath, though loud enough for Trista to hear, muttered, "You needn't fret, Fritz. Her rather lopsided state is the result of nothing more than a lost shoe." With the briefest hint of a grin, Nicholas turned to her and arched a brow, as did his "good man," who peered at her rather curiously beneath a pair of bushy gray eyebrows.

Nicholas clapped this Fritz on the back. "Trista, meet Frederick Otto Hamilton. A man of stout English-German heritage, possessing the keenest of wits, the sharpest intelligence and a decided knack for running the smoothest of households. Ah, yes, and my good friend. He's been with my family for years. If he likes you, he may allow you to address him as simply Fritz. If not..." Nicholas raised both brows, then shrugged, as if suddenly at a loss for words, and cast the servant a slightly baffled look.

Frederick Otto Hamilton's keen eye took but an instant to appraise Nicholas's beautiful bride, for just as Trista was about to resign herself to her theory that all these stone-faced male servants in London were somehow related, the corner of his mouth lifted ever so slightly and, in a rather pleasant voice that shattered her theory, he intoned, "A pleasure, my lady. You may call me Fritz. Welcome to the family."

Trista flushed like a dutiful little wife and clasped his extended hand. "Thank you, Fritz..." She paused when Peter, laboring with her trunks, pushed past them to enter the house. For a moment, her eyes lingered on her friend, a servant in her husband's home, in *her* home. Her brow grew troubled and she swung her gaze to Nicholas, only to meet the scowl darkening his features once more.

"Shall we, madam?" His tone was brusque and drew a raised brow from Fritz, though Trista hardly noticed, for the firm hand at her back urged her through the doorway into a massive foyer.

With widening eyes she viewed the three-story entrance, the mahogany walls bathed by the flickering candlelight of an enormous gilt chandelier suspended in the center of the hall. Her head fell back and her eyes slid along plush golden velvet wall hangings, then across carved mahogany railings on the second floor and down the impossibly wide staircase lying directly before her. Unaware that her mouth had parted slightly with her surprise, she continued her appraisal of the fine rosewood and mahogany furniture and the thick Persian carpet, soft and plush beneath her stockinged foot. Through an opened doorway to her right she glimpsed a cozy fire burning in a richly appointed room and grew increasingly aware of the delicious aroma of something sweet and enticing wafting through the house.

Firm pressure against her back guided her up the staircase to the second floor and a wide set of mahogany doors. Fritz pushed the doors open and stepped aside as Trista entered what was to be her chamber, or so Nicholas brusquely informed her as she wandered about the room.

It was all of the palest pink, from the silk damask wall coverings to the huge velvet-draped bed lying opposite floor-to-ceiling windows. A large mahogany armoire occupied one wall, and opposite that, a cozy fire burned before a plush velvet chaise. Through another set of doors lay a dressing room, containing a luxurious dressing table and all the necessities for a pampered maiden's toilette. As she turned to Nicholas, her eye was drawn to an enormous vase of pale pink roses on a table beside the bed.

"Oh, Nicholas..." She lifted a hand to the delicate pink blossoms. "Such gorgeous flowers."

Nicholas's gaze fixed upon the tawny skin of his wife's slender back, revealed by the low cut of her dress. "Mmm...gorgeous," he murmured. Then, as Trista turned those jade eyes upon him, he muttered, "Polly's touch, I believe. You'll meet her soon enough. Tends to the kitchen, the garden and such. She's Fritz's wife. If you need any...you know, the things you women do, she can assist you. Now, if you'll excuse me, I'll see you at dinner."

With a furrowed brow, Trista stared at the door closing none too softly behind him. No doubt *he* had also pondered the enormity of their situation and wished that perhaps he had battled his insomnia within the safe confines of his room in that grand Leighton manor rather than tempting fate, and losing. His taste for brandy that evening had saddled him forever with a wife, capable only of invading his home and disrupting his life. A woman forced upon him, and for whom he felt little compassion or desire. The same woman who had allowed herself to be ruled by her wayward passions, despite every warning, every firm resolution that she should keep herself from the one man capable of rendering her bereft of moral fiber.

"I was truly bewitched that fateful night," she murmured wistfully as her fingers lightly played over the fragile rose petals. "Uncaring of my family, with nary a thought. Caught in that silken web he wove about my common sense. Surely he thinks me no better than some strumpet eager to bear my bosom before him."

With a troubled sigh, she turned from the roses and contemplated her unopened trunks lying at the foot of the bed. Her fingers lifted the latches, then raised the lid of one. As her eyes fell upon the flimsy silk gift from Adelle, she drew an unsteady breath. "These past few weeks his vices, his certain faults—dear God, his complete lack of regard—have been obscured with a mere glance from him, much less a touch of his hand. He need only strut those slim hips or enter a room and I care naught for anything but the feel of his skin beneath my hands, pressed against my bosom. Oh, wanton soul that I am, 'tis the harshest punishment of all to bear this burden."

Willing the tears from her eyes, she lifted several garments and moved to the armoire to set about unpacking, if only to take her mind from her thoughts. As she swung the armoire doors wide, her first thought was that she had been mistakenly put into someone else's room, for several gowns hung neatly beside a narrow column of drawers containing a woman's undergarments. Upon closer inspection, however, she realized that the exquisite gowns carried Adelle's label and were definitely her size. With a dumbfounded expression, she pulled forth a stunning scarlet silk dress with the tiniest of cap sleeves and a low scooped neckline. Replacing this, she shook her head and drew another forth, though at first she wondered if this flimsy garment even *was* a dress. Made of a sheer, soft fabric, which looked almost like the finest of netting, the dress consisted of several strategically placed pieces of shimmering gold silk that appeared to be strung together to form some semblance of a gown. Trista raised a skeptical brow and wondered if perhaps this was one of those gowns one simply had to see off the hanger.

With a piqued curiosity, she peered into the drawers and drew forth several pairs of the sheerest silk stockings. Her fingers brushed over more silken fabric and she lifted what looked to be a shift and chemise from the tumble of satin and lace, only to feel the color climb in her cheeks at the transparency of the fabric. Who was to wear these things?

"Oh! So sorry, my lady. When you didn't answer my knock, I thought you might be asleep."

Trista raised flushed cheeks to the tiny gray-haired woman peering curiously at her from behind the armoire door. With a hastily murmured apology, Trista replaced the scandalous undergarments and shoved the drawer closed.

"Polly Hamilton, at your service, my lady." Clear brown eyes slowly assessed the newest addition to the family, from the tips of the stockinged toes peeking beneath the stunning gown to the cheeks still pink with some embarrassment. Polly nodded. "Nicholas has never been found lacking in his eye for a beautiful girl. However, I do believe the man has outdone even himself. My lady, you bring a long-awaited breath of the purest loveliness to this household. When I heard that Nicholas was bringing home a bride, and with only a week's notice, well, I was certain she was something to behold. That boy never disappoints me!" Her softly rounded face broke into a wide smile. "Ah! I see you've found a few surprises." Pushing the armoire door wide, Polly bustled past Trista and began to sort through the gowns, as if in search of one in particular. "Had that poor seamstress working around the clock. Not that Fritz and I were idle! Oh, heavens no, the house had to be spotless! Now, what was that seamstress's name again? Adelpha? Ada? Oh, whatever, but mark my words if she isn't carrying a torch for him . . . Ah, here it is."

Much to Trista's chagrin, Polly pulled forth the scarlet silk gown and, with the utmost care, hung it on the armoire door. "My lady, dinner will be served very soon and I must help you to dress."

"I can't wear *that!*" Trista squeaked.

"Oh, but you must." Polly's nimble fingers plucked the band of flowers from Trista's head, then turned her with practiced hands and bent to the long row of buttons. "Your husband requested this dress specifically."

Trista bristled. "I suppose Nicholas always gets what he wants."

"Indeed he does, my lady. Always."

Trista sighed resignedly and peered over her shoulder with a growing curiosity. "You've known Nicholas for some time?"

"Oh my, yes. Fritz and I have been with the family for many years, even before Nicholas was born. 'Tis difficult to believe that thirty years has passed. Nicholas was the only child, you see." The hands stilled upon Trista's back. "And he is the finest of men, my lady. You should be very proud to be his bride."

"I—I . . . yes . . ."

Polly resumed her task and her tone grew whimsical. "Why, it seems like only yesterday that he first set foot on a ship, and only four years old at the time. My, my . . . I can still see him, so eager to be off to a new home in the colonies."

"Oh . . ." Trista frowned. "He's so often referred to as a Yankee, I simply assumed he was born in the colonies."

Bending to help Trista from the gown, Polly replied, "His father was a Yankee, that could be the reason. And though Nicholas was born here, my lady, he spent the majority of his young life in Virginia. Oh, now there's a *truly* beautiful place."

"You've been there?"

"Oh my, yes! My lady, we sailed with the family and remained in Virginia for, oh, some fifteen . . . no, eighteen years! How we missed England. 'Tis our home, after all."

"The family was indeed very lucky to have such loyal employees that would travel such a distance with them."

"My lady, the Brennans are an exceptional family. We've long considered ourselves the lucky ones, even after that awful tragedy." The tiny form bustled past Trista toward the dressing room before Trista could find her voice.

Tragedy?

Polly emerged carrying a porcelain washbasin and pitcher. As Trista tended to her toilette and mulled, Polly rummaged through her drawers, muttering softly to herself as she selected the proper undergarments. "I do hope you like roasted quail and venison stew, my lady. 'Tis Nicholas's favorite. Such a hearty eater! Always had that insatiable Brennan appetite."

Trista started. Surely she didn't mean to imply...

"No doubt your children will inherit that charming quality, as well."

Children? Surely the woman understood the nature of this marriage... or did she? Didn't the separate quarters alone attest to the chasteness of this arrangement? Or had Nicholas led the servants to believe otherwise? She had further cause to question her husband's motives when she dressed in the sheer undergarments and scandalous gown. The gown was cut so low, Trista quaked in fear that she would pop from the thing with every breath she took, and the tiny cap sleeves offered her slender arms little modesty. The bodice and waist fitted snugly and fell to a full sweeping skirt, draped at her hip with a sassy bow.

"So beautiful you are, my lady. That Nicholas surely has an eye!" Fluttering about the blushing girl, Polly tucked a few stray curls into Trista's coiffure, then tugged the sleeves of the gown down yet again, as Trista insisted on pulling them up almost over her shoulders. "My lady, these sleeves are meant to be worn *down here!*"

"But I feel as if I will walk away without the dress."

Polly's knowing eyes flickered over Trista's swelling bosom. "My lady, believe me, the dress is going nowhere. Now, off you go. I believe Nicholas is waiting in the library. And I must tend to dinner."

With an overwhelming feeling of anxiety, Trista left the haven of her room and descended the wide staircase, fiercely clenching her cold hands against the swishing silk skirts. Tugging at her sleeves once more, she glanced at the high curves of her bosom pushed provocatively from her gown and groaned inwardly. Flaunting her charms before a man who detested the very sight of her was utter foolishness. He must know she felt this way! How he must relish forcing her to his bidding, engaging in some battle of wills.

"I'll give him a bloody battle!" she huffed half-aloud. Tugging her sleeves down where they belonged, she thrust her bosom forward and swept into the library.

Chapter Nine

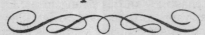

At the sound of rustling skirts, Nicholas turned from his contemplation of the crackling fire to find his breath momentarily caught in his throat. His gaze narrowed upon the challenging green orbs and the haughtily lifted chin before dipping to the abundant display swelling above the scarlet silk. With a difficult swallow, he scowled and forced his attention to the fire once more.

"Good evening, madam," he growled into the flames. "I trust you are settling in comfortably?"

"Yes, quite comfortably." She lifted a brow at his harsh tone and hesitated, her eyes sweeping his fiendishly handsome form. Despite his black mood, he stirred her blood no small measure. Drawing an unsteady breath, she moved to his side in search of that which he found so fascinating in the flames. After a moment, she spoke with forced levity. "Will Ivy be joining us this evening?"

Nicholas found his eye unwittingly drawn to the light of the fire playing upon her profile, aware of her dewy scent engulfing him. His gaze found the full curve of her lips and lingered, until she turned those emerald pools upon him, shattering his reverie and reminding him that she had spoken.

"What...? No...no, Ivy has returned to school. No one else will be joining us." He scowled yet again and turned back to the fire, clasping his hands behind his back, if only to keep them from tearing that gown from her. Blast that Adelle and all her damned ideas! He certainly didn't need this tawny-skinned nymph prancing about in a half-dressed state if he was to abide by his promise not to take her to his bed. His bed? Ha! The girl would be lucky if she didn't find herself contemplating the ceiling of this very room, very soon.

"I see." A slender hand rose to the bodice of her dress, and the slight movement nearly proved Nicholas's undoing. "The clothes . . . they're all lovely, though I fear I may have been remiss in my assumption that your request for this particular dress had something to do with a dinner party."

"What? Oh, yes . . ."

"Nicholas." She turned to face him, her voice perched precariously on the brink of profound agitation. "I will not be told what clothes to wear or, for that matter, what manner in which to conduct myself. My behavior heretofore may have caused you some concern, and justly so, but I assure you that I am well aware of the proper manner in which to dress."

"Woman, I care naught for what you choose to wear upon your back."

Trista stared at him, dumbfounded, and wondered again at the reason for his ferocious mood. "But Polly said you requested that I wear *this!*"

Gazing upon his achingly beautiful wife, Nicholas knew a frustration like none he'd ever experienced. Struggling to retain his control, he spoke through gritted teeth. "Trista, 'twas but a fleeting thought, and I only happened to mention it to Polly when she asked if I had a preference. Henceforth, wear whatever you damn well wish."

"Ah, then the gown does not please you?"

Nicholas's eyes narrowed on the challenging expression sweeping across the lovely features. "It pleases me."

For a moment, Trista's heart fluttered. Even with this permanently affixed scowl, he was still the most dashing, the most handsome . . .

"Excuse me, sir, but dinner is being served."

Nicholas acknowledged Fritz, then held an arm to his bride. As he tucked her hand beneath his arm, he warned in a low growl, "I will say this but once, wife. Do not test my patience or you will find your circumstances dramatically... altered."

Trista had little chance to ponder his intent, for she was led into a magnificent dining room and seated at the foot of the elegant table. Her eyes swept the luxurious white damask table linens, the polished sterling flatware and the crystal goblets sparkling in the dim candlelight. Opposite her, at the far end of the long table, was the only other place setting, visible through an enormous lead crystal vase brimming with white roses. A steaming bowl of delicious-looking soup lay before her, and as she leaned forward to sniff the enticing aroma, her eye was drawn to a flat, black velvet box lying beside her plate.

All too aware of Nicholas's lingering presence beside her, she laid trembling fingers upon the box and lifted wide eyes to her husband.

"A wedding gift, Trista," he muttered distractedly.

"I cannot accept this, Nicholas. I have nothing for you."

"I never expected anything, madam." He leaned down beside her and lifted the lid.

Trista gasped. Nestled within the black velvet interior was a spectacular triple-strand necklace of brilliant oval diamonds, which increased gradually in size to join at an enormous teardrop diamond pendant.

Trista's breath caught in her throat as Nicholas carefully lifted the piece and tilted it to catch the flickering candlelight in its brilliant facets. Dimly, she was aware that he loomed close beside her, half facing her, with one arm draped casually about her chair. His spicy scent invaded her bedazzled senses and his face in profile drew her attention momentarily from the necklace.

"This piece has been in my family for some time, almost as long as this house. It holds tremendous sentimental value." His eyes narrowed upon the brilliant stones. "It was given to my mother by my father, many years ago."

Trista was struck by a rather curious thought. "Forgive me, Nicholas, but I seem to remember that you said your family was a hardworking, rather unremarkable lot. Certainly without the means..." Her words trailed off as Nicholas turned a cool gaze upon her.

"I spoke the truth, dear inquisitive wife. They *were* hardworking, and for that reason, at that time, decidedly unremarkable. However, as a result of their diligence, they achieved a success far beyond their dreams." For a moment, his tense features softened, and with a finger beneath her chin, he brought her eyes to meet his. "Contrary to what you undoubtedly believe, not all the rich are idle."

She sputtered with instant indignation. "I have never once paused to admire the frivolous existence enjoyed by many Society folk! Nor do I believe the sums they regularly squander at gaming houses found their pockets through any of *their* doing! Indeed, I find their dallying at those social clubs and posturing over tea and cakes decidedly superficial and completely inane and..."

To Trista's horror, Nicholas suddenly threw back his head and roared with laughter. She clenched her teeth, her hands gripping the edge of the linen tablecloth as he lowered twinkling eyes to her.

"Madam, you *are* full of surprises." His expression grew increasingly bemused as hers grew increasingly vexed, and he shifted position, unconsciously dropping his hand from the chair to her back.

Trista pursed her lips. "You're laughing at me, and I would like to know why."

"Either you're a hypocrite, Trista, or you were doing a damned good job of pretending to enjoy yourself during your brief visit."

"And what was I supposed to do? Sequester myself in my room for days on end, popping forth only when the conversation consisted of something more than exchanges of pleasantries about the weather or, of course, whenever *you* happened by to cause some great commotion and ruffle everyone's feathers?"

A flicker of amusement scudded across the bronzed features at the images her words inspired, yet his eyes found her parted lips. "And do I ruffle your feathers, wife?"

All too aware of the sudden change in his manner, and of the hand stroking like a whisper along the length of her spine, Trista found her wrath dissolving with horrifying ease and her eyes drawn treacherously to his mouth...a perfectly shaped mouth for a man, not too wide, with firm, even lips.... He pressed her toward him.

Suddenly frantic to break his spell, she spoke the first thought that found its way to the tip of her tongue. "The soup is getting cold."

At that moment, the side door burst open and Fritz, bearing two huge steaming platters, took three steps, maybe four, into the room. Encountering Nicholas's ominous glower, he promptly turned on his heel and hastened from the room.

Fritz's interruption could not have been more perfectly timed, for it served to jar Nicholas to his senses and he quickly straightened. He spoke far more roughly than he intended. "Stand up. I can fasten this around your neck, if you'd like."

"Oh...of course," Trista murmured, rising to her feet and presenting Nicholas with her back. The necklace felt cool and heavy against her skin, though the fingers brushing against her neck were very warm, sending shivers along her spine and a trembling through her limbs. Seeking to break the strained silence, she glanced over her shoulder and ventured airily, "'Tis such a beautiful necklace, I cannot help but wonder why your mother does not choose to keep this piece."

"My parents died a twenty-three years ago."

His voice was a low growl, and the words he spoke sent a chill through her. She flushed profusely, embarrassed at her glib remark. "Nicholas, I'm sorry. I had no idea."

Silence, again, hung about them like a shroud. She felt his hands fall from her neck and she turned, raising a hand to the brilliant pendant resting between her breasts. Her heart lurched as his smoldering eyes fastened upon the huge gem. "Thank you, Nicholas. 'Tis the most exquisite gift I have ever received."

In response, she was presented with a deepening scowl and a sweep of fierce blue eyes. "I find that my appetite for food is sorely lacking this evening, madam, and my mood renders me an unfit dinner companion. Therefore, I shall leave you to enjoy your repast alone." The side door burst open again and Nicholas shot Fritz a black look, then muttered under his breath, "I'm going out." With that, he turned on his booted heel and strode from the room.

The following day brought little relief from the dampness and clinging chill hovering about the manor. Nor did the night's rest, what little was achieved, serve to ease the tension brewing between the newlyweds. Indeed, Trista all but wore a path in the carpet of her room as she stalked back and forth before a crackling fire, mulling over Polly's remark that Nicholas had left the house very early that morning and would not be returning until dinner, if then, which was a good six hours away. Her anger mounted, stilling her feet momentarily and marring her delicate features as the vision loomed of him at a gaming table, going about his leisure, leaving her to face the lingering, worried looks from Polly and the empty chair opposite hers at the long dining table. How dare he cast her aside! She resumed her path for a moment, then, finding the four pink walls unbearably confining, she ventured from her room to test the carpets on the first floor.

The heady aroma of a bubbling stew wafting through the air and the cozy fires lighted in hearths throughout the house tempted Trista to cast aside her troubled thoughts and revel for a time in the soothing atmosphere. Yet one thought continued to gnaw at her. Perhaps Nicholas had fled from naught but the mere loathsome sight of *her.*

Her wandering took her through a short corridor into a wide hallway along the length of the back of the house. As she passed before open doorways, she peered into each room, pausing to admire the rich furnishings and simple, understated elegance of her new home. She lingered at one particular room, marveling at the impossibly high ceilings and the curved wall of windows draped with luxurious lengths of rich creamy velvet. On a clear day she could imagine the sun streamed through that wall of glass and played upon the cream and pale blue carpets. The room was sparsely furnished, relatively empty save for a cluster of elegant Louis XIV chairs surrounding a beautiful piano.

Her feet stilled before the instrument, and hesitantly, almost reverently, she lifted slender fingers to brush over the ivory keys. The rich sound of that one chord echoed through the room, so clear and true that Trista couldn't resist another...and another, and before she realized, she was seated at the low bench and her fingers were sweeping over the keys. To her pleasant surprise, the pieces that had become her favorites over the years of study came to her memory with startling ease.

Striking the final chord of her most favorite Mozart piece, she drew a deep breath, smiling with pride, and lifted her eyes momentarily. What she saw caused her breath to catch in her throat and her smile to vanish instantly.

Nicholas leaned against the doorjamb, arms folded over his chest, observing her with a strange look upon his face. With a sinking heart, Trista realized that the relaxed manner in which he stood seemed to indicate that he had occupied that stance for some time. He had doffed his topcoat and any waistcoat he'd been wearing, leaving only the broad expanse of crisp white cotton, with its billowing sleeves and tightly wound stock, to cover his torso, while the deep blue trousers fitted snugly about his muscular thighs then disappeared into polished black boots. Indeed, he looked more than dashing, and Trista became acutely aware of this as he sauntered toward her and her eyes met his, so incredibly blue as the meager light of the day reflected off the azure depths. She could only imagine their brilliance beneath a dazzling sun.

"You needn't stop on my account," he told her in a tone that revealed little of his mood. He paused at the side of the piano to stare rather intently at her.

"Oh...I didn't realize that you were home...I mean, listening." Trista rose from the bench on legs so suddenly shaky that her hands fell to the keys, the notes she inadvertently struck sending a discordant echo through the room. Wincing, she managed a wan smile, then stared down at her fingers. Why in heaven's name was she behaving like a nervous twit?

"My mother used to play." The deep resonance of his voice obliterated the last vestiges of the piano's echo. "I'm certain those keys haven't produced a melody as fine as she was capable, until now." His gaze caught hers, peering from beneath the sweep of dark lashes. "You play beautifully."

Flushing anew, Trista averted her eyes. "Thank you. I hope you don't mind that I took the liberty of wandering about."

"Why would I mind?"

"Well . . ." She gave a noisy swallow. "I fear that I know not what to do with myself all day if you insist upon keeping these hours."

Nicholas gave her a strange look and frowned. "Do whatever it is that you women do. I know less of those trivialities than you, dear wife."

Trista felt her anger bubble up inside her. "I'm frightfully sorry but I am as unaware of those 'trivialities' as you. I fear you have taken a wife whose father deemed it unnecessary to foster only acceptable maidenly behavior and encouraged other pursuits. Hence, my dilemma."

"Call it what you will, though I'd like to think it a godsend," he muttered beneath his breath. "The house is at your disposal, Trista. Indeed, feel free to venture out and about, as well, for some shopping . . . and don't tell me you find *that* in any way distasteful. Your sex's fascination with that pastime is no pursuit, dear wife. I'm quite certain 'tis instinct, which requires little in the way of either fostering *or* encouraging."

"One can shop only so much."

Momentarily, Nicholas's brooding eyes locked upon her. "You needn't concern yourself with my ability to keep the larder stocked while you purchase another item you simply cannot live without. I do have the means to keep you despite any such tendencies."

Trista lifted her chin and looked coolly at him past her prim, upturned nose. "I was in no way implying anything to the contrary."

As he studied her proud features, Nicholas grew increasingly aware of the challenging, almost belligerent tone in her voice, the very same glint in her flashing eyes, almost as if with this innocuous conversation she was waging some battle with him. A frown crept across his features and deepened into a scowl. "Fine. So shop a little, attend those damned tea parties, visit your aunt. But I demand that you never venture forth unescorted. Take Fritz or the coachman whenever I'm not available. Highwaymen abound in these parts, and I don't relish the thought of rescuing you from those blackguards."

Trista stared at him, then shuddered. "I may forego a good many of those expeditions if only for that reason."

"Ah, an even better idea. The library is at your disposal, if you are so inclined. The piano here, the gardens and the stable, as well. You've only yourself to blame if you find yourself with nothing to do."

"The stable?"

His expression grew decidedly bemused. "Yes, madam, that crude structure used to house horses and varying species of rodents. You're familiar with this oddity?"

Trista gave him a chilling glare. "Vaguely. I was beginning to wonder in which of these rooms you were keeping Nero, though I would not be at all surprised to find him reclining upon some satin pillow at White's Club, since he seems the equine version of his master."

"Oh, he's a gambler all right. A quick, sure eye, fast on the take, undaunted by adversity." He inclined his head and, to Trista's surprise, revealed even white teeth in a dazzling smile. "However, he has never had luck with the women in his life."

"Indeed, then in light of your recent *bad* luck, I would venture to say that he is one up on you in that respect, Nicholas."

"You may be right, madam, only because I sincerely doubt that there has ever existed a mare with as waspish a tongue as yours."

"Perhaps, although I detected in that noble animal a certain stoutness of heart, an innate sense of respect and consideration. I find it a trifle difficult to believe that any mare has ever deemed it necessary to unleash her waspish tongue upon him. After all, 'tis the nature of the beast that fosters anything less than a warm response."

"And here I'd always thought those scathing words forever poised on the tip of your tongue were rehearsed countless times during the day."

Trista sniffed. "Neither you nor your mercurial moods have ever caused me the briefest moment of pause during my day, you arrogant man."

"Indeed. Then you possess a rare talent, my lady."

"Albeit an acquired talent."

"Is that so?"

"And one that I find continually *forced* upon me whenever you are about. 'Tis a circumstance that leaves me with something less than a smile upon my face at day's end."

Nicholas folded his arms over the broad chest that Trista was finding difficult to ignore, despite their sparring, and his smoldering eyes slid over her troubled features. As his gaze lingered on her mouth, his tone grew softer, almost husky. "I am well aware of your aversion toward this arrangement, my lady, and can only hope that the simple passing of time will bring about a softening in your manner, if not an acceptance of the way of things."

His tone, coupled with the heated intensity of his eyes upon her mouth, caused Trista certain discomfort, and much to her chagrin, she felt a blush warm her cheeks. How *could* she allow him to have this effect on her yet again, and in the heat of an argument, at that? Easing her way from behind the piano, she paused before him. "'Twill take far more than the mere passing of time, Nicholas. Now, if you will excuse me..." With her head lifted determinedly, she turned toward the door.

"Where the hell are you going?" he barked.

"To the stable, my lord, if you must know. I find myself in need of the pleasant company of your noble beast and those varying species of rodents dwelling in that crude structure. Do you mind?"

As she peered over her shoulder, Nicholas was suddenly struck by the coy arch to her brow, the saucy lift to her shoulder. His eyes slid over the jade-and-cream striped satin gown hugging the fullness of her bosom and narrow waist, and he found himself wondering if she was all too aware of the effect she had upon him. Despite their less than warm exchange, the urge to sweep her into his arms and bear her to the softness of his bed became nearly overpowering. Indeed, the more she fought and resisted him, the more she chose to avoid him, the more he wanted her. Damned woman!

He managed a casual shrug. "No, I don't mind. I've work to do."

"So you will be gone for the remainder of the day?"

How she no doubt hoped for this! In another moment, if she did not remove that gown and those beckoning eyes from his sight, she would find herself precariously close to complete ravishment. "No, my work in the city has been accomplished. I will be tending to business from my study." He gave her a curt nod. "Enjoy yourself, madam." Sweeping his arm toward the door, he allowed her to pass before him from the room, then hesitated to admire the sway of her hips as she moved quickly down the corridor. He lingered thus for some time, a frown troubling his features, before he turned and, with no small measure of reluctance, headed for his study.

With some direction from Fritz, Trista found the stable nestled among a tall growth of trees some distance from the house. The structure was sturdily built of stone and brick and quite large, with stalls for a dozen or more horses. The familiar scent of horseflesh and polished leather assailed her senses, and her skirts rustled along the hay-strewn dirt floor as she peeked into each of the empty stalls. With mixed feelings, she wondered if there was another maiden in the

PLAY THE

scratch-off game
and get as many as
SIX FREE GIFTS . . .

HOW TO PLAY:

1. With a coin, carefully scratch off the silver area at right. Then check your number against the chart below to find out which gifts you're eligible to receive.

2. You'll receive brand-new Harlequin Historical™ novels and possibly other gifts—ABSOLUTELY FREE! Send back this card and we'll promptly send you the Free Books and Gifts you qualify for!

3. We're betting you'll want more of these heart-warming romances, so unless you tell us otherwise, every month we'll send you 4 more wonderful novels to read and enjoy. Always delivered right to your home. And always at a discount off the cover price!

4. Your satisfaction is guaranteed! You may return any shipment of books and cancel at any time. The Free Books and Gifts remain yours to keep!

NO COST! NO RISK!
NO OBLIGATION TO BUY!

You'll look like a million dollars when you wear this elegant necklace! It's a generous 20 inches long and each link is double-soldered for strength and durability.

More Good News For Subscribers Only!

When you join the Harlequin Reader Service®, you'll receive 4 heart-warming romance novels each month, delivered to your home. You'll also get additional free gifts from time to time, as well as our subscribers-only newsletter. It's your privileged look at upcoming books and profiles of our most popular authors!

If offer card is missing, write to:
Harlequin Reader Service, 3010 Walden Avenue, P.O. Box 1867, Buffalo, NY 14269-1867

MAIL THIS CARD TODAY!

BUSINESS REPLY MAIL
FIRST CLASS MAIL   PERMIT NO. 717   BUFFALO, NY

POSTAGE WILL BE PAID BY ADDRESSEE

HARLEQUIN READER SERVICE
3010 WALDEN AVE
PO BOX 1867
BUFFALO NY 14240-9952

NO POSTAGE
NECESSARY
IF MAILED
IN THE
UNITED STATES

whole of England who, like she, found this stable more comforting than all the plush elegance that house had to offer. Ha! Perhaps she *was* daft to seek solace in a place such as this.

Her feet stilled at Nero's stall, and with some surprise she found Peter tending to the sleek stallion, massaging a clear ointment into the muscled rump and sinewy legs. Glancing up from his work and meeting her gaze, Peter hesitated a moment, then wiped his hands on a rag dangling from his pocket and ambled toward her. With a pained look in his eyes, he said softly, "Trista...I—I mean, my lady..."

"Oh, Peter..." she breathed, shaking her head. "Please, you mustn't treat me with such formality. We've known each other far too long for that, despite these circum-stances."

Peter opened his mouth to speak but found himself rather rudely interrupted by Nero, who gave a soft nicker of rec-ognition upon spying Trista and thrust his wet muzzle through the wooden slats in search of a parasol.

"Good day, my friend, I fear I have but one small treat." She drew a carrot from the deep pocket of her skirt. With a laugh, she relinquished the treat, then scratched between those pricked ears. "Isn't he magnificent? I'd wager he's a wild one."

"On most days," Peter replied as he patted the sleekly arched neck, though his gaze was fixed on Trista. "Not to-day, though. Not after last night's ride. I've been rubbing him down all day with salve, just in case."

Trista frowned. "What happened last night?"

Shaking his head slowly as if in disbelief, Peter replied, "Lord Brennan...he came in here last night with the look of the devil himself in his eyes. Bridled him up real quick...no saddle...and off they went. Not for very long, but it must've been a hard ride, for Nero was soaked with more than rain, and he didn't stop wheezing until long af-ter they returned. But *he* was still here, long after that, and, more than likely, after I tucked in for the night. Standing there at the doorway, staring out at the house through the rain. Didn't say a word. Scares you a little, man like that, almost as if he's battling some devil inside.''

Trista stared at the horse, feeling her heart tripping along a tad lighter at the news that Nicholas had not sought the gaming houses to wile away his evening. Her eyes strayed to the stable door and she envisioned his broad-shouldered shadow against the portal, silent, brooding. Could it be that he, too, found comfort in this place, or had this *arrangement* driven them both from that elegant home simply to avoid dealing with each other?

Swinging her gaze to Peter, she was met with that pained expression once more. "He has been good to you?"

"Yes ... both kind and generous ... and more. 'Tis what makes it so hard to detest the man, Trista. He has given me work ... here, tending to the grounds and the stable and aboard his ships. He has paid me handsomely and has promised that I will sail with his crew very soon. 'Tis what I long to do. And he allows frequent visits to my family.''

"But who tends to the farm?"

"My younger brothers." He swallowed hard and Trista's eye was drawn to his bobbing Adam's apple. "I had to leave, Trista. After what happened between us. I had to get away from that village ... that life. So I came to London, unskilled, and couldn't find work. I realized that I had little choice but to do what my father had done. Then I found Lord Brennan's ships and he hired me on. Asked if I was a good honest worker. Took me on my word, Trista. He's been so good to me, but it tears at me to know that he has taken you as his wife! What a cruel twist of fate!''

Trista lowered her eyes. " 'Tis almost too cruel a twist."

Peter's voice grew strident. " 'Tis nearly too much to bear ... to stand idly by while he puts his hands all over you ... stares upon you like he will have you for supper ... then bears you to his bed! How can I allow this?"

"Oh, Peter, you must, for he is my husband. Though you must also know that things are not as they seem. We do not share a ... a ...''

Peter stared upon her with widening eyes. "Dear God! What measure of a man would take as a wife the fairest of all maidens, then keep himself from her?"

Trista flushed at his words. "This marriage is not based upon affection, Peter. 'Tis one of convenience, solely for the purpose of saving face." At his perplexed look, she hesitated. "We were found in rather compromising circumstances by my aunt and her husband, as well as the Duke of Leighton...in his home, no less. They deemed it necessary that we marry simply to stave off the scandal that would have tarnished the family for years. 'Tis not a pleasant arrangement, to be sure."

"Dear God, Trista, then be gone! Flee from here! I will take you! You must know that I feel only the most honorable of feelings, that I hold you in the highest regard, despite what happened between us." Shamefully, he averted his gaze. "I allowed my feelings for you to...to...I wanted you for my wife! You are so beautiful...and I fear I destroyed whatever there was between us with that...that attack upon you...those vile things I said—"

"No, Peter, please, you must stop this."

"How can I? Trista, you married a man for all the wrong reasons! I care naught what happened! You must leave here!"

Regretfully, Trista shook her head, feeling her heart go out to her friend. "I'm so sorry to have hurt you and, God's truth, I would wish for any fate but this. But I cannot flee from my vows or my responsibilities as Nicholas's wife. I fear shirking these would weigh far more heavily upon me than accepting this fate." Laying a hand gently upon his sleeve, she gazed beseechingly into the troubled brown eyes. "All is forgiven, Peter. You are still my dear friend."

His beefy hand covered hers, and his voice was thick with emotion. "If 'tis all I can hope for, then I shall gladly stand beside you simply as friend. Though you must know the depth of feeling I have for you, that I would do anything for you, Trista. If you need me, if he...perhaps, attempts to force..." His hand gripped hers. "If you should ever change your mind and wish to leave this place, simply ask...."

"Thank y—" Her words trailed off as she detected, out of the corner of her eye, a slight movement at the stable door. Turning, she nearly jumped from her skin as she met Nicholas's stormy glare, fixed upon her hand beneath Peter's.

Chapter Ten

Trista snuck her hand from beneath Peter's, only dimly aware of her friend's embarrassed cough as he hastened to resume his work. Her heart thumped erratically within her chest and her gaze darted to a pile of hay beside the door. How long had Nicholas been standing there, listening? Better yet, when had he acquired this infernal talent for prowling stealthily about? Why the devil wasn't he working?

Silence filled the air, a hanging stillness all the more muffled and confining due to the heavy fog and mist. Nero grunted, eliciting a singsong cooing from Peter as he made himself overly busy tidying up before rather conspicuously removing himself from the stable.

Silence again. Trista couldn't bear it a moment longer. Lifting her gaze, she found her eye instantly drawn to the large, fluffy white pile of fur at Nicholas's feet.

"What a beautiful dog! Oh, Nicholas..." She extended a hand and the dog bounded with an eager yelp and a feverishly wagging tail right into her arms. Unable to suppress a giggle, Trista lifted her eyes to her husband and gushed, "He's wonderful! So cuddly! What a love!"

Nicholas stared at her, completely taken aback at the ease with which she brushed aside his anger, his entirely justifiable rage at finding her all but cavorting with his stable hand. Her Peter. *Her* Peter!

Yet in spite of himself, his fury sputtered and dwindled before her unabashed display of almost childlike wonder with this dog. How guilelessly disarming, how utterly fascinating, and he found himself staring with an intent far flung from rage. Indeed, the more she cooed and petted and allowed that blasted animal to lick her hand and rub his furry back against her, the more Nicholas yearned, for the first time in his life, to sprout another set of legs and call himself canine, as well. At long last he found his voice. "That's enough, Bo. Come here."

"Oh, what an adorable name! Bo!"

His scowl deepened. Both Trista and the dog reacted as if neither had heard him, Bo completely ignoring the command, and Trista cooing and giggling and stroking.... "Bo darling, I've always longed for a dog like you. Poor Maggie's consumed by fits of sneezing around animal hair. She can barely abide Gypsy. Did you hear that, Nero? A fine mare Gypsy is, tall at the shoulder, sleek, with a decidedly frisky nature, but certainly no predisposition for a waspish tongue."

Nicholas raised a brow, then bellowed, "Bo! Down, boy! Now off you go."

Bo stared at his master as if uncomprehending that harsh command, then gave a muffled bark but made no move to obey, which caused Nicholas to wonder at his wife's effect on his animals. First Nero's show of defiance and now the damned dog, as if her mere presence incited some resistance from them. Perhaps she had cast her spell upon them, as well. He shook his head as if to rid himself of these ridiculous imaginings, his eyes following Trista's fluid movements as she straightened and Bo settled at her feet.

"Did you require something, Nicholas?"

"What? Yes, as it turns out, I have some business in the city to which I must attend this evening."

A winged brow lifted almost imperceptibly at this news. "And will you be gone very late?"

"Perhaps, 'tis hard to say."

"Nicholas, I certainly hope that you will employ discretion with your affairs apart from this house."

"My lady, rest assured that I deem discretion a priceless commodity and employ it liberally in all my business dealings."

" 'Twas not business to which I was referring."

"Indeed. And would you suggest that the prudence you have exercised *not* apart from this very stable be the standard by which my behavior is measured? If so, madam, then I fear you have bestowed upon me complete freedom of rein to frolic and romp as I please."

Trista ground her teeth in frustration. "If you are referring to my behavior with Peter, you have once again stumbled upon the wrong conclusion. 'Twas an innocent exchange between friends."

"Is that so?" With mounting anger, he took several steps toward her, his hands on his hips. "I suppose you would have me grow accustomed to such intimate displays with all the gentlemen fortunate enough to find themselves called friend, eh?"

"Certainly not!" Trista huffed. "Peter and I have been friends for years. Why, we grew up on adjacent farms. Surely you knew that! He is like a brother to me!"

"Hardly an exchange befitting a brother and sister," he growled. "For God's sake, Trista, the lad is mooning about like a wounded calf, wearing his broken heart upon his sleeve and glaring at me as if he yearns to drive a stake through my heart. That, my dear bride, is infatuation. And you are offering nothing but encouragement."

"What? And what would you have me do, Nicholas? Keep myself ensconced within that imposing manor, avoiding contact with those I have known since long before *you* disrupted my life for fear that the slightest friendly response be viewed as a brazen display of my easy virtue?" She trembled, proud and glorious in her anger. "I resent your implication. You have not taken as your wife an immoral gaming house wench!"

"You've done little to convince me otherwise."

The moment the scathing words passed from his lips, Nicholas wished with all his might that they had not. He made the slightest movement toward her, opening his mouth to speak his apology—to tell her he'd never once thought such a thing—when suddenly, from nowhere, her hand shot out and, with a mighty whack, laid a stinging blow upon his face. His jaw snapped shut. With a frustration he'd never thought possible, he watched her flee from him through the fog.

For several moments he remained thus, staring at the path she'd taken and hating himself for behaving like an utter fool. Little wonder the maid sought the company of others.

He released his breath and looked down at Bo, sitting docilely at his feet. He glowered at the animal, quite certain that he detected the slightest mocking lift to the damned dog's brow.

"Yes, I am well aware that I deserved that," Nicholas muttered. "I suppose you would also like to wreak your vengeance upon me. My loyal friend, do not assume that I would be as forgiving of your scolding. Your mistress occupies a place all her own within my heart. Now, be off with you."

With a muffled yelp, Bo bounded from the stable and followed the path toward the house, leaving Nicholas to find solace alone, yet again. As Trista did, in her room, for what remained of the day and evening and throughout a restless night, which brought her little in the way of sleep or relief from her troubled thoughts. Indeed, she arose before first light to stoke the fire and tend to her toilette and was soon stomping about, laying ruin to Nicholas's character.

Green eyes flashed and long legs strode purposefully before the fire; fists were clenched tightly against crisp lavender skirts that swung to and fro with her pacing. The satin shimmered in the early morning sun playing upon the polished wood floors, serving to enlighten those less distracted that it was a glorious day.

The cad. To suggest that she should strive to achieve the most prudent manner in order to prove herself worthy of a higher regard than that bestowed upon those pub wenches of ill repute! The conceit! Indeed, he should consider himself fortunate to have escaped with only the imprint of her hand against that bronzed cheek after his scathing remark. A well-aimed knee and a swift kick in the shin would have eased her plight, however momentary. Try as she might to banish them from her thoughts, the words he had spoken served as a constant reminder that the one man capable of seducing her will from her despised her for that very reason.

"He thinks himself some swank, fashionably bred nobleman of the highest regard, commanding only the most humble response from his lowly wife, that same wife he so gallantly plucked from the jaws of humiliation and despair! No doubt he expects me to bow before him, forever grateful for his having stooped so low. Ha! 'Tis *he* who should be humbled! He took advantage of a mere innocent..." She paused and chewed on her little finger. "However willing she may have been, though 'tis of scant consequence..." She scowled at the fire, her voice ringing through the chamber. "He should have known better! Ha! Had I not chosen to acknowledge my fault in the matter, he would be hanging from some tree by now."

She paused and stared dumbstruck into the fire. "I saved his blasted hide! Ooooh, that blackguard!"

A light tapping upon the bedroom door drew Trista's attention and she bade Polly enter, then resumed her pacing. Polly took one look at the blazing eyes, the clenched fists, the determined set of her jaw, and heaved a weary sigh.

Nicholas had indeed chosen well a woman of determination and pride, though perhaps he had chosen too well, for this maiden appeared to have achieved naught from the night's rest but a refreshed obstinacy. Polly clucked to herself and set about straightening here and there, though the mistress had seen fit to make her bed and tend to her toilette alone. Perhaps to vent some of that frustration. Then again, perhaps she, like Nicholas, had not disturbed the bed and had instead dozed fitfully slouched in a chair before the fire, awakening with a grunt to resume all that scowling and brooding. And both refusing to eat! Whatever was she to do?

Her thoughts lingered on the man closeted in his study below, the man pacing about, not unlike his wife, then slumping in his chair to stare entirely unseeing at whatever lay before him.

In all her years with the family, she had come to know and respect the intensity, the fierce stubbornness, the unyielding pride in family and work, and had accepted the inevitably surly dispositions from time to time. But never had she seen Nicholas behave in this manner, and so foolishly at that!

"My lady, I have prepared a delicious breakfast," Polly ventured gamely, casting an expectant look at the younger woman. "Fresh berries and cream . . . crumpets. You cannot live long without food, and besides, you will have to venture forth from this room at some point."

Trista's feet stilled at the images Polly's words inspired, and she felt her stomach rumble in response. "That sounds delicious."

"Then we'd best tend to your hair, my lady."

Trista waved a hand. "'Tis of no consequence to me."

"But you would like to look your best."

"Indeed, and for whom?" A winged brow lifted haughtily and she grumbled, "Certainly not for my husband, who sees fit to spend more of his time away from this house than in it."

"My lady, 'tis only business that takes him from this house. I'm quite certain that were this work not of such importance, he would be forever at your side."

Trista gaped at her. "Whatever made you think I would want him there?"

Polly shrugged. "My lady, were you not hidden away in this room you would realize that your husband returned quite early last evening and has no intention of leaving again for some time."

"Mmm, how very nice for him. But I will have you know that I have *not* been keeping myself hidden away. 'Tis only that I find him insufferably stubborn and thickheaded."

"He is a man, after all, my lady. You were expecting something different?"

For a moment, Trista stared blankly at the older woman. "I suppose I knew not what to expect."

Clucking softly, Polly clasped Trista's hand and led her to sit upon the bed. "Marriage, even to the most humble of men, is a frightening endeavor. But you, my lady, have taken a husband quite unlike a typical man.''

''Ha! A man whose ego knows no bounds, whose ability to twist my words is surpassed only by his ability to twist my every action.''

Polly laughed softly and shook her head, patting the girl's hand soothingly. ''He is so very much like his dear father. I can still remember the battles Jason and Caroline used to have. Why, they shook the very timbers!'' Her smile faded. ''However, lest you judge Nicholas too harshly, perhaps you should realize certain things about the man you call husband.'' The soft brown eyes peered intently at Trista. ''My lady, I have known him to be the most generous, kind and thoughtful of men, capable of charming an entire roomful of men and women alike, if the mood suits him. Yet he possesses a strength of will to match his desires, his need to avenge his family name and to right that wrong committed so long ago.''

Trista's eyes fell to her hand still clasped within Polly's warm embrace. ''I know so very little of Nicholas...other than...''

''Just as I suspected. Swept you up with his charm and good looks and uttered not one word about himself, didn't he? So very much like his father.''

Trista squeezed the other woman's hand. ''Tell me, Polly. I must know.''

Polly gave a wistful sigh. '''Tis difficult to know where to begin. It was all so long ago, and to this very day I'm still not quite certain of the exact events. Nicholas was only three at the time, I believe, when it happened, though I know not *what* exactly. You see, his father, Jason, had sworn to Caroline's father that he would salvage Trent Shipping for the old man before he died. Then one day, Jason decided to move the family from London to Richmond very quickly, and to my eye *too* quickly. He took Caroline from this very house, a house that had been in the Trent family for generations, the house in which her father died. Why, it nearly broke poor Caroline's heart!'' Polly shook her head. ''Trent Shipping was lost and Jason never returned, of course, for tragedy struck. You see, Caroline never recovered from a fever she contracted on that blasted ship, though I, for one, believe 'twas a broken heart she suffered from. She grew weaker and weaker while Jason worked harder than any man is capable, along with his sister's husband, Joshua Cooper, to build a shipping industry based in Richmond. Oh, they prospered immeasurably. Aye, but he worked himself to death, especially after Caroline died. 'Twas an obsession with him, this success, as if it would avenge the loss of his wife and ease the humiliation of his one failure. He died, weak, broken, terribly bitter. 'Twas an awful tragedy from which, I fear, Nicholas is still recovering.''

Trista swallowed past the dryness in her throat. ''Nicholas must have been very young when he lost them both.''

''Oh, yes, my lady, barely a lad of seven, though it was as if he had already lost them once his mother became so ill and with his father constantly gone. He was always an independent boy. I don't believe he realized the extent of his loss until much later, and by then he had developed the same obsession as his father.''

''Surely he was too young to understand what happened.''

''Indeed he was, but Joshua soon filled his ear with the story and taught him the trade. Nicholas has since taken over the business quite successfully.''

''Then why is he here, if he has found such success?''

''My lady, the man you call husband is no dallying fop, eager to recline upon his laurels. Indeed, a man like he requires far more than a weighty purse in his pocket to call himself happy. Besides, you find yourself in the most wealthy, the most exciting of all cities in the world. There is far more than business to be conducted within its limits.'' Polly leaned closer and winked at her. ''Perhaps he sought a wife.''

Trista scoffed. ''I find that a trifle difficult to believe. Nay, I would venture to say that Nicholas has come here for other reasons. To reclaim this house, for one.''

''And who could blame him! Indeed, he insisted that the house be restored as such. It was in a sad state of disrepair,

my lady, after so many years. The Trents had little in the way
of money to afford servants to manage the place. Then, after Jason and Caroline left, the house sat empty for eighteen years. 'Twas at the time that he entered Oxford that
Nicholas sent both Fritz and me back here to look after the
estate. He came during holidays and weekends to aid in the
reparations."

"And now he's returned." Trista searched the softly lined
face for answers. There was far more here than simply a
philandering rogue. Nicholas was after something. "He has
returned to avenge his parents' death."

"Oh, my lady, I am not at liberty to discuss anything
further...even if I knew of such things...." Polly hastily
looked away. "Nicholas does not offer forth much about his
business dealings, nothing, as a matter of fact, but...
well...you see, I come from a long line of rather *curious*,
resourceful women, who find a tongue held in check more
of a temptation than a deterrent." The grip on Trista's hand
intensified, the soft brown eyes beseeching. "My lady, from
what little I can gather, I fear that Nicholas may be in danger."

"What? Whatever are you talking about?"

"I did not mean to alarm you! 'Tis just that the stature of
the individuals with whom he is dealing...one never
knows..."

"Never knows what?"

"My lady, I, more than anyone, wish I knew! He is so
secretive, so absorbed with this, so very much like his father I fear he will suffer the same fate!"

Trista patted the older woman's hand. "'Tis enough for
me that this has caused you such distress. I will confront
Nicholas...."

"No! You mustn't! He will know 'twas I who planted the
seed of your curiosity! Oh, how my tongue runs away with
me! 'Twas always my problem, you know, and Fritz detests
it so." She patted Trista's hand once more. "I only meant to
soothe your troubles. Surely now you see your husband with
different eyes."

"They remain the same eyes, Polly, though my husband is far clearer to me now. I thank you for offering forth that which he has seen fit to keep from me." Trista plucked idly at her sleeve. "I presume your curiosity and resourcefulness have not failed you in discerning that ours is not a typical marriage."

"My lady, I would not wish upon you a typical marriage, though you both seem bent upon that very thing. You are not remiss in assuming that I am well aware of the circumstances surrounding your union. However, do not fool yourself, for my deduction required little in the way of peeking through keyholes and making myself overly busy outside of partially opened doors. No, 'tis more than obvious, and a terrible shame, if you ask me."

Trista rose and moved to the windows overlooking the stone circular drive, feeling her cheeks flame beneath what she mistook as Polly's insinuation. "You speak truth, Polly, for 'tis both shameful and humiliating."

"My lady, I meant nothing of the sort. I would never seek to impose my judgment upon either you or Nicholas, or the events that led to the marriage. I care naught for that! I'm merely suggesting that perhaps you should consider setting your differences aside before they become a barrier to your happiness, my dear. Oftentimes, 'tis that which is left unsaid that poses the greatest threat to a marriage."

"He has said enough already," Trista muttered half to herself, then swung a troubled gaze to Polly. "And are you also suggesting that I overlook certain of these differences in light of Nicholas's troubled past? I fear I cannot, for I find his lack of good fortune a poor excuse for bad manners and an unabashed surliness while storming about like some pigheaded lout!"

A smile tweaked the corners of Polly's mouth. Ah, but Nicholas had surely met his match! She sighed, completely at a loss with this maid, who certainly exhibited some rather pigheaded tendencies herself. "My lady, perhaps the slightest softening of manner... some small effort..."

Trista released her breath, lowering her gaze to the brilliant emerald weighting her left hand. "Dear Polly, I shall

be forever grateful for your kindness. However, I fear that
the very circumstances from which this marriage was born
will be the reasons for its demise.''

"Not if you try, my lady! Perhaps with time..."

A movement from below drew Trista's attention. She
turned to the window and gasped. "Gypsy!"

With a shriek of pure unadulterated joy, she bounded
from the room, down the wide staircase, through the massive entry and past an openmouthed Fritz with a dazzling
smile.

"Gypsy!"

Her unbound tresses flying, she streaked across the wide
stone portico and down the steps toward her beloved horse,
standing beneath a shady elm. Peter stood beside the chestnut mare with reins in hand, patting the finely arched neck
and cooing softly. Momentarily, his eye was drawn to the
tall, broad-shouldered form pausing at the open doorway to
stare with a burning intent upon his wife.

"Oh, Peter! Oh, darling girl, how I've missed you so!"
She rubbed the soft muzzle, between the pricked ears, then
patted the sleek neck. "Oh, but you look wonderful! Ian has
been taking such good care of you, eh, girl? You haven't
even missed me, have you?" Tearing her eyes from her beloved mount, she grinned at Peter. "How on earth did she
get here? Did you...?"

"Aye, Trista...I..."

"Oh, Peter!" Without a moment's thought, she threw her
arms about his neck and planted a smacking kiss upon his
reddening cheek. "'Twas too kind of you! Oh, you are so
terribly thoughtful!"

With obvious distress, Peter attempted to set her from
him. "'Twas not I...I—I mean, I rode back for her...at
your husband's order, Trista. I left early last evening and
only just returned. He bade me fetch her as quick as I
could."

Trista's heart plummeted to her toes, her breath momentarily snatched. "I would never have guessed...I mean,
perhaps I should thank him..." Turning toward the house,

she halted abruptly as she was met with the broad planes of her husband's chest not a hand's breadth from her.

"That will be all, Peter," his voice rumbled above her.

Swallowing past a huge lump in her throat, Trista closed her eyes upon his white shirt, dimly aware that Peter mumbled some reply before clucking softly to Gypsy and leading her to the stable. A myriad of thoughts flooded her brain, though none as vivid as her sudden awareness of the soft chirping of the birds around them and the warm breeze gently ruffling her hair against her cheek. Hesitantly, she opened her eyes and was about to turn from him, when the firm touch of his hand upon her arm stilled her movements. "You may thank me now, wife, and in the proper manner befitting a bride."

Before she had time to ponder his meaning, Trista felt a powerful arm slip about her waist to crush her against that tall frame. Her eyes flew wide. She barely glimpsed the blazing eyes, the stern set of his jaw, before his mouth descended upon hers with a force that sent her senses reeling. His mouth flamed over hers in a kiss so fierce with suppressed passion that she sagged against him, struggling for one breath, for some release...but none came. He bent her back over his arm until she thought she would sink to the ground. And then his mouth released hers and she gasped as the warmth of his lips caressed her throat.

"Thank me...again and again, sweet wife...I'll get you a hundred horses...just keep thanking me." His voice rasped against her ear, his palm rubbing over the satin covering her breasts. And then his mouth captured hers again, hungrily, his hands branding her with the boldness of his touch, tempting all troubled thoughts to flee. But she could not allow herself to surrender to temptation, no matter how sweet, and she struggled against him, pressing her palms against his chest.

At that moment, the distant rumbling of horses' hooves upon the winding dirt drive stilled Nicholas's hands, and he lifted passion-glazed eyes to the black coach moving speedily toward them. As the vehicle drew closer, he spotted the familiar white head of the passenger, and his hands relaxed slightly against Trista.

Realizing her opportunity, Trista twisted from his grasp and ran to the house, clutching her skirts with one hand as she struggled to contain the tears threatening to spill from her eyes.

It took far more than sheer force of will for Nicholas to refrain from chasing after her. With a grim smile, he turned to assist the old gentleman from the coach.

"I was not expecting you until later this afternoon," Nicholas said.

The white-haired gentleman fixed a keen gaze upon the younger man. "Were it not of the utmost importance, I would not have imposed myself upon you until the arranged time. However, your rather untimely, shall I say, premature, departure early last evening prevented you from witnessing a rather interesting exchange between our friends."

Nicholas lifted a dark brow. "Indeed, I am most interested." He held an arm toward the house and the old gentleman moved forward slowly.

"Truly the finest of days to enjoy beneath yonder elm with one's lovely bride. 'Twas your new bride, Trista, was it not?"

"Aye," Nicholas murmured.

The old man leaned heavily on his cane. "I achieved only the briefest glimpse, but she looks to be quite beautiful."

"Aye, that she is."

"Now I can understand your eagerness to see that she become your wife. A woman such as she could drive a man to distraction."

"Aye, more than a distraction, but worth it."

"And does she know anything of your plans, or the part she has come to play?"

"She knows nothing."

"Do you think that wise?"

Nicholas shrugged. "The proper time for telling her has not presented itself."

The older gentleman paused and laid a trembling hand upon Nicholas's sleeve. "'Tis not wise to delay telling her. Trust me, it would serve you well to take her into your confidence, for the longer you keep this from her, the more difficult she will find it to understand that you felt it necessary to do just that. She is your wife. She loves you." The voice filled with an emotion Nicholas could not fathom. "Nothing should come between that love, or the love of family."

The portal swung wide and Nicholas graciously ushered his guest toward the study. As he moved through the corridor, his mind reverberated with the words spoken not moments before. Of course, she should be told, but how in God's name could he explain this to her when they seemed incapable of engaging in normal conversation? And love? Why, they had yet to achieve some small measure of acceptance of each other! Upon what depth of feeling would she draw to find some level of understanding of his pursuits?

Distractedly, he ran a hand through his hair, then hesitated, for he detected the faint scent of her lilac fragrance still clinging to his fingers. Instantly, his mind filled with images of her pressed against him, soft and supple beneath his hands, and his desire burned with an intensity so fierce he gave serious thought to abandoning his guest and racing up those stairs to ease his passions with her upon that blasted pink bed. Instead, he pushed the study doors wide and bade his guest enter, then, with a last glance toward the stairs, pulled the doors closed behind him.

Chapter Eleven

The mother duck and her four baby ducklings wove an erratic path across the pond, their paddling feet sending tiny ripples over the otherwise smooth surface. The sunlight played upon the water and warmed the thick grass and wild heather growing in lush thatches surrounding the pool. A soft breeze stirred the leaves of several large elms and momentarily cooled Trista's cheeks as she stared into the pond's brilliant depths. Idly, she twirled a stem of grass between her slender fingers and loosened the top few buttons of her shirt, the very shirt she had snatched from Ian so long ago, along with her beloved trousers.

Her eyes strayed to Gypsy grazing nearby. The mare lifted her head to peer anxiously at the family of ducklings waddling from the pond. The sleek chestnut coat still glistened from the effects of their hard ride, and she snorted as the ducks meandered about directly beneath her nose.

Trista sighed and leaned back on her elbows. She'd been quite lucky to stumble upon this secluded spot, tucked away on the edge of Nicholas's property, well hidden from the main path by a tall growth of brush. She had ridden the perimeter of the property and had paused on a grassy knoll to view for the first time the grand manor she now called home—that immense stone structure, all three stories of it, with tall narrow windows and a large stone portico supported by thick columns. An imposing structure, indeed.

She eyed the pool, then, with a sudden thought, slipped her shoes from her feet and rolled the rough trousers to her knees. Jumping to her feet, she strode through the grass and into the warm pond, pausing when the water reached just past her knees. She wiggled her toes into the soft mud and swept her hands through the water, reveling in the feel of it threading through her fingers. Cupping her hands, she splashed the water over her cheeks and across her throat, then paused to coax Gypsy to the water, but the mare ventured only so far as the edge of the pond to drink, eyeing her mistress suspiciously.

"Oh, come now, girl. Methinks you've become a rather timid lass of late. Nero will think you weak of heart, and you wouldn't want that, for he is the finest stallion in all of England. 'Twould serve you well to impress—" Her words were cut short as Gypsy suddenly lifted her head in the direction of the path, ears pricked and nostrils flaring.

Through the thick brush, Nero emerged with Nicholas astride. A cool assessing eye swept over the rolled-up trousers, the parted shirt, to settle upon the tumbling cascade of chestnut curls. She looked like some woodland nymph frolicking about, like a child. Yet, as he pulled on the reins, halting Nero at the pool's edge, and his eyes fell again to the parted shirt, Nicholas was certain he had not taken a child as his wife.

Trista hastily drew the neck of her shirt together. "Your guest has departed?"

Nodding, Nicholas raised a dark brow and the corners of his mouth lifted faintly. "'Tis an interesting riding habit. Perhaps Adelle neglected to mention this latest fad, though the style suits you . . . rather well." Indeed, the cut of the trousers emphasized the tiny waist and slim-hipped, long-legged form, while the shirt did little to conceal the high curves of her bosom. As his appreciative gaze traveled slowly over her again, Nicholas gave serious consideration to procuring an entire wardrobe of these trousers and shirts for her.

"I find trousers far more comfortable than any skirt," she replied, wondering why she suddenly felt so small and helpless standing in this blasted pool. "Indeed, I find I enjoy riding like a man."

"Madam, I sincerely doubt any man has ever done such justice to a shirt and trousers. Despite the clothes upon your back, I would wager you ride far better than most men."

Trista peered at him closely. " 'Tis a trifle shocking that you would deem a woman as capable as a man."

"The woman of whom I speak is far from the typical sort. However, notwithstanding the obvious difference in physical strength, a woman is as capable of mastering a skill as any man. Perhaps even more so."

"Indeed, and why is that?"

"I've found women capable of an inner strength far surpassing that of most men. And, of course, a woman can employ a finesse born of her tender touch to master the most difficult of tasks, while a man's strength may prove a hindrance at times." The strong hand on the reins tightened as Nero made a playful move toward the mare he apparently found very much to his liking, though the object of his desire merely gave him a sidelong glance before tossing her head sassily and strolling away to graze. Nicholas shifted in his saddle. "You should have postponed your ride. I would have liked to show you the grounds myself."

Trista shrugged. "I hadn't a notion that you wished to ride along."

"Consider the request a permanent one from now on."

Didn't the man ever tire of staring upon her? Feeling her cheeks grow warm, Trista bent to sweep her hands through the water. "Gypsy was a wonderful surprise. Thank you."

He nodded and looked as if he meant to have her for lunch.

"The grounds, the home, are truly magnificent. All one could ever desire." Her eyes locked with his. *Desire*... Why in God's name had she chosen that word?

With some difficulty, she swallowed and attempted to take a step toward the water's edge, only to find that her feet had sunk well past her ankles into the muck along the bottom of the pond. Indeed, she could barely move them. Offering a weak smile, she struggled as inconspicuously as possible with her dilemma. "Polly tells me that the home has been in your mother's family for some time. 'Tis an admirable thing you have done, restoring it so wonderfully.''

"It was the least I could do." The dark head inclined curiously. "And what else did dear Polly find necessary to tell you?"

As casually as possible, Trista shrugged and gritted her teeth in some semblance of a smile as she sought to free at least one of her feet. "Oh... she told me of your childhood... of your parents and your life in Richmond."

Nicholas gave a short laugh. "That woman possesses the most flagrant inability to keep her tongue in check."

Trista ceased her struggle with the muck. "That's highly unfair! Why, if it weren't for Polly, I would no doubt wander through the rest of my life completely ignorant of my husband's past, knowing of him only that which he deems me worthy, which, to date, has been absolutely nothing!"

"'Tis hardly a question of your worthiness, little she-cat. You are continually passing the harshest judgments upon me, do you realize that?"

"Only judgments of which you are most deserving."

"Indeed." He paused momentarily as his eye was drawn to the sunlight playing upon the golden streaks threading through the tousled mane tumbling about her shoulders. "Trista, believe me, I have not kept the story of my life from you, as unremarkable as it may be, for any reason other than that the proper time has never seemed to present itself. You would have to agree with me on this. Besides, I don't believe you ever *asked*. I would venture to say we were both rather... distracted with other far more interesting pursuits."

"And foolishly distracted, at that."

"Speak for yourself," he murmured in reply, then slid to his feet beside Nero. His movements startled Trista, and the gleam in his eye set her heart palpitating. Did he realize she was his prisoner, ensnared by the cold muck shackling her ankles? She watched him carelessly loop the reins over a small thatch of brush, then settle himself comfortably on the ground, leaning back on one arm and dangling the other over a raised knee, his eyes fixed upon her. "Tell me, wife, what it is you would like to know, that is, if dear Polly neglected anything. I promise I shall do my best to remain *undistracted.*''

Ha! Trista trailed one hand idly through the water. "I would rather that you tell me what you wish me to know. I've always found that the memories one finds most vivid reveal more of a person than any telling of a sequence of events."

"As you wish," Nicholas replied, his eyes sweeping the clearing. "This pond...I remember this from when I was quite small. My mother and I would come, and she'd spin her tales of the ducklings that ventured about and the thrush that perched overhead to sing. After we settled in Richmond, she still talked of this place."

"You must miss her very much," Trista murmured softly.

"Indeed, I miss them both." For a moment, their eyes locked, and time hung suspended for them until Trista glanced away, cheeks flushing profusely.

"I...it's lovely," she said. "I can see why your mother found it so captivating. Though surely Richmond must be beautiful in its own way."

"Without question, the Virginia countryside knows no rival. I trust you will find our home there equally as lovely, once the time comes to return."

Trista stared at him. "Return?"

"Of course, once my business is complete."

Trista blanched. He intended to take her from her home, from all she knew to a place of heathens and cutthroats, a lawless land where people didn't even bathe!

Nicholas gave her a bemused look. "You needn't look so stricken. Many have found great fortune in that land of promise, for opportunity abounds for those desirous enough to work for it. You've nothing to be afraid of...except for an Indian or two lurking about."

"Indians?"

"You needn't fret, my lady, for your husband wields a hefty blade of his own, quite capable of scalping a few of those red-skinned savages."

"Scalping? Savages!"

"But only if they threaten to abduct you to one of their villages on the prairie or attempt to burn down the house."

"What? Oh, Nicholas, you cannot mean to take me there...I cannot, I will not go, do you hear me? Never! I shall remain here and gladly confront any of the highwaymen threatening to accost me...rather than...oh...oh... Nicholas!"

Suddenly, and to her extreme dismay, Trista lost her balance. With her feet firmly mired in muck, she frantically sought to remain upright, her arms wheeling feverishly, but to no avail. With wide eyes and a high-pitched scream, she plunged backward into the water, completely submerging, then resurfacing to sputter and struggle to get her feet beneath her. Through a tangle of hair, she watched Nicholas plunge into the water, felt his hands grasping for hers. Frantically, her hands clawed for his, then, with a gurgled scream, she felt the muck give way and again submerged. Sputtering and choking, she thrashed about, then felt powerful arms slip around her, and suddenly she was crushed against his chest. Clinging to him with one arm, she gasped for breath while one hand feverishly sought to sweep the tangled curtain of sodden hair from her eyes.

"Cease your wiggling!" Nicholas muttered as he struggled to retain his footing and make his way from the pond with his baggage. He reached the bank and deposited her on shaky legs, slipping his arm about her waist as she swayed.

Gazing upon the wide eyes peering up at him through the veil of hair, he was suddenly overcome with the humor of the situation. The smile tugging at his mouth evolved into a rumbling chuckle deep within his chest, which only grew more difficult to contain the stormier her gaze became. Green eyes blazed at him and he self-consciously raised a fist to cover his mouth, then turned and forced a horrid imitation of a cough to cover the laughter threatening to overcome him.

"Had I known you would react so violently, I would never have jested about the Indians," he drawled.

Grinding her teeth in frustration, Trista swept his hand from her waist, placing hers on her hips. "Jested? You addlepated dolt! I find little humor in this situation!"

"Oh, give it a rest, Trista. I'm no Society patron to whom you must forever present a stiff upper lip, though the sight of you in those damned trousers, tumbling backward into that pond would surely crack the most hardened of all *proper* visages." The lopsided grin reappeared despite her ominous glowering. "Have you always had this tendency toward clumsiness, my lady, or is it something you have recently acquired?"

"'Tis neither," Trista ground out through a clenched jaw. "My feet were stuck."

"Stuck?" Nicholas stifled a chuckle. "Why in God's name didn't you tell me? I would have assisted you."

In reply, she simply glared at him as haughtily as her disheveled appearance would allow.

"Ah, I see, your stubborn pride wouldn't permit the asking of something so simple of me. I shall never understand the intricate, unfathomable workings of the female mind," he mused, as if half to himself, and his eyes raised heavenward for a moment. "And woe is me to have taken for all eternity a woman far from the typical sort and, without a doubt, doubly baffling!"

Trista leveled a cool look upon him. "From what little I have gleaned, I would venture to say your wont is to rise to any challenge, and the more baffling the better."

"You know me well, wife." The sudden smoldering gaze dropped to her breasts, enticingly revealed by the sodden shirt and thin shift molding the swelling curves. "You're cold."

With a gasp, Trista pulled the clinging fabric away from her taut nipples, then turned her back to him. "I...I should fetch Gypsy..."

Her words caught in her throat when he moved close to her, his hands rubbing gently but, oh, so insistently against her upper arms. She turned to him, her eyes lowered, her heart thumping frantically. She felt the firm pressure of his hands at her arms, holding her, and her breath was released in a soft rush. "Nicholas . . . please . . ."

"Let me warm you. . . ."

Trista closed her eyes. A dull buzzing began in the deep recesses of her brain. Every fiber of her being stood poised, as if suspended, waiting for the release of his hands upon her skin, his mouth over hers . . .

"Nicholas . . . 'tis not what I want . . ." Her lips parted in the softest of sighs as his fingers moved like a whisper to the remaining buttons of her shirt, parting the fabric and sliding the garment over her shoulders to fall in a soggy heap at her feet. His lips brushed softly against her bare shoulder, then moved to the base of her throat, where his tongue gently tasted her skin and a shudder of pleasure rippled through her. His touch was so gentle, so coaxing, yet Trista could sense the force of his restraint in the slight trembling of his hands and the huskiness of his voice in her ear.

"What else could you possibly want, my sweet seductress? This . . ."

His fingers traced her skin just above the lace at the top of her shift, over the high curves of her breasts to meet at the deep cleavage. He made quick work of the tiny pink ribbon as Trista stood, trembling, and she gasped as he parted the thin fabric and her breasts spilled forth.

"Oh, lovely, sweet wife . . . how can you deny me . . ." His voice was a husky whisper, his mouth molten fire along her throat, her collarbone, to the soft mounds he pressed to his face.

Sagging against him, Trista clutched at his shoulders and liquid fire coursed through her. His mouth claimed her flesh with slow, gentle kisses, an infinite tenderness that swept her along on his swelling tide of passion. With every caress, every kiss, he coaxed, he teased, and she had to draw from the depths of her resolve to speak.

"I must deny you . . . and myself." She pushed softly against his shoulders. "Nicholas . . . please, you must listen to me."

His mouth stilled at one rosy peak to suckle with whisper-soft strokes as his fingers brushed the tender sides of her breasts. "I can barely think...how can you expect me to listen?"

"You must." Gently, she raised a trembling hand to ease his mouth from her, only to find her fingers grasped in his, then pressed to his warm lips.

"This had better be worth it," he murmured against her fingers.

"Please...Nicholas..." Her free hand plucked at his, still upon her breast, and with a slight shake of his head, he lowered it to her waist.

"You expect too much of me, sweet wife." He nibbled at her fingertips until she snatched her hand from his to clutch at the parted shift.

"No, 'tis you who expects too much, Nicholas, and you must heed me...this time."

His passionate gaze settled upon one ringlet nestled between her breasts and his voice grew thick with emotion. "How can I? How can you?"

She turned from him, struggling with the ribbons of her shift and a stubborn will that waged a battle with her passionate soul. And then a powerful chest pressed against her back, strong arms slipping about her waist, warm lips brushing against her neck.

"You have inflamed my very soul, woman. Speak now, before I lose control and take you...here, upon the grass...against yonder tree, in the damned pond."

With a gasp, Trista fled his embrace, struggling for breath as she watched him draw his shirt from his back. Her eyes widened as he moved slowly toward her, the sculpted symmetry of his torso, bathed a golden bronze beneath the sun, momentarily snatching her breath away. He stopped before her and swept the shirt about her shoulders.

"I am incapable of coherent thought with you as you are," he said huskily, drawing the shirt over her breasts. "Cover yourself with this, and perhaps I will be able to concentrate some small measure."

And what of me? she moaned to herself as her eyes strayed to the sleek-muscled chest and bulging arms hanging at his sides. For a brief moment, she considered giving free rein to her wanton soul. She drew a steadying breath and clutched his shirt close. "I fear you have me rather confused regarding this marriage of convenience."

" 'Twas a statement made in haste and one that I have regretted ever since. Forget I ever spoke those words. I have."

"I fear I cannot, for I desire that arrangement far more than any other at the moment."

His eyes narrowed upon her and his voice bore a hint of sarcasm. "Forgive me if I have a bit of trouble believing that, Trista. Your response several moments ago does not lend your statement much credibility."

"To the contrary," she replied, feeling the color rising in her cheeks with her growing indignation. " 'Twould appear my response was somewhat lacking in zeal, for we are decidedly far from testing the softness of this grass at the moment, wouldn't you agree?"

"We're closer than you think."

"Nicholas, you must heed me!" Fixing an agitated glare on his hooded visage, she heaved a troubled sigh. "In the wine cellar, before we . . . rather, as we were about to . . ."

"I remember the scene well."

"I recall your words that you would not . . . proceed . . . if I were not willing."

"Indeed. I would derive little pleasure from forcing my passion upon you, though that was hardly the case. 'Tis indeed the sweetest of my memories that you were more than willing."

"In body, aye, there is no denying that, though admitting as much weighs heavily upon me."

"A burden you bring unnecessarily upon yourself."

Trista shook her head slowly. " 'Tis the heart that is unwilling, Nicholas, despite the bodily response I cannot deny. It's the very reason for my despair. I fear I will never find peace within myself and as your wife if I must forever battle my will."

For several moments, her words hung between them, only the sound of a bird's call filling the sun-dappled air. Then his voice, low like a deep growl, rumbled from the depths of his chest. "You realize you are denying me my rights as your husband."

"And what of mine?" Jade eyes flashed angrily at him. "Surely you would not subject me to this despair simply for the sake of your precious rights?"

His jaw tensed beneath a stormy brow. "I had little idea you were so miserable."

"Not entirely! 'Tis just that so much has happened in so short a time, I've barely had a moment to think! Dear God, a scant few weeks ago, marriage was the furthest thing from my mind! Indeed, contrary to popular belief, my venture forth into Society had little to do with finding a husband!"

Nicholas gave a derisive snort. "You would be remiss in assuming that women of your beauty run rampant through the streets of London or any city, for that matter. Indeed, 'tis a sorry testimony to every London gentleman that an entire fortnight passed before you were presented with your first proposal and nearly a month before you found yourself wed."

"Don't mock me, Nicholas, I simply wish to make the best of the situation, and I presume you desire the same." He grunted in reply and folded his arms over his chest. "I need time to grow accustomed to you, your home, to come to know the man I married, in ways other than those most intimate."

"Time. I see." He all but glowered at her. "Lest you require some reminder, Trista, I am no eunuch able to live beneath the same roof with a wife who looks like you and keep myself from her for months on end. It would be testing the very limits of my patience. However, in deference to your wishes, may I ask how long a time you will require to become so accustomed?"

"I know not how long it will take, Nicholas! 'Tis highly unfair to ask such a thing."

"And what you ask is in no small way unfair?" he roared, and with two long strides stood before her, roughly gripping her arms. "How long, Trista? A month? Two? Ten? If ever?"

"I don't know!" she cried, twisting in his grasp. "Take your hands from me!"

"Not until you listen to me," he ground out. "You may have all the time you wish, for I respect your desires, though I may not find your methods at all to my liking. However, tread lightly, little wife, and do not test my patience overmuch. There is little telling how much I can bear."

The biting comment bubbled forth. "You can always ease your starved passions on your gaming house wenches or even Bianca, for that matter, for I'm quite certain she would be eager and most willing."

The fierceness of his gaze nearly drove Trista's breath from her as he leaned very close and growled, "Still your vicious tongue, wife, lest your shrewish words drive me to do that very thing. 'Tis no doubt what you wish."

Trista felt a tremor pass through her. "In all truth, I would rather you not seek the arms of another, but if you feel you must..."

"I have every intention of abiding those vows I spoke with you, madam, and rest assured, it will be a cold day in hell before I seek the arms of another. 'Twould serve you well, however, to remember that at any time I may choose to ease my 'starved passions' with you, willing or not. Do you understand?"

"I shall remember."

Releasing her, he added beneath his breath, "So be it. We'd best get back or Polly will have my hide if she has supper on the table."

Nodding in response, Trista watched as he whistled to the horses, and found herself wondering how a man so fierce could fear a lashing from that tiny woman. While his back was turned, she hastily tended to her shift and donned his shirt, rolling the sleeves to her elbows and knotting the tails at her waist. She lifted her eyes as he wordlessly led Gypsy to her and assisted her into the saddle before mounting Nero. He reined the stallion sharply about and dug his booted heels into the animal's sleek sides, which brought a startled snort from the steed before he leapt forward at his master's command.

Trista urged Gypsy along closely behind them, though the mare hesitated with an uncertainty born of unfamiliarity as they plunged through the brush. However, once on the open meadow, the mare strained against the bit for her head, which Trista gave without hesitation. Nicholas seemed bent upon some kind of race to the manor, and she was certainly more than game. The mare lunged forward after the mighty stallion, racing just ahead of her, and within moments pulled alongside the ebony steed.

The wind whipped Trista's unbound tresses about her and caught in her throat as her lips parted in a wide smile and her heart pounded with exhilaration. For several moments, the horses ran stride for stride, sweeping smoothly across the lush fields as if their hooves barely touched ground. Trista chanced a quick glance at her husband and was surprised to find his eyes upon her, at once challenging, yet full of some emotion she could not fathom. Her smile faded for a moment, then, as Nicholas spurred Nero once more, she leaned closer to the mare's pumping neck and urged Gypsy faster. However, the mare stood little chance of beating the mighty stallion, due more to her lack of stature than lack of heart, and she followed just at his heels as they skidded to a halt before the stable.

Sliding from her saddle, Trista gasped for breath, her eyes lifting to find Nicholas close beside her. "You're an exceptional rider," he said. "You're quite a pair, not unlike Nero and myself."

"Perhaps Nero would favor the gentle touch of a woman sometime, hmm?"

Nicholas looked at her as if she were mad. "Don't even think about it, Trista, for you would find yourself on your round little bottom, if not on your head, before you realized. It took me nearly six months to break him and he still gives me trouble from time to time. He's much too dangerous for a woman."

Trista cast him a mocking glance, then handed Gypsy over to Peter, who quickly led the horses to the stable. With arms folded over her chest, she cocked her head and remarked sassily, " 'Twas you who said a woman was as capable as any man, was it not? Or does that thinking apply only in situations where there is little chance of danger? Like sewing or gardening, for instance, two idle pastimes that require an infinitely tender touch and therefore hold little fascination for the male mind.''

Nicholas gaped at her and bellowed, "Hardly! I would advise the most accomplished of all horsemen in the same manner!''

"But your remark was quite obviously directed to women.''

Grinding his teeth in frustration, Nicholas replied, "It's not for lack of anything but strength that would prove to be your shortcoming, Trista. Nothing more.''

"Ah, therein lies your problem, Nicholas.''

"Problem? In God's name, what problem?''

"In situations where you call upon physical prowess, I call upon...*charm.*'' His look of utter stupefaction brought a small smile to her lips and she could not resist the feeling of self-satisfaction that swept over her.

"Charm? Ha! No man has ever *charmed* a horse into complacency, Trista.''

"Perhaps because a man would never think of trying. Now, I feel in need of a warm bath. I shall see you at dinner, hmm?'' With that, she turned on her heel and strode purposefully toward the manor, even as his bellowing voice all but begged for a response.

"Heed me well, Trista! Don't even think twice about it. Rest assured, I will feel little compassion when you nurse your sore backside and a bruised ego. Do you hear me?'' With an angry scowl, he glared after her retreating form. "Women!'' he muttered beneath his breath, even as he paused to admire the swing of her hips in those blasted trousers.

Charm, indeed! Though if any woman were capable of taming a wild beast with nary but a sloe-eyed glance, it was she. After all, hadn't she accomplished that very thing with him, in spite of himself? Charm... The idea was worthy of some thought.

Dark brows drew together over a pensive gaze. Perhaps there was more than one way to achieve all that he desired. There was no denying that his resounding lack of success with her thus far required some rethinking of his methods. Damn! This marriage had rendered him a passion-crazed dolt, at once foolishly proclaiming himself desirous of a loveless marriage yet panting after her as if he wanted the exact opposite.

His eyes narrowed in thought. Perhaps the lady was susceptible to a pleasant, engaging manner offered forth by a most charming and gracious husband. If he were to sheathe his passions for a time and devote his energies to wooing his lady, perhaps he would achieve that which he desired above all else: her complete surrender. With a smile of unabashed self-satisfaction, he turned and strode toward the manor.

Chapter Twelve

*B*lackmail.

With a furrowed brow, Nicholas stared at the word his quill had traced at least forty times upon the parchment.

Blackmail. Was it possible?

Shoving a hand through his hair, he gave a disgusted sigh and pushed his chair from the desk. His troubled gaze settled upon the cozy fire before him, his constant companion in this room where he spent so many hours. The gentle flames offered little in the way of advice, but he found a moment's solace staring into the fire, until the clock over the mantel chiming the hour of ten drew his attention. He rubbed a hand over his weary eyes, then grimaced into a cold cup of tea sitting upon his desk.

The midmorning sun slanting through the windows fell upon the parchment and drew his eye once again. "Archibald Sleeth," he muttered to himself. "Methinks you conceal a sly nature beneath that foppish demeanor. Indeed, my fault lies in not seeing past your massive girth and lewd manner to the wily fox capable of blackmailing himself into the good graces of London Society." And what a ticket. Sleeth alone had the evidence to achieve a defamation of character so complete, his prey was willing to abide by his rules. Those papers he'd recovered from his departed brother, Oswald, must have contained that proof. And where did that leave him? Nicholas wondered. Indeed, he had much to offer in the way of a hefty purse to obtain that information. He was certain, however, that Sleeth's greed extended beyond the coin in his pocket to the company he kept, or rather *used to* keep. He feared he would be of little use to Sleeth in that regard, for he'd been all but banned from Society and bore the reputation of scoundrel as a result of his infatuation with his ever-so-desirable wife.

His thoughts strayed to the prior evening's rather pleasant dinner conversation and, more important, to Trista's engaging response to his purposeful and ever-so-gracious manner. She'd bestowed the most genuine of smiles upon him when he had assisted her from the table and offered his arm to lead her to the parlor to enjoy a glass of sherry before the fire. Her light touch upon his arm and her lilting voice had caused him no small measure of discomfort, and he'd purposefully seated himself opposite her lest she settle too closely beside him on the settee. And there he had found his attention captured as she chattered on about God only knows what—*he* surely couldn't recall much, except that the fire did marvelous things to the color of her hair and her skin. He drank in her movements, feasting on the manner in which she toyed with her earrings or plucked at the lace at her sleeve. Her fingers were long and slender, the nails not overly long and perfectly tended. He had a distinct recollection of wondering how they would feel scratching at his back when he brought her to the heights of passion.

Damn. He cleared his throat, willing his mind to clear, as well. He rose and stretched his arms over his head, feeling the corded muscles along his neck and shoulders resist at first, then loosen, as he rolled his head to and fro. With a disgusted snort, he ventured down the corridor to the foyer, where he paused to peer up anxiously at the closed set of doors to the pink bedroom. Scowling at the silence that filled the house, he continued to the portal and flung the door wide. He stood with legs braced apart, his hands thrust into the pockets of his dark breeches. A movement in the distance drew his attention and his eyes narrowed on a vehicle approaching with some speed, evidenced by the billowing cloud of dust left in its wake. Scowling yet again and muttering something about respect for a man's privacy at such an hour, he slammed the portal closed and turned to

seek solace in his study once again. A high-pitched sound
from the kitchen, however, altered his course and he moved
to ease that door open slightly and peek inside.

He was met with a cloud of what he could only surmise
was flour, the same white powder that covered his wife from
head to toe. As she was turned away from him, he allowed
himself a good long look. Her pale pink cotton gown was
covered with flour, the sleeves rolled to her elbows. Her hair
tumbled in careless floured ringlets about her flushed
cheeks. Her apron bow was askew. She had about her a look
of grim concentration, her tongue just peeking out of her
mouth, her brow knit determinedly as she bent in earnest
over the dough she furiously kneaded. She looked positively delicious.

Pausing for a moment, she sniffed and gingerly ran the
back of her arm over her nose, completely unaware of
Nicholas's presence. "Baking bread. Such an obedient little wife I've become."

Nicholas's brow lifted, then his attention swung to Polly
as she bustled about the kitchen. "'Tis hardly a token of
obedience, my lady. Indeed, 'tis a worthy endeavor to un-
dertake for a maiden unaccustomed to such things. I must
admit, I never expected to find you up with the sun to assist
me."

Trista shrugged and continued kneading the lump of
dough before her with such determination Nicholas could
not help but wonder what frustrations she sought to allevi-
ate by pounding so. "I found sleep a trifle elusive last night.
In all truth, I stirred long before the sun." She drew a deep
breath and muttered, "I would have never thought baking
bread could be so tiring."

Without a moment's pause, Polly quipped, "'Tis not
normally so, though when one pounds upon something as
if it were the broad shoulders of the man causing her such
vexation, then I suppose a certain degree of weariness could
be expected."

Trista gaped at the woman, then started abruptly as
Nicholas chose that moment to burst into the kitchen to
announce the arrival of some unexpected visitors. Trista felt

the heat of his gaze upon her and brought a self-conscious hand to her hair, unwittingly depositing a lump of flour amidst the glossy locks.

She bade him good-morning. "Are you expecting a business engagement this morning?"

He leaned back against the table close beside her and folded his arms over his chest, musing on this engaging skittishness. "Nay, not this morning. And you, Trista, perhaps a secret admirer or two?"

The twinkle in his eye stilled the hot retort on the tip of her tongue and she lowered her eyes to her hands, buried in the mound of dough. At that moment, the door burst open and Fritz bustled into the room, then paused openmouthed at the sight of the lady of the house. "The Countess Catalani and her niece Bianca have arrived. They await your pleasure in the parlor, my lady."

"Oh! I cannot believe . . . oh, what a mess I am!" Feverishly, Trista sought to sweep the dough from her hands and the flour from her dress, at the same time tugging at her apron strings.

"Let me help you," Nicholas offered with a smile.

He towered above her, his touch remarkably gentle, and Trista found herself growing decidedly flustered beneath his ministrations. She stared at his hands smoothing over hers.

"You're not wearing your wedding ring," he observed, his thumb brushing over her ring finger.

A shiver raced through Trista and her eyes darted to the gold band encircling his sun-bronzed finger. "I . . . I have it here..." she stammered, lifting an unsteady gaze as she drew one hand from his and pulled the emerald ring from her pocket. Without hesitation, he took the ring and slid it upon her trembling finger, his eyes meeting hers.

"You have beautiful hands," he murmured.

Trista's heart flip-flopped and she could do naught but draw breathy little gasps and gaze upon his handsome features so close above her. She nearly swooned when he raised one hand to pluck the lump of flour from her hair. His fingers swept the stray tendrils from her face, then cupped her chin, tilting her face to his. "Such a rare beauty I find in my kitchen. Whatever did I do without you, hmm?'' The smoldering eyes suddenly twinkled mischievously and he gave her a lopsided grin that melted her soul. "Shall we greet our guests, my lady?''

Nodding dumbly, she swept the apron from her waist and laid a trembling hand upon his arm, then allowed him to lead her to the parlor.

Esme, resplendent in a pale yellow traveling suit and matching plumed hat, turned with a smile at the rustle of Trista's skirts, then started abruptly when her eyes swept over her niece. *"Cherie,"* she cried, rushing forward in a flurry of skirts and sweet perfume to embrace Trista. Grasping her niece's hands urgently, Esme whispered close against her ear. "Darling, I simply *had* to see how you were faring. *Mon Dieu,* I had little idea things were so awful!'' As if as an afterthought, Esme nodded perfunctorily at Nicholas, looming at Trista's side, then fixed a worried gaze upon her niece.

"It's so good of you to come,'' Trista replied tenuously, feeling Nicholas's hand rub slowly against the small of her back.

"Why, we simply *had* to, darling!'' Bianca's throaty reply filled the small room and caused Trista's spine to stiffen despite the soothing strokes of Nicholas's fingers. Swinging her rounded hips saucily, Bianca sashayed toward them, her feral black eyes riveted upon one tall bronzed figure.

Trista's jaw tensed as her eye swept over the daringly low-cut crimson satin gown that hugged Bianca's full bosom and trim waist to perfection, and she willed herself to keep from glancing at Nicholas to see if he'd noticed. How could he not! To Trista's eye, the gown seemed entirely inappropriate for this time of day, though if one were bent upon seduction, it was a perfect choice. But the hat! Some godawful concoction of feathers and plumes that no doubt screamed some fashion statement, though Trista knew not what. Yet her heart hammered within her chest as she watched that she-cat pause before her husband and part those scarlet lips before reaching up on tiptoe to brush Nicholas's cheek in a feather-light kiss.

"Nicholas, it has been far too long," that dusky voice murmured, her musky perfume enveloping them. Her expression grew somewhat miffed at Nicholas's silent nod, and her eyes flickered over him to settle for the first time upon Trista. "Why, cousin! Is married life not agreeing with you? Such a rumpled mess you are!"

"You found me in the midst of baking bread. Had I known you were coming..."

"Baking bread!" Esme shrieked. "What in heaven's name for, *cherie?* Certainly your husband is not forcing you to cook?"

"Hardly," Trista replied with a chilling glare at Bianca, who muffled a dramatic giggle behind her hand. "However, I certainly don't think it below me to prepare a meal for my husband if he so desires. To be perfectly honest, I find it quite enjoyable and was up to my elbows in flour and dough when you arrived."

"Seems a rather odd pastime so frightfully *early* in the morning for a newly wedded bride," Bianca ventured in a throaty voice. "One would think at this hour you would be dragging yourself from a tumbled bed and your husband's arms."

"Bianca!" Esme swung a stormy glare upon the sleek figure in crimson.

"My wife is not one to loll about for the better part of the day," Nicholas remarked, his gaze upon his wife. "I consider myself blessed that she is capable of tending to my needs as well as her own pursuits in a most charming manner."

"How very *efficient* of you, Trista," Bianca snorted derisively, then hastened from her spot before the low table as Fritz appeared bearing tea.

"Please, sit for a while." Trista swept a hand to the pair of settees. She seated herself, glancing beside her for Nicholas, but found that he chose to remain standing behind her, his hand upon her shoulder.

Her gaze wavered and she forced a weak smile when his hand moved slowly to the base of her neck, and she nearly jumped from her skin when he leaned close to her and murmured, "Darling, I have a bit of work to do. If you should need me, I'll be in the study."

Lifting her gaze to his, she felt the breath driven from her in a soft sigh as she met the tender look in his eyes. For several moments, she was caught in the spell he wove effortlessly about her.

"Countess, forgive me, but an inordinate amount of work awaits me and I must therefore take my leave. It was good to see you again." He gave Bianca a brief nod before his gaze captured Trista once more. "Enjoy your visit, sweetheart," he said, then, much to the surprise of every female in the room, he brushed his lips softly over her forehead and sauntered from the room.

"What that man does for a simple pair of breeches," Bianca observed huskily, her eyes fixed unabashedly on Nicholas's departing backside. She jumped as Esme deliberately slapped her arm. With a sidelong glance, she huffed, "Well, it's true!"

"That's hardly the point!" Esme scolded in a fierce whisper. "'Tis extremely bad taste to speak so loosely of another woman's husband! Now, behave yourself or I will be forced to banish you to the coach!"

With an elaborate flounce of her shoulders and a pretty little pout, Bianca settled herself to peer with burning intent upon her cousin.

Esme heaved a weary sigh and grasped Trista's hand. "*Cherie,* you seem to have adapted rather well to the circumstances, though 'tis a wee bit unsettling to find you in the kitchen, attired as you are."

"I'm grateful that Nicholas allows me to do as I please," Trista replied, ignoring Bianca's derisive snort.

"Well, thank heavens... Oh, *cherie,* a letter from your father came yesterday!" Esme drew forth an envelope and handed it to Trista. "Open it, for heaven's sake. You must be anxious for his return, though, I must admit, I am not!" Esme fanned herself with a gloved hand. "Of course, 'tis for no other reason than the atrocious state of your circumstances, for which I bear full responsibility. We sent word, but Lord only knows, he may return before the news reaches him. Oh, no, whatever shall I do then?''

Lending her aunt half an ear, Trista scanned the letter. "It seems he has to extend his trip indefinitely. Some unanticipated problems arose while they were in Italy. He knows not when he will return."

"He shall return soon enough." Esme patted Trista's hand. "I realize you must be dreadfully miserable adjusting to your situation, but need I remind you that your father will undoubtedly agree with the manner in which your indiscretion was handled."

Trista shook her head. "Lest you harbor some misconceptions, Aunt Esme, 'tis simply my father's prolonged absence that weighs upon me, not my desire to see him return to alter my circumstances in any way."

For a moment, Esme stared openmouthed, then raised her brows with surprise. "*Well!* Let me say that I am certainly astonished, but pleasantly so! Not a moment has passed since your wedding that I have not fretted over your welfare and scolded myself to no end for allowing that—that seduction."

"You bear no blame for that. Rest assured, I hold only myself accountable. Now, cease your scolding and enjoy some of Polly's tea."

Esme clasped her breast and closed her eyes. "Ah, *cherie,* you have lifted the stone from my soul!" Her eyes flew open, suddenly twinkling devilishly. "Though 'tis certainly no hardship to make the best of things when you recline in the lap of luxury, no? I trust he is generous with you?"

The porcelain teacup rattled in the saucer as Trista's hand wavered in pouring tea. "He has been . . . quite generous, yes. . . ."

"I should say so!" Bianca sniffed as she leaned forward to stare openly at the emerald ring on Trista's finger. "Though one would certainly wonder where Nicholas acquires his wealth. Oh, but of course, 'tis his *gambling* luck that has served him so handsomely. Indeed, to hear Uncle Dom tell it, 'tis a wonder Nicholas still *has* a business, for he spends nearly every moment in White's." The feral black eyes narrowed upon Trista. "'Tis your undeniable lack of breeding, no doubt, that enables you to find comfort in allowing your husband to gallivant about the gaming houses. Hmm, I feel in need of a breath of air. If you will excuse me." With a flounce of her skirts and a haughty lift of a rounded shoulder, she sashayed from the room.

"Don't stray too far!" Esme called after the crimson figure, then shook her head. "Pay her little heed. The talons of envy claw at that one, though her behavior of late has caused me to question *her* lack of breeding before attributing all the blame to her broken heart."

Trista managed a shrug despite the hammering of her pulse. Perhaps Nicholas did indeed still practice his old habits....

"Speaking of broken hearts..." Esme sipped daintily from her tea. "I had occasion to see Kendall Barry the other day. He looks well, I suppose, considering Nicholas made a laughingstock out of him. In any event, he asked about you. He was always such a proper young man. But, don't misunderstand me, there was pain in the poor boy's eyes."

"Time heals," Trista replied. "And how is Dominic? Business is good, I hope."

For a moment, a shadow passed over Esme's lovely features, her skin a sudden ghostly white. Trista's heart skipped a beat and she placed her teacup on the table without taking her eyes from her aunt. "Aunt Esme, what is it?"

"Oh, nothing, really." Esme contemplated her gloved hands clutched in her lap, and her lower lip trembled. "Darling, I am so ashamed. I never meant to and...oh, you needn't worry. I'll be fine."

"Aunt Esme, something is amiss! You must tell me!"

Esme clutched at her niece's hands and raised brimming eyes. "Oh, Trista, I fear Dominic has squandered nearly his entire fortune at the gaming tables. 'Tis the business of which he speaks constantly, nothing else. I have been so foolish! His mother, the Marchioness...you remember her, *cherie,* that awful old woman... she has been well aware of our dire financial state for some time. Indeed, she threatened more than once to disinherit Dominic if he failed to control his gambling. But rather recently I found him in my jewelry box…oh, I cannot bear it! He intended to barter the earrings I received from Mother on the day I wed Gaston! We had an awful quarrel … he said some dreadful things to me and informed me that we had no money left to pay his gambling debts. His mother has cast him off. He's quite desperate. You see, the family jewels, which comprise the majority of those I have, belong to his mother, as does the house. He has no claim! 'Tis utterly dreadful … so humiliating! I am nearly at a loss, not to mention what this has done to my marriage."

Trista gaped at her aunt. "I can scarcely believe it! What on earth shall you do?"

Drawing a lace handkerchief from her reticule, Esme dabbed at her pinkening nose and sniffed, then raised a brow and leveled an astonished look upon Trista. "I was not so naive as to relinquish *everything* to him when we were married, for heaven's sake! He still believes I came to him with almost nothing, which, in all truth, is a dreadful lie. Now mind you, I am in no way suggesting that a marriage be based upon untruths. However, a woman has to be careful, especially with money, and doubly so at my age. The truth is that Gaston left me with a small fortune, which your father has kept safe for the past year."

"And you intend to use those funds to pay off the gambling debts?"

Esme gave her niece a startled look. "How foolish do you think I am?"

" 'Twas not foolishness that came to mind. It was love."

"Love?" Esme gave a hollow laugh. "Darling, perhaps at one time I would have sacrificed so much for love. For Gaston, yes, without hesitation. But Dominic is not Gaston. Indeed, I have come to realize that I put relatively little thought into marrying Dominic. Perhaps I was lonely and frightfully vulnerable to charm and dash. We had such fun. But a marriage cannot be based solely upon this! No, rest assured, I will flee from him before I starve with him or relinquish the fortune Gaston earned from good honest work. Such loyalty Dominic does not deserve. Indeed, I have reason to believe he has been unable to keep himself unto me. You needn't look so shocked, *cherie*. 'Tis dreadfully commonplace these days."

Trista stared at her aunt. "I find that scant justification. I know not what to say. I wish there was something I could do."

"Thank you, *cherie*. You might consider hosting a lavish little party or something to break the dreadful monotony. Trust me, London is no place to be if everyone is afraid to socialize."

"Afraid?"

"Why, of course! Ever since poor Chorlis Beckwith met her dreadful fate, no one will open their doors for fear of the murderer doing such a thing in their very own boudoirs! *Mon Dieu,* the Duchess has yet to fully recover from her shock, much less the dreadful effects on her social life." She patted Trista's hand one last time. "Enough of that! Shall we see where our bothersome Bianca is hiding herself?"

Bothersome, indeed. They found Bianca forthwith, clinging rather dramatically to Nicholas's arm as she scurried to keep pace with him striding down the corridor.

"Your wonderful husband here was just showing me about," Bianca purred, her scarlet nails clutching at Nicholas's sleeve until he pried himself from her. "I was so looking forward to viewing the second floor." She pouted and gave Nicholas a slanted look.

"Not today," Esme hastened to reply, and none too gently grasped Bianca's bare arm to steer her toward the front entrance. "We mustn't overstay our welcome, now. Trista, 'twas divine to see you. Monsieur Brennan . . ." She paused and peered closely at Nicholas. "Take the best care of my niece."

"Nothing but the best, Countess," Nicholas replied, slipping his arm about Trista's waist.

They followed their guests onto the porch and watched silently as the footmen assisted them aboard the black coach. Trista waved as the coach rolled slowly from the manor, then stared thoughtfully after the vehicle.

"Did you enjoy your visit?" Nicholas asked.

"'Twas pleasant enough, though I glimpsed a side to Aunt Esme that left me rather surprised. And Bianca's manner has remained just as offensive."

Nicholas folded his arms over his chest and seemed entirely too amused. "Is that so?"

Trista raised a brow. "You know very well the manner to which I am referring. You needn't behave as if you're immune to the woman's charms. Nicholas, I am well aware that your infatuation with that Italian she-devil began long before our vows were spoken."

The corner of Nicholas's mouth lifted slightly. "It would appear, dear wife, you're in need of some reassurance."

"Reassurance? Ha!" Trista folded her arms over her chest, her toe tapping against the stone porch.

Nicholas grinned devilishly at her. "Denying that she is an attractive woman would only arouse your suspicions."

"Hardly suspicions! You played the smitten suitor to a tee, chasing her about the drawing room, stealing a kiss here, a squeeze there!"

He gave a short laugh. "Bianca has certainly filled your head with lies, which I'm certain you had little trouble believing. However, in your haste to label me rake and scoundrel, you failed to consider the source, sweet Trista, and her motives. Perhaps the thought never occurred to you that she was inventing lies simply because she viewed you as a threat."

"Hardly a threat! Indeed, whenever she or Aunt Esme were about, I went to great lengths to exhibit a remarkable lack of interest in you! Besides, one could easily deem your behavior with her encouraging."

"Trista, I can assure you, my reasons for associating with her had little to do with any depth of feeling, regardless of her more obvious assets."

Trista frowned at him. "You make it sound as if you were using her—"

"Shh..." His voice dropped to a murmur as he pressed a finger to her lips. "Why speak of the woman when her attributes are few and pale in comparison to those of the maid before me—the sleek long limbs, this silky chestnut hair ablaze with golden fire, and skin as soft as thistle-down." His hands cupped her face, his fingers about her neck, his thumbs brushing her jawline. "In her wildest dreams, no maid in the whole of Europe could ever hope to embody so completely everything I desire in a wife."

Trista's unsteady gaze lifted to settle upon the skin at the base of his throat, left exposed by the open neck of his shirt. Despite the fierce intensity of his manner, she was suddenly struck by the vulnerability of his bare throat. The desire to press her lips to that warm skin suddenly became over-whelming, and a trembling began deep within her. Swal-lowing past a parched throat, she heard only the blood pounding in her ears as her eyes swept up to find his gaze focused on her mouth. Her eyelids fluttered and her lips parted of their own accord as his mouth descended gently upon hers. His lips moved slowly, tasting, lingering like dew upon a flower, and Trista's world spun crazily. Molten heat spread through her as he teased her with his sweet kiss, plucking at her desires, awakening in her a yearning to cast aside all her fears and become his.

His hands at her shoulders pressed her closer for a mo-ment, then he lifted his head to stare with passion-filled eyes into her very soul. "Your kiss is warm and sweet, wife, and arouses in me that from which you should flee this very moment." His voice was a husky whisper as he eased her from him, and Trista's breath was released in a soft sigh. He drew a deep breath, his hands rubbing against her shoul-ders. "While you were visiting with your aunt, I received word from a business associate that my presence is required at a meeting. The location is a good day's ride, and I must leave today."

Trista fought the sinking feeling in her belly. "When shall I expect your return?"

"A week, maybe ten days hence. 'Twas rather unex-pected, but the gentlemen with whom I'm meeting desire to make a rather substantial investment in Brennan Shipping, and I've an entire shipment of goods to oversee. It's imper-ative that I be there."

"Of course," Trista murmured, willing the disappointment from her voice. "It will be rather lonely here."

His arms drew her close against him. "Just keep yourself out of trouble and off Nero's back." At her look of complete innocence, he raised a brow. "If you wish to go anywhere, summon Fritz."

Trista nodded and mumbled a reply, more than a trifle unsettled that his impending journey should leave her with such a hollow feeling. Perhaps his charming manner of late called forth these feelings, though, as it turned out, she found herself missing far more than simple companionship.

She did, however, find a myriad of activities with which to occupy her time. Indeed, she awakened very early each morning to ride Gypsy about the grounds, as she felt in need of physical activity, and the weather allowed it. She lingered several times at the pond to bathe in the sun, though she did not venture again into the water. Midmorning found her with Polly in the kitchen, either to assist or simply to perch on a nearby stool and chatter idly while peeling fruit or vegetables. The piano captured her fancy for an hour or two each day, as did Nicholas's extensive library, which kept her awake into the wee hours of the morning. She ventured to the stable to visit with Peter and Nero and also ventured about the house. One afternoon found her gazing with a burning curiosity at the closed set of double doors directly across the balcony overlooking the front entry, just across from her own room. She hesitated but a moment before peering for the first time into her husband's chambers.

Stepping into the massive room, she grew instantly aware of the clean smell of *him* mixed with that of richly polished mahogany. The mere smell of him sent her senses reeling for a moment and she paused, allowing her eyes to slowly sweep the room. The walls were of a deep mahogany, as were the double set of large armoires between three tall windows draped with creamy velvet. The late afternoon sun spilled into the room, casting rectangular shapes across the thick carpets and polished planking floor. The room was sparsely furnished, with a small table and several large chairs upholstered in the same creamy velvet as the draperies, which also adorned the four thick posts of the massive bed. Trista's heart skipped a beat as she gazed upon the crisp white sheets upon which her husband found sleep every night. Before she realized, her hand lay upon his pillow, and when she pressed it to her face, tears stung her eyes.

She held the pillow to her breast as she turned from the bed, her fingers trailing lightly over a table laden with his toiletries, an ache looming in her throat. Dear God, but she had no idea she missed him so!

Just as she spun about to flee the room and the myriad emotions, her eye fell upon a mussed pile of papers lying atop a small desk near the corner. A sudden curiosity about his business dealings prompted her toward the desk. At first she peered hesitantly at the pages of scribble and scrawl, then, after a moment, began to shuffle the papers about. Her eyes scanned the parchment, noting her husband's bold scrawl on several of the pages. She stared at his signature for a moment. To her eye, the sure sweeping strokes spoke volumes of the man.

With a smile, she swept the page aside, then started. At the top of the page beneath was the name Sleeth, underlined several times. Below there were notes on places and dates, of which she could determine nothing. Then farther down the page was the word *blackmail*. Frowning thoughtfully, she placed the page aside and was about to scan the next one, when Polly's voice calling her from below brought a frightened yelp to her lips. With great care, she swept the papers together as she'd found them, replaced the pillow upon the bed and, with one last quick glance about, treaded silently from the room.

Chapter Thirteen

Beneath an enormous yellow moon arcing a path across a cloudless sky, the coach slowed to a stop before the manor. The stillness of the warm night air was broken by the sounds of the horses shuffling their hooves and wheezing from their exertion. Before the footman could attend to the task, the coach door burst open and Nicholas alighted. He muttered to his coachman, then scowled at the moon, well into its nightly journey. With a weary sigh, he mounted the stone steps and strode toward the opened portal, where Fritz stood rather sleepily.

"Good evening, my good man. 'Twas not necessary to wait up for me, you know," Nicholas muttered as he stepped into the dimly lit foyer and swept his topcoat from his back.

Rubbing his bleary eyes, Fritz grumbled, "You know very well if it were up to me, my head would have been long upon a soft pillow by now. 'Tis a ghastly hour to be up and about. Though it was the lady of the house that kept me from sleep."

Nicholas paused in his scanning of various correspondence, left for his leisure upon a table nearby. "Indeed. And what was she up to?"

"She was rather determined to await your return in the parlor these three nights past. As has been her wont, she failed to keep her eyes opened past ten o'clock, so I thought it best to stoke the fire lest she catch a chill."

"That was thoughtful of you, Fritz. I'm certain she would appreciate your devotion. I take it she's still in the parlor?" At Fritz's nod, Nicholas said, "I'll see to her. Thank you."

"Very well," Fritz grumbled as he turned to amble off to bed. "I trust your meeting was successful."

"Remarkably so," Nicholas replied in a distracted manner as he dropped his coat into a chair and peered at the half-closed parlor doors. "Worth every mile traveled." Moving toward the parlor, he muttered over his shoulder, "Have a good night, Fritz."

The older man's reply was lost on Nicholas as he gently pushed the doors open and stepped inside the room. Immediately his eye was drawn to the figure curled upon the settee facing him, and his breath caught in his throat at the sight.

The pink silk robe shimmered like a lustrous pearl in the soft firelight, serving only to emphasize the smooth tawny skin of the one nestled within its folds. With one arm tucked beneath her head, she lay upon her side, her legs drawn up, trapping the robe beneath slender thighs. As he stepped nearer, Nicholas's gaze lingered for a long moment on the smooth curve of her hip enticingly displayed by the silken fabric. With a leisure borne of too many days spent away from her, his eyes caressed the gentle sweep of curved legs, over the sash knotted at her waist to the neckline draped primly around her throat. One stray lock tumbled over her shoulder to rest coyly against the smooth silk folds that hid her bodice from his seeking gaze. A flame ignited deep within him as he stared at her lips, parted with her slow, even breathing. The fire bathed her skin with a rosy blush and shadowed the long sweeping lashes resting upon her cheeks. She indeed slept peacefully.

As if caught in a wondrous spell, Nicholas moved forward and lowered himself beside her. Hesitantly, he raised his hand to rub the lock between his fingers, marveling at the streaks of molten gold curling softly within his grasp. Slowly, he pressed the lock to his lips, inhaling the lilac fragrance. A fierce desire flooded over him, nearly driving him to tear that blasted robe from her sweet body and make her his. His breath caught in his chest as he leaned closer until he could hear her soft breathing. Her warmth enveloped him, all but driving him insane with the promise of her unbridled passions. With the blood pounding in his ears, he raised a shaking hand to the fold of her robe, only to pause when he detected a slight movement out of the corner of his eye.

Curled beside the hearth, in what had become his favorite spot, was Bo, eyeing his master rather suspiciously. Nicholas scowled at the animal. Bo merely pricked his ears and uttered a soft "humph!" in greeting. Beneath Nicholas's fierce perusal, Bo barely flinched; indeed, he all but ignored every attempt to show him the door and lowered his muzzle to rest upon his front paws. He heaved what could only be called a weary sigh, then settled himself comfortably and peered casually from beneath raised eyebrows.

Gritting his teeth in frustration, Nicholas cast his sleeping wife a longing glance, then scowled upon his silent tormentor once more. "Have you no compassion for a tortured soul, my friend?" he muttered under his breath. "Or are you so damned loyal that you seek to protect her from me even as she sleeps? I suppose I'll soon receive a lesson on the merits of employing charm versus muscle when training a damned dog." With a sudden thought, he whispered hoarsely, "Boy, outside! Outside! And if you're good and you stay out there for an hour or so, you'll receive a bloody treat!" Rising agilely to his feet, he patted the side of his leg and moved quickly to the door, with a prancing Bo at his side.

He returned alone to the parlor, wearing a self-satisfied grin, and silently seated himself at a safe distance upon the settee opposite Trista. He feasted upon her for a moment, then his eye fell to the book lying upon the table before him. He leaned forward to see what author had captured her fancy for the night, but he froze when she stirred upon the settee. With a soft sigh, she snuggled against the plush cushions and turned, lifting her arm over her head. Beneath Nicholas's passionate gaze, the silken robe parted to reveal the fullness of her breasts pressing against the thin white batiste of her nightgown. The smooth skin swelled over the low scooped neckline, drawing Nicholas none too reluctantly from his chair.

Almost reverently, he gazed upon her, noting the determined tilt to her chin, even in repose, before his eyes swept lower to her exposed bodice. With a groan, he lowered his lips to brush softly over those high curves, breathing deeply of the fragrant warmth of her skin. His senses reeled as his mouth traced over her collarbone and along the slender column of her neck. She moaned softly in her sleep and his heart leapt when he felt her fingers in his hair, drawing him closer. He paused until the sound of her even breathing assured him she still slept, then pressed his lips to the hollow at the base of her throat. As soft as a whisper, his hand moved to cup her breast and his mouth brushed along her jaw, then gently caressed her parted lips. He tasted of her sweet breath, then spread kisses across her nose and over her cheeks. She stirred again, arching her back in her sleep, her hand sliding along his back.

"Nicholas..."

Blood thundered in his ears and his touch grew bold. With ease, he swept the robe aside and caressed her belly through the thin fabric, then ventured lower still to draw the gown up over her thighs. Murmuring softly, he lowered his mouth to tease the pale pink nipples taunting him through the sheer fabric as his hand brushed over the smooth skin of her thighs. The softest of sighs escaped from her parted lips and her legs fell open at his touch. Nicholas nearly lost control. His fingers delved and found what he sought, so warm, beckoning with a sweet promise, and he moaned with pleasure. "Trista...my love..."

An insistent scratching at the front door, accompanied by a persistent whining, which perched precariously on the brink of a full-fledged bark, drew Nicholas's attention. Raising his eyes heavenward, he nearly roared with a frustration he'd never known possible. His movement caused Trista to stir and mumble incoherently in her sleep, then turn again on her side and draw the robe about her. Clenching his jaw so fiercely it hurt, Nicholas stared at her, feeling his

passion replaced by a sudden overwhelming and entirely il-
logical desire to kill his mangy animal.

"Damned nuisance," he growled, hastening to bade the
dog to enter. With a yelp, Bo bounded through the portal,
right past his stern-faced master and into the parlor, where
Nicholas found him eagerly greeting his mistress with a few
well-placed licks upon her nose. To Nicholas's chagrin,
Trista's eyes fluttered open and her nose wrinkled as she
turned her head to avoid Bo's hearty greeting.

"Bo...darling...please..." she murmured sleepily, then
laughed softly when Bo settled himself before her. Rubbing
her eyes, she stifled a yawn, then started as her sleepy gaze
fell upon her husband standing just inside the room. Instinctively, one hand reached to draw her robe about her as
she sat upright and smoothed her hair from her face.
"Nicholas...you're home."

Though he purposefully kept his distance from her, his
eyes swept over her flushed features for any hint that she had
been aware of the intimacy they'd shared not moments before. "Indeed. 'Tis good to be back."

Stifling another yawn, Trista rose shakily to her feet. "I
trust your trip was a success."

"Aye." His unflinching gaze followed her movements as
she carelessly knotted the sash at her waist, then bent to rub
Bo's head.

"You're pleased?" she asked softly, rubbing her hands
over her upper arms.

"Very."

She attempted to stifle another yawn behind her hand.
"I'm terribly sorry, Nicholas, but I'm so dreadfully tired.
Could we talk of your trip on the morrow? 'Tis not for lack
of interest, you know."

"I know."

With a feeling of utter helplessness, he allowed her to
brush past him, then, like his obedient canine, followed her
from the room. His gaze lingered on the silk robe billowing
about her as she slowly climbed the stairs before him. At the
top of the stairs, she turned to him and laid a hand gently

upon his chest. The gesture seemed entirely guileless, but Nicholas nearly jumped from his skin in anticipation.

" 'Tis so good to have you home," she murmured sleepily, then rising on her toes, she leaned forward and brushed her lips over the day's growth of beard on his cheek. Her voice murmured softly in his ear. "I missed you. Good night...." Before his arms could wrap fiercely about her, she turned in a sweep of pink silk and made her way to her chamber. Pausing at the doors, she glanced wearily at Bo standing expectantly at her side, then lifted a twinkling gaze to Nicholas. With a smile, she pushed the doors open and allowed the dog to precede her happily into the room.

For some time, Nicholas stared at the closed doors, pondering his state of complete befuddlement with his wife. It seemed uncanny that a man capable of managing a hugely successful shipping business should be rendered incapable of a single coherent thought while in the presence of his wife. Indeed, one could easily surmise from his actions that he was completely enamored of the beautiful Trista.

Another thought occurred to him sometime later as he studied a smoldering fire in his darkened room, cradling a snifter of brandy, reluctant to confront the coldness of his bed. What prevented him from entering his wife's chamber that very moment, taking that which he longed for day after day and deep into the night, every night, his desires so fierce he nearly screamed aloud with frustration?

The amber liquid swirled about in the glass he lifted to his lips to drain with one long gulp. He set the glass down none too gently upon the table before him. His eyes fell from the fire to his torso, revealed by his half-parted shirt, and almost unconsciously his hand rubbed against his chest and corded belly, as if to test the firmness of the muscles beneath the bronzed skin. He snorted in disgust and closed his eyes upon the fire.

" 'Tis not a physical flaw that keeps her from you," he muttered half-aloud. "If only it were that simple to remedy."

A sputtering from the fire drew his attention and his eyes narrowed upon the gentle flames. Time. She no doubt required *more* of it while he felt perched on the brink of insanity because of it. He had never been a patient man, though circumstances of late had all but forced it upon him. Indeed, all he seemed capable of doing lately was wait...for Maurice to lay the bait, for Sleeth to bite, for one more roll of the dice in his favor so that this sham of a transaction could take place and he could finally see his plan to an end. Blast it, but it all seemed suddenly beyond his control.

And then there was the matter of his wife. All the charm he had employed, every sweet word and action born of love, and here he sat, *alone,* while she sought dreams as an escape from her cruel fate. Perhaps it was his realization of this that prevented him from seeking her warmth in the dead of night, finding his solace with her beneath a haunting yellow moon that slid silently across the planking floor. How he longed to ease the bitter grip revenge had upon him, to bury himself within her warmth, to tell her that he needed her, that he longed to tell her everything but couldn't solely because he wished to protect her.

If only revenge weren't such an unforgiving mistress.

Thus, he listened to the stillness creeping about him with a mounting frustration that threatened to sweep aside the last threads of his patience, and with that most warm and comforting and near at hand: a bottle of brandy.

The first dusky pink rays of sunlight peeking over the horizon bathed Gypsy's coat a fiery red and brought a promise of warmth to the brisk morning air. The mare snorted, eager to be off from atop the grassy knoll, despite the strenuous pace of the ride thus far. Her mistress, however, was of a different mind altogether and settled in her saddle to enjoy the day's awakening.

After a time, she swung Gypsy's head about and guided the mare toward the manor. She kept the reins tight and felt anxiety gnaw in the pit of her belly at the thought of encountering her husband, the very man who had haunted her dreams all through the night.

She was more than certain he'd detected her discomfort in the parlor last eve after she'd awakened with the flush of her passion staining her cheeks. And *such* passion for a dream— It was as if his hands had been upon her, his breath soft against her face, his voice murmuring, "My love..."

She groaned half-aloud, drawing a grunt and a snort from Gypsy. Indeed, the dreams hung suspended in the foggy recesses between her fantasy and reality. For one brief moment, she'd felt his presence beside her as she'd slept, then a filmy mist had descended over her, drawing her effortlessly into her dream. She'd opened her eyes and he'd loomed in the darkness, his naked body a sculpted shadow. She'd slipped again into darkness, then her lips parted beneath a whisper of a kiss that tasted of warm, sweet brandy. Wraithlike fingers of warmth had swept her gown aside and tenderly caressed her skin, drawing her into the depths of passion. With languid movements, her arms clung to the vision of her husband close above her, drawing him nearer until the molten heat bubbled forth from within her. The warmth had suddenly ignited and flamed over her skin, lifting her higher...and higher still, until a thousand brilliant stars blazed within her and she tumbled into the recesses of her dream once again.

"You're certainly about rather early this morning, Trista."

The deep voice snatched her from her musings with a start and brought the color high in her cheeks. Her breath caught in her throat as she found Nicholas standing close beside her. His satisfied grin nearly proved to unseat her, and his manner did little to assure her that her dreams were not in fact reality. Dressed in an immaculate black topcoat and trousers, with matching cravat at the starched collar, he presented a fiendishly handsome demeanor that sent her blood racing through her veins. She clutched at the reins to still her hands.

His eyes were all over her. "Would you care to dismount?"

With a shrug, she looped the reins over Gypsy's neck, then leaned forward to swing her leg across the mare's back. Her breath caught when Nicholas's hands slipped about her waist to lift her clear of the saddle. Her flailing arms finally stilled about his neck as he lowered her with painstaking care to the ground, the entire length of him pressing unabashedly against her.

His look was one of such innocence that Trista found herself wondering if perhaps she had imagined his intent. As her feet touched ground, however, his hands lingered at her waist and a twinkling began in the depths of his eyes.

"Your rather late return last evening has not kept you from an early rising," Trista managed, easing from him.

"Indeed. I have an urgent meeting this morning. I know not when I shall return."

"I see," she replied, feeling the old familiar irritation blossoming to life within her. "Is this work of the same nature as that of your trip?"

Nicholas gave her an odd look. "This morning, yes. However, the business this afternoon is of a more personal nature."

"Such as?"

"My, we're rather inquisitive today."

"Indeed, *we're* rather tired of being kept uninformed of *our* husband's so-called business."

Nicholas folded his arms over his chest. "So-called business, Trista?"

She pursed her lips. "Business, gambling, call it what you will. I sincerely hope you refrain from squandering your time and your fortune at some gaming table, Nicholas. Indeed, Kendall mentioned to me some time ago that Dominic had lost no small amount to you."

"Ah, your ever-so-reliable source."

Trista scowled at him. "I swear, Nicholas, if you are in any way involved in Dominic's financial ruin, in the virtual destruction of my aunt's life..."

Nicholas gave a hollow laugh. "If your dear uncle has found himself in such dire straits, 'tis not solely on account of my good fortune. Admittedly, he has lost a goodly sum at my table, but I assure you, the man's lack of skill has not proven a deterrent. Surely you didn't think me capable of winning the man's entire fortune." His eyes twinkled devilishly. "Even *I'm* not that good, love."

Trista glared at him. "How very cavalier of you, Nicholas, to admit it. Aunt Esme would indeed be pleasantly surprised at this remarkable show of humility. After all, 'twas she who threatened me within an inch of my life each and every time you ogled me in an improper manner."

"One would think ogling in and of itself was improper."

"Indeed! And you are a master! Stalking about like some sleek panther, stealing kisses, turning my world upside down! What was I to do?"

"You married me, of course. I always knew you were an intelligent woman."

"I exhibited a rather marked lack of intelligence in that cellar with you."

"Whatever it was you exhibited, I wish you'd do more of it. You're not regretting it, by any chance?"

Biting her tongue, she flashed him a murderous look and abruptly turned to fiddle with Gypsy's saddle. The sudden pressure of his chest against her back brought a trembling to her limbs. Her legs all but dissolved when his hands slipped about her waist and his voice sounded close to her ear. "I'll never regret it, sweet wife, no matter how long you keep me at bay. I can assure you, Dominic Catalani will soon reap his just rewards."

Something in the self-assured tone of his voice brought the blood quickly to Trista's legs. She spun in his arms. "How certain of the man's doom you sound."

For an instant, his expression grew harsh and his eyes blazed into hers, then he lifted a hand to cup her face. "You must trust me, Trista."

"What the devil are you saying?" She pushed with mounting anger against him, but his arms held her pinioned. "Has this something to do with the death of your parents . . . the loss of your business? Damn you, you cannot keep this from me, Nicholas!"

"Trust me" was all he muttered before his mouth claimed hers in a fiery kiss that left her trembling with far more than rage. And then he turned and was gone, mounting Nero in one swift movement and shoving booted heels into the horse's sides.

Trista watched them for the briefest moment before she gave full vent to a resounding bellow of frustration. Then, without a moment's hesitation, she ran to the house, bursting through the front portal, where she skidded to an abrupt halt before Fritz's raised brows. With a pretty little smile, she clasped her hands behind her and ambled off down the hall toward the study, all but whistling a cheery tune, such was her desire to fool the man. When he disappeared from sight, her pace quickened until she reached Nicholas's study and as covertly as possible slipped inside.

To his desk she flew, her hands sweeping feverishly over the jumble of documents strewn about. She searched drawers, scanned the pile yet again, until she all but stumbled upon it, lying on the very edge of the table.

She knew not what she was looking for, of course, though this had to be it. It appeared to be some kind of legal document, dated April, 1797, and bearing two signatures. Though they were faint, Trista could make out Trent as one signature and Oswald Sleeth as the other. From what she could discern, the agreement was for a rather large and expensive shipment of goods to be purchased by Trent Shipping from Sleeth for transport to the colonies. She glanced up from the parchment to stare blankly out the window. So, this Oswald Sleeth fellow and no doubt his relative, whom she knew rather well, were somehow involved with the Trent family business. And Nicholas. Perhaps in his scheme of revenge. And what of this blackmail? With a thoughtful frown, she lifted the parchment to study the page beneath. A lump of cold dread formed in the pit of her belly as she scanned what appeared to be an itinerary of sorts and several columns of numbers, amounting to a hefty sum. At the top of the page was written "Catalani."

Dear God, Nicholas *was* the cause of Dominic's gambling debts! What an enormous sum to win from a man over a table! Poor Esme! Had Nicholas no honor?

With a racing heart, she stared unseeing at the columns of dates beside each number, until it occurred to her that the dates were nearly consecutive. With a frown, she swept the pile of papers together as she'd found them. Before she turned to leave, her eye fell on the top page. In the upper corner, traced a number of times, was "Trista."

"Stubborn man!" she huffed to the silence filling her room. She hastily smoothed her jade traveling suit into place and bent to the mirror, poking and tucking at her hair, then grimacing at the result. "Off he goes once again to conduct his business, whatever it may be, thinking that I shall await him like some docile and ever-so-obedient little wife! Ha! Arrogant man! How well I know his activities are far from the usual realm." She stalked about the room in search of her blasted reticule, muttering to herself. "What are you up to, Nicholas? So adept are you at playing the gallant husband, plying me with your charismatic charm, such that I'm left painfully and quite contentedly unaware. Ah, but you are a master. How easily I play into your hands. And who could possibly resist! Methinks the gentlemen with whom you conduct your affairs stand little chance of besting you. But what is your game, my cunning husband? Ah, here it is...."

Plucking the reticule from beneath a tangle of silk stockings, she flung her gaze about in search of her plumed hat. "No, I must be as sly a fox as he, even more so. If he won't tell me what I wish to know, I'll find out for myself." She allowed herself a very self-satisfied little smile. "Your only mistake thus far, dearest husband, was to underestimate the curiosity and resourcefulness of your wife."

At long last, she managed to locate both her hat and her gloves and summoned the coach, claiming to be in desperate need of a shopping sojourn. Once on her way, she gazed at the passing countryside and mused on her rather rebellious mood of late. Perhaps being told what to do one too many times had brought this on. First she'd had to play by Society's rules, and now Nicholas was demanding she play by his. No more! She would do as she pleased and Nicholas could stomp about in fury until he was blue in the face. To her manner of thinking, it would be the only occasion heretofore where such behavior was warranted.

A short time after the coach reached the city's limits, Trista bade the coachman deliver her to White's, then settled upon her seat, purposefully ignoring his wary look. When the vehicle slowed to a stop sometime later, she peered from her window, past the bustling city streets, in search of the establishment that had become her staunch nemesis.

She was struck by the rather unimposing nature of the building itself and realized she had expected some gaudy, ornate facade that literally screamed of the iniquities conducted within its four walls. Indeed, the elegant structure with its lovely bay windows would lead one to believe White's was a respectable business establishment, if not an exclusively posh club catering to the very rich and elite. Certainly not a place where a man could squander an entire fortune with a scantily clad courtesan on either arm.

Trista remained thoughtfully gazing at the entrance to the club for some time, carefully observing the many patrons arriving and the scant few departing, until a flash of color farther down the street drew her attention. Her heart skipped a beat as she recognized the pale blue, silk-clad figure of Clothilde St. John, the beautiful courtesan, sashaying along on the arm of some tall escort. An enormous plumed hat perched coyly atop her auburn ringlets hid from view the face of her escort. As the couple reached White's entrance, however, she paused to allow her gallant gentleman to open the door for her. As Trista's eye fell for the first time upon this gentleman, she felt the blood drain from her face and her heart lodge in her throat. Nicholas!

Chapter Fourteen

"I say, Brennan, 'tis a trifle surprising to find *you* here," Archibald Sleeth snorted, peering over his cards at the tall man looming beside the gaming table. "Indeed, even more so at this time of day. Your conspicuous absence of late would lead me to believe that your luck has changed remarkably for the worse since you wed, eh?" The beady eyes slid from Brennan to the voluptuous form of Clothilde St. John ascending the nearby stairs. His tongue lapped at the spittle collecting in the corners of his slackened lips as he strained to keep the pale blue confection within sight. "Or perhaps 'tis the company you keep apart from the marriage bed that consumes all that beastly Yankee energy."

Nicholas leveled a steely gaze upon the repulsive man whose massive girth rendered useless any corset designed to contain him within his clothing. Indeed, with every wheezing breath he drew, he appeared on the verge of popping from his orange topcoat. With a cool smile that never quite reached his hooded eyes, Nicholas drawled, "To the contrary, my wife has brought me nothing *but* luck, for business has never been better. As for the company I keep, I would wager you'd agree that any man with half his senses would face the hangman's noose before straying from the woman I consider myself blessed to call wife." Cocking his head, he lifted a sardonic brow. "Methinks, however, that you, Sleeth, appear in dire need of some remedy to restore what little prowess you once wielded with the fairer sex. Or perhaps 'tis simply your lack of a good scrubbing that women find offensive. In any event, I had thought to linger here but a moment, but your game, if not your disposition, looks as if it could use some life. Gentlemen, may I?''

Without hesitation, Nicholas seated himself at the table and loosened his topcoat, eliciting a furious ''Humph!'' from a nearly apoplectic Sleeth. Drawing a thin cigar from his coat, Nicholas struck a match and smiled wickedly at Dominic, who was seated at Sleeth's side.

The Count shot Nicholas a black look and reached a shaky hand to gulp from his ever-present glass. "Your presence is not appreciated, Brennan.''

Nicholas grinned devilishly. "Your luck has seen better days, I take it? You needn't fret overmuch, Catalani. I will do all that I can to go easy on you today, though just this once you must try your best to do your part, as well." Ignoring the Count's blustery reply, Nicholas swung his gaze to the white-haired gentleman seated opposite, very much aware that the familiar twinkle of mirth in the depths of the green eyes was meant solely for him. "Monsieur Maurice, a pleasure, once again. It's been quite some time since we shared a table. Indeed, I've recently taken myself a bride and find, much to my pleasure, that my penchant for cards has been replaced by more ... *constructive* pastimes."

A smile tugged at the corners of the wrinkled mouth as the white-haired gentleman nodded cordially at Nicholas. "Brennan. My congratulations and best wishes, though judging by your manner, one would conclude that marriage sits rather well with you. 'Tis awfully refreshing, I must admit." Heaving a sigh, the elderly man shifted in his chair and raised a troubled brow as he eyed his cards with disdain. "Have a care for me, as well, Brennan, for Lady Luck has not found favor with me for some time. 'Tis a trifle disconcerting with business as sluggish as it has been of late. Thank heavens I saw fit to retain a goodly sum against the advent of such troubled times."

The old man hesitated a moment, as if lost in thought, though Nicholas's keen eye observed that the feigned preoccupation lasted only until Sleeth's beady eyes fastened with a decided intent upon the older gentleman.

Reel him in slowly, Maurice, Nicholas muttered to himself, then swung his gaze upon Dominic, who appeared rather hopelessly lost within his cards and frightfully unaware of his cohort's intent. Based upon his experience with the man, Nicholas had to wonder if his preoccupation was a carefully orchestrated ruse, as well, or, as was far more likely, simply further proof of the man's stupidity. The old man's voice snatched Nicholas's attention once more.

"'Twould seem, Brennan, that several of my choicest purveyors have found doing business with Brennan Shipping equally, if not more lucrative than with my small company, much to my dismay. Your familiarity and good standing with your business compatriots in the States has served you well, for they are indeed a prosperous lot, willing to pay far more for English goods than I can achieve."

"Yankee scum they are, nothing more," Dominic muttered, raising his empty glass to his lips. With a scowl, he slammed the glass upon the table and gritted his teeth in abject frustration, his glittering black eyes fixing upon Nicholas. "Good for nothing curs stealing from the pocket of every Englishman."

Nicholas relaxed into his chair, though the tic in his cheek and the ferocity of his gaze were adequate tribute to the ire Catalani's words evoked. He was, however, far too disciplined a man to allow his anger to get the better of him. Indeed, his determination to see his plan to fruition rendered his anger but a fleeting irritant.

"On the contrary, Count," Maurice remarked, looking Catalani square in the eyes. "'Tis the hardworking Englishman that benefits. The ability of those 'Yankee scum' to pay more for the goods enables a merchant like myself to acquire the goods initially at a much higher price from the English supplier. And I would be eager to do so, knowing full well that a ready market awaits me in the States."

Nicholas's dark brows rose. "If 'tis a ready market you seek, my good man, perhaps I could acquaint you with several of my business contacts in the States. I feel compelled to remind you, however, that hard work, a bit of luck and the shrewdest of business minds achieved the prosperity they now enjoy. In short, fairness in price is essential.''

"I would expect nothing less," Maurice replied, nodding his thanks to the younger man. "Very well. I need only locate someone with the goods to sell." A wizened brow lifted in Nicholas's direction. "I take it your generosity does not extend so far as to steer a few of those suppliers my way, eh, Brennan?"

"Uh...that may not be necessary," Sleeth interjected, nearly leaning out of his chair with anticipation. Beads of perspiration dotted his protruding upper lip and he licked at them feverishly.

"Indeed?" Maurice bestowed a stiff smile upon the loathsome man.

"I know of a gentleman in need of a merchant to transport his goods. Indeed, he has hesitated in retaining the services of the larger shipping companies—" the puffy lips twisted into what could only be described as a sneer and the beady eyes slid for a moment to Nicholas "—like our Yankee friend Brennan's company, for fear of an unfair price. I can hardly say I blame the man."

Nicholas bestowed upon Sleeth a disparaging sweep of steel blue eyes and directed his remark to Maurice. "My first inclination would be to wonder in what ghastly hovel Sleeth stumbled upon this 'gentleman.' His mere mention of the word 'gentleman' would lead me to seriously doubt the man's credibility, if not wonder at the underhanded means by which he no doubt achieved these 'goods.'"

A wave of the older man's hand in Nicholas's direction snapped Sleeth's sagging jaw shut and brought a self-satisfied smirk to the mottled face. Maurice laid his cards facedown upon the table and peered curiously at Sleeth. "Regardless of Brennan's misgivings, I'm rather interested in the nature of the goods and the sum your gentleman had in mind. When may I have occasion to meet the fellow?"

"Oh, in good time, rest assured," Sleeth hastened to reply, nearly rubbing his hands together with glee. "'Tis a goodly sum he requires, though one that I'm sure you will gladly pay, knowing the profits you will reap upon resale in the States.'' With a sidelong glance at Dominic, who stared morosely into his glass, Sleeth pasted on a smile and turned once again to Maurice. ''The man has retained me as his adviser....''

''Aha! And there you have it!'' Nicholas shook his head with disgust. ''Need you any further proof this 'gentleman' is nothing but an addlepated dolt!'' With a snort, he slid his chair from the table. ''Your conversation has rendered me in dire need of a stiff drink. If you will excuse me, *gentlemen*.''

Sleeth's eyes narrowed upon the departing broad-shouldered figure. ''Brennan is no doubt *the* most arrogant, cocksure bastard I have ever had the misfortune to encounter.''

''Indeed...'' the older gentleman mused as he swung his gaze from Brennan, knowing full well those same broad shoulders hid a lopsided grin from view. Pausing to sip from his glass, he started abruptly, recovering his composure before either Sleeth or the Count took notice. His eyes narrowed upon the jade-clad female form perched hesitantly just inside the double doors to the gaming room. She looked so much like her mother had at that age it was almost eerie, and Maurice found himself staring dumbly at her for a moment. She glanced about nervously, her gaze darting so fleetingly past their table it was difficult to discern if she'd noticed his two companions. Then, displaying a surprising fearlessness, she followed an elegantly attired, heavily painted courtesan up the flight of stairs nearby.

Feeling the blood thumping through his veins, Maurice forced himself to sip casually from his drink, though the gaze that lingered once more after Brennan was full of anxiety. Drawing a deep, steadying breath, he fixed a half smile upon his face and turned once again to Sleeth, with a growing sense of unease that their best-laid plans were on the verge of running amok.

''Clothilde St. John?''

Trista's voice rang through the dimly lit salon, drawing several daintily arched brows from the scattering of elegantly attired women lounging about on plush velvet chaises. The auburn-haired woman lifted dazzling blue eyes to Trista, and a soft, secretive half smile, for which she had become notorious, parted her rouged lips.

"And who may you be, darling?" Clothilde's voice was as deep and husky as she was dainty and petite, and for a fleeting moment, despite her anger, Trista felt frightfully naive and coltish, completely intimidated by the woman's sophisticated and highly polished veneer.

As she gazed upon this stunning creature, Trista reminded herself that she had determined to confront her rival and fight for her husband, if need be. Though she could scarcely blame him, or any man for that matter, for Clothilde was exquisite, petite yet voluptuous, with an innocence despite her seasoned experience. "Trista Brennan is my name. Perhaps if we could speak privately..."

Clothilde stared at her for a moment. Rising gracefully to her feet, she murmured to he woman beside her, then floated past Trista in a cloud of heady perfume.

With her eyes fixed upon Clothilde's tiniest of waists and the cascade of artful ringlets tumbling down her slender back, Trista followed in her perfumed wake, thinking that clawing the woman's eyes from her head would prove far more satisfying at the moment than any civilized conversation. Crushing her reticule in trembling hands, she drew a breath to still the anger quaking in the pit of her belly. She'd come to confront her husband, to seek the truth from him, to force the issue if need be. Yet in the face of his possible betrayal with this—this—*feline,* all Trista could envision was life without him. Her heart wrenched with unspoken grief. He might be an arrogant cad, a stubborn, headstrong beast of a man, but God help her, she wanted him all to herself.

She followed Clothilde down a narrow hall, her assessing eyes searching for some flaw, some hideous growth sprouting from the woman's saucy hips, or perhaps a limp from those perfectly tiny feet swishing beneath the satin of her skirts.

'Tis my awful bearing of late that has driven Nicholas from me, Trista lamented to herself.

Through the dim hallway they proceeded and into a small parlor, richly and tastefully decorated in cream velvet.

Dear God, how beautiful she is. How could I ever hope to keep a man like Nicholas true to his vows when temptations such as she abound. Grinding her teeth in frustration, she perched self-consciously upon a deep overstuffed chair, only too aware that Clothilde all but melted into the velvet folds of the chair directly opposite.

Such a fool she was, to marry a man desired by so many. Perhaps he found his wit challenged far more by this creature...perhaps his beautiful eyes twinkled with mirth whenever she was about...perhaps her kisses stirred his passions far more than those of his cold-blooded wife, whose foolhardy attempt to keep herself from confronting her growing feelings for him served only to thrust him into the arms of another.... She almost sobbed aloud. *How I love him!*

At this sudden dawning realization, Trista's heart leapt—indeed, it fairly soared—and a soft smile parted her lips. *I love him! I love him?*

"Mistress Brennan? Are you quite all right?"

Trista started visibly as Clothilde's husky voice shattered her reverie, and for a moment she stared dumbly at the other woman. "No! I'm fine...really...." Growing uncomfortable beneath the woman's penetrating gaze, Trista lowered her eyes and sought to retrieve her anger from the depths of the boundless joy that filled her heart. After a moment, she drew a deep breath and lifted her eyes. "I have come to ask you to keep yourself from my husband."

If Clothilde was even remotely taken aback by Trista's bold statement, she succeeded in concealing it. Her lips parted in a soft smile that dissolved into a throaty laugh, which drew a perplexed frown from Trista and fiercely renewed anger.

"How dare you mock me!" Trista flared, rising to her feet. "'Tis not sufficient that you flaunt your sordid alliance with Nicholas for all of London to see! You must also make a mockery of me to my face!"

A delicate auburn brow arched as Clothilde remained comfortably within her seat. "Darling, I'm afraid you're a trifle muddled, for 'tis no sordid alliance."

"Is that so? I take it you're in love with him. And he with you, no doubt. Well, Miss St. John, you shan't snatch him from me without a fight, and a bloody good one I'll give you, at that, for I love him, as well! Though you may not think a country miss capable of it, I can swing my hips and thrust my bosom as provocatively as even you, which I intend to do, with fervor, I might add, until you are but a fading memory! Do I make myself understood?"

"Indeed." A soft smile teased the corners of the Cupid's bow that was Clothilde's mouth. "I feel compelled to point out, my dear, a decided fault in your logic, if I may. 'Tis not my wont to associate, at least beyond simple friendship, with any man, regardless of his many attractive qualities, when I am more than certain that he is very much in love with his wife. And may I say that I can certainly understand why."

Trista gaped openly at the other woman. "What did you say?"

"Your husband—whom I adore, by the way, for he is a rare find, in a husband as well as a friend—Nicholas loves you."

"Y-you're not . . . I mean, he's not . . . he does?"

"Darling, throughout the years, Nicholas and I have developed a special friendship, one which could never endure a love affair. Besides . . ." The crystal gaze grew wistful. "I never stood a chance once he met you. Oh, he never said as much, but he never had to. By the looks of it, I would say he hasn't even confided this to you." An auburn brow rose wickedly. "I can only imagine why."

Feeling rather dazed, Trista lowered herself to her chair once more. "I'm dreadfully sorry . . . I had little notion. And when I spied you together, 'twas my first thought that you were . . ."

Clothilde waved a perfectly manicured hand. "A reasonable conclusion for a woman to draw when she is hopelessly in love, though one can't help but wonder why you harbor such doubts about him. Unless, of course, he knows not of your feelings. Methinks perhaps 'twould be best if he did, eh? I would wager his devotion to you will become readily apparent...rather quickly." With a throaty laugh she mused, "I suppose we shan't see much of him then, and you much of anything but the ceiling above his bed, hmm?"

. Trista flushed. "I shall be sure to...enlighten him. I would appreciate, however, if you were to refrain from mentioning our little meeting to Nicholas."

"It will remain our secret. I must say, however, that I'm rather pleased to meet you at long last. You see, you're a rather notorious young woman, Trista Brennan, for you've captured London's most eligible bachelor. And I'm not speaking only of the ring upon your finger, for 'tis only a symbol, which can easily be rendered meaningless." With a wry laugh she remarked, "Infidelity is an everyday occurrence. No, you've stolen his heart, snatched it from beneath his nose, if I were to guess. How delicious! And the legions of women in London who so wish to be you!"

Trista grimaced. "Legions, indeed! Whatever will they all do without his unwavering attentions?"

"Ha! If only that were so, perhaps 'twould not be so heartbreaking." Clothilde shook her auburn ringlets and her gaze settled upon Trista's perplexed frown. "I am in earnest, my dear. 'Tis no swaggering brute you call husband. To be sure, 'tis his aloof manner, a certain bearing that proves forever irresistible despite his infuriating lack of interest. You see, no one had ever captured his fancy until you."

Trista stared at the other woman for a moment. "Surely he fancied a maiden or two here, for goodness' sake! Why, he all but made his home beneath this roof, from the tales I've heard."

"And tales they should remain," Clothilde advised. "Admittedly, he has spent a considerable amount of time here rather recently, though I'm quite certain his motives had little to do with squandering his fortune or acquiring a ladylove for the evening. A business matter, I believe, though he tells me little of *those* doings, and I do not see fit to niggle. You see, there was a time when Nicholas patron-ized our tables but once or twice a year, if that, for he was never a wagering man. And rest assured, many a comely wench awaited his return with eager anticipation. Hence, my suspicions were aroused, and *their* many prayers answered, when he began appearing with startling regularity, forever in the company of the Italian Count and that repulsive Mr. Sleeth.'' Clothilde shuddered delicately. ''Why Nicholas would share a table with that lecher is beyond me. And certainly another oddity, hmm?'' Leaning forward slightly, she spoke in a low, conspiratorial tone, though her blue eyes twinkled mischievously. 'I wonder if Nicholas is indeed aware of Mr. Sleeth's...how shall I put this...penchant for young boys.''

''What! I wouldn't know.'' Rising to her feet, Trista managed a smile. ''I'd best be going. Thank you.''

''Oh, you needn't thank me.'' The throaty laugh filled the small salon. ''Be gone to your loving husband, my dear, before I allow my jealousy to get the better of me, eh?''

Closing the door softly behind her, Trista glanced hesitantly down the deserted hallway and heaved a weary sigh. What to do? Of a sudden, confronting her husband no longer seemed the intelligent thing to do. Snooping about, however, if done with the appropriate discretion, just might serve to ease her concerns. Determinedly, she set out in what she hoped was the general direction of the stairs, only to realize the tall, broad-shouldered figure striding purposefully toward her down the narrow hallway was none other than her husband. The smile that parted her lips and brought a dazzle to her eyes faded with his every step as she grew increasingly aware of the undeniably murderous look leveled upon her. Unconsciously, her feet stilled beneath her as the blood pounded with deafening urgency in her ears and her mind flew for the proper words, some lame excuse. Ha! A bold lie was necessary and nothing less...though perhaps three simple words would do: *I love you*.

''What the hell do you think you're doing?'' Nicholas growled, roughly grasping her arm.

The reply caught in Trista's throat and she gazed with widening eyes into his, blazing with the ferocity of his unrestrained anger. Unceremoniously, he forced her down a side hallway and against the wall, then loomed close above her, his jaw clenched as tightly as the fist at his side.

Trista offered little resistance, though her ire stirred like a sleeping lioness within her and she attempted to jerk her arm free from the iron grasp. Winged brows swept together and her lips parted with an indignant gasp as his hold remained about her like a vise.

"Nicholas! My arm!"

"I'll give you your arm and more, you little fool." His hold upon her eased, though his foreboding tone and the glint in his eye held Trista pinioned to the wall. "What the hell are you doing here? And don't bother telling me you've suddenly developed a fancy for cards."

Pursing her lips, Trista groped for words, her rage mounting at his every word. "I just so happened to be passing by."

"Is that so? Another of your sojourns into the city for tea or shopping, is that it? I know you too well, wife, well enough at least to recognize an outright lie." His eyes glittered dangerously into hers and she suddenly realized how fierce a man he could be. "So helplessly naive and too spoiled for your own good. If, for just this once, you were the typical sort to be found lollygagging about couturiers' shops, I would be a happy man."

"Spoiled!" Trista exclaimed, instantly furious. "Why, you addlepated lout!"

"Spare me the childish name-calling, Trista."

"Ooh! I'll spare you nothing, you pigheaded, half-witted simpleton!" With all her might she shoved against his unresisting bulk and achieved only a frustration and a helplessness that knew no bounds. "Let me pass, you ninny! You're the fool, not I!"

"You're damn right I am," he growled, grasping her hands in his and leaning his weight upon her. "I should have had my head examined for taking a willful child for wife. Conjured up by Lucifer himself, you were, and I helplessly your victim right from the start." The chill in his eyes, the curl to his lip, belied the words he barely murmured. "The face of an angel, a body to torture any man and the myriad, fathomless workings of a spoiled child-woman's mind." His gaze lowered to her mouth and lingered long enough for Trista's pulse to begin an erratic thumping that had little to do with her anger.

In spite of herself, she reveled in his powerful length pressed against her. With an inward groan of pure helplessness, she felt her breasts swell against his chest and the liquid heat spread like wildfire through her limbs. Unconsciously her lids lowered and her lips parted, beckoning him from the depths of his rage.

With a growl, Nicholas thrust her from him, eliciting a gasp of shock from Trista.

His eyes narrowed fiercely upon her. "You may have rendered me at times a weak-kneed fop, witch goddess, a state that I abhor and will somehow control. However..." The steely eyes flashed a warning and the lips, which not moments before loomed so invitingly, now curled with a sardonic twist. "It will be a cold day in hell before you muddle my plans as efficiently as you have my brain. Heed me well, Trista, I do not take kindly to being spied upon by my own wife."

"'Twas all you left me!" Trista huffed in defense, her voice ringing clearly through the hallway. "You know me well, ha! I am no simpleminded wench content to sit idly by while her husband plots to see his revenge to fruition! If you insist upon treating me like a child incapable of fathoming your schemes, then indeed I shall take matters into my own hands!"

"To hell with trusting me, eh?"

"Trust? How can *you* speak so nobly of trust when 'tis the very thing you refuse to embrace? Your entire scheme shan't tumble about you if you confide in me, Nicholas. Besides, I'm beginning to believe this revenge of yours has done nothing but bring heartache and financial ruin upon my family."

"You know nothing of the matter."

"Indeed, I don't, and left to my own devices, I've come to wonder if perhaps I myself don't play some type of role in all this." Tears stung her eyes, and she paused but for one breath. "Tell me, Nicholas, are you perhaps using me as you've used Bianca, as some little doxy to keep at your convenience?"

White-hot anger leapt in his eyes and he loomed dangerously above her. "If 'tis indeed my intent, I'm doing a damned poor job of it. Rest assured, you have proven nothing but a distraction from the very start, in all truth a damned nuisance! This has nothing—do you hear me— nothing to do with you."

"Then why do you so relentlessly pursue Dominic if not to seek your revenge? 'Tis not for want of coin, of that I'm sure. And what of Sleeth and this blackmail scheme?" The telltale flame leaping in his eyes spurred Trista on without hesitation. "Oh, yes, I have an inkling of this, as well. What has that wretched man to do with all this? Are you perhaps in cahoots with him? Or perhaps that white-haired gentleman I spied at the table below? Surely as your wife I have a right to know!"

The tic in his jaw and the painful coldness in his voice were all Nicholas revealed of a frustration burning out of control. "'Tis a right that you must earn, wife. Until then, keep out of my affairs." With that, he turned on his heel and disappeared around the corner, leaving Trista stunned, openmouthed and desperately fighting the sudden tears welling like a gushing spring.

"Blasted arrogant man!" she choked, then, in spite of herself, gave full vent to her humiliation, her frustration and anger, and the tears streamed from her eyes. With a sniff, she searched within her reticule for a handkerchief, which only threatened to elicit another barrage of tears when her search proved futile.

"What good are these silly little bags." She sniffed again, drawing herself up and dabbing at her eyes with the lace trim of her cuff. "Of course, only a child would be found about with no handkerchief."

Drawing a deep breath, she touched a hand to her hair, then hastened down the hallway in search of a rear exit to avoid further confrontation with her husband. She needed to think, to regroup, to determine whether she could bear loving a man who harbored naught but scorn and contempt for her, a man as consumed by revenge as he most certainly was.

So engrossed was she within her troubled thoughts that she was entirely unaware of the bulky figure squeezed tightly into a space designed for nothing more than a broom or two. As she passed, the beady eyes gleamed with anticipation and the puffy lips curled into a sneer of a smile, despite the perspiration running in rivulets across his brow and down the bloated body. Prying himself free from his hiding place, he peered after her and nearly rubbed his hands together in glee. Then, with a wicked snort, he turned and ambled off in the opposite direction, his twisted mind mulling over all that he had overheard.

Chapter Fifteen

The booted heels dug fiercely into Nero's heaving sides, eliciting a reluctant snort and a toss of that black head before the mighty steed responded with a burst of speed. Sleek black legs swept over the narrow dirt road as if suspended just above the winding thoroughfare, the black-clad rider crouched low over the animal's steadily pumping neck. The wind whipped viciously at the ebony mane, serving as a constant reminder of the force behind the menacing black clouds threatening their wake. Of this the rider was grimly aware, and his softly spoken words pricked the animal's ears and urged him onward at an even faster clip.

Nicholas had scant desire to be caught in a rainstorm. He'd be damned if he'd allow anything further to threaten his sanity, though a good dousing from Mother Nature would certainly be in keeping with the events of the day. Grudgingly, he had to admit progress had been made, the stage set, the trap carefully laid to ensnare the man he sought. It was only a matter of time.

Time. His nemesis, indeed, for patience had never been a virtue to which he aspired, though the chaste and gracious husband he'd found himself playing of late would certainly cause one to wonder at his aspirations. His derisive snort pricked Nero's ears once again and the animal whinnied in reply. Absently, he murmured to the horse as the vision of his green-eyed wife loomed through the wind blurring his sight. The knot of frustration tightened low in his belly. Her foolhardy actions had nearly proven his undoing; indeed, one hastily spoken word from those softly parted lips could have rendered his best-laid plans grossly amok. Damn, if Maurice hadn't spied her lurking about...

That Maurice had never met Trista, yet had seemed to recognize her, caused Nicholas not a moment's pause, so entirely relieved was he. Then again, he was wont to allow his thoughts to stray to that moment in the hallway when he'd nearly swept her soft tempting body into his arms and kissed her sweet mouth. If she'd but lifted a hand invitingly...

"To hell with everything else, eh?" Nicholas snorted in disgust, ruing his weakness for her, even in the face of his anger, then raised his fist in frustration as huge pelts of rain splashed upon his upturned face. With a certain helplessness, he reined Nero back a notch as the clouds descended upon them and the rain fell in torrents.

"Ah, what the hell!" he bellowed defiantly into the shower as his hand remained firm on the rein despite the water streaming down his face. If Nero wondered at his master's sanity for not taking refuge beneath some nearby elm, his unflinching pace gave little clue. The huge black eyes flickered hesitantly as his master bellowed heavenward. "'Tis my penance, I presume, for treating my wife so harshly! So be it, and I shall gladly endure it, for I will *not* allow that woman to completely upend my life! Vixen, she is—ah, but I never feasted my eyes upon one so comely." Almost reluctantly he slowed Nero to a walk and raised a rain-sodden arm as if to prove his point. "And therein lies the heart of my problem. Admit it, you bumbling fool! She has ensnared your heart so completely, wound you so tightly about her finger with that dance of seduction she has played upon you, she could tear your life asunder, lay complete ruin to your plans and, with the promise of but one kiss, leave you begging for more. Ah, but I love her with boundless passion! And prove it to her, I will...again and again. What better way to pass all this damned time, eh, Nero?" With a wicked grin, he urged the horse onward with an urgency that had little to do with getting himself out of the rain.

When he arrived at the manse, the rain had eased to a gentle shower. Impatiently, he glanced about for some sign of Peter, then shouted into the gathering gloom. When the stable proved deserted, as well, he hastily tended to Nero, muttering to himself as he did so. The constant squishing of his feet inside his water-clogged boots brought a scowl to his features, which dissolved into a ferocious bellow when he turned to leave the stable and nearly planted a foot in a pile of horse droppings. The scowl blackened with every noisy step he took toward the house, though once he was perched just outside the front portal, his features softened.

"Ah...home at last. A warm hearth, a warm bed, a warm woman..."

With some surprise, Nicholas found the foyer deserted, unlit save for a lone candle flickering softly upon a low table. No Fritz to welcome him, and certainly no warm woman. With a frown, he gave a vigorous shake of his wet head and peeled the sodden topcoat from his back. His waistcoat followed to land in a heap at his feet. His fingers stilled upon the buttons of his shirt as a soft thump and a yelp drew his attention.

"Bo! 'Twould seem you're what's left of a warm welcome, eh, boy?" His smile dissolved into a look of utter stupefaction when the dog bounded past him without a moment's pause. To hell with man's best friend.

A muffled sound of laughter from the direction of the parlor drew Nicholas from his musings and he strode purposefully, and rather noisily, in that direction, muttering beneath his breath. Upon pushing the parlor door open with a force he would soon regret, he was met with a warm and cozy scene.

Nestled before an inviting fire, upon the floor no less, were his wife and Peter. A warm hearth...a warm woman...*and another man*. Peter? Damn her! She'd *never* looked at him like that...that sweet secretive look reserved for...lovers. As the door banged unceremoniously against the wall, their smiles faded and they glanced up in unison to meet Nicholas's suddenly stormy visage. For one painful moment, a blinding jealous rage threatened his sanity.

"Get the hell out," he growled at a pale and flustered Peter, who, along with Bo, beat a hasty retreat with head bent low and eyes averted.

Nicholas's gaze flickered coldly over his wife, who was rising hastily to her feet. She seemed atrociously uncomfortable, consumed by guilt no doubt, though when he moved a pace into the room, her eyes darted to his boots and the merest hint of a smile teased her mouth. As her gaze rose, the telltale blush crept from the prim lace at her throat and suffused her cheeks with a brilliant pink. Her reaction left little doubt in his mind that the rain had rendered his trousers and shirt a second skin, laying to rest any suspicions she might harbor regarding the state of his manhood.

He clenched his fists at his sides, nearly consumed by his desire to crush her in his arms before he wrung her little neck. "He's not to step foot in this house again," he ordered, deriving some perverse pleasure from her gasp of outrage.

"How dare you!"

He took a step toward her, his hands itching to feel her, touch her, yet he knew the moment he laid a hand upon her, every last ounce of his will would flee. "I dare whatever I damned well please, madam. This is *my* house, you are *my* wife, and that stable boy of yours is *my* servant. And you shall all do as I say."

She sputtered and sucked in her breath like a flustered little kitten. "Ooh! You beast! I am no man's slave! You bloody arrogant bastard!"

Nicholas had but a moment to ponder where she'd honed such talk before she flew at him in a frenzy, her fists pounding against his chest, claws bared and legs kicking at him. She spewed forth a stream of language that only served to lift one corner of his mouth as he struggled to entrap her in his arms. Which he did, until she burst forth with a shrill cry and planted her heel painfully into the arch of his foot. With a bellow of rage, he released her, the movement bringing her head up sharply beneath his chin, snapping his mouth shut with a painful click. In a flash, his arms swept about her, crushing her to him, and he found himself, in spite of everything, lowering his head, his mouth seeking hers... needing to feel her surrender, to know that in some way she was his. And for the most fleeting of seconds, he felt it... in the softness of her lips melting beneath his, parting to receive his tongue... and then she bit him.

"So cocksure you are, Nicholas," she breathed, shoving herself from his arms and eyeing him coolly, despite his murderous look. "How you glower and bark and stomp about like a foolhardy knave, then expect a mere touch of your mighty hand to sweep it all aside. How very..."

At that moment, Peter burst into the room. "Lord Brennan, sir?"

White-hot anger surged through Nicholas, and for a moment he forgot about the painful throb of his tongue. "Get out!" he bellowed to an ashen-faced Peter.

"But, sir, I..."

"Now!" He took two steps toward the younger man.

Peter flinched but stood his ground. "But, sir... the horses, sir... I... I believe you may have, er, forgotten... that is, er, you left the stable door ajar, sir, and the horses have, uh, run off, sir."

Nicholas stared at the other man, acutely aware of the muffled sounds beneath the fist Trista pressed against her mouth. He turned and glared at her, and she simply sucked in her cheeks and gave him a wide-eyed innocent look. "You find humor in this, woman?" he barked.

She shrugged helplessly and bit her lip against the giggles that no doubt threatened to engulf her.

Nicholas released his breath and shoved a hand through his hair. "Very well," he muttered. "Come with me, Fleming, we've work to do." And with that, he turned and followed Peter from the room.

The slam of the front portal shook the rafters of the huge house and jostled the perfume within the lead crystal bottles adorning Trista's dressing table. Her hand upon her brush stilled in its nightly task of taming her wayward curls and her eyes flew instinctively to her reflection in the gilt-edged mirror.

The evening breeze stirred the sheer curtains at her windows and brushed softly against her bare skin, serving to remind her that she wore only a thin chemise. Her gaze dropped momentarily to the high curves of her breasts and her bare shoulders, bathed a tawny hue by the flickering candle at her side, and she heard naught but her pulse drumming insistently in her ears as heavy footsteps drew nearer to her door. Before she had the chance to reach for her silk robe, lying just beyond her fingertips, her door flew open with a bang and a stormy-eyed Nicholas strode purposefully into her room.

His step faltered when his brooding gaze settled upon her for several long moments and his scowl deepened when she returned his glare unflinchingly, making no move to cover herself. With a sound akin to a low growl, he spun from her and stalked angrily to her armoire, flinging the doors wide to grumble and search through the contents. After several moments of fumbling through drawers and creating complete disarray, he emerged and tossed his spoils upon the bed, then loomed close above her.

He flung a brawny arm toward the gown upon the bed, though his gaze found its way to settle upon the tiny pink silk bow at the top of her chemise. "Get dressed, wife," he growled. "We're going out." With that, he turned on his heel and exited her room as noisily as he'd entered.

"Infernal man!" she huffed, turning back to her reflection and glaring at the fevered and flushed she-devil that met her stormy gaze. The hand upon her brush tightened fiercely. "He thinks me some feebleminded nitwit, eagerly awaiting his every command with breathless anticipation! 'Get dressed, wife'? Ha! I shall get myself dressed when I so please and in the manner I please, Lord Brennan! And to bloody hell with you!" Tossing her brush aside with disgust, she stalked angrily to the bed and plucked at the chosen gown with a look of utter stupefaction. "Surely the man has lost his mind!"

Her fingers slid disbelievingly over the shimmering gold silk swatches, which appeared to be constructed into some semblance of a gown by the sheer, flesh-toned underfabric.

Her jaw sagged as her gaze slid from the gown to the flimsy excuse for a chemise lying innocently upon the bed. Her fingers trailed over the transparent fabric and her cheeks flamed at Nicholas's boldly apparent intent.

"He wishes to parade me before him like some cheap, gaming house wench, displaying myself to all those with eyes in their heads. 'Tis an outrage! An utter disgrace! Why, I will never allow such a thing! If he thinks for one moment he can force me to his addlepated bidding..." She thrust the garments from her, turning to retrieve her silk wrapper, when her eye was drawn once again to her reflection in the mirror. This caused her a moment's pause to reflect upon *her* intent not moments before as she'd sat serenely before that mirror.

So Nicholas had chosen *not* to behave in keeping with her plans, though this was certainly no surprise, as this was his wont. Hardly reason to toss aside her scheme and embark upon yet another entirely futile and foolish squabble over his domineering manner. Her heart had realized some time ago that she loved him, domineering manner be damned. It was high time that a carefully and skillfully executed scheme of the most wicked of seductions be employed to tame that wild beast. To hell with all her blasted pride. He was, after all, worth far more than that to her.

"He loves you," she reminded herself as she turned a speculative eye once again upon the bed. "He's simply behaving like any typically foolish, stubborn man." Sweeping the gown from the bed, she held it against her and turned to the mirror. Lifting one hand to toy with her hair, she cocked her head and gave her reflection a careful assessment. Such a scandalous dress ... certainly one to which only a saucy dish like Bianca could do justice.

A dark brow lifted devilishly as a mischievous little thought wriggled into her mind. Spinning from the mirror, she tossed the gown upon the bed and hastily removed her chemise to don the much sheerer version. As she turned to the mirror once again, her breath caught in her throat and the heat of her blush rose to her cheeks. The sheer silk clung to her every curve like a second skin, accomplishing little in the way of concealing the pale pink nipples straining against the fabric. With her eyes fixed languidly upon her reflection, she toyed with the tiny ribbon joining the chemise at the valley of her breasts and imagined undressing before penetrating blue eyes....

With a mental shake, she roused herself from her musings and bent hastily to the task of arranging her hair exactly as she deemed fitting for such a gown...and her plan.

When Polly entered the room sometime later, she took two steps, then skidded to an openmouthed, dumbstruck halt.

"Oh, Polly, there you are," Trista chirped over her shoulder, turning her back to the woman and lifting her hair. "Perhaps *you* can manage all these buttons."

For a moment, Polly wallowed in confusion, her eyes sweeping the slender figure before her, settling upon the long row of gold silk-covered buttons extending from the nape of Trista's neck to an area just below the girl's rounded derriere. As she tended to the buttons, her eyes flickered over the mass of golden-streaked ringlets tumbling in artful disarray from atop Trista's head nearly to her waist. An unusual coiffure...and an unusual dress, as far as she could see. Certainly did the girl's slim-hipped figure justice, for the gown clung to her clear past her hips to the middle of her slender thighs before fanning out in a sweep of shimmering gold silk. How the girl could walk, she hadn't a notion.

"Well, Polly, what do you think?" Trista turned about with a radiant smile.

Polly's mouth fell open. "Why...I...I..."

"You don't think the rouge is a bit too much, do you?" Trista turned to the mirror and peered closely at her reflection, touching a finger gingerly to her powdered cheek and perfecting a pout that showed off her full lips to perfection. "I thought 'twould be fun for a change." Straightening, she turned slightly from side to side, enjoying the play of candlelight upon the shimmering swatches. The gown fit her to perfection with not an ounce of extra fabric to pinch, from the deep neckline to the fan at her knees. The sleeves sat just at her shoulders in a huge pouf, then flowed like a second skin, ending in a point just below her wrist. Artfully placed silk swatches swirled from below her derriere, rising to barely cover her breasts, which were poised precariously, almost overflowing the gown. In fact, she found if she moved in just the right manner, the barest hint of a nipple would peek from behind the gold silk. This brought a small smile to her rouged lips, as did the precise manner in which the gown all but hugged her rounded bottom.

"Adelle, you are a master...." she murmured to herself, then swung her sultry gaze upon the still openmouthed Polly. "Polly, if you don't find your tongue, I will deem your blatant staring in that manner an all-encompassing approval of my attire." Leaning forward slightly, she winked conspiratorially and a soft smile parted her lips. "Is it truly not the most wicked concoction?"

Polly's head bobbed and she stared wide-eyed at her mistress. "Indeed, my lady... wicked, indeed. Lord Brennan, he shan't be pleased."

Trista gave a throaty laugh as she turned to the open jewelry box atop the dressing table. "Oh, he will be more than pleased, of that I'm certain. 'Twas he who demanded I wear the gown."

Polly gave the back of Trista's tousled head a troubled look. If Lord Brennan had indeed demanded such a thing, which, in light of his recent foul mood, seemed altogether likely, it was no doubt some foolhardy attempt to bait his wife. Nothing more. Surely Trista realized this?

Apparently not, for she seemed intent upon a little baiting of her own, and Polly could do naught but mumble to herself when Trista lifted the exquisite diamond necklace from its resting place.

"I believe this will do quite nicely. Polly, do you agree?"

Nodding dumbly, the older woman clasped the necklace about Trista's neck and attempted to keep her eye from straying too frequently to the gown, the tousled mane, the rouged lips and cheeks... She shook her head, wondering if she could possibly get herself safely from the house before Lord Brennan laid his eyes upon his willful wife. She harbored little doubt the man's rage would bring the rafters crashing upon them once and for all.

Trista was nearly halfway down the entry stairs when Nicholas emerged from the parlor. In the scant few seconds before their eyes met and the blood drained from Nicholas's face, Trista's heart began an erratic thumping.

Such a magnificently handsome man he was. His hair had grown rather wild and untamed but gleamed richly in the flickering candlelight and seemed to add just the proper touch of devil-may-care arrogance to his demeanor. As her eyes met his, she wondered if his sudden pallor was altogether due to her purposefully saucy bearing, or if perhaps the brandy she'd detected gracing the air about him had finally gotten the better of him. The steely gaze he narrowed upon her, despite the hand he offered to assist her the last few steps, did little to ease her mind, though the tic in his jaw served as inspiration to carry out her scheme to the end.

"Good evening, Nicholas," she murmured in as husky a voice as she was capable, her lips parting in a soft half smile. She purposefully stilled her feet upon the last step, directly before him, and was suitably rewarded when his hooded gaze slid first to her rouged lips, then to the diamond pendant twinkling saucily between her breasts. Only when his breath was released in a soft rush did Trista realize she held hers, as well.

"My..." she breathed, raising a slightly trembling hand to play upon the crisp white shirt covering what she knew to be the broadest chest in all of England. "You cut such a fine figure, Nicholas."

Quick as a flash, her hand was encased in a viselike grip and her eyes flew to his, which were still fixed rather intently upon her cleavage. After a moment they lifted, and his lip curled in a sardonic smile. "Whatever game it is you're playing, wife, I am more than willing. However, before we embark upon this evening and all that it holds for us, let me simply warn you that you'd best be prepared for the consequences. Do I make myself clear?"

"Whatever do you mean, Nicholas?" she asked in a teasing voice, drawing her hand from his, which suddenly appeared to radiate a heat capable of searing her skin. With a husky laugh, she cooled her fingers upon the jewels at her neck and tilted her head coyly. " 'Tis no game that I play, rest assured. I simply find myself rather... *frisky* this evening. Perhaps we shouldn't linger."

A dark brow lifted and Nicholas offered his arm. "As you wish."

As he led her through the front portal to the waiting coach, Trista was all too aware of his heated gaze upon her, so much so that she marveled at his ability to maneuver himself through doorways and into small coaches without taking his eyes from her. Once seated opposite her inside the velvet interior, he fixed a permanently hooded gaze upon her.

After a time, Trista licked her lips in a most provocative manner and drew a rather unsteady breath, peering at him through lowered lashes. "Would I be remiss in assuming your rather obvious ogling attests to your approval of my attire?"

"You look good enough to eat."

He didn't move. He didn't have to; his powerful presence enveloped Trista like a flame. A wanton sigh escaped her parted lips. His gaze dipped once again to her breasts, and the passion aroused in the depths of his eyes drew Trista forward upon her seat until but a handbreadth separated her aching bosom from his powerful chest. Beneath the sweep of gold silk, her stockinged legs trembled and her fingers gripped the soft velvet cushions at her side. Dimly, she grew aware of the rasping of her breath as her eyes fell to his mouth so very near hers. With all her being she ached for his lips upon hers, his hands upon her skin. Very slowly her eyes rose to his and locked, and with a breathless sigh she half whispered, "As do you, my gallant knight."

At that moment, the coach lurched, jolting Trista forward off her seat. As powerful arms swept about her, she instinctively reached out to brace herself against a fall, a dreadfully ineffectual attempt at best as one hand glanced uselessly off Nicholas's shoulder and the other fell directly in the proximity of his turgid manhood, of which she became startlingly aware.

With a gasp, she snatched her hand from the contact and her eyes flew to his, which flamed with an intensity that took her breath away. His hands upon her upper arms held her pinioned so closely against him that she felt his breath upon her face, the heat of his chest searing her bodice.

"Perhaps you require further proof of my appreciation," he murmured, his eyes dropping to her parted lips.

The words caught helplessly in her throat as her every intention to play the wanton seductress scattered to the four winds. She felt his hand catch at the back of her head and suddenly she was in his lap, clutching at his shoulders as his mouth found her throat. She gasped as his hand captured one breast and his mouth swooped over hers, parting her lips with a fiery kiss that left her breathless. An uncontrollable trembling seized her limbs as his mouth worked its sweet magic upon hers and his thumb brushed urgently against the swelling peak of her breast. The unleashed hunger he displayed aroused that joyous ache of languid longing deep within her and she clung to him, arching her back against him.

From deep in her throat a soft moan escaped, eliciting a low growl from Nicholas as his mouth released hers and he shifted her in his arms so that she lay half-reclining against the plush cushion. His dark head bent and she felt his lips upon her skin, his breath hot upon her flesh as his hands cupped her breasts to his face. With one slight movement, he released the swollen mounds and spread fiery kisses over the thrusting peaks.

Reveling in the sensual tide sweeping over her, Trista caught her hands in his hair and pressed him closer to her, needing the feel of his mouth upon her aching flesh. When his hand slipped beneath her gown to part her legs, she offered scant resistance and lifted her hips wantonly to ease the molten urgency building within her. His hand caressed her thigh, then slipped easily within her chemise, finding the pulse beating beneath the soft tangle of chestnut curls. For a moment, his head lifted and his burning gaze roamed freely over her unbridled charms, then swept to her mouth, parted slightly with her breathless gasps.

With a soft moan, Trista drew his mouth to hers once more as her legs fell open to receive his knowing touch, the gentle teasing strokes that instantly fanned the flames of her passion.

"Oh…yes, Nicholas," she murmured against his mouth as that wondrous coil of white-hot passion threatened to burst within her and the heady feel of him pressed her deeper into the cushions.

"Ah, Trista, you're so ready for me, love…." His voice rasped against her throat. In one swift movement, he pulled her beneath him and hastily drew the tangle of gown to her hips.

Whatever his intention was then, Trista would never be sure, for she found herself nearly thrown from the seat as the coach lurched to a sudden, jarring halt. With a scathing curse borne from the depths of some horrendous frustration, Nicholas eased himself from her and hastily drew her upright, sweeping her skirts aside with a muffled oath. Once she had retained some semblance of modesty, he ducked his head and threw the coach door open with a nasty bang.

"What the hell is going on, man?" Trista heard him bellow to the driver. A slight smile teased her mouth as trembling fingers adjusted her bodice over her flushed breasts and smoothed the gown about her hips. As she raised a hand to press against the flaming skin of her cheeks, Nicholas reappeared at the coach door with a look of murderous intent marring the chiseled features. When his eyes met hers, his expression softened. For several moments he stared at her as if he were about to say something, then apparently thinking the better of it, he averted his gaze and gestured to the coachman.

"One would think the man had never sat his rump upon that lofty chair," he grumbled, scowling in the direction of his rather flustered employee. "Nevertheless, we can be somewhat grateful that we shan't be jostled about for at least a few hours' time. We've arrived, Trista." His eyes flickered over her to settle upon her tousled hair. "You are up to it, are you not?"

"Oh...of course," was all she managed with a slight smile as she reached for his extended hand, though with all her heart she wished to remain right where she was.

If Nicholas was in any way of the same mind as she, his behavior offered little insight, for he gallantly offered his arm and swept her along the shadowy back street toward a noisy entrance to a huge, brightly lit establishment. As she hurried along to keep pace with her stoic husband, Trista couldn't help but hope that this was not a place where a slightly disheveled maiden still glowing with the flush of her unbridled passions, in a dress that revealed far more than it concealed, would be found conspicuous.

Her step faltered, for their passionate interlude had left her more than a trifle weak-kneed and rather lacking in gumption at the moment. In all truth, she felt quite languid and all aglow, capable of only sloe-eyed glances and breathless sighs, one of which escaped as she slanted a look at her husband.

He appeared no worse for wear and in possession of all his faculties. Even his shirt was without a single wrinkle to mar the smooth, fitted lines. How *did* the man manage it?

A shrill, high-pitched giggle accompanied by a round of bawdy guffaws drew Trista's attention to a smart black coach that had pulled before the entrance. The vehicle's door burst open to allow passage of a cloud of thick smoke and a huge scarlet plumed hat, accompanied by a black-haired woman wearing an atrocious concoction of feathers and plumes to match that of her hat. Her liberally painted mouth parted in a wide, wicked smile as she turned on rather unsteady legs to slap playfully at the masculine hand extending from the coach to brazenly fondle her derriere. Eyes heavy with kohl batted suggestively as she leaned toward the coach and grasped that eager hand in hers, drawing it to her swelling bosom.

Trista watched in stunned disbelief as the unseen escort took full advantage of the wench's easy virtue, slowly fondling the heavy breast, then roughly squeezing the nipple.

The woman, apparently used to such behavior, gave a throaty laugh and made no move to discourage him. To the contrary, she reached within the dark coach and pulled his head to hers, parting her full lips to extend her tongue to slip and dance about the eagerly opened mouth of her escort. They lingered thus for several excruciatingly long moments, causing the bile to rise in Trista's throat at the vulgarity of such a display. Averting her gaze, she wondered how this could repel her so completely when Nicholas's lovemaking not moments before had captured her so passionately in its rosy glow.

Winding her fingers more tightly about the muscled arm at her side, Trista turned to follow Nicholas through the entrance, from which emitted the sounds of tinkling laughter. Just as she began to wonder exactly what type of establishment this was, a vaguely familiar voice from behind her drew her attention once more to the brazen couple.

Her jaw fell open and her feet suddenly refused to move as her eyes fell upon Kendall Barry alighting with some difficulty from the coach. This was due perhaps to the manner in which his dark-haired companion all but clung to him, running her painted nails over his chest, then lower to fondle between his legs as she giggled playfully. Or perhaps the brew that had gotten the better of his "lady friend" had also rendered him a trifle wobbly-legged.

Despite his obviously altered state, his look of openmouthed stupefaction as his eyes met Trista's attested to a somewhat lucid manner, and he gripped the arm of his companion rather hastily as if to keep his legs beneath him.

Trista was smartly reminded that she was staring in a most obtrusive manner when Nicholas's deep voice murmured close to her ear, "Darling, ogling is a sport best confined to one's mate, and certainly not one to be practiced and perfected upon those whom you've cast aside with broken hearts. 'Twould appear your onetime inamorato has not seen fit to mend the error of his ways."

Trista swung a puzzled look upon Nicholas as they proceeded through the entrance into an enormous, brilliantly lighted foyer. He glanced at her and gave a soft laugh. "This may come as a bit of a shock, sweet wife, but the regularity with which young Barry has frequented establishments such as this, on the arm of... *ladies,* for lack of a better word, such as she, has not altered in the least since you rather soundly made a laughingstock of him. 'Twould be a feather in your cap no doubt to think that 'twas you who drove such a kind, noble young gentleman to seek such forbidden pleasures, but alas, 'tis not so. You see, long before you captured his fancy, he was well acquainted with such pleasures and was known to keep the company of several ladies of ill repute. I wouldn't doubt that he intended to maintain that life-style even after your marriage." His hand rubbed along her slender back. "Now, aren't you in the least bit grateful that you bear the name Brennan?"

"I never would have guessed! Why wasn't I told of such behavior?"

Nicholas gave a wry laugh. "Surely you don't think that *I* would have wasted my breath sullying his blue-blooded character? Darling Trista, you never would have believed me. However, not everyone would deem his actions noteworthy in any way to a prospective bride. Indeed, 'tis rather customary behavior for gentlemen of his kind and widely accepted practice in Society. To be sure, 'tis the fellow that keeps himself from such goings-on who is guaranteed to raise a few brows."

Trista could only nod. As her eyes flickered over the crowd noisily milling about, she found her musings on Kendall hastily tossed aside. As her gaze fell upon the sea of gowns and the women wearing them, the color climbed higher and higher in her cheeks, for her gown was undoubtedly the most modest of those on parade. Just then Clothilde St. John sailed past in a sweep of silk and heady perfume, clinging to the arm of her tall blond escort and bestowing upon Trista a saucy wink as she passed.

Nicholas pressed a cool glass of pale gold liquid into Trista's hand and murmured close against her ear. "Champagne, darling, to give your mouth something to do besides hang open in that manner."

"I—I...where the devil are we?"

Nicholas swept a brawny arm about. " 'Tis the infamous Covent Garden you find yourself in, playground of the nouveau riche and those more inclined to passing their evenings with a gay, lively crowd rather than in the stodgy company of those swank and fashionable and insufferably boring. Perhaps you would rather we scurry over to Almack's to posture and pose the night away."

Trista stared at the cockily raised brow towering above her and sipped from her glass, first one delicate sip, then a second, followed by a huge gulp that nearly drained the glass and obliterated the last vestiges of doubt in her abilities to behave according to her plan. "Oh, never that, husband." Her airy reply and the saucy smile she bestowed upon him over the rim of her glass drew a look of surprise from Nicholas. Trailing a finger lightly over the satin of his waistcoat, she inclined her head and peered coyly at him. "No, since we are here, and appropriately dressed for such a place, I see no reason why we should not...*indulge* ourselves."

And indulge herself she most assuredly did, finding the champagne very much to her liking as well as the company of the couple seated beside them within their box to enjoy the circus. With every sip of her champagne her manner grew more lighthearted, and she chattered on unceasingly with the buxom blond courtesan and her overly eager escort, who, to Nicholas's keen eye, seemed intent upon ogling Trista's ripe bosom with far more fervor than was appropriate.

In fact, as the night wore on, Nicholas could not help but wonder at his sudden role of grumpy, glowering ogre, simply looming at her side or fetching yet another glass of champagne while attempting to keep her within his sight. He realized that he had no one to blame but himself for foolishly thinking that he could parade his winsomely beautiful wife in a racy gown and not expect the men of the city to take notice. It all set the blood churning within his veins. At one point, when a particularly young, fresh-faced lad bumped rather obviously into Trista, then allowed himself the liberty of steadying himself by placing one hand about

her waist and the other at the curve of her hip for a clumsy
squeeze, Nicholas had to wrestle the overwhelming urge to
level the lad with a swing of his fists.

And to all of this, Trista appeared blissfully unaware,
smiling whimsically at him as she chattered on and on,
praising his choice of such a place and expressing every wish
to visit again very soon. To this, Nicholas offered a grunt of
a reply as he eyed her full glass with disdain. He would have
been better served this evening *not* indulging his damned
male ego. If his purpose had been to cause a horrific stir to
ease his week's worth of frustrations, which he supposed
had been his intention all along, she had certainly made a
mockery of him with one sultry swing of those slender hips.
With a snort of self-disgust, he allowed his eyes to sweep for
the thousandth time over the lush curves and willowy hol-
lows of her body, all but served up for the taking in the
blasted gown. He never should have let her step foot from
the house.

He grumbled and muttered for the better part of the evening and ruminated on their unfinished business within the
coach. When Trista raised her arm to greet some newfound
friend, his breath caught in his throat and his never-lagging
manhood leapt to attention. The seemingly innocuous
movement caused her dress to slip and one pale pink nipple
to peak tantalizingly from the gown. Just as Nicholas was
about to sweep his coat from his back and fling it and his
squirming wife over his shoulder and bear her to the coach,
a fellow well into his cups jostled Trista's extended arm and
sent her entire glass of champagne tumbling down the front
of her gown.

The fellow hastened to apologize, his manner all the more
gracious and obliging as he stared with rapt attention at the
clinging bodice. The pressure of a firm hand at his elbow
accompanied by a chilling glower from Nicholas, however,
sent him hastily on his way. With a last glance after the
clumsy oaf, Nicholas swung to take Trista's hand firmly in
his and found himself grinding his teeth in frustration as the
buxom blond courtesan swept before him to take Trista by

the arm and lead her away. Over one plump shoulder he managed to hear her say that the powder room was just around the corner.

Chapter Sixteen

"There... that should do." Trista patted her damp bodice one last time with a towel, then fanned herself with it as if the slight breeze would accomplish the last of the task. Laying the towel aside, she hastened a quick glance at her reflection and touched a hand to her hair, then to her lips, which owed little of their rosy fullness to any liberal application of rouge. Indeed, the flush staining her tawny skin and warming her belly was due entirely to the sweet champagne, and as she turned to the door, she reminded herself to sip slowly.

Her brows drew together in a perplexed frown as the doorknob refused to turn beneath her fingers. Surely her friend the courtesan had not mistakenly locked her in. She tried again, turning the resisting knob and pushing all her weight against the solid oak door. Glancing about for a key, she gave a sigh of relief and a short laugh as her gaze fell upon another closed door opposite.

She chided herself as she turned to open what was surely the proper exit and not some soundly locked closet door. However, that knob proved as unyielding as the first. Before she had a moment's time to ponder her situation, a slight breeze filtered softly into the room, sweeping gently against the back of her neck. With a grateful smile parting her lips, she swung about to greet the newcomer. In the fleeting second before the room went completely black, she glimpsed a broad-shouldered, black-clad figure looming in the open doorway, then a gloved hand pressed forcefully against her mouth, denying the horrified scream threatening to erupt.

Roughly, she was drawn against the solid frame of her captor and a sinister voice rasped hoarsely against her ear, "You managed to escape me once, didn't you? And into the vile arms of your Yankee Brennan I left you on that fateful night. I should have taken you then, instead of that little whore Chorlis. She proved to be quite unremarkable beneath me, you know. Not anything like you will be."

Eyes wide in terror, staring into the inky blackness, Trista struggled ineffectually against him, her efforts eliciting a sneer of a laugh. "You cannot escape me, little Yankee's whore."

Trista jerked violently as she felt a hand roughly fondle her breasts and rank breath fall ragged upon her cheeks. "Aye...I shall have you..."

Foul-tasting bile rose in Trista's throat and she pushed with all her might against the rough fabric of his coat. With a muffled growl, her captor shoved her against the door, ramming his knee between her trembling legs. Trista gasped in stunned horror as his hand released her mouth to tear clumsily at her bodice and clutch at her derriere.

"Oh, God...you're vile!" Trista spat, twisting frantically against him, her hands clawing at his face and along his shoulders. A muffled sob escaped her as she felt the proof of his manhood pounding against her belly with every painful thrust of his hips. She cried out in pain and humiliation, recoiling yet again from the insane laughter filling the tiny room.

And then, as if from a great distance, she became aware that his intent had changed...had grown entirely menacing.

His hands rose to span her throat, clumsily at first. Then, as his movements became frenzied, the pressure at her neck increased.

Frantically, she clawed at his hands, but his grip only grew stronger. The blackness became a spiraling emptiness, devoid of all but the brilliantly flashing points of light exploding in the recesses of her brain.

Suddenly, he surged against her, crying out hoarsely against her throat and, for a moment, releasing his hold about her neck. From the depths of what little consciousness remained, Trista lunged from him, flinging herself with a cry into the blackness of the tiny room. Frantically, she groped about with trembling hands spread wide, sliding helplessly against the walls, then sending the mirror crashing from its perch. With a mind-numbing terror, she felt him turning toward her, then nearly screamed in sudden desperation as her flailing hands slid over what felt for a fleeting moment like a doorknob. With a panicked cry, she whirled, clawing at the darkness. The doorknob seemed to materialize within her grasp and the icy clutch of fear upon her heart lifted to allow a glimmer of hope. The knob turned easily within her grasp and she lunged against the door, flinging it wide.

A spray of cool air engulfed her and she spun to slam the door upon the monster, who chose most unfortunately to clutch at her sleeve, one arm extending through the partially open door. As Trista fell with her entire weight against the door, his arm and what most assuredly was the aged oak gave a mighty crack, followed by a bone-chilling howl of agony.

Trista spun and lurched down the hall, struggling to maintain her footing. A sea of faces whirled about her, as if borne from the very nightmare that had created the villain still recoiled within the powder room. A dull buzzing droned in her ears, her vision blurred and she jostled recklessly into a cozy group, only to right herself without a hint of apology. She stumbled amidst the swarming tide of humanity that penned her within its suddenly garish and grotesque facade, and her flight became a panic-driven surge. A hand grasped hers in its steely warmth and she twisted from that hold with a choked sob, flinging herself through the crowd and the exit into a cool night air.

She knew naught of the soft breeze caressing her fevered cheeks or the masculine voice raised with obvious concern trailing in her wake. Nor did she pause to acknowledge the couples staring lingeringly after her as she stumbled along the cobblestones. Tears streamed unheeded from her eyes, blurring her vision and enveloping her in a wave of helpless confusion. With a choking sob, she sank to her knees, clutching at her belly to ease the coil of revulsion deep within her and completely unmindful of the familiar pair of powerful arms that wrapped about her and swept her easily from the street. Those same arms bore her to the waiting coach, a soothing voice reverberating through her senses, the strong beating of his heart easing her fears. She clung to his shoulders, drawing strength from that sturdy breadth and the familiar masculine scent emanating from the fine cloth of his coat.

And then she was enveloped within the plush warmth of the coach and drawn close against her husband. Her arms wound about his neck and she buried her face into his chest, choking on the sobs that racked her slender frame.

With a troubled sigh, Nicholas relaxed against the seat as best he could and drew her head tightly against him, wrapping his arms about her, waiting in silent frustration for her story. It was not long in coming.

He listened in silence, gently running his hands across her tense shoulders and down the stiffness of her back while a muscle twitched menacingly in his cheek and his eyes blazed with a fury that would see justice done without fail. And when her tale ended, he lifted her swollen, tearstained face to his with a finger lightly beneath her chin and pressed the softest of kisses against her mouth.

"I shall get this demon, darling Trista, whoever he is," he vowed, gazing with a fierce intensity into her bleary eyes. "Of this, you can rest assured."

Drawing her head against him once more, he wrapped his arms tightly about her and buried his face in her hair. They rested thus for the remainder of the ride.

With Trista nestled snugly in his arms, Nicholas strode purposefully through the entry, past an astonished Fritz, and mounted the stairs. Over his shoulder he muttered instructions to the wide-eyed servant and, at the top of the stairs, proceeded left, toward his room.

Trista offered little resistance when he kicked his door open and proceeded into the shadowy room. With infinite care, he placed her upon the creamy velvet chaise and knelt before her, taking her hands in his and pressing them to his lips. His eyes fastened upon hers and he lifted a hand to caress the curve of her cheek, then rose as Fritz entered bearing a silver tray. The servant retreated silently, closing the door softly in his wake.

Nicholas turned and doffed both topcoat and waistcoat, tossing them carelessly upon a chair nearby. The lead crystal decanter sparkled brilliantly in the glow of the fire's softly leaping flames as he poured a liberal draft of the warm brandy into two crystal snifters, then he moved beside Trista and pressed a glass into her hand.

She appeared lost in thought, completely unmindful of him for the moment, and he found himself groping for the proper words. He sat beside her silently, contemplating first his drink, then the fire, before finally allowing his eyes to feast again upon the beauty at his side. Without thought, he lifted a hand to brush a stray tendril from her cheek, and much to his surprise found his hand suddenly covered with hers as she pressed his fingers in a most loving manner against her cheek. For a moment, she rested her head upon his hand, then turned to press her lips against his palm. Drawing his hand to her lap, she sipped slowly from her glass. She sighed softly and her eyes fell from the fire for a moment to the hand resting within hers. Her fingers stroked those lean and brown encased within hers, smoothing over the gold band and playing gently upon his knuckles.

In spite of himself and a restraint he knew would be tested sorely this evening, Nicholas found her innocent touch stoking his passion, making him all too aware of the bed beckoning over his shoulder. Now was not the time for seduction. She needed comfort, a loving touch, not the unleashed passions of a lusty, long-denied, ever-so-eager husband. He averted his gaze, drained his glass in one gulp and set it aside, then nearly started when she spoke.

"You know, I believe the first thing I loved about you was your hands." She appeared unmindful of the jolt her words sent through him and continued with the slow, exquisite torture she performed upon his hand. "'Twas only later that I realized your hands speak volumes of the man concealed beneath." Emerald pools lifted to hold him captive. "Physically, so incredibly strong you are, stubborn and proud. Yet I have come to cherish far more what lies beneath your carefully tended veneer." Her fingers pressed against his chest where his heart hammered an irregular beat, and her lips parted. "Nicholas, my darling husband, love of my life, I need your tender touch upon me this evening and every evening hereafter... not simply to sweep the stain of this horrendous deed from my skin, but to make me wholly, completely your wife. To lie with you upon yonder bed, beneath you, within your warm embrace... to know that I do not love in vain."

"Oh, God... Trista, love, never in vain." He swept her fiercely into his arms, the same powerful arms that trembled as his words caught in his throat for a moment, then tumbled forth against her hair. "God, how I have yearned to feel you thus, hear those words spoken from your sweet lips, my love. Aye, that you are, Trista, darling sweet angel. For love you I do, with all the passion a man is capable of."

She lifted her face to his and he lowered his mouth to play softly upon hers, reveling in the eagerness of her response. He felt her tremble and his hands slid to her shoulders, drawing her gently against him as he willed his passions to subside for a time. He held her close, his lips pressing soft kisses against the corners of her mouth, her ear, her cheek, her delicate jawbone, as her lilac fragrance enveloped him, bringing the blood to pound in his veins and his desire to rage like a flame ignited.

Her lips parted in the sweetest of moans. Unable to resist, he drew her close, his lips against her throat, feeling her arch against him. He lowered his head to nuzzle her breasts, his hands sliding slowly up her spine to the beginning of that endless row of buttons, which earlier in the evening had captured his fancy more than a scant few times.

With a seductive smile curving her lips, she leaned toward him and lifted her hair to aid his task. While his fingers plucked at the buttons with an expertise upon which Trista chose not to reflect, he resisted the nearly overwhelming urge to tear the damned gown from neckline to waist and to hell with the buttons. His impatience threatened to get the better of him when she lifted slender arms around his neck, pressing the entire length of her supple body against him and brushing her lips softly over his. His fingers faltered upon the buttons and he caught her fiercely to him, running his hands over her hips to ease her high against him.

He buried his mouth in her neck. "If you wish to see this gown in its present state ever again, you've got to let me see to the damned buttons."

Trista obliged, lowering herself to the chaise once more, though the sloe-eyed glance she slanted at him belied the innocence of her raised brows. Indeed, she displayed all too well a knowledge born of some baser instinct as her fingers unfastened the buttons of his shirt, then spread the cotton wide, boldly caressing the furred chest and the muscles beneath. His task was again waylaid when she leaned forward to press her lips to his skin, her hands playing a siren's song upon the corded ridge of his belly.

"You smell so wonderful," she murmured, sweeping feather-light kisses over one brawny shoulder as her fingers eased his shirt aside.

"Trista...I can't...you've got to help me..." The words were a low rasp emitted through clenched teeth, and he swallowed past an unusually parched throat as she lifted doe eyes to his.

"Perhaps if I turn around," she offered, drawing her hands from beneath his shirt and turning her back to him. His fingers indeed flew to his task. When she rose to slip the gown from her shoulders, his eyes flamed over the firm roundness of her derriere, all but served up at eye level.

He sat immobile as the dress fell to the floor. The blood pounded in his ears as his eyes traveled slowly over the slender back and incredibly narrow waist before sweeping over the gentle curve of her hips to long slender legs encased in silk stockings. His breath caught in his throat as she turned to him, lips parted invitingly and eyes hooded as her fingers toyed provocatively with the tiny bow at the top of the sheer chemise. His eyes fell immediately to her breasts and he nearly groaned aloud at the sight of her.

"Nicholas, love... you're ogling," she murmured huskily, her fingers slipping the silk straps from her shoulders before tugging gently at the bow.

Nicholas ogled all right, and his passion flamed beyond control as she leaned forward until the silky fabric parted enticingly, then slid to her waist and her breasts spilled free.

The soft firelight played upon their swelling fullness, caressing the smooth skin and highlighting the pale nipples blossoming before Nicholas's eyes. His world reeled when she slipped one hand about his head and drew his mouth to her breasts.

"Love me, Nicholas... please..." she moaned, clutching at his shoulders when his mouth found her pulsating skin.

With a moan of the purest pleasure, Nicholas slid the chemise over her hips to fall in a heap at her feet. He reveled in the smooth curve of her legs as he caressed their length, slipping the silk stockings to the floor, before removing the heavy diamond necklace from about her neck. His mouth stilled in the deep valley between her breasts and he pulled her hips against his chest until he felt the soft curls between her legs brush against him.

This nearly proved his undoing. With a groan of sweet agony, he slipped his fingers beneath her derriere until he found the warmth pulsing between her legs and she moaned sweetly in response. With an urgency that threatened, he swept her into his arms and strode to the bed, his lips finding hers in a searing kiss that tore at the last threads of his restraint. She turned in his arms, resting upon her knees, and he felt her breasts nuzzling his chest, the soft swell of her belly caressing his stomach.

"You're trembling, darling..." she murmured against his mouth, her hips nestling provocatively against his. "Do I please you?"

"Aye." His hands spanned her waist, easing her from him momentarily, if only to shed his clothes. "You please me nearly too much, sweet wife, for I fear...you test my will...sorely."

She made little effort to ease his plight, perhaps from an innocent lack of comprehension, and her tongue began a soft teasing of his. He groaned and all but tore the shirt from his back, fumbling feverishly with the top of his trousers.

"Let me, darling," she offered, sweeping his hands aside, "'Tis a lusty wife you have taken to your bed...one who wishes to undress you as you have done so many times. Surely you don't mind?"

"N-nay..." he rasped hoarsely with eyes closed as her deft fingers made quick work of the buttons, then slid his trousers to the floor in one swift movement. He heard her soft intake of breath and his eyes flew open to find her resting on her heels, staring upon that which no doubt loomed from between his legs. "A lusty wife should not be frightened of that which she has aroused in her lusty husband." He reached for her.

"I'm not frightened," Trista replied, raising a hand to his chest, stilling his attempt to lay her upon the bed. "'Tis just that it—I mean...*you* are so...big." Her fingers trailed lightly over his chest, then ventured gamely down his belly to linger at the tangle of dark hair nestling his swollen manhood. "Perhaps if I were to touch you..."

Without a moment's hesitation, he seized her fingers in his and drew them to his lips. "If you were to do that, love, this would be over before we even have a chance to begin."

Wide emerald eyes lifted to his and her lips parted in surprise. "What? Do you mean I can never touch you *there?*"

Nicholas laughed, lowering his mouth to play upon hers, his hands finding her breasts. "You may touch me *there* whenever you desire, sweet innocent. Rest assured there will be adequate time later for all your eager exploring. At the moment, however…'' His mouth followed his hand to brush gentle, teasing kisses over her swollen nipples.

"Of course…later…" was all she murmured as he eased her against the downy softness of his bed and parted her thighs with a sweep of his hand.

Slender fingers played softly through his hair as Nicholas buried his face in Trista's neck and tasted of the dewy fragrance of her skin. He felt her breath against his shoulder return to a slow even pace and began to wonder if perhaps his lovely bride slept. A breathy sigh of contentment and arms that wrapped about him served to remind him that she was still awake, and he rose above her to gaze with wonder into the hooded emerald depths.

The firelight played upon the tangled swirl of burnished chestnut ringlets fanning the pillow beneath her and curling softly against her flushed cheeks. Her love-swollen lips curved into a gentle smile and her lashes swept over those smoldering eyes as she drew his mouth to hers for a lingering kiss.

"You are pure enchantment," Nicholas murmured, brushing his lips softly over hers, his thumbs stroking the wayward tendrils from her brow. Lifting his head, he allowed his gaze to linger on the smooth perfection of her skin, bathed rosy by their sensuous lovemaking. "I have never known such a passion, nor has my heart ever beat with so fierce a love." He lowered his mouth to hers once more. "You have slain the wild beast, my sweet wife. I am forever yours."

"Oh, 'tis the sweetest of joys to hear you speak those words," Trista sighed, drawing his head to nestle against her throat. "It seems for so long I have feared the love that has gripped my soul and made me long for you…in every way, wanton soul that I am."

"A wanton soul for which I will thank God every day hereafter," Nicholas murmured. "You never had reason to fear, my love, for stubborn beast that I am, I yearned for you in much the same manner, if not more." He rose above her and traced the sweep of her cheek. "In all truth, I believe I fell in love with you when I first felt the sting of your hand upon my cheek, even after I so nobly rescued you from your Mr. Sleeth. So fiery-tempered you were, incredibly young and beautiful. I was but a pawn in your dainty hand from that day forward.''

"You never spoke as much," Trista replied with a slanted look. "I hadn't the slightest notion."

"Indeed. And would you rather I laid my soul upon your doorstep, alongside that of noble young Barry and a host of other love-smitten swains, painfully vulnerable, breathlessly awaiting the crunch of your heel twisting with deadly accuracy into the very heart that beats for you alone.'' He gave a soft chuckle, his fingers toying with a stray lock curling winsomely against the high curve of her breast. '' 'Tis spoken from the heart, darling innocent. I had little reason to plead my case. 'Twas rather painfully apparent from the moment we first met that you desired naught but a cheerful farewell from me, in spite of your decidedly warm physical response to my advances.''

"You displayed a remarkable lack of restraint with regard to those advances, despite the feelings you managed to keep at bay." A soft sigh escaped her lips as his head bent to nuzzle her breasts.

"Some things a man can't control." Nicholas's lips brushed over the engorged peaks and he cupped the soft mounds to his face, feeling his manhood swelling to life within her once more. "Had I but known the pleasure that awaited me . . . aye . . .'' His voice grew hoarse as her hands played upon the flexing muscles of his back and he positioned his hips more snugly against hers. "I would have snatched you from beneath the prim and pristine noses of those who watched with hawklike scrutiny over you . . . and proclaimed my undying love for you, then borne you to my bed to have my lusty way with you." He rose above her, his eyes blazing a fiery passion as he moved inside her with infinite slowness.

His reward was immediate, for she moaned softly and boldly caressed the sinewy arms at her sides. "And I would have come willingly."

" 'Tis easy to say now, love, beneath me as you are...."
His breath caught in his throat as her legs wrapped about his
hips to draw him deeper within him.

"Perhaps, though I was but a stubborn wench. Oh,
Nicholas..."

"Yes, love..." he murmured against her parted lips as his
rhythm remained slow, caressing, intoxicating her with its
sweeping flow. "I shall hereafter remind you whenever
you're becoming insufferably stubborn—"

"Darling..."

"Yes, love..."

"Must you talk so much?"

With a sound akin to a low growl, Nicholas claimed her
mouth with his and the only words spoken until dawn were
the most tender words of love.

Perhaps the faraway hoot of an owl or the early morning
stirrings of the countryside awakened Trista from a dreamless slumber. Or perhaps some instinct roused her when her
hand fell upon the warm sheets at her side, only to find them
bare of the muscled torso she sought even in her sleep. She
sat upright, sweeping a hand across her bleary eyes, and
peered into the dim light filtering into the chamber. Her eyes
swept over the hearth, which had long since lost its cozy
warmth, and fell upon the silhouette of her husband standing motionless at a tall window. A breeze fluttered the sheer
curtains on either side of him but he appeared unaware of
the cool air as he stared at the pale gathering light of dawn.

Shoving the sheets aside, Trista swung her legs over the
side of the bed and felt a soreness between her thighs, reminding her of their enchanting night of passion. A blush
warmed her cheeks as she mused on her own rather wanton
behavior, though the warmth of Nicholas's response laid to
rest any fears she could ever harbor regarding her "duties"
as his wife. And such welcome duties they were, she
thought, and a soft smile curved her lips as her eyes roved
lovingly over that long-legged form. With a sigh, she pad-
ded across the cool floor and slipped her arms about his lean
waist, pressing her breasts against his back. She felt his

hands instantly cover hers and she bestowed a kiss upon the bronzed skin then laid her cheek against him.

"Something troubles you..." she said.

"Aye." Save for the thumb rubbing against her hand, he remained motionless, staring upon the ghostly mists lifting from the moors. His voice rang deep and husky, as if borne from the depths of some hidden emotion. "Somewhere out there lies a man who, when I find him, will know a terror many times worse than that he has inflicted upon you. Until then, I cannot rest, knowing that he walks about, awaiting another chance to harm you. Aye, killing him would be too gentle a punishment."

"Nicholas! You mustn't even speak of such things! Surely you can't possibly mean to have the man's blood upon your hands."

With a wry laugh, he turned and caught her fiercely against him, burying his face in her hair. "My love, I bear the stain of no man as yet upon my hands, and though I have sought revenge with a dauntless pursuit, never has the desire to see justice done burned with such intensity within me. Trista, love, if any harm were to come to you, I would be a man insane."

With his fiercely beating heart beneath her ear and his steely arms wrapped protectively about her, Trista wondered how any harm could possibly befall her. She nuzzled her cheek closer against his furred chest. "Darling, I am safe within your arms, beneath your roof. I am certain no harm will come to me. Now please, come to bed with me." She peered up at him and smiled softly, her fingers tracing the planes of his back, then sweeping against the high curve of a firmly muscled buttock. "'Tis far too large a bed for me alone. Besides, I find myself a trifle chilled and in need of your warmth...."

In one swift movement, Nicholas swept her into his arms, then with two determined strides reached the massive bed and tumbled her among the rumpled sheets. With startling ease, he rolled onto his back, pulling her on top of him, and clasped her hips to his with two large hands cupping possessively about her rounded bottom.

Trista's breath caught in her throat as his mouth closed over one thrusting pink nipple to suckle slowly, lazily, as if intent upon performing that "duty" with the most infinite care. One hand caressed the downy softness of her lower back and drew her even closer against his swollen manhood, which throbbed against Trista's belly.

"You're so incredibly beautiful," he said thickly, his lips playing upon the curves of her breasts. "I could never get enough of you, you know." His eyes swept over the tumbled, flushed beauty perched breathlessly above him. "You are my sustenance...my very life's blood...all that I could ever need or desire." With a groan, he pulled her parted lips to his, his hands slipping beneath her hips to stroke with infinite tenderness.

With a gasp, Trista eased her mouth from his and rose up against his chest. "Nicholas. I wish to please you, as well."

With a husky laugh, Nicholas nuzzled her breasts. "Oh, but you do please me, angel wife. You could never do anything but that, try as you might."

"You are an impossible man." Trista sighed until the stroking of his fingers within her became almost too much to bear. "Darling, let me love you..." Without hesitation, she slid slowly down his torso, her hands caressing the corded muscle along his ribs. "You too are beautiful to my eye, so much more captivating to gaze upon with your sleekly muscled body. 'Tis perfection..." Rising on her knees on either side of him, she brushed her lips softly over the sweep of fur covering his chest, then followed the path of dark hair as it tapered to a narrow line over his belly. She reveled in his sharp intake of breath as her palms stroked his lean hips and her breasts caressed that which lay potently between his legs. "Do I please you, love?"

A strangled groan and blazing blue eyes served as adequate encouragement to proceed with her task and eased the slight trembling of her hands. Her gaze dropped and all movement stilled as her widening eyes beheld that which she sought. Almost unconsciously, her fingers brushed tentatively over his hip, then stilled, trembling. "Nicholas...

I..." Her gaze fluttered self-consciously to his. The entire length of his sinewed body appeared as if it were a tightly coiled spring on the verge of release, and Trista swallowed at the sudden dryness in her throat. Her eyes flickered back to her hand once more. "I...I know I should not be frightened or unsure, but you..." Her breath caught in her throat for a moment and her fingers fell gently against the heated flesh, then stroked the smooth length. "Why, Nicholas, it's so smooth to touch...so very warm..."

Her next words went forever unspoken as Nicholas rose from the bed like the fiercest of lions and pulled her beneath him with a sweep of one powerful arm. In a single movement, he parted her thighs and slipped inside her, pressing her into the bed, his mouth poised over hers. "Your lesson must end, sweet witch, for though I am willing, I fear I cannot bear it. Perhaps later, and we shall try again."

"Mmm..." was Trista's only reply as she pulled his mouth to hers.

Chapter Seventeen

With eyes closed, not in slumber but in infinite pleasure, Trista reveled in the heady sensation of a warm mouth nuzzling the length of her back with the slow, caressing strokes of a tender lover. A large hand slipped about her waist to press its heated palm against the tautness of her belly before drawing her down flat against the sheets. Firm lips replaced the hand and brushed over the downy softness before venturing lower to nuzzle the chestnut curls between her legs. Trista's fingers caught in his hair to draw him nearer and a soft sigh escaped her lips, only to be cut short as a curt knocking upon the bedroom door drew her reluctantly from the depths of passion and brought Nicholas's head about with a groan.

Clutching the tumbled sheets about her, Trista eyed her husband with appreciation and a growing dread as he slipped from the bed and strode purposefully to the door. Her thoughts lingered but a moment on the perfection of flexing buttocks and long, sleek-muscled legs before she nearly dived beneath the sheets as he unceremoniously flung wide the bedroom door.

"What is it, man? Can it not wait until the sun has at least reached its zenith?" Nicholas bellowed to a rather red-faced Fritz, whose eyes flickered nonchalantly over his very naked lordship before peering with a decided curiosity to the tangled mass of sheets.

"Er, Lord Brennan, the sun *has* reached its zenith...some time ago, I'm afraid." A wizened brow lifted at the grunt he received in reply and his gaze flickered once more to the younger man. "Indeed, 'tis not the hour of day which brings me to your door, though 'twould ease Polly's plight if you were to pause for a moment . . . to eat. However . . ." At Nicholas's stormy expression, he continued in a lower voice. "A message arrived a short time ago, sir, from Maurice. I believe 'tis a matter of some urgency."

Nicholas took the proffered slip of paper and scanned it, running a hand carelessly through his dark hair. "Aye, you did right, Fritz. Have Peter saddle Nero at once. And instruct Polly to prepare a tray and a warm bath for Mistress Brennan. Oh, and have her things moved into my room . . . permanently." He turned, then paused with his hand upon the door. "Thank you, Fritz."

Trista's eyes searched Nicholas's brooding scowl, which was leveled upon the paper still clutched in his hand as he closed the door behind him. She sat upright upon the bed. "Is something amiss?"

He shrugged, though his forehead remained furrowed as he looked up at the vision upon his bed. At the sight of Trista, his scowl softened and one dark brow rose wickedly. "Whatever could be amiss in this world with a maiden so fetching reclining upon my bed, hmm?" With two long strides he reached the bed and leaned over her—one knee upon the sheets. "Nothing that one sweet kiss could not ease. . . ." His lips brushed unhurriedly over her parted mouth until a hand pushing against his chest brought his head from hers.

"I do not wish to detain you," Trista murmured, pulling the sheets to her neck in a meek attempt at modesty.

A lopsided grin slid across his features. "'Tis not a matter within your control, my love." His gaze fell again upon the note and his tone deepened. "Were it any matter but this, rest assured that neither of us would see the other side of yonder door until the morrow . . . if then. However . . ." His hand softly stroked the curve of her hip through the sheets as his eyes found hers. "'Twould seem my scheme will come to fruition on this very day and I will finally taste of my revenge." Gently, his fingers traced the curve of her cheek. "'Tis odd indeed that I could suddenly deem that pursuit rather inconsequential at best, for that madman that haunts you still roams freely about."

Trista pressed his palm to her lips. "Were you to keep me warm and cozy beneath these sheets until the morrow, that madman would still roam freely about, Nicholas. Tend to your matter."

He kissed her lingeringly, then with a reluctant sigh rose from the bed to search for his long-forgotten trousers. "I must, however, hasten to Maurice. He's the bait and I would never risk his...situation. Now where in God's name are my boots!" A scowl furrowed his dark brow and he stalked about the room with trousers and shirt slung over one brawny arm, peeking beneath the chaise and a low table for his ill-placed boots.

"Over here, darling." Trista gestured beneath the bed. "So this older gentleman has aided your cause?"

"Immeasurably." Nicholas slipped the shirt about his back, then hastily tended to his trousers. "Were it not for him, I would have spent months attempting to identify the man responsible for my parents' deaths. As it was, Maurice told me his name upon our first meeting and our scheme to entrap the man was born at that time." A dark brow rose wickedly. "My greatest thanks, of course, is that I was left with much more time on my hands to woo you, dear Trista, and for that I will forever be most grateful to him."

"And to what end does this Maurice offer his much-needed aid?"

"He is after the same man for reasons he deems personal and of little import to my cause. Don't ask me Maurice's full name for I know not who he is, Trista. Had he not proven the most faithful and trustworthy of cohorts, I would have pursued the issue. I trust him, 'tis as simple as that."

Trista plucked at the sheets. "You're certain he has not led you to seek your revenge against an innocent man—innocent, at least, of the crime you avenge—for his own purposes?"

With a last mighty pull on his boots, Nicholas moved close beside her upon the bed. "Darling, he knows of things...my family history. Time does not allow for me to explain this entirely to you, but he was privy to some information many years ago from the rather loose-tongued brother of our friend Archibald Sleeth."

Trista's mouth fell open. "Sleeth? Why, I thought you and he were..."

"Corroborators? Hardly that, Trista. His brother, Oswald, was involved many years ago in some rather shady business dealings on behalf of a young Italian Count."

"Dominic..." The word was uttered just above a whisper.

"Indeed, 'twas your beloved Esme's husband, though he was no husband of hers then, to be sure, and 'tis certain she would have found little to interest her in a spoiled and no doubt financially beleaguered young Count. Desperate, to boot, so much so in fact that he risked doing business with Oswald Sleeth."

"Do you know of their scheme?"

"Know it? I'm relying on it myself! My mother's family owned Trent Shipping. In essence, Oswald, acting on behalf of Catalani, contacted my father, who was managing the business at the time. In exchange for a tremendous sum, Oswald promised to deliver a valuable cargo to my father for shipment to the colonies. Times being what they were, my father rather hastily agreed, despite the substantial drain on his cash reserves, and delivered on his end. However, before the goods were received, Oswald made off with that small fortune, split the spoils with the nearly bankrupt Catalani and left my family in financial ruin. Unable to locate Sleeth or his benefactor, my father was left with no alternative but to sail for the colonies. My mother died shortly thereafter and he, as well."

"A tragedy, indeed." Trista's hands rubbed softly against his. "One can understand your deep-seated desire for revenge, though I am at a loss as to your scheme to entrap Dominic now. Can you not simply provide evidence..."

Nicholas gave a caustic laugh. "'Twas indeed my only stroke of bad luck in this whole affair. Apparently, Oswald retained some type of evidence, which I never had opportunity to acquire. After his death, his brother managed to lay his hands upon those documents. Since then, he has been blackmailing Catalani, draining him of what precious little funds remain. However, I believe that Sleeth sees Catalani as his ticket into a Society that has forever been denied him." A sharp rapping at the door drew Nicholas hastily to his feet and he reached for his topcoat. "Tonight, love, I shall explain it all to you." His gaze flickered over her sitting amongst the rumpled sheets, which had fallen from her shoulders unheeded. He groaned and bent forward to kiss each rosy breast, eliciting a soft gasp from Trista.

"Really, Nicholas... 'tis all you can think of at such a time."

"Rest assured, the vision of you thus shall play havoc with my senses until I return." His lips pressed against her palm one last time before he rose from the bed.

"Be careful, love," Trista murmured, rising to her knees without hesitation to clasp her arms fiercely about his neck and press her body full against him. "My dearest wish is to spend many more nights in this bed with you. Come home to me safe, my love."

"Have mercy, passion goddess. You're making this much more difficult than it already is. You've little notion..." With one last, lingering kiss, he eased himself from her, pausing with his hand poised upon the doorknob. "Wait here, inquisitive little mouse, where Fritz can watch over you. And you needn't fret over my safety. I love you far too much to allow the likes of Sleeth or Catalani to bring about some premature end to our sweet paradise. Until later, love..."

And with that, he closed the door behind him, leaving Trista to stare with an all-consuming longing at the space he left painfully unoccupied, clutching at sheets that still smelled of him, and battling a gnawing dread in the pit of her stomach as his purposeful strides along the marble faded into a foreboding silence.

A cool breeze ruffled the emerald-and-cream striped satin sleeves and toyed playfully with the wayward tendrils escaping the loose chestnut knot atop Trista's head, bent low in thought. Despite her absorption in her troubled musings, which left her unmindful of the beauty of the day, her eye fell upon an enterprising squirrel scurrying to and fro searching for his daily quota of food amongst the rosebushes. She observed his efforts for a moment, then, with a sigh, shifted her weight upon the stone bench and bent her thoughts once again to the hands clenched in her lap.

"Ah! And what better spot to view the blushing rose of womanhood than in this lovely garden! One couldn't have set the stage any better."

With a startled gasp, Trista whirled about to confront Archibald Sleeth, posing rather obviously with walking stick and stockinged leg extended, his pompous manner hardly in keeping with the fetid stench permeating the air about him. He waddled forward on pudgy legs, pausing to peer down his bulbous nose at her. With a confident sneer of a smile, he leaned toward her and snorted, "Surprised to see me?"

"Be gone!" Trista commanded with a dismissing sweep of her arm. "Or my husband shall toss you from this house, lowly swine!"

Sleeth uttered a high-pitched, maniacal giggle, which jiggled his belly and set Trista's teeth grinding. "'Tis an undeniable fact that your husband is, as we speak, in the midst of a wild-goose chase, and the pleasure that gives me prevents me from properly administering some punishment for that remark."

Trista felt the blood drain from her face. "You're bluffing. You've no idea where my husband is."

"Is that so? Could you perhaps be suggesting that my message this morning, a message of extreme urgency, I might add, from that old fellow Maurice, was not credible? I think not. Your husband took one look at it and mounted that big stallion of his with little time to spare." His shrill laugh pierced the air. "Nay, 'tis you who are bluffing, and 'tis your second mistake. Your first, in case you're interested, was flapping that tongue of yours such that it carried quite nicely through White's. Revealed your husband's scheme in such a beguiling manner, I must admit I thought 'twas part of the plot. Ah, but even Brennan isn't *that* clever.'' The puffy lips twisted in disgust. "Certainly not half as clever as I.''

"You're mad.''

"Oh, nay, my dear. Rest assured, I am in complete control of my faculties.''

"Where have you sent Nicholas?''

"In good time, Trista. You've little to fear for his safety, for my scheme requires him to remain very much alive. Actually, I've simply created a bit of a diversion for a time. You see, I needed to get *you*, dear, the love of that Yankee vermin's life. And he shall pay handsomely for your safe return, on this I am counting, and methinks not foolishly so. I'd wager the man would lay down his life for you. 'Twill matter little to him, after all, that his scheme to entrap Catalani will fail miserably in the end. Now, if you will so oblige me, fair one. We haven't all day, you know.''

Trista stared uncomprehendingly at the pudgy arm extended to indicate the flagstone walkway leading from the garden to the side of the house. "You must be joking!'' she cried in disbelief. "I will no more oblige you than—''

Quick as a flash, his hand encased her upper arm, yanking her nearer as something very hard pressed into her ribs. "Oh, you will oblige me, you little hellion, for 'tis no impotent pistol I wield.'' His face loomed so close above her that Trista had to avert her head lest his fetid breath cause her to retch. "And you shall, of course, think twice about fleeing or calling for help. You see, I was once an apt pupil of a very ruthless man who enlightened me to the many ways one can use a pistol without actually killing. I could simply leave you without the use of your legs for the rest of your young life.'' The maniacal cackle sliced through the pounding in Trista's ears. "I'd wager Brennan would have scant use for a cripple, eh?''

"You're a vile, miserable wretch,'' Trista hissed through clenched teeth, willing her legs to remain unmoving even as Sleeth's hand at her arm and the pistol against her side steered her down the path.

Sleeth gave a hoarse cackle. "I've been called far worse, dear Trista. Aye, better that you not waste your breath blaspheming my character, for 'tis a feat that has been accomplished many times over."

"And no doubt rightly so!" Trista spat as they emerged from the garden and Sleeth steered her around the perimeter of the house. Upon spying the black coach and three attendants lying in wait, Trista mused sarcastically, "And no doubt you've a pistol digging into each of their ribs, as well?"

"In a manner of speaking, aye, though 'tis indeed a barb well aimed that you deem me unworthy of coming by so handsome a vehicle in the typical manner."

"Sleeth, you are a man bent upon achieving naught but ill-gotten gains. Why should I assume otherwise?"

"No doubt Brennan appreciates such a keen intelligence. Methinks perhaps I shall demand far more than originally intended...." His voice trailed off thoughtfully, then he yanked roughly on her arm, urging her along. "The coach—ah well, my lady, as you can see from the familiar crest upon the door, your *dear* Uncle Dominic has seen fit to leave this handsome vehicle and its men at my disposal. In essence, they work for me."

"Is that what you lowly swine deem blackmail? Then Dominic, as well, has been in your employ for some time now."

"The man may be an addlepated half-wit at the gaming table, but he is not a complete fool. Now, dear Trista, turn about nicely and wave to your friends hovering there on the front stoop. Smile...that's it. And I shall wave, too. Such nice people they are. A trifle simple, if you will, but what could one expect of a man like Brennan. Birds of a feather. Now, climb aboard, no fuss...hurry along, my dear. That atrociously somber-looking fellow looks as if to question us. Don't make me shoot him, Trista...smile once more for good measure." With a heave and a mighty whoosh, Sleeth squeezed himself through the coach door and plopped heavily upon the seat opposite Trista.

Trista stared for a moment at the black pistol he drew from beneath his topcoat and turned menacingly upon her, and with a helplessness never before known to her, she swung her gaze to the window. A movement from the corner of the house drew her eye and she met Peter's troubled brow.

In the scant few seconds that their glances met, Trista willed all her fears to scream with a bloodcurdling chill from the depths of her eyes. She had little time to wonder if Peter had gleaned even an inkling of the trouble in which she'd found herself, for the coach leapt forward, obliterating all view of her home and loved ones and sending Sleeth slamming against the side of the coach with a grunt.

Trista's blazing eyes settled with contempt upon his vulgar bulk. "With what sordid lies did you fill their heads that they would stand idly by while you kidnap me?"

"Why, Trista, 'twas an entirely believable tale, at least for the time being. I am such a faithful friend of the family, you know. Why, I even have use of the Catalani coach, which certainly adds to my credibility. I was but hastening to deliver you to your dear Aunt Esme, who is rather distressed of late over her 'situation' and has taken to her bed. Knowing of your unfailing devotion to the poor woman, of course your servants deemed it fitting to allow me to escort you quickly to her side. By the time they realize otherwise, if ever, 'twill be far too late."

He gave a loathsome, self-satisfied grin, which brought a disgusted snort from Trista, though her eyes remained fixed upon that firearm. She'd never seen a pistol before but was well aware of the danger. Indeed, as wont as she was to indulge her whims, she was not about to test the accuracy of Sleeth's shot. Besides, common sense told her that he'd rather leave her unharmed, and Nicholas, as well. If a hefty purse was all he was after, so be it. She'd gladly pay him any sum; indeed, she'd oblige his every fancy to ensure the safe return of her husband.

Her eyes flickered to his, which gleamed like tiny black marbles in the sweat-streaked face. Better that he not be too aware of her eagerness to please. There was no telling of what depths of depravity the man was capable. His eyes fell to her heaving bosom and Trista groaned inwardly, hastily averting her gaze lest she view some debauched notion brewing in his brain.

His harsh cackle momentarily threw her off guard. "Aye, you are as fetching a wench as I've ever seen, enough, perhaps, to show a man like myself the . . . well, the error of his ways, so to speak. Indeed, methinks having a maid such as you perched upon my arm would serve me far better than a passel of young lads, however fetching they may be. Aye, 'twas my original intent on that day we met, dear Trista. Surely you can see my point? Society would never look with disfavor upon a beauty like you and would instead assume I possessed some rather delightful qualities that you found enchanting. And I suppose I could force myself to service you every now and again, if only to keep you content." Ignoring her gasp of disbelief and the look of revulsion she made little attempt to hide, Sleeth narrowed his gaze upon her and mused thoughtfully, " 'Twould be far more worthy of some thought if you were not worth so much to Brennan. Alas, my dear, the thought of sampling your virtue pales in comparison with the fortune I shall soon have within my grasp."

" 'Tis a pitiful commentary on your life this eagerness to avail yourself of any means to achieve some social stature."

"Is that so?" Suddenly, he loomed from his seat, and his face, hovering very close to hers, twisted into a vile sneer. "And what would you know of my life? You've little notion what it's like to exist within this ugly, bloated body, to forever view the open contempt and disgust no soul makes any effort to hide beneath a dainty handkerchief! Bloody fools, they make a mockery of me to my face and clasp to their breasts such swaggering brutes as your husband! Aye, but he has the ticket, good looks *and* wealth. In their eyes, he embodies everything they could ever yearn to be. And he obtained the ultimate prize in you, to boot." The beady eyes swept coldly over Trista's shocked features until he settled back in his seat with a heavy sigh. "Nay, Trista, you could never know this lowly state."

Despite the slight tug at her conscience and a nagging pity for the man, Trista remained all too aware of the pistol leveled unflinchingly upon her and the steely purpose underlying his demonic intent. "I shan't waste my time judging you. Rest assured, my every thought is with my husband . . . and his safety."

A corner of Sleeth's puffy lips lifted mockingly. "Ah, then you shall indeed behave as I instruct, if only to save his hide. Tsk, tsk, Trista. Such a martyr you've become, and all for the love of that Yankee bastard. Have you no thought for your own safety?"

"'Tis of little consequence if some harm were to befall him."

Sleeth snorted in disgust. "Ugh! How fortunate I was to have escaped such a fate! To love so completely at the risk of one's own life!"

Trista's eyes fixed on the revolting man swimming in the excesses of his flesh and sweat. "There are those, such as you, who live their lives in search of wealth and social standing, or perhaps dedicate themselves for years to a purpose. In spite of the joys in attaining these goals, 'tis a true love that makes one's life worth living, nothing more. And I pity you, Sleeth, not for your futile quest for social acceptance at any cost or for the physical attributes you have been dealt, but for your soul, which has never known such a love."

Sleeth dismissed her words with a wave of his pudgy hand, and Trista swung her gaze to the windows once more. As the sloping countryside gave way to the clatter of city cobblestones, her every thought remained with her husband.

With a mighty bang, the salon door slammed against the wall and Nicholas's towering form lunged through the doorway.

"Where the hell is Maurice!" he barked impatiently to the two women, who leapt to their feet, lips parted in startled gasps as they beheld him.

Clothilde St. John was the first of the pair to find her voice, though one dainty hand remained comfortingly upon the arm of the other woman, who clutched a handkerchief to her trembling lower lip. The woman's disconcertion stemmed not entirely from Nicholas's stormy glower above a fiercely clenched jaw in dire need of a sharp razor. Nor could her tearstained cheeks lay all blame upon the manner in which Nicholas had chosen to conduct himself upon barging unannounced into the ladies' private salon, interrupting what had proven a rather painful confiding of the woman's troubles to the ever eager ear of Clothilde St. John. Nicholas, however, appeared unmoved by the woman's teary-eyed regard, though his gaze lingered upon her for a moment and the frown knitting his brow deepened before he glanced away with a subtle shake of his head to fix a scowl upon Clothilde.

"Nicholas, what a surprise," Clothilde purred.

"Is Maurice here?" Nicholas growled, sweeping past the pair to glance hastily about the deserted salon. He shoved an impatient hand through his hair, then nearly threw both hands into the air in frustration. "Where the hell can he be?"

"I have not seen Monsieur Maurice for some time, Nicholas," Clothilde replied. "Have you tried his residence?"

"Of course I've been to his residence!" Nicholas bellowed, an angry red suffusing his face.

Clothilde turned to whisper something to the other woman, who beat a hasty retreat through the opened doorway. Turning once more to Nicholas, Clothilde waved a hand after the other woman and explained, much to Nicholas's chagrin, "Poor girl is suffering from a broken heart, though one finds it difficult to feel sorry for her. Indeed, we're schooled from the very start to keep our hearts uninvolved with our business lest this very thing occur. Ah, so giddy she was last evening, so looking forward to Covent Garden on the arm of her special beau. Indeed, he keeps a particular room for them here. Tsk, tsk. 'Twould seem the fire has died, for he simply vanished last evening, just after one of the circuses, no doubt victim to the charms of some other woman. Pah! And a fool, to boot, claiming today that he cannot see her due to an injury to his arm obtained God knows where, as if she would ever believe that!'' Clothilde shook her head and gave a knowing sigh.

"My heart goes out to the poor woman, Clothilde, but 'tis no social call that brought me here. I must find Maurice.'' With a disbelieving shake of his head, he stalked about the room, mumbling beneath his breath as if thinking aloud. "He summoned me to his residence . . . 'twas an important matter . . . one that could not wait. Yet when I arrived, his man appeared rather shocked to see me, and even more so when I asked for Maurice. He claimed that Maurice had left just before I arrived, along with a messenger sent to inform me to meet him, regarding our business deal with Archibald Sleeth. He knew not where Maurice had gone but suggested I try here.''

With a wave of her hand, Clothilde chided lightly, "Ah, and there you have it! Have you searched downstairs? Really, Nicholas, I'd never imagined you could be so dense.''

"Blast it, woman!'' Nicholas stormed, throwing his arms into the air once again. "Of course I did, and he's nowhere to be found! Don't you see? I never *received* the second summons! His messenger had departed just before I arrived! The summons *I* received indicated he wished to meet me at his residence. . . .'' A frown scudded across his features, which suddenly turned thoughtful, and his voice dropped low. "Or did he?'' His face paled and he whispered hoarsely, "Damn . . . a trap.''

"Nicholas! Where are you going?'' Clothilde cried as he brushed past her into the hallway.

"I'll search the whole damned city if I have to!'' Nicholas bellowed over one shoulder as he strode purposefully to the stairs, only to skid to a halt as Peter's hell-bent flight up those stairs nearly caused a collision. "Fleming! What the hell . . .''

"Lord Brennan . . . thank God I've found you. . . ." Peter gasped between breaths, welcoming the steadying hand of his employer upon his shoulder. For a moment, his eyes flickered to Clothilde as she hurried toward them, then slid back to Nicholas. "It's Trista . . . Sleeth . . . he came not long after you left. Claimed he was there on behalf of her sick aunt. Took her away in Catalani's coach. Only . . . they didn't go to her aunt."

"Where, man? Tell me where he's taken her!"

"The . . . the old warehouse down at the end of the docks. I f-followed them there. 'Twas her eyes when she left. Lord Brennan, she was so frightened . . . and I s-saw a pistol. Th-thank God I found you."

Nicholas stared long and hard at the younger man, willing the murderous thoughts from his head for want of much-needed rational ones. "And Sleeth was alone, you say . . ."

"Aye."

"Dominic was not waiting at the docks?"

"I didn't see him or another coach, Lord Brennan. I fear I was looking out for your wife, sir."

A flicker of a smile tweaked at Nicholas's mouth as he clasped Peter on the shoulder. "You're a hell of a lad, Fleming. I shan't forget this. Now listen closely. There are several things I need you to do for me."

Chapter Eighteen

Despite the silken tie that held her captive against a sturdy wooden beam, Trista's wrists still ached from the pressure of her bonds as she struggled futilely against them. To make matters worse, Sleeth had seen fit to stuff what was no doubt his most vile-smelling handkerchief into her mouth, lest she feel compelled to cry out.

A twisted man he was, and by the sounds of it, making a career out of stalling. His voice, along with that of an unknown man, carried to her through the dusty, mildewed air that hung oppressively about the enormous warehouse. From what Trista could gather, Sleeth had summoned the man to this godawful place in order to see to the completion of a business transaction: the delivery of an agreed-upon amount by the other man in exchange for goods from Sleeth. The other man apparently intended to comply with Sleeth's wish, for he indicated that he had indeed brought the funds. He refused, however, to hand over the money until Sleeth's benefactor made an appearance and the promised goods were delivered. Sleeth was insistent that his benefactor would arrive very shortly and simply wished to examine the funds for accuracy, a wish the other man refused to grant. Both men appeared intent upon maintaining their positions, though by the shrillness of Sleeth's voice, Trista harbored little doubt that he was fingering the concealed pistol with more than an idle thought at the moment. Whoever the unsuspecting soul was, he'd best see himself and his funds safely from this hovel and to bloody hell with the business.

At that moment, an enormous rat scurried directly over Trista's foot and she would have screamed in terror had a door nearby not burst open, allowing a brilliant shaft of sunlight to stream into the warehouse. Sleeth's voice echoed shrilly throughout the cavernous space, raised not quite an octave above his normal pitch. "D-Dominic...indeed, 'tis a surprise..."

"I don't doubt that for one moment, Sleeth. Indeed, 'twas a shock to be found so ill-informed of your plans." The cultured voice rang smoothly, accompanied by a slow, measured tread of highly polished heels upon the wooden floor. When Catalani spoke again, the irritation was markedly evident in his voice. "You can well imagine my chagrin when Brennan's lad Fleming appeared at my door...yes, Brennan sent him. A shock to you, as well, eh? He very graciously informed me that you'd suddenly decided on a change in our plan. What the hell is going on? If you are attempting to hoodwink me in this, Sleeth, I'll have your bloated ass slung up on a tree."

"Is that so?" Sleeth's low growl was accompanied by a sudden intake of breath from the other two men.

"Sleeth, what is the meaning of this?"

"Dear God, man, put the pistol away."

"I shall sheathe this mighty weapon when and if I please, you pompous asses. Until such time, you shall listen to *me*. Now, over there, both of you...hands up...that's it. Oh, and, Maurice, you can do me the pleasure of sliding your nice black bag over here. Such a tidy little sum."

"You've lost your mind, Sleeth," Catalani remarked dully. "You shall never achieve what you desire."

"Oh, and I have achieved naught but painful indigestion groveling with the likes of you!" Sleeth spat. "Indeed, the astonishing regularity with which you have chosen to gamble away what little fortune you still possess has left you unworthy even of blackmail, my dear Count! You've no money, and certainly have been found lacking in social stature of late. I would have been a fool to continue in this scheme with you as a partner!'' Sleeth heaved a heavy sigh and laughed hoarsely. ''Besides, Maurice here and your Yankee Brennan were on to us, no doubt from the very start. They were partners, corroborators. You needn't look so shocked, Dominic. 'Twas all a very carefully laid trap. The prize? Perhaps you'd better ask Maurice. I've other matters on my mind at the moment.''

''I—I can scarcely believe it,'' Catalani muttered. ''How in hell did they know?''

''Perhaps I can enlighten you, Count,'' Maurice offered in a tone dripping with sarcastic graciousness. ''Are you perhaps familiar with an Oswald Sleeth? Perhaps a friend of yours at one time, eh?''

''N-not quite...''

''Ah, then a business acquaintance, I presume.''

''I—I...''

''Oh, for bloody hell's sake, Catalani!'' Sleeth sneered. ''The man obviously knows the connection between you and Oswald. Why deny it?''

''But how could he possibly know? Sleeth, you assured me that you were the only soul in possession of that information. The documents...''

'' 'Twas not documents that proved your involvement in the ruination of Trent Shipping,'' Maurice replied. '' 'Twas the rather loose-tongued Oswald Sleeth, who, over a bottle of fine brandy, told me every last detail of your wretched scheme to recoup your financial stability. To my eye, your streak of bad luck commenced long ago when you first conspired with Oswald Sleeth. 'Twould seem your choice of conspirators has not improved over the years.''

''Hold your tongue, old man!'' Sleeth ordered.

''Oh, you needn't wave your mighty pistol my way, Sleeth. I shall keep my opinions to myself. I feel compelled, however, to inform you, Count, that your true faux pas those many years ago occurred upon the selection of Trent Shipping as your prey.''

''Oswald selected Trent Shipping. 'Twas not I! He assured me a company of that size would not be missed...and that the owner of the company was a useless old man barely one step from the grave!''

The old gentleman gave a short laugh. "That useless old man had recently turned the reins of the company over to his new son-in-law, Jason Brennan. Brennan, yes. 'Tis no coincidence, Count, for Jason Brennan was Nicholas's father. 'Twas Nicholas's family you ruined. The financial blow you dealt them forced them from the country, killed Nicholas's mother and Jason eventually, as well. For this loss, Nicholas Brennan has sought revenge upon you with a vengeance, and I have but aided his cause."

"You?" Dominic's voice rang shrilly. "Who the hell are you?"

The old man chuckled softly. "I am Maurice Renaurd, your father-in-law, to be exact. Esme's father. Perhaps she has spoken of me."

Dominic's response was lost upon Trista as her legs suddenly collapsed beneath her and she slumped against the wooden beam. Maurice Renaurd? Her mother's father? The man she'd never known because of some dreadful family rift that had never been repaired? Her head reeled with the news. Had Nicholas known with whom he'd conspired? Did her father have any inkling?

"And once I'd received the news that my daughter had indeed wed a man I knew to be every kind of scoundrel, I *had* to expose you for what you are. My relations with my daughter being what they were, she would never have believed me were I to have appeared after so many years to blaspheme the character of her new husband. No, 'twas an altogether different tactic that I had to employ. And Brennan, with his relative anonymity and thirst for revenge, provided the means to ingratiate himself into your circles. His remarkable ability at the gaming table, coupled with your remarkable *lack* of the same, laid the way to your financial straits and our realization that this was our opportunity. You see, we had no definite plan, as yet, as to how we would entrap you. With your poor luck, however, the opportunity presented itself with relative ease. Indeed, you can well imagine my pleasant surprise upon overhearing you and Sleeth arguing over his apparent blackmailing of you. This aided our cause immeasurably and you were quite financially desperate far sooner than we'd expected. So desperate that you fell very nicely into our trap, with the help of Sleeth, of course, who rose to the bait, relying upon that same scheme Oswald conjured up so long ago. Only this time, my floundering little shipping company was the prey and Archie here your solicitor.''

"I—I can scarcely believe it! This is an outrage! I shall not stand here a moment longer—''

"Sit down, Catalani,'' Sleeth instructed in a rather bored tone, and Trista imagined he waved the pistol for effect. "I'm dreadfully afraid you're not going anywhere at the moment.''

Catalani uttered a high-pitched, disbelieving laugh. "And *you* were aware of all this, Sleeth?''

Sleeth's voice remained impassive. "Nay, only that Brennan and Renaurd here were in cahoots. I knew not why, nor do I care.''

Dominic's shriek filled the hollow warehouse. "Do tell me! How did you stumble upon such vital information while I remained blissfully ignorant?''

"In good time.''

"Listen to me, you blackmailing swine! Our deal is off, do you hear me? As far as I'm concerned—''

Sleeth's wicked cackle accompanied a scraping of heels upon the floor, moving toward Trista. "Save your breath, Catalani. 'Tis I who wield the power, lest you forget. Need I remind you that you, not I, bear the guilt of that deed committed against Brennan's family, one to which you've all but confessed to Renaurd here and no doubt Brennan, as well. And as far as your sordid tale of blackmail, why, 'tis simply your word against mine, Catalani. You see, I've little use for you any longer, for I've acquired another, shall we say, ace in the hole.''

Quick as a flash, Sleeth was at Trista's side, releasing her from the wooden beam, though he left her bonds secure and the gag in place. Rather roughly he grasped her arm and pulled her hastily from her prison, thrusting her into the space before Renaurd and Dominic.

Trista's wide eyes flew to those of the grandfather she'd never known, a wizened, white-haired gentleman, elegantly attired despite his stooped frame, wearing a look of such confusion and pain that he gripped the side of a crate for support. His gaze met hers unflinchingly, and in their depths, Trista glimpsed the pain and loneliness he'd suffered over the years as a result of the foolishly and hastily spoken words so long ago that had driven his family from him. Of their own accord, her feet moved toward him, only to be forcibly stilled as Sleeth's hand upon her arm yanked her to his side once more.

"We've no time for family reunions now, Trista."

"What in God's name are you doing, Sleeth?" Dominic cried. Trista stared at him. It was obvious the Count had not weathered well the events of late.

His hair hung long and unkempt, pushed hastily from his eyes with an annoying toss of his head. Though his clothes were elegant, they appeared as if he'd spent many a night within them tossing and turning upon a very uncomfortable bed. Perhaps that lack of sleep had caused the pallor and sunken eyes above the stubbled jaw clenched with his anger. Even as his eyes swept contemptuously over her, Trista kept her gaze fixed upon him, quite certain that she felt something akin to pity for the man, a pity jaded by a fierce loathing.

An evil chuckle close to her ear drew Trista from her thoughts as Sleeth rubbed the pistol idly against her arm. "Why, I thought it only seemly to invite Mistress Brennan to our little party. After all, 'twas she who so graciously enlightened me, albeit innocently done, of course, that Brennan and Renaurd were up to something. Were it not for her, I'd surely be spending the rest of my days inside Newgate prison with *you*." Sleeth's contemptuous sneer fixed purposefully upon the Count. "As it is, however, I've thought of a much better plan to accomplish my task. You see, Trista makes for such a lovely hostage, and her husband is far wealthier than you shall ever be again, Count. Indeed, I'm quite certain he will gladly pay a handsome sum to see her safely returned to him, and could no doubt be very easily convinced to make do with seeing *you* imprisoned for the rest of your life, while I go off on my merry way with a heavy purse to keep me company. 'Tis all so very simple, though you weren't to hear of it until much later, Count. I hadn't anticipated Brennan disrupting *this* plan by tipping you off.''

Dominic's face grew a deep mottled purple and his Adam's apple bobbed uncontrollably. "I...you...you miserable excuse for a man. If you think Brennan will let you get away with such a thing, you're more fool than I! Indeed—'' Dominic's fear-glazed eyes darted to the pistol and he gulped again. "Sleeth, perhaps together we could manage a plan...take Trista here to another country...perhaps one of those heathen African places where we could obtain a bloody fortune for her. Indeed, I've heard tale of the slavery markets...no telling what fortune a fetching wench such as she could bring...far more than Brennan would pay...if you would just hear me out on this.''

Sleeth stared disbelievingly at Dominic for a moment before erupting into a gleeful cackle that snatched the desperately pleading look from the Count's face in an instant. "You truly are too much, Catalani. You will, of course, forgive me, but I've little desire to conspire with the likes of you any longer. Indeed, I bear no blame for the crimes you've committed, and I shan't ease your plight in any way by whisking you out of the country! For God's sake, man, Brennan would kill us both before we made it to the outskirts of London! Besides...'' A pudgy hand trailed lightly up Trista's arm to rub against her cheek, which she turned angrily from him as her stomach recoiled. Sleeth's mouth twisted lopsidedly. "Methinks you underestimate this wench's worth to the Yankee.''

As if struck by a sudden thought, Sleeth swept his gaze about the shadowed interior, over the piled crates and dusty, gloomy crevices where a man could easily hide himself. For a fleeting moment, he experienced a mind-numbing terror that he would not succeed. However, with all the bravado of a man tasting of freedom from the wretched life he'd led, and much to his misfortune, he allowed his manner to become a trifle gloating and careless.

"Brennan? Indeed, I know you lurk in the shadows . . . awaiting your chance, perhaps? Let me remind you that 'tis a loaded pistol I hold tightly against your lovely wife's ribs."

Silence again filled the warehouse. Trista flinched as Sleeth's hand slid with bold familiarity over her ribs, pausing at the full curve of the underside of her bosom. Her eyes darted frantically about the warehouse, searching for some sign, some movement that Nicholas would come to her aid before . . . Her breath caught in her throat and the bile rose threateningly as Sleeth's vile hand slid slowly, painstakingly, over the fullness of her bosom.

"Ah, and such a soft, round woman she is . . . a delight to touch, I must admit. One finds it difficult to believe you'd risk losing such a wench. . . ."

Of the exact sequence of events that followed, Trista would never be quite certain, for through her tear-filled eyes, everyone, everything, seemed to move at once. Vaguely, she glimpsed a look of murderous intent seize her grandfather before he uttered a scathing oath and lunged toward Sleeth. At that precise moment, apparently realizing his opportunity to flee, Dominic shoved the older man from his path and thrust himself toward the only visible exit. This was indeed the Count's final stroke of bad luck, for in the instant before the world became an inky blackness filled with a myriad of brilliant stars, Sleeth, uttering a strangled cry, lifted the pistol from Trista and pulled the trigger.

It was a credit to his eye that the lead ball found its mark, plunging squarely into Catalani's chest and propelling him into a tangled mass of crates. Indeed, for so corpulent a man, one would have thought the sudden impact of brawny Yankee sprawling atop him from behind would have rendered Sleeth nothing but a spongy mass aquiver upon the floor. As it was, he managed to get his shot off before rolling to the planks with Nicholas straddling his massive bulk, rendering the pudgy arms useless with one steely arm and the force of a muscled leg.

Through the haze of a thousand twinkling lights and the dreaded realization that his plan had gone atrociously awry, Sleeth squinted painfully at the blazing eyes and fiercely twisted jaw of the man astride him. For one paralyzing moment, as he felt the sharply honed blade pressing coolly against his throat, he thought the Yankee would kill him. Brennan's next words, issued menacingly through gritted teeth, served only to seal that fate.

"Just give me one more reason, man...just one...."

From the shadows where she'd fled, Trista lunged forward, uttering a cry through the wretched gag. Her movement drew Nicholas's gaze and the pressure of the knife eased upon Sleeth's throat, making the man nearly apoplectic with relief. With a shuddering sigh, Nicholas drew Sleeth to his feet, albeit a wobbly stance, then thrust him into the waiting hands of a pair of able-bodied constables in tow.

While one of the men restrained a squirming Sleeth, the other moved to Catalani's limp form. After a moment, the constable turned to the group and proclaimed in a voice bereft of any emotion. "The bloke's dead as me own great-grandmother, God rest her soul."

Trista slumped against Nicholas while he cut her bonds free and eased the gag from her mouth. Wrapping his arms fiercely about her, he claimed her parted lips with his in a kiss that melted into a trembling embrace. Clinging to his shoulders, inhaling of the deep masculine scent that was his alone, Trista reveled in the many words of love, of despair, that tumbled effortlessly from his lips.

Lifting her head from his shoulder, she gazed expectantly into his eyes, running a hand lovingly over the stubbled jaw. "You're not angry with me for ruining your plans? If I hadn't spoken so foolishly..."

"Shh...love..." he murmured hoarsely, drawing her head close once more. "How could I ever be angry with you when you are all that I live for? The rest is of little consequence."

"Thank God you came," she whispered against his shoulder. "How did you find us so quickly?"

Nicholas laughed shortly. "It was your ever faithful friend Peter, a brave lad, indeed." A finger lifted Trista's chin. "Apparently something in your eyes when you left the house with Sleeth told Peter that you were afraid. So he followed you, then tracked me down at White's." A soft smile teased Nicholas's mouth. "A remarkable lad. Truly a fine boy."

Trista gave him a skeptical look despite the grin tugging at her mouth, as well. "Ah, so you admit you've judged him too harshly in the past."

"Perhaps a trifle harshly..." The azure gaze narrowed upon his wife's self-satisfied smirk and he drawled, "Which is not to say that I still don't believe the lad is smitten with my wife and henceforth shall find himself aboard my next ship sailing for the States, which is what he longs to do."

Trista turned and her eyes fell upon the old man resting wearily against a crate. With tears welling in her eyes, she eased from her husband's arms and moved slowly before the old man, taking a gnarled hand in hers. For several long moments, she kept her eyes on his fingers, trembling slightly within her grasp, and wondered what he must be feeling at such a time. So many years... so many words still unspoken. He was a stranger to her, yet a stranger whose eyes, when she lifted hers, glimmered with the undying hope of a family reunited, of a love for a grandchild yet to be expressed.

The words trembled upon her lips. "Grandfather, you know who I am?"

Tears sprang into the aged eyes and he nodded slowly. "Yes, my dearest Trista, you are my Helene's lovely daughter. Forgive an old man his sins, my dear. Forgive me for the years I have missed."

As the tears slipped from her eyes, Trista embraced him, feeling the fragile bones shaking slightly beneath his fine topcoat. "I could do naught but forgive you, Grandfather." A gentle touch at her shoulder drew Trista's head about.

Nicholas swept a lock of hair from her cheek. "I've another matter that requires my attention, love. Of course, I must see to Catalani and ensure that Sleeth does not squirm away. Perhaps Maurice could accompany you back to Esme's. Peter is awaiting you outside with Catalani's coach." He paused as his gaze found Maurice. "Indeed, 'tis a time for your family to be alone, methinks."

"Lest you've forgotten, you, too, are family, Nicholas," Maurice replied, clasping the younger man's outstretched hand. "You've little notion the number of times I wished to confide in you, especially once you'd married my dear granddaughter."

Nicholas nodded and gave the old man a reassuring smile. "Of course. 'Tis a relief simply to be done with it."

The wizened face captured Brennan's gaze. "Nicholas, your efforts were not in vain."

A wry smile tilted Nicholas's mouth. "Would that I could proclaim thus at day's end and I will be a man at peace. Now, be off with you, eh?"

Despite the firm smack of his lips against hers amidst a powerful embrace, Trista could not help but ponder Nicholas's parting remark. Her thoughts lingered but a moment, for she and Maurice found themselves graciously ushered to the waiting coach by a much-relieved Peter, who followed closely behind them.

Had Trista but known of the heavy pistol concealed within Peter's coat or his razor-sharp gaze as it scanned the streets, perhaps her thoughts would have strayed once again to her husband's remark. As it was, she talked softly with the old man seated opposite, drawing him from his thoughts and never once considering that far more lay in wait for her than she could ever imagine.

Chapter Nineteen

Closing the bedroom door softly behind her, Trista moved through the hallway and down the staircase. She stared unseeing at the magnificent foyer of the Catalani mansion, her ears straining for the sobs echoing from her aunt's chamber, sobs of remorse, loss. No matter that one's husband was a scoundrel, he would be missed. But these were also sobs of joy, of a daughter reunited with the father she'd stubbornly refused to acknowledge, the man who at that moment perched lovingly at his daughter's side, offering his consolation, his seasoned words of wisdom.

Trista paused at the bottom of the staircase as Emerson slipped noiselessly past her bearing a tray laden with warm tea and a cool cloth for his mistress's aching head. He paused at Trista's side and her startled gaze met his.

"Just between the two of us, miss, the Count shan't be missed much in this household. Made the Countess dreadfully unhappy. Rest assured, 'tis but a scant few tears she sheds for him." With the merest hint of a reassuring smile, Emerson nodded, then resumed his path up the stairs.

With a shake of her head, Trista turned and spied Peter lingering just outside the doorway leading to the kitchen. He lifted his head as if to appreciate better the aroma of something very tasty wafting through that door, when it burst open and Aileen scurried past with a start and a giggle as she spotted him. Bestowing a smile upon the young maid, who brushed past her with a blush and another giggle in Peter's direction, Trista hastened to Peter's aid.

"I'm quite certain Cook could manage some semblance of a meal to fill your aching belly," she remarked. "'Tis the least any of us could do as a token of our thanks. Were it not for you, Peter..."

"Oh, Trista, 'twas not I but the quick thinking of your husband that saved the day," Peter replied, edging toward the kitchen door. "He's a good man. Aye, the very best. If I can't be your husband, he's the man I'd surely choose for you, God's truth. Did he tell you? I'll be sailing with his next ship! A regular seaman I'll be!" He flung the door wide and disappeared with a grin.

Just as Trista turned toward the foyer, the front portal burst open and Bianca, on the arm of Kendall Barry, sashayed through the entrance.

"What the devil are *you* doing here, Trista?" Bianca squawked with characteristic sarcasm upon spotting her. "No, don't tell me. That ever-so-handsome husband of yours has finally come to his senses and thrown you from his house to grovel and mewl upon our doorstep. Ha! Kendall, darling, was it not *painfully* evident to us from the very start that this would prove the little tramp's fate?" Bianca swept an enormous fan from beneath her arm to tap Trista lightly upon the sleeve in a manner that was none too soothing. "Too bad dear Uncle Dom shall send you packing the instant he hears of this."

Resisting the urge to raise her eyes heavenward in a silent plea, Trista forced her voice to be calm. "'Tis not the reason for my visit. Perhaps if I could speak with you...alone, Bianca. I mean no disrespect, Kendall."

Before a rather pale-faced Kendall could utter some reply, Bianca burst forth in a rush. "Ha! As if you *ever* gave him a hoot of respect! You can hardly expect the man to show you any kind of sympathy in your time of shame, much less oblige you in any way! You really are too much, Trista!" A dark brow arched and gleaming eyes slid over the silent young man at her side. "He's such a gentleman, offering me a lift in his buggy after another of Darcy Langston's dreadfully vapid afternoon teas. One wonders how truly bored the women of this town must be." She lifted heavy-lidded eyes to Trista. "So sorry, Trista, but I feel 'twould be awfully rude to send Kendall on his way. Whatever it is you've to say to me, say it here…say it now…then be off with you, eh?"

"As you wish," Trista conceded, deciding that the last thing she would do was soften the blow for Bianca. "There has been an accident. I'm afraid, in the melee, Archibald Sleeth shot Dominic. He's dead, Bianca."

Whether from sincere shock and despair or simply for effect, Bianca raised a trembling hand to her brow and, with a strangled groan, proceeded to swoon right into Kendall's arms. Trista rushed forward to assist Kendall, who appeared to be laboring with Bianca's weight. This proved a trifle surprising to Trista, for despite her voluptuous figure, Bianca couldn't possible weigh enough to prove cumbersome to a healthy young man. Giving the matter but a moment's thought, Trista glanced up as Emerson descended upon them.

The servant bent hastily to the task of righting Bianca, though as he moved to support much of the girl's weight, Bianca managed a brilliant recovery and steadied herself by leaning heavily upon the older gentleman's arm, whereupon he escorted her into the parlor.

Trista turned to Kendall, concerned at the pain-racked expression torturing his handsome face. Her words of consolation poised on the tip of her tongue, only to be left unsaid as her eyes fell to his hand, which dangled uselessly from the arm he clutched painfully to his side. Her eyes widened as she viewed the mottled purple hand swollen to twice its normal size, his entire arm bulging within the confines of his topcoat. Perhaps this dreadful injury was to blame for his peaked countenance and the shifting eyes that refused to meet hers.

"Kendall! Your arm, for heaven's sake! What happened? Have you seen a doctor?"

"I was on my way when I met with your cousin," Kendall offered weakly, raising his good arm to steady himself against her. " 'Tis no doubt far more serious an injury than

I'd suspected. I should hasten to get help...but I fear I am so weak."

"Oh, for heaven's sake, allow me to assist you." Trista grasped his arm and guided him to his waiting buggy. She helped him aboard, mindful that he rested his entire weight upon her and the driver.

He settled against the seat and lifted a pain-racked visage. "Would you perhaps see me safely to the doctor? I—I fear I can barely sit upright."

With a glance toward the mansion, Trista hesitated a moment, pondering whether she should inform someone of her plans. As Kendall appeared in dire need of immediate attention, she decided against it, and mounted the buggy steps, settling opposite him.

As the buggy moved swiftly from the manse, Kendall appeared to make a remarkable recovery. He straightened himself with ease, the agonized look sweeping from his face as quickly as the streets passed them by. A fleeting sense of disquiet plagued Trista as she observed him. The moment his dark eyes met hers, a cold dread prickled up her spine. Perhaps it was the suddenly harsh planes of his unshaven face that proved the clue. Or perhaps the cruel twist of his lips, which rendered his handsome face a demonic visage. He did not speak, but merely watched her eyes dart to his hand, his arm, again and again as the memory of the terror waged upon her in that tiny powder room blazed anew for each of them.

The rasping voice that gnawed with familiarity despite her terror...the arm outstretched, clawing desperately for her, only to be crushed beneath her weight slamming against the door....

Trista's tongue refused to move, blood rushed with deafening urgency in her ears and she stared, eyes wide in terror, at the man she'd once considered a suitable beau, the very man that had killed Chorlis Beckwith and no doubt intended to do the same with her.

"Y-you..." she whispered hoarsely, feeling her heart lurch sickeningly as Kendall grasped her arm and leered wickedly at her.

"''Tis a bit of a shock, eh?'' he growled, twisting her arm painfully behind her. "Had it not been for your rather pushy cousin, I'd have been able to finish you off in my own good time, which is half the fun, is it not? Ah, but I'll make do. One has to marvel at your ability to fall into traps so easily.''

Trista's world reeled as that dreaded mind-numbing terror descended upon her. "Why . . . ?''

"Need you ask, Yankee whore?'' He wrenched her arm once again until she cried out in agony. This seemed to please him in some horrendously debauched way and a cruel smile twisted his lips. "Is that what you do beneath your Yankee cur night after night? Tell me, will you cry out in pain at the exquisite torture of lying beneath me? Tell me!''

Trista stared terror-stricken at his face, twisted with all his demons. No words could reach him, she realized with a growing dread as he settled upon his seat and fixed his dark eyes upon her. His moods seemed like quicksilver, as if he were a tightly coiled snake on the verge of unleashing his venom with nary but the slightest provocation. A maniac, with whom she knew naught how to deal.

"Oh, and don't get any ideas.'' From within his coat, he withdrew what to Trista's eye appeared to be a finely honed carving knife, complete with an intricate ivory handle. He fondled the blade in a distracted though somewhat loving manner, then eyed Trista curiously. "Rest assured, my beautiful Trista, 'twas not you who drove me to such lengths. However, you can well imagine my rage upon learning that 'twas *I* who had locked you in that wine cellar with your rutting stag husband. A cruel twist of fate, wouldn't you agree? Ha! To learn that I had played no small hand in thrusting you into Brennan's arms, sealing my fate as the suitor played false. Aye, 'twas a laughingstock you made of me! And for that you shall pay dearly!'' The knife tapped rhythmically against Kendall's thigh, though the movement appeared an unconscious one. "To my eye, taking you now would simply be recouping that which would have been mine,'' he remarked almost offhandedly, then shrugged. "I will, of course, forgive you your lack of virtue, though 'twill pain me greatly!"

Awash in helplessness, Trista watched as he settled quietly once more upon his seat. She cringed when his eyes slid slowly over her hair, then fell to her heaving bosom. Save for the muscle twitching in his jaw, he displayed little emotion for the remainder of the ride. When the buggy finally slowed to a stop, she nearly jumped from her skin and glanced about her like a frightened animal. Kendall roughly grasped her arm to shove her from the buggy.

"I have a special place for us, lovely Trista," he mocked, shoving her through the rank, narrow alleyway. Trista shrank from him, stumbling over a pile of rotting vegetables whose stench nearly caused her to retch. Kendall laughed cruelly. "Walk along nicely now and do not—do you hear me—do *not* cause a scene. 'Twould prove a dreadful disappointment were I not to sample your charms, but if I must I will kill you with a swipe of this blade if you make one move. Do you understand me?"

Before she could reply, Kendall gave her a shove that sent her sprawling against a heavy oak door. Before she could regain her footing, much less her wind, he thrust himself against her, pinning her back to the solid wood. He dropped his lust-filled gaze to her bosom. "Methinks I will have a taste of your charms before we enter. 'Twill lend us more of an air of lovers, don't you agree?" He seized the lace at her throat and tore her gown to the waist. Like some lust-crazed animal, he feasted his eyes on the display, then lowered sagging lips to her flesh.

Vainly Trista twisted against him and shoved with all her might against his injured arm. This she regretted immediately, for with a bloodcurdling scream, he slammed his fist into her cheek, driving her head against the oak with a dull thud and bringing the tears to stream from her eyes.

"I thought I told you no false moves!" he spat. "I will use this knife when you've had enough of my fists, do you understand?" Roughly, he yanked her from the door, then flinging it wide, shoved her into the gloomy interior. "This way, Trista . . . up the flight of stairs."

She did as she was told, the wrenching of her arm and the knife concealed beneath his coat leaving her little alternative. She stumbled up the dimly lighted stairs, conscious only of the dull throbbing in her jaw and of *him* directly at her back, urging her onward toward her doom. Tears blurred her vision and the image of Nicholas loomed suddenly within her mind, drawing a wrenching sob from the depths of her panic, and she stumbled once more.

"Get up!" Kendall commanded, yanking on her arm, which brought a cry of pain to her lips.

Trista managed to reach the top without enduring another beating and realized dully that they were at White's. A rough hand at her elbow propelled her along, though her feet seemed incapable of movement and she tripped and stumbled, sobbing anew as they grew closer to Kendall's "special place." With a yank on her arm, he slammed her into the wall, nearly knocking her unconscious, and thrust his hand deep into his pocket, retrieving his keys. Wielding those and the knife, which he waved menacingly for good measure, he inserted the key in the lock and pushed the door wide. Without further ado, he grabbed her arm and thrust her into the darkened interior. Slamming the door behind him, he whirled and pinned her against it with a force that drove what little breath remained from her lungs.

With a sob, she slumped against him, pounding her fists uselessly upon his shoulders as his mouth sucked greedily at hers, then lowered to spread painful bites across her breasts. The darkness became a void, Kendall's hideous grunts melding with the drone filling her ears and obliterating all but the soft panicked cries she uttered. "Stop...God... Nicholas..."

From the depths of that void a voice reverberated through her senses, sent the blood coursing through her veins with unabashed hope and brought Kendall erect with a start.

"It would serve you well to take your hands from my wife."

With a strangled cry, Kendall whirled, taking Trista with him as he held her tightly against him, pressing the knife to her throat, his eyes searching frantically in the darkness.

A lone match flared, illuminating the profile of the man reclining easily within a chair not ten paces away. Rather casually, he lowered the match to a candle resting atop the table at his side, bathing the room in a soft light that reflected off the polished black of the pistol he leveled at Kendall. Cocking his head, he regarded Kendall through hooded eyes, in a manner not unlike that he employed when contemplating the purchase of a horse. Crossing one booted foot over his knee, he slid his gaze to his wife. The azure eyes flamed as they beheld the swollen, tearstained face, then fell to the gaping bodice and exposed breasts. A tic in the lightly stubbled jaw intensified and his voice crackled through the stillness.

"Take your hands from my wife or I shall put a hole in your head, man."

The calmness of Nicholas's voice seemed only to inflame Kendall all the more, perhaps because the Yankee appeared to regard himself in complete control of the situation, an opinion that Kendall was nearly on the verge of sharing. The hand wielding the knife trembled visibly at Trista's neck and his eyes popped from his head like huge saucers.

"You Yankee vermin, have you no eyes in your head!" Kendall shrieked. "'Tis *I* who hold the knife to your wife's throat! You shall do as I say!"

"I think not."

Kendall's eyes narrowed upon the entirely impassive face of his opponent. His hold upon Trista tightened, drawing a gasp from her and a flame of rage barely held in check from Brennan's eyes. "Ah...so you seethe with anger, Brennan. Perhaps you shall seethe with something more when you watch me take your wife upon this very bed!"

Despite Trista's gasp of horror, Nicholas's only reaction to the man's threat was the idle fingering of the pistol held almost casually within his grasp. "Do not force me to kill you, Barry. Release my wife, now."

With a high-pitched laugh bordering on the hysterical, Kendall snorted, "You can't possibly kill me! Brennan, have you lost your mind! I've a knife. Do you see it? 'Tis at your precious wife's throat! You would never risk her life in such a foolhardy manner!''

"Methinks the fool is the man who sorely underestimates the accuracy of my shot.''

"'Twould be a miraculous shot at best, and you could kill *her* instead!''

"At this range, the odds are in my favor.''

For a moment, Kendall simply stared at the other man, weighing the coolness of Brennan's responses. Then, as if driven by the demonic purpose that had possessed him, Kendall cast Brennan a challenging glance and slowly slid the knife from Trista's throat to the top of her chemise. With a sweep of the blade he sliced through the stays, causing the flimsy garment to sag from her trembling body.

Trista's breath caught at the back of her throat and the room spun before her eyes as she felt Kendall's hot breath panting upon her neck and sensed the presence of the knife just above her naked breasts. An uncontrollable trembling seized her limbs and her legs buckled beneath her as the cold blade slid with painstaking slowness between her breasts. Through tear-filled eyes, Trista gazed helplessly upon her husband.

"Oh, Nicholas, please...stop him. If it means risking my life, so be it. I cannot bear it...."

This drew a maniacal giggle from Kendall as he toyed idly with the blade upon her breast.

"Go on, Brennan, indulge the lady.''

"On the count of three, release her or her wish shall be granted.''

"Never...you would never attempt it!'' Kendall snorted, dropping his gaze momentarily to Trista's heaving bosom. "She really is quite lovely.''

"One...''

"Idle threats shall serve you naught, Brennan! She shall be mine or she shall die with me...straight through the heart!''

"Two...''

"Never! I shall never allow it! You bastard—"

"Nicholas! Please . . ."

"Three . . ."

Chapter Twenty

Precisely one month after the day Kendall Barry was laid to rest, Trista stood beneath the stone-columned portico, leaning peacefully against the short wall surrounding. She idly swept an enormous lace fan before her to afford some respite from the warmth of the day. Shielding her eyes from the late afternoon sun, she allowed her gaze to scan her husband's land, *her* land, before settling upon the trio enjoying lemonade beneath a shady elm.

Esme, despite her parasol, was no doubt cursing beneath a carefully tended smile the custom of heavy mourning clothes. Black suited neither her coloring nor her mood of late, which had been deemed by some Society matrons to be a brilliant and graceful recovery from the awful blow fate had seen fit to deal her. Trista, however, knew better. After hastily and ever so efficiently shipping a blustering Bianca back to Milan to be taken in hand by the Marchioness—a fate Bianca undoubtedly deemed worse than death itself— Esme had set up a tastefully understated town house in London by virtue of the funds she had retained from her marriage to Gaston and those gambling debts of Dominic's that Nicholas returned to her. In addition to reacquainting herself with her aging father, Esme was attempting, albeit halfheartedly and with a decidedly wicked sparkle in her dark eyes, to fend off the scores of eager gentlemen vying with one another to become the shoulder upon which she should ease her grief. As sure as the next day's sunrise,

Trista knew Esme's stint as grieving widow was to be bliss-fully short-lived.

Trista's eyes slid to her grandfather, seated beside Esme. It was difficult to imagine a man so small and gentle wreak-ing such havoc upon his young family so long ago. Beneath that shady elm, with his daughter chattering at his side, he appeared at peace, as if those past demons had finally been put to rest.

The slightest breeze teased the damp tendrils lying against Trista's cheek and she fanned herself a bit faster as she con-templated the rich auburn head of the woman seated op-posite Esme. Isabel Kingsley, who, with one innocent business jaunt about the Continent, had so completely en-amored Winston that Trista still could not believe the transformation. The thought filled Trista's heart with joy, as did the unabashed warmth and affection brimming from Isabel's eyes, which strayed long and often to Winston, who was strolling leisurely about with Nicholas. Her father's step was light, jaunty even, and the frequent smiles he bestowed upon his lady friend were filled with sentiment reserved for lovers alone. Marriage was in the air, no doubt. Trista's only hope was that the gala event would take place before her "condition" proved a hindrance.

At the thought, her hand moved unconsciously to press against the soft curve of her belly, still taut and unyielding yet harboring a tiny being born of the love that filled her with endless joy. Her eyes slid to Nicholas's tall form and she felt her pulse quicken at the mere sight of him. He had paused to wave an arm over the landscape, Winston listen-ing with rapt attention at his side. Trista's gaze caressed her husband's profile, so rugged and imposing even when he smiled that beloved lopsided grin. He had whooped with joy at her news of the baby, sweeping her off her feet and lust-ily bearing her to their bed to discover for himself the se-crets of his wife's changing body.

Trista fanned herself heatedly for a moment as a rosy blush suffused her cheeks. Such a rogue, aye, but she loved him for it. Loved him with a boundless passion, and would have just as much had he not saved her life, even killing a man to do so. She still marveled at his cleverness in deducing that Kendall was indeed the Boudoir Murderer.

The woman Clothilde had been consoling when Nicholas had burst upon them at White's was indeed the very same woman that Trista had so blatantly ogled that night at Covent Garden, the woman upon Kendall Barry's arm. The very arm Trista had crushed in the powder room door and the excuse Kendall had offered forth to his lady friend for keeping himself scarce. To Nicholas's eye, that proved too much a coincidence to ignore.

After sending Trista and her grandfather back to Esme's with Peter as watchful escort, Nicholas had returned to White's, where the woman tearfully confessed to Kendall's increasingly violent nature and his decided "preoccupation" with acquiring an innocent and pure Society maiden as his wife; a preoccupation that had apparently become a twisted demonic obsession.

The woman had revealed that Kendall kept a room at White's and had taken to spending nearly every night there. This was due, she explained, to his deteriorating relationship with his father, who flagrantly disapproved of his son's debauched life-style and had thrown a drunken Kendall out on his ear on more than one occasion. Nicholas had requested access to the room, which the woman had hesitated to grant until Nicholas had confessed his urgency to speak with Kendall alone on a matter of extreme importance. Never one to deny a tall dark Yankee anything, the woman had complied, leaving Nicholas to lie in wait for Kendall Barry. Not for one moment had he imagined that Kendall would arrive wielding a knife pressed menacingly against Trista's throat.

Trista shuddered at the memory. How blissfully naive she had been, falling into Kendall's vile hands without forethought. Indeed, she had been so blinded by her own expectations, by a fierce stubbornness, that she'd entirely misjudged nearly every soul she'd met upon arriving in London. Had she but realized her ignorance and naiveté instead of allowing Peter's bumbled attempt to seduce her to instill in her a fear of deception so fierce that she'd been blinded by it. That very fear had nearly proven her undoing.

Her eyes met those of her husband across the tree-shaded expanse and her lips curved in a smile. How odd that the thought of her safe country life, one that a scant few months ago she would never have abandoned, now seemed a dreadfully lonely existence. Gazing upon the face of her beloved, she knew she would travel to the ends of the earth and back with him, confronting wild buffalo and legions of those Indian savages, safe within the cocoon of a love she'd never imagined. How she had misjudged him!

"Ah, my lady, there you are."

Polly's voice behind her startled Trista from her thoughts and she greeted the woman with a smile before swinging her gaze to her husband once more.

Trista's preoccupation did not go unnoticed by the other woman, who gave a knowing smile and remarked, "Word about London has it that your husband is a hero, my lady."

A faint smile tugged at the corner of Trista's mouth and her eyes twinkled mischievously. Turning to Polly, she lifted her nose a notch and sniffed. "My dear Polly, you more than anyone know that from the moment I first met him, I never once thought otherwise."

And with a sly wink, Trista gathered skirts in hand and swept from the terrace to join her husband.

* * * * *

Harlequin Historicals®

Now that you've been introduced to our March Madness authors, be sure to look for their upcoming titles:

From Miranda Jarrett—

COLUMBINE—Wrongly convicted for murder, Lady Diana Grey finds herself on her way to the American Colonies as an indentured servant.

From Ana Seymour—

ANGEL OF THE LAKE—The warm-hearted story of a widower, wracked with guilt, and the woman who teaches him to love.

From Kit Gardner—

THE DREAM—A stiff-necked boarding school teacher is defenseless against the charm of a handsome, carefree lord who has set his sights on her.

From Margaret Moore—

CHINA BLOSSOM—Raised as a pampered Chinese slave, a young Englishwoman must adjust to 19th-century British society.

Four great stories that you won't want to miss!

MMANB

HARLEQUIN PROUDLY PRESENTS A DAZZLING CONCEPT IN ROMANCE FICTION

 One small town,
twelve terrific love stories

JOIN US FOR A YEAR IN THE FUTURE OF TYLER

Each book set in Tyler is a self-contained love story; together,
the twelve novels stitch the fabric of the community.

LOSE YOUR HEART TO TYLER!

Join us for the second TYLER book, BRIGHT HOPES, by
Pat Warren, available in April.

*Former Olympic track star Pam Casals arrives in Tyler to
coach the high school team. Phys ed instructor Patrick
Kelsey is first resentful, then delighted. And rumors fly about
the dead body discovered at the lodge.*